NAHIA

Faerie Legacy Series, Book 3

PATRICIA BOSSANO

WaterBearer Press

NAHIA

Faerie Legacy Series, Book 3

Published in the United States by WaterBearer Press
Escondido, CA 92030
www.WaterBearerPress.com

Because of the dynamic nature of the Internet, any web addresses or links contained in this book may have changed since publication and may no longer be valid. The views expressed in this work are solely those of the author and do not necessarily reflect the views of the publisher, and the publisher hereby disclaims any responsibility for them. Any people depicted in stock imagery provided by Thinkstock are models, and such images are being used for illustrative purposes only. Certain stock imagery © Thinkstock.

Cover design and art by Tamra Gerard

Identifiers:
ISBN: 978-0-9994-346-0-4 (hc)
ISBN: 978-0-9994-346-1-1 (sc)
ISBN: 978-0-9994-346-2-8 (e)
Library of Congress Control Number: 2017914938
BISAC: Fiction, Young Adult Fiction: General / Fantasy / Magical Realism / Fairy Tales, Legends & Mythology / Coming of Age / General / Epic / Saga

This is a work of fiction. All of the characters, names, incidents, organizations, and dialogue in this novel are either the products of the author's imagination or are used fictitiously. Any resemblance to actual persons, living or dead, events, or locales is entirely coincidental.

Manufactured in the United States of America

WaterBearer Press Edition: October 2017

Al correo de las brujas y las brujitas,
May we live on and prosper.

Acknowledgments

As with *Faery Sight* and *Cradle Gift*, *Nahia* transferred to the page thanks to the support and encouragement of my family, who prompted me to dream—particularly when the safe reality I lived in disappeared. Thank you Blanca, Kelsey and Remy, Carmen, Alex, Nicole, Julio, Martín, Esteban, Majito and Leo, Silvia, John, Linda and Camila, and all my aunts, uncles, cousins, near and far, for believing in me. I am forever grateful to the friends who I consider extended family, and who contributed to this book with their magical artistry, unconditional support, and enthusiastic sponsorship—couldn't have done it without you: Paul, Tamra, Johnnie, Sherry, Christy, Michele, Natalie, Jodi, Lynda, Drienie, and WildBound's fantastic PR team for taking me to the next level.

A most radiant thank you to: Luis, María, Esteban, Renee, Carolyn, and all my grandparents for your trans-dimensional guidance in my journey.

Also, a special thanks to a young man my daughter and I met on June 26, 2016. We stopped in Barstow, at a Pilot station on Lenwood Road; he was hungry and we had an extra sandwich. He asked where we were headed and I said, to a new beginning with my books. Instead of a perfunctory 'thank you' he chose to bless my journey, and what an unexpected karmic boost that turned out to be!

To you, the reader, I thank you for picking up this book; I hope Nahia's blend of fantasy and realism will inspire you to believe that we can be as magical as we choose to be.

W⊕RLD WISD⊕M ⊕N FAERIES

Faery: Also fairy, faerie, fee, fay, fae, fey, wee folk, little people, people of peace, fair folk. In folklore: one of a class of supernatural beings, generally conceived as having a diminutive human form and possessing magical powers with which they intervene in human affairs.

Faeryland: A place of ethereal beauty, enchanting. The imaginary realm of faeries. Any enchantingly beautiful region.

Seelie Court: An assembly of faeries (trooping faeries) inclined to do good though they can still be considered harmful pranksters.

Unseelie Court: An assembly of malicious faeries, who will do harm to others, including humans, for their own entertainment.

Solitary Faery: One who does not associate with others of their kind.

Trooping faeries organize themselves in matriarchal communities ruled by a Faery Queen. For safety reasons, to maintain their privacy, and to help things grow with their brilliant energy, faeries live underground even though they are creatures of light—veritable rays of sunshine! The first of their kind came into being in Italy, where the sun is said to shine at its loveliest. They spread to different parts of the world during the expansion of the Roman Empire, seeking remote locations to set up their underground realms, learning the language of their host countries and adopting the more intriguing customs practiced there, as an act of silent diplomacy.

The innate power faeries have to wield and transmute the energy inside their bodies is called Glamour, and they use it to astonishing though limited effect; faeries are not all-powerful. Glamour allows them to live in the same world as humans, but in a different dimension. They usually choose forested locations for it is their practice to develop a symbiotic relation with their habitat and share in its longevity. A faery will grow normally to the age of fifteen, but afterward her body will change at a rate of one year for every fifteen human ones. For example, a faery that has lived 140 calendar years will look like a 23-year-old human, because she is sharing in the lifespan of her forest home. Sadly, emotional maturity does not court the vast majority of faeries until they're well into their two hundreds.

Although Glamour accounts for the Faery Queen's gift of Future Sight, only rare specimens are considered reliable seers. They view Future Sight as a potential weapon and being mostly peaceful; they ignore it and hope never to have need of it.

The Faery Queen is by far the most proficient wielder of Glamour. From her down to the lowliest member of her court, Glamour is used at varying degrees of intensity to emit the brilliant appeal that makes them irresistible to humans. Beguiling females and formidable males alike use the Glamour in their bodies to perform basic shape-shifting feats, cast domestic spells, give plain Cradle Gifts to babies, and cause annoying bewitchments. But when used at its highest degree, by a ruling Queen for instance, she can overcome insurmountable odds, change the weather, and endow infants with life-altering gifts of character.

Faeries do *not* have wings but thanks to Glamour they do have the power of vertical and horizontal motion; a skilled faery can fly faster than a diving falcon.

All faeries exist inside colorful auras powered by Glamour, which accounts for their luminous orb appearance. The aura serves to insulate them from the elements, mostly by regulating their temperature. However, in moments of grave danger it can also become a protective shield. A faery's eyes are the same color as her aura, and her hair is always streaked to match.

An adult faery's height (female or male) ranges between ten and eighteen inches, although they can shape-shift to most anything they wish, including an adult human. Nevertheless, most faeries are so content with their shape and size they rarely indulge in copying others.

The dimension faeries inhabit and their auras prevent humans from seeing them with the naked eye. For a human to catch a glimpse, or to recognize a glowing orb as a faery's aura, she must exert the Glamour in her body to purposely grant him the gift of Faery Sight. That is by far the most direct method. There are two other ways, but be warned, they are bound to test a human's determination and drive him to give up before he achieves success. A human must know of a portal into the Faerie Dimension, in itself a difficult piece of information to come by. He must enter said dimension during the full moon on a Midsummer Eve (risking punishment if detected) to be rewarded with the sight of traditional faery reveling on that special night of the year. Or he can attempt to intercept a group of traveling faeries, assuming he knows of their path and timeline. He must hide and await the caravan's passing, all the while looking for them through a self-bored stone (a smooth, flat stone with a perfectly round hole through the middle caused by its tumbling in a brook or creek). Happening upon such a contraption is as improbable as acquiring a faery troop's detailed travel plans.

While faeries share the full gamut of human traits, a faery's qualities are significantly heightened, for better and for worse. The vast majority of them can carry out peaceable, fulfilling lives in the *central* portion of the trait gamut. If the inner workings of *all* faeries are considered a conundrum, and their thoughts, emotions, and instincts plagued with paradoxes, it is because faeries' attributes as a species have been defined by the notorious minority compelled to highlight extreme ends of the scale.

Usually the Faery Queen and the older members of her court are seen as the wisest because their focus is to find balance; they've recognized it as the path to achieve great success and to avoid catastrophic failure. In their youth faeries are mostly impatient, self-absorbed, frivolous and insensitive to others, which makes them prone to bouts of wickedness. Faeries tend to act on the principle that one good (or bad) turn deserves another; trouble is, their perception can be sometimes seriously flawed, and more often than not their reaction is sadly disproportionate to the action that caused it.

As they grow older, the creases in their character smooth out. They see their individuality as part of the collective unit, they discover their purpose, and their temperament slants toward amiability and patience. When faeries acquire a taste for tolerance they take to practicing it with an earnest desire to please. They find the joy in assisting others and can become obsessed with improving the world by deploying their boldest gifts for the good of the troop.

In the Faerie Dimension, the whole troop functions in a way that is equivalent to that of a human family, but with some structural differences. Unlike lesser members of the Faerie Court, who typically prefer a single partner with whom to increase the troop's numbers, a Faery Queen is wont to choose temporary male consorts in her quest for change and variety. It is not uncommon for a Faery Queen to have multiple consorts throughout her lifetime. As faeries can live upwards of six hundred years, it is noteworthy a queen needs *alone* intervals, and sometimes the gaps between consorts can last whole centuries.

Because they share the planet with humans, and with an eye on smoothing the way for future relations, faeries began their now traditional practice of appearing in a household soon after a birth and bestowing Cradle Gifts upon the newborn child (favorable or otherwise, depending on her mood or how she perceived her reception). In recent centuries and owing to their natural curiosity, faeries expanded their original function and began meddling in human affairs, to the detriment of diplomatic interests.

For the most part, they stick to their kind, but there is the occasional report of a faery-human marriage, which nearly always ends badly—the faery bride's varying moods and erratic attitudes drive the man to act out, and when his confusion and frustration peaks, she conveniently releases herself and returns home, wondering why she ever left in the first place.

Aside from botched inter-species marriages, faeries and humans get on quite well, so long as they are unaware of each other. Inevitably, a faery's curiosity and desire to intrude will drive her to meddle, and a good number of such instances can be merely annoying or disruptive. However, there is one practice that cannot be labeled so mildly.

Possibly the most hurtful thing faeries have been driven to do by their frivolous penchant for snooping is to steal beautiful human infants (before they are christened) and replace them with changelings. The faery's reason for acting as she does ranges from a simple fascination with beauty to raising a strapping human to do the heavy lifting (especially accurate in the case of a solitary faery); whatever the case, they don't display any regard for what the loss of a child means to a human parent, perhaps because in the bosom of the troop it is all for one and one for all.

It should be noted, most Faery Queens consider baby stealing a punishable breach of faery-human etiquette, but consequences and their severity do vary from one troop to another.

PART I

1882 T⊕ 1961

It is hard to contend against one's heart's desire; for whatever it wishes to have it buys at the cost of soul.

Heraclitus

Chapter I

Funeral

Citadel of Santillán, at the foot of the Western Pyrenees, Spain

The dying leaves of the large beech tree shivered in the blustery fall afternoon. From her spot on one of the lower branches, Nahia scowled at the sight below, her aquamarine eyes fixed on the wooden box the humans meant to lower into the ground. She refused to accept the fact that her beloved birth sister, Celeste, was inside.

"I bet I know what's on your mind," Sendoa whispered close to her ear, interrupting Nahia's brooding.

"I bet you don't," she whispered back. "I still can't believe she's in there. Decomposing."

"I know. It is a vile human custom to box and bury their loved ones, cheating nature of what is hers."

"Exactly. Celeste should have been buried naked, straight into the earth so her dormant energy could go back to everything around her, same as we did with her mother when she died."

Sendoa scooted closer to her on the branch. "But unlike Paloma, Celeste didn't die in the Faerie Realm."

Nahia sniffed moodily; yes, it came down to that. Celeste hadn't died in the Realm because she'd chosen to live in Santillán instead. Nahia pulled off the hood of her cloak, exposing her turquoise-streaked curls. She frowned at the cluster of humans gathered below: Celeste's husband, their three children, and Celeste's first grandchild, who had already grown into a young lady. Nahia bit her lip and looked away from the girl, her gaze passing over the Citadel walls and toward the majestic Pyrenees rising in the distance.

Unbidden came a chain of memories so vivid, Nahia felt transported to

3

the past, to the beautiful day when Celeste had married the human Etienne St. Michel.

Celeste had looked absolutely radiant. Etienne by her side was the most handsome creature Nahia had ever seen—which was saying something, because she had been around male faeries all her life and she knew firsthand there could be no comparison.

Nahia brushed away her tears, remembering everyone's reaction when impetuous Celeste had kissed her enchanting groom, *before* they were even pronounced man and wife. She shifted and resettled on the branch, indulging bitter thoughts of the old argument Celeste and Etienne had ignored long ago. Sighing, she leaned toward Sendoa and spoke. "If only they had chosen the Realm of Faerie instead of Santillán as their permanent home, they certainly wouldn't be burying Celeste today! They would have been absorbed into our magical dimension, and benefited from a much longer lifespan!"

Sendoa's eyes seemed to laugh at her. "So now you'll dredge up old regrets and sink to your neck in long-gone memories of you and Celeste?"

Nahia flared her nostrils and her lip twitched. What a nuisance that Sendoa should know her so well. She opened her mouth to tell him off, but changed her mind mid-breath and whispered back, "I am working my way there, just leave me to it." Sendoa bumped her shoulder with his. Although she wouldn't acknowledge it, Nahia felt a rush of gratitude; Sendoa must feel the loss of Celeste keenly too, even if she hadn't been *his* birth sister.

On Sendoa's other side, a few feet away, Nahia could see the grave profile of another male faery, one who had long ago favored Celeste, to the point of going against faery lore and bestowing his first kiss on her, a human! Amets had done it in spite of the price he'd have to pay; when she died, Celeste would take his heart into the light, condemning him to wander the earth without it.

With grim fascination, she watched Amets rock absentmindedly as he too stared at the wooden box. *What had happened to him the moment Celeste exhaled her last? Had the full effect of his choice hit him like a bolt of lightning, turning his breast into a brittle, empty husk overnight?*

Nahia shuddered, returning her glance to Etienne who stood by the head of the coffin, his hand resting resolutely over the lid. Though he looked old, as if he might not be able to shoulder the weight of Celeste's death, Nahia fancied him determined to stay connected to his wife until the last second. The faery felt a sudden surge of empathy toward him, despite the forty-some years she'd begrudged him the share of Celeste's heart he'd had.

How time had flown!

Nahia sank deeper into a sea of bedtime tales and memories, down, down, all the way down to a night in 1819, when the human Paloma had been discarded at the entrance to the Faerie Realm, under a curse and without the smallest hope of it being lifted, with the baby in her womb ready to come out. By choice, the Keeper of the Forest, a unicorn named Basajaun, intervened and allowed Paloma into the Realm where she gave birth to Celeste, while at the same time, deeper in the Realm, in Handi Park, the Faery Queen, Oihana, gave birth to Nahia. By daybreak, three new beings had been admitted into the magical Dimension of Faerie; two humans and one more faery to the troop. From there, their lives had unfolded forever and deeply intertwined.

Nahia and Celeste had grown up free of care in the Realm of Faerie until Paloma's death set off a chain of life-altering events. Because the curse hadn't been lifted while Paloma lived, Celeste had felt compelled to avenge her mother's death, which exposed her to the human Realm she'd never known, and from whence Etienne came into her life, for better or for worse.

The faery and the human's path split amid assurances from Celeste they would forever be birth sisters. Nahia watched her leave hand in hand with Etienne, stubbornly fancying she would one day return. Certainly, Celeste had been true to her word and Nahia, who would not be denied, demanded and had gotten almost equal time with them in Santillán and in the Realm. In the blink of an eye their days were filled with the laughter and chatter of Celeste and Etienne's three children. Another blink, and Exteban, Xiomara, and Bastien had become adults.

Nahia clucked her tongue, irritated anew by Celeste's incomprehensible decision to shorten her passage through the planet by so significant a period. Sendoa automatically bumped her shoulder again.

"We are both sixty-three years old, but Celeste is dead! Did you see her in there?" Nahia's urgent whisper came out as a hiss. Sendoa grimaced. "Her skin all crisscrossed with wrinkles. Her once beautiful mane of brown hair all lusterless and threaded with countless silver strands, and she looked so small! Shrunken and brittle inside a box, whereas I . . . ." Nahia didn't finish her sentence, keenly feeling the injustice. The faery looked and felt like an eighteen-year-old, and Celeste could've too, had she stayed in the Realm, where their bodies had developed normally until their fifteenth year, and afterward changed at a rate of one year for every fifteen in the human dimension. Why would she renounce the Faerie Realm with all its magical advantages?

"She didn't look as bad as that to me, Nahia," Sendoa interjected kindly.

"The gray hair, maybe. But you must admit, she was as lively and beautiful as ever, even when she got quite ill toward the end. You just never got over the fact that she chose to leave the Realm—and you."

Nahia scowled and looked away from him.

A gentle breeze brought with it the distinctive scent of lilac; Nahia turned in time to see the Faery Queen, Oihana, alight beside her.

My own mother is over six hundred years old and looks twenty years younger than Celeste, Nahia thought sourly. She put her head on her mother's shoulder, unable to stifle the sob that escaped her throat.

"It'll happen to all of them," Nahia said, looking down on Celeste's children; she loved the three of them as if they were her own. She sniffed and resumed complaining in urgent whispers, "I attended each of their births and my Cradle Gifts were the first gift those children ever received! And I promised Celeste I would protect them all, never harm them, *not even a hair on their head*—how much easier it would be if only they lived with me in the Realm."

Oihana put her arm around her daughter and kissed her forehead. "It was their choice, my love. And don't forget, we too shall go into the light one day."

Nahia's hands balled into fists as Etienne bent over the coffin, placing a kiss on the wooden lid. They began to lower it into the ground, and Nahia's heart fluttered desperately in her chest. Oihana held her tighter. On Nahia's other side, Sendoa fumbled for her hand; she grabbed it and squeezed. She couldn't breathe.

Just as Nahia thought she would lose control and do something rash, like extract Celeste's body from the box and take her to the Realm for a proper burial, she became distracted by the sight of Celeste's granddaughter, Alaia. The girl was shifting from one leg to the other, glancing toward the sky as if asking for patience. Judging by the curled lip and the way she morosely played with her braid, not even bothering to look aggrieved, Nahia imagined the girl must be sulking about the unfortunate fact that Celeste's death was taking away from her own wedding preparations.

The intense dislike Nahia felt for Alaia momentarily smothered her sorrow, but only until two men started shoveling dirt over Celeste's coffin. She watched the whole family gather as one around Etienne, except Alaia, who continued to mope a couple of feet away from the others.

Oihana must have felt Nahia tense up because she suddenly said, "Remember, she is young and a big event is coming up for her—"

"That is *no* excuse," Nahia hissed wriggling away from her mother's arm. "Let's give our condolences to Etienne so we can leave."

Nahia and Oihana willed themselves off the branch and descended gracefully. As soon as their feet touched the ground, mother and daughter shape-shifted to human height and stood under the shade of the tree, waiting for Sendoa to join them. He did so promptly, as did Amets, but he stood to the side, staring around blankly, as if excluding himself on purpose.

When Etienne looked up and saw the small group, he warmly gestured for them to approach. The two male faeries bowed but stayed respectfully behind while the ladies condoled with the family.

Alaia acknowledged the faeries with a jerky nod as they passed, but she didn't close in, nor did she linger for the emotional exchange following. *Perceptive of her,* Nahia thought acidly, as she walked into the embrace of the rest of Celeste's human family, where teary sentiments were expressed and sincere promises not to drift apart were made.

The four faeries, led by Nahia, left as soon as Oihana hinted it was polite to do so. They shifted back to their respective heights of under two feet and took to the air. They rose above the mountaintop and over the waterfall to enter the cradle of the Western Pyrenees. They passed Moon Dancer Lake and Oihana continued on to Handi Park, the underground home of the troop, while Nahia and Sendoa stayed in the Arboretum, where stood the Hall of Glamour they had built years before as a gift for Paloma. Together, they watched Amets float idly by on his way to Celeste's old home in the grotto.

Nahia hovered distractedly over the large boulders damming the creek, tossing pebbles into it. "Xiomara looked lovely today, didn't she? Sad though she was, it is remarkable how her inner beauty shines through."

"She did, and it does," Sendoa said whittling a stick he'd picked up at the site of Celeste's grave. "I think it's sweet how devoted you are to her—but do you think it's proper for a faery godmother to have a favorite child?"

"So what if I favor Xiomara above the two boys? I am not their mother," Nahia bristled. "And anyway, you know very well that I *do* love all three as if they were my own, and I never singled out Xiomara or made my preference obvious to the others."

"I see—so do you exclude Xiomara's daughter from your statement, so others will know there are things about Xiomara you don't like? Or is it simply you do not love the girl, Alaia, as if she were your own?"

Stumped, Nahia paused mid-hover and frowned at him; his silver aura had begun to glow in the creeping darkness beneath the canopy.

When she failed to reply, Sendoa stopped whittling and looked at her expectantly. Tears pooled in Nahia's eyes but she blinked them away irritably. She dropped the fistful of pebbles in her hand and drifted over to sit by him, meshing her sea-green aura with his. "Am I a vile creature? I know I've been prejudiced against Alaia all along, but I could never help my dislike of her, even when she was an innocent infant. I think it was predestined!"

Sendoa looked startled by Nahia's admission. "I think it's mutual," he blurted. "Don't ask me how but I've always felt Alaia was predisposed to hate *you*. Perhaps she envied your beauty, just like she envied her own mother's and Celeste's. She can't be called *pretty*, she's not musical, and she's not artistic. She likes structure and rules, and she can't approve or appreciate the behaviors that mark us and which her other family members treasure so."

Nahia nodded. "I just can't be drawn to her, and I know I helped exclude her from us!"

Sendoa put his arm around Nahia and patted her shoulder soothingly. She sniffed and wiped her eyes with the back of her hand. "And now the girl is preparing to marry—just like Celeste, just like Xiomara! Xiomara was only twenty-three years old when she chose to marry, and I still can't understand why human women are so willing to tie their lives to a man's. Do you know what I did once?" Nahia said thoughtfully, leaning into Sendoa with the air of someone ready to confess a misdeed. "I went behind Celeste's back, and I told Xiomara about the faery way, how a Faery Queen has multiple consorts throughout her lifetime but *never* a husband."

"Did you, now?" Sendoa laughed and shook his head.

"I did!" Nahia smirked, feeling like a praiseworthy rebel. "Xiomara laughed at me though, and told me, 'I'm not a Faery Queen, Nahia, and besides, I love my Andrés sooooo much!'" She repeated the words doing her best imitation of the apple of her eye, and Sendoa rewarded her with another smile and shake of his head.

Night fell and it was full dark under the canopy where Nahia and Sendoa sat at the edge of the creek. Under the mighty oak, at whose foot was Paloma's grave, their glittering auras bled into one another, encapsulating their voices. "Are there any faery secrets you *didn't* tell Xiomara about?" Sendoa asked playfully.

Nahia grinned. "You know I imparted to her all the tales of the wondrous childhood her mother and I shared, and she put them all in a book. Sweet girl—she called it *Faery Sight*, and she keeps it hidden in Santillán."

"Let us hope it stays hidden," Sendoa said, giving Nahia a squeeze. "Time to turn in."

They rose together and the two orbs wended leisurely between the trees on their way to Handi Park.

Alone in her chamber that night, Nahia stretched on her nest and pondered her losses so far—Celeste to Etienne, and Xiomara to Andrés. Except now, Celeste was lost for good—gone into the light, out of Nahia's reach. It washed over her anew how much she would miss her sweet birth sister.

Sleepily, Nahia's thoughts turned to her own mother and she heaved a relaxed sigh. She trusted Oihana would live forever, always be the Faery Queen, which would allow Nahia a single partner rather than consorts. She began to wonder with increasing delight who was to be *her* partner. If Celeste and Xiomara had found one, then surely she, Nahia, could find one as well.

Until a distressing awareness struck her: *If I want to mimic Celeste's and Xiomara's lives, does that mean I'm obsessed with humans?* Admittedly, their strength and vulnerability enthralled her, but there was an even more intriguing, fascinating aspect, and it was the passing of traits, like imprints of themselves, from mother to child. In Xiomara, Nahia constantly saw features and expressions she knew to be Celeste's or Paloma's. The boys too—Bastien had Celeste's smile, and flecks of gold flashed in Exteban's brown eyes, just like they had in his mother's.

The faery's aquamarine eyes lit up in the dark chamber looking like two disembodied points of light; she was a little jealous, because full-blooded faeries did not work that way. No two faeries were alike. Would anyone ever see *her* imprint in another being?

Chapter 2
A Faery's Blunder

In the weeks following Celeste's burial, Nahia descended to the Citadel in Santillán two more times in close succession. She grudgingly attended Alaia's wedding (to a human Nahia cared nothing about) out of love for Xiomara, but couldn't bring herself to even wish the couple joy. They had buried Celeste barely two weeks before, and she strongly felt the wedding should have been postponed.

Five months after that, Nahia and Oihana joined the human family once more to bury Etienne, who had passed away. As ever, Xiomara, Exteban, and Bastien showed their warmth and attachment to Nahia and Oihana, but the Faery Princess couldn't help feeling a distancing had begun. Who was bringing the sense of rupture to their relationship? Was it her or was it them? Nahia feared it was her—she couldn't stop thinking all the love and magic, which had marked their relationship in the past, had been buried with Celeste.

Nevertheless, Nahia stubbornly kept in contact with Xiomara, in order to hear the news about each family member. As the months turned into years, Nahia often found herself urging her favorite to visit the Realm, with or without invitation.

"Remember, Celeste and I renovated the gateway to the Realm precisely so you could come as often as you like," Nahia would say, emphasizing it had been Celeste's idea to fit the cliffs on either side of the waterfall with concealed stairs leading in and out of the passage behind the curtain of water. Until then, Wizard's Pass had been near-impossible to use.

Even with that option available to them, when Nahia tallied up the children's visits over the last four years, she came up sadly short of the numerous gatherings they'd had while Celeste lived. She would then repeat to herself, *It's been a long time since they were children—they are adults now.*

"But my Xiomara is coming for Autumnal Equinox," Nahia told Sendoa one morning, shaking off her gloomy thoughts. "I do hope she stays a few days—and the boys too, of course."

"That would be nice. It has been a full three months since we last saw them."

Nahia hardly slept the night before the equinox; she rose from her nest before sunup, and dressed for the day. She went to Moon Dancer Lake and propped herself on the branch of her favorite blue spruce near the shore, to wait for her guests. By midmorning, she at last saw them come out of the wooded hills on the west shore and let out a sigh of relief.

Nahia flashed over the water toward them, cutting a frothy V on the tranquil surface as she went. They paused and pointed eagerly toward her.

"Good morning!" Xiomara called out from where she stood between her brothers. Bastien waved and Exteban grinned, shading his eyes with his hand. Without slowing, Nahia slid from water to shore, shifting to human height the moment her toes touched the sand.

"So glad you're here," Nahia exclaimed, going from Xiomara to the boys, embracing them warmly before scolding them. "You've stayed away too long!"

Xiomara linked her arm with Nahia's and kissed the faery's cheek. "I'm so sorry—I have no excuse other than the days keep getting away from me."

"There is so much work to be done; Santillán is so large," Exteban added, walking around to Nahia's other side.

Bastien got in front of all three and walked backwards as he cajoled his faery godmother, "Between cattle, horses, and crops, there aren't enough seasons in the year for us humans to manage it all!"

"Oh—you are going to hear about it now!" Exteban teased his brother.

Nahia frowned at them. "You know how I feel about that. Much as I loved her, I have to say it: it's your mother's fault you have to work as you do!"

For a reply, Bastien picked her up and twirled her in a mock dance. Nahia's complaints were momentarily forgotten in laughter; it was like old times.

They spent the day hiking and talking until it was time for lunch. Nahia knew they looked forward to this part because to enter Handi Park, not only would she reduce them to faery height, but she would treat them to the gift of flight; faery-style, through energy distribution as faeries don't have wings.

"You won't get me this time," Bastien said, and Nahia gave him an arch look, accepting the challenge.

As children, unable to hide their excitement, they had giggled and wriggled when the faery placed her hand over their solar plexus, causing a whirl of tickling energy to converge there. As adults, only their broad grins betrayed their outwardly relaxed bodies.

Determined to get a reaction out of him, Nahia dispersed Bastien's weight without warning and fast enough to lift him a few inches off the ground. Before he had a chance to drop back down, she commanded the swirling energy to propel him upward, at which point he couldn't hold back an exhilarated whoop.

"This is by far my favorite of your skills!" Bastien shouted gleefully.

Satisfied, Nahia turned to Xiomara and Exteban, who experienced a similar sensation although not as intense as Bastien had asked for. Once airborne, they joined their pirouetting brother in good humor. The four of them dipped and bounced over the Arboretum on their way to Handi Park.

Celeste couldn't have left them a better legacy than her love of the outdoors, so meals underground, much as they appreciated the clever setup, were a practicality to be dispensed with quickly. After they were fed and watered, Sendoa whisked Exteban and Bastien away to indulge in their own exploration of the Realm, leaving Nahia and Xiomara to themselves.

Arm in arm, the ladies strolled back to the edge of the forest enjoying the warm breezes of dying summer; the white sandy shore of Moon Dancer Lake stretched before them and Nahia, who knew Xiomara well enough to sense something was up, said, "Out with it."

Xiomara laughed, unable to contain her excitement, "My Alaia is with child!"

Nahia's amused smile froze on her face and seconds began to tick. *I will have to give a Cradle Gift to Alaia's child*, she thought with a stab of hostility. Yet Nahia would not hurt Xiomara for the world; for her sake, she must hide the petty, irrational dislike she harbored against her daughter, but she couldn't summon even the swiftest of congratulations.

The faery turned away from Xiomara's expectant glance before the silence became awkward, or worse, made plain her dislike of the girl. Nahia busied herself with a closed pine cone she picked up. She held it in her open palm, and as Xiomara looked on, the faery directed her energies toward it. Soon, a glowing heat enveloped and dried it, forcing the cone to open and release its seeds.

"You have such creative force," Xiomara mused running her index finger over the seeds on Nahia's palm. "Let's pick a special place to plant them," she added excitedly, "and these will always be my grandchild's trees!"

Nahia's brows quirked. It was supposed to have been a distraction until the subject could be changed or until she thought of something to say. She hadn't meant for Xiomara to take her flustered display as a congratulatory gift. But as there was no taking it back, and more trees in the Realm were always a good thing, Nahia looked at Xiomara with what she hoped was a delighted expression and declared, "Of course—we will do just that."

They strolled through the Arboretum until they found a sunny clearing to plant the seeds.

"Thank you, Nahia, this means so much to me."

The faery nodded, wondering if a couple of trees could give Alaia the sense of belonging she'd never had. *Probably not*, thought Nahia. *The trees are not even for her, they are for her child.*

"I can hear my brothers," Xiomara said, rising from the stooped position she'd been in while planting.

"That's right. We're close to the shore where we were supposed to meet them."

As the weeks advanced and the baby's birth approached, Xiomara's anticipation of her first grandchild increased exponentially, and Nahia at last settled that she *would* give the baby a Cradle Gift, only if she didn't have to see Alaia in the process. Into her argument, Nahia wove Sendoa's comment about the dislike being mutual, knowing Xiomara would not be able to deny it. She put Alaia's aversion to all things faery in such a way Xiomara, anxious to make amends, readily agreed to help Nahia visit the baby, undisturbed by its mother.

The baby arrived, a boy, and Alaia named him Calisto, which means *most beautiful* in the Basque language. Nahia humphed when she heard this, thinking it arrogant of the new mother, although it did increase her curiosity to visit the child and see for herself if such a name was deserved.

As planned, Nahia descended into the Citadel and visited Calisto on the eve after his birth. She flew in through the nursery window and found Xiomara holding a small bundle of white blankets—a tiny fist poking out of them. A quick glance around the room told Nahia they were alone, just as Xiomara had promised.

Looking radiant with anticipation of Nahia's approval, Xiomara crossed the room as the faery shape-shifted to human height, her arms already extended to receive the baby. "So this is the luckiest, most beautiful grandchild who has ever lived—"

Her own words still hung in the air as Nahia looked down at Calisto, and something quickened inside of her. She couldn't quite put it into words—maybe it was the alert expression in his eyes, maybe the downy softness of his blond head, maybe the heartbreaking pout that screwed up his mouth at precisely the moment their eyes met.

"Calisto," Nahia whispered, entranced. "Most beautiful indeed." The overwhelming conviction this particular child belonged in the Faerie Realm sent shock waves through her; something she'd never experienced with any of the others, not even Xiomara! At that moment, reason left her completely.

Nahia looked guiltily at Xiomara's glowing face and then back at the baby. She hardly knew what she was doing. In a breathless moment, less than a quickening heartbeat, she shifted Calisto and herself to faery height and fled through the open window. Nothing mattered, only that she should have this baby for her own.

CHAPTER 3

No Remorse

Holding Calisto to her breast, Nahia flashed over the walls of the Citadel toward the waterfall high above the mountains. Within seconds she had flown over the jagged rocks which Etienne had long ago named Vulcan's Palings, and which formed the northwestern boundary of the Realm. She skimmed the tops of trees advancing toward the white sandy shore of Moon Dancer Lake, and then dived into the Arboretum.

In the gloom beneath the canopy, her pace slowed. *What to do—where to take Calisto?* Nahia knew her mother would not immediately approve of what she'd done, so Handi Park was out of the question, at least until she could soften Oihana to the idea. But before she could figure out how and what exactly she would tell her mother, the perfect place popped into her head.

"I will take you to your great-grandmother's home," Nahia said happily as she sped over the elderberry lane toward the grotto, which had been Paloma and Celeste's home for many years. The place was convenient and livable, as it was there Celeste's children liked to spend some nights on longer visits to the Realm.

Nahia congratulated herself on her display of foresight when choosing to maintain it. The grotto was equipped with a fresh-water spring and hearth, plus all the original furnishings from Paloma's time, such as the table with chairs set around it, glass plates and cups all in primary colors—made at Handi Park. The large bedstead remained too, complete with bedding and a trunk at the foot of it, full of old gowns.

Nahia spared a loving glance toward the Hall of Glamour and the Great Oak, which her turquoise aura briefly illuminated as she passed. The old landmarks refreshed themselves and new, fanciful outlooks flashed before her eyes; she would give up her royal chamber in Handi Park and raise Calisto by herself. Nahia glided over the lane, merrily cooing to the baby, "The grotto will be our new home, and you're going to love it."

As she approached the hidden entrance, Nahia parted the profuse jasmine tendrils with a swift motion of her hand. The hollow echo of wooden wind chimes resonated throughout and followed them into the dark interior. She motioned deftly toward the hearth and a cheerful fire immediately crackled to life.

The baby started fussing and a fleeting sense of responsibility flashed across Nahia's mind, prompting her to consider more pressing matters. *How often do infants eat?*

She floated over the bedstead frowning at Calisto. "What would you like?"

The baby screwed up his face and began crying in earnest. Nahia placed him in the middle of the large bed and backed away, pondering. A happy recollection slipped through his wailing and into her head; a new fawn had been born just a week ago.

Nahia left the swaddled baby writhing stiffly on the enormous bed. "I will be swift," she called back as she darted into the night in search of the doe and her fawn. With a small offering of peaches and nuts hastily gathered, Nahia dashed directly to the brushwood she knew the doe had chosen as her shelter. The doe took the offering and allowed the faery to milk her. In no time, Nahia's skillful direction of energy caused plenty of milk to splash into the sac she'd conjured to collect it. She stroked the doe's neck and whispered her gratitude before taking to the air again.

She could hear Calisto's lusty cries as she approached the grotto—maybe she shouldn't have left him alone. "Can't be undone now," she told herself. The baby was furious, red-faced and sweaty, having worked himself up into a rage, but even in that state, Nahia still found him most beautiful.

She shifted to human height along with the milk sac and picked up the screaming baby from the bedstead. Although agitated by his incessant crying, Nahia foresaw that the tickling sensation in his solar plexus, when she triggered the shape-shift, would shock Calisto right out of his fit. She changed him back, and the hysterical crying did stop, but before she could even consider feeding him, the pitiful hiccupping noises left over from his angry fit needed to die down as well.

Nahia paced with him in her arms, bouncing him lightly and singing the kind of songs she loved to make up describing the scenery at hand. When he was no longer red and tense, she offered him the tip of the sac filled with milk and Calisto began suckling at once. Nahia knew he didn't understand a word about the colorful cups or the busy mosaics covering the walls of the grotto, but she did feel him relax as she sang, and was satisfied.

Having had his fill, Calisto appeared drowsy. Careful not to disturb him, Nahia placed him on the bed again. She lay on her side next to him and propped on her elbow, she watched his eyelids close; movement beneath them started right away, making her wonder what a human infant could possibly dream about. She fell fast asleep hoping Calisto's dreams might be about flying.

A few hours later, Calisto's fussing woke her from a sound sleep. Nahia's eyes adjusted to the golden glow of the fire and she let out a terrified scream. An enormous, shaking hand loomed directly above her, and she ducked, covering her head with her hands. It took Nahia a couple of seconds to realize that she must have shrunk back to faery height in her sleep, which meant Calisto was almost twice her size. Nahia rose out of bed, heart hammering in her chest, and shifted to human height. She saw no light seeping through the jasmine curtain, which told her morning hadn't broken yet. She turned a bleary, resentful eye on Calisto.

She retrieved the milk sac from the bedside table where she'd left it, climbed back on the bed and scooped the baby into her arms. As he fed, Nahia began thinking perhaps she'd been too rash. It hadn't occurred to her loss of sleep would be involved. She reflected on how different it had been with Celeste's babies—Nahia never had to worry about feeding or changing them, or putting them to sleep; she only played with them and handed them back to Celeste or Etienne at the hint of any troublesome behavior.

When Calisto stopped drinking Nahia leaned back on pillows, placed the baby over her breast and commenced rubbing his back, just as she'd seen Celeste do. She closed her eyes but couldn't doze; Xiomara and Alaia had popped into her mind for the first time since she'd left the Citadel.

Nahia squirmed uncomfortably. *What a situation to have put Xiomara in. What had she told Alaia happened with the baby?* A frustrated moan escaped Nahia's lips. "What must Xiomara think of me!" Calisto gave a little shudder and breathed evenly; asleep again. She put him gently on the bed, and fell into a fretful slumber, trying to lessen the suspicion that she might have made a mistake.

The sound of leaves being ruffled drew her out of a shallow sleep. She opened one eye and saw Calisto, still snuggled against the blanket she'd bunched up between them as a precaution, in case her height shifted unconsciously again. She glanced toward the jasmine-covered entrance and detected daylight beyond. Someone was floating there, staring at her.

"I thought I'd find you here." Sendoa's gravelly voice made her squirm again; she'd been found out.

Careful not to wake the baby, Nahia rolled out of bed and resumed faery height.

"So everyone knows?" she asked, wringing her hands nervously.

Sendoa nodded. "It was soon after midnight when the Aspen Grove outside Handi Park came to life with Xiomara's plea."

Nahia grimaced and bit her lip—she had taught it to Celeste and her family. Aspens, being a living colony stretching for miles and miles, would carry messages through their root systems, surfacing intermittently over valleys and mountainsides all the way to the Realm. Nahia could almost see poor, desperate Xiomara; her arms around the trunk of the nearest Aspen outside the Citadel, whispering word into the required gash on the bark, about what Nahia had done.

"I'd forgotten about that—" Nahia said giving Sendoa a tortured look. "I take it my mother knows too?"

Another curt nod. "She sent me to find you."

Nahia sighed. Sendoa had been in her life from the beginning, always a friend, although more often than not, an accomplice. "So you're here to take me in," she said, not bothering to hide a note of drama in her voice. "Is she very angry?"

"Never saw her more so—at first she wouldn't credit what the trees were whispering, but as the message became more insistent, and you were nowhere to be found, she had to believe it."

"What did Xiomara say?"

"To give her grandchild back. Yes, very brief, but you know how eerie it is to hear the trees—they spoke over one another in their raspy, rustling voice until we were dizzy with the message coming from all directions."

Nahia nodded, glancing at the baby. "I don't want to wake him," she whispered. "We will wait a while and then go to my mother."

Sendoa shrugged and floated over to the table, where he made himself comfortable. He gestured to the placemat next to him and Nahia took it. "What was your master plan anyway?"

Chastised by his grave expression but reluctant to acknowledge how reckless her behavior had been, Nahia stifled a groan and replied in a steely voice, "I was going to raise Calisto here, with me."

Sendoa clucked his tongue and shook his head. "But you're not anymore?"

Nahia rolled her eyes. "I guess without Alaia's consent, my mother would never allow it—and I can't very well hide within the Realm. You know between her and the Keeper of the Forest, they know everything." She was annoyed with herself as much as with the situation—only a few hours ago she'd been determined to raise Calisto on her own, against all odds, and now she couldn't deny the overwhelming sense of relief she felt at the prospect of giving him back.

"What made you do it in the first place?"

"I don't know! I lost my head—I'd never seen such a beautiful baby as this—not even a faery one!" Nahia cringed at how frivolous her reason sounded; she wanted to add something of more substance but the broken sentences forming in her mind hinted at peevish whims she wasn't ready to express.

Sendoa looked unconvinced at the baby, as if he'd seen better. "Your reasoning doesn't bode well," he said, but didn't have a chance to say more or to further prod Nahia, as Calisto began to stir.

Rather than reducing him to faery height, Nahia chose to disperse the baby's weight and they used his blanket as a sling. The two faeries made an interesting sight with the large baby suspended between them as they wended through the forest to Handi Park.

Nahia heard the raspy whispering of the trees before they reached the Aspen Grove. As they got closer, she could tell more words had been added to the original message, and she had no trouble figuring out whose they were: "You fiend—give me back my son!" Of course, Xiomara had had no choice but to tell Alaia what happened. Nahia hung her head and they continued to cross the grove through a viciously hissing, leafy tunnel.

With grim relief, Nahia spotted the ivy-covered mound through the thinning tree trunks—the hidden entrance to Handi Park. Nahia, Sendoa, and the baby in his hammock pressed through the ivy in the spot known only to troop members. They descended ten stories through the central shaft, surrounded by the tiered exhibition stands notched on the earthen walls.

They reached the circular receiving hall at the bottom and Nahia still hadn't said a word—the hissing of the trees and Alaia's righteous demand still buzzed in her head. She followed Sendoa's lead, gliding past the bubbling spring radiating its bluish light and toward one of the twenty-one doorways in the receiving hall. She allowed Sendoa to pull her through the one marked with the royal amethyst lantern, all the while keeping an eye on Calisto.

Nahia exchanged a nervous glance with Sendoa before she rapped on Oihana's door with her free hand.

"Come in." The terse command didn't bode well.

Nahia trembled as the door opened and they passed into the room. They floated straight over to the queen's bed and deposited the baby on it. Calisto was sound asleep thanks to the swinging motion of the sling during their journey. Sendoa excused himself with a curt bow and left the way he came, closing the door behind him.

"I would not have believed you capable of such a thing! My stars!" fumed the Faery Queen as soon as they were alone. "Tell me you didn't stoop to leaving a changeling in place of this baby—what is his name?"

"Calisto," Nahia replied stiffly, feeling the sting of her mother's displeasure, "and no, I did not leave a changeling."

"Well, thank the stars for *that*," Oihana snapped, and it seemed to Nahia her mother's amethyst eyes flashed as if to add, *that* would have been the last straw!

Oihana pursed her lips and frowned at her daughter. Nahia shrank out of the way as she swept past her and out to the terrace. Nahia followed, although she kept a respectful distance. Mother and daughter stood in tense silence for a few minutes, looking over the veranda at the softly lit underground dwellings of the troop, their gardens, and the winding trails connecting them all.

Nahia could see her mother gripping the banister as if she would squeeze the lifeblood from it.

"You must simply give him back," Oihana said at length, looking steadily at her daughter. "He certainly is a beautiful baby, but that is no excuse for what you've done. I can't believe my own daughter has acted on the basest impulse our kind can display! I dearly hope you didn't do this to spite Alaia—"

Although doubt had begun to roll like waves through her mind, Nahia held her mother's penetrating glance. Could she really have done it just to satisfy her ill will? "I really can't understand what happened! I looked at him and something pierced my heart or my mind—I don't know! All I know is I had to take him from there," Nahia burst out in a wounded voice. "Am I really a despicable, baby-stealing faery? If you think I have it in me to deprive a mother of her child, then it must be so!" Nahia cried out plaintively, her eyes darting back toward the small, sleeping bundle on top of the bed, and the ache in her heart stabbed her again. *So what if I lose some sleep during his infanthood? He'll grow out of it soon enough.* "I can care for him so much better than her!" she exclaimed as she wrung her hands, looking at Oihana through her tears and hoping for understanding or forgiveness—she wasn't sure which.

"A child is her mother's treasure, and no one can steal or replace the bond of love between them. By attempting it, you've only magnified the dislike between you and Alaia, and now you must outdo yourself to repair the harm you swore you'd *never* inflict on any descendant of Celeste's."

Her mother's words washed frostily over Nahia and she hung her head, *I harmed Alaia—I didn't keep my word.* But soon a mitigating thought occurred to her. She hadn't inflicted bodily harm, not to Alaia and definitely not to Calisto. In fact, where he was concerned, her intention had been, and still was, to care for and provide the happiest life Celeste's newest descendant could hope for.

Oihana grazed Nahia's cheek, startling her out of her confused thoughts.

"I will give him back," Nahia sniffed dejectedly, but her expression cleared as soon as her mother kissed her. "I see no point though in returning him until nighttime," she added, determined to have Calisto for at least one full day.

"I will allow it," Oihana replied.

Trying to keep contrition out of her tone, for she had worked it out no real harm had come from her actions, Nahia went to silence the trees. They had been hissing nonstop since morning and it was time they stopped. She deliberately ignored Alaia's demand but responded to Xiomara's plea, reminding her of the promise made long ago to Celeste; she, Nahia, would watch over her birth sister's family. Never would she hurt any of them, not even a hair on their heads. "Be assured Calisto will be returned shortly after nightfall," she exhaled the promise with a heavy heart.

Nahia left the Aspen Grove without waiting for a response and spent the rest of the day with the baby, introducing him to the other faeries as Celeste's newest descendant. They cooed and crooned over him, gave him faery milk, and fought over who would rock him to sleep, which under normal circumstances would have been approximately every three hours, but with so many fairies fawning over him, Calisto was rocked and fed without respite for the entire day.

As dusk approached, Nahia didn't feel nearly as mutinous at the thought of returning him to Santillán, confident things would be patched up—how could they not? And as with the others, she'd be able to oversee Calisto's development in Santillán and in the Realm—she counted on Xiomara for that. Nahia's fancy launched her to the future; she could already see the seedlings sprouting and Calisto's forest thickening near Moon Dancer Lake. Happy thought!

She bathed the baby and dressed him in clean silky garments and swaddled him for the journey. Ignoring Oihana's warning, to start earlier rather than later to avoid further injury to Alaia, Nahia and Calisto, already at faery size, left the confines of Handi Park well after the sun dropped behind the Cantabrian. Cradling the baby, Nahia leisurely crossed the Arboretum, she passed into the forest, then skimmed over Moon Dancer Lake and bounded over the ridges and waterfall.

Nahia scowled at the Citadel as it came into view below them. She liked the feel of Calisto in her arms, and the thought of returning him to his mother did not sit well. A sudden chilly sense of doubt overtook her spirit: *What if this is the last time I see him?*

She entered the nursery and sulkily deposited Calisto in his crib; she placed her hands over him, directing the shape-shift one last time. The baby whimpered a little, but did not cry, and Nahia smiled, endeared. Just as she began to wonder why Xiomara wasn't there waiting for them, Nahia experienced an unpleasant shock as she spotted Alaia lurking in the shadows, glaring at her, her face distorted with rage and revulsion.

Unabashed, Nahia glowered back, finding she couldn't shed the old bitterness; Alaia simply infuriated her. Perhaps Nahia had deluded herself into thinking that because the abduction hadn't exceeded a full day, it could all be forgiven and forgotten. As it was, Alaia's scorn and fury, swollen beyond reason in Nahia's opinion, shook her with prickly anger.

Stepping out from the dark corner where she'd been skulking, Alaia seethed, "Leave here and *never* return."

Nahia's face flushed, blindsided by the finality of the demand. Clearly, Calisto's brief abduction had given Alaia the perfect excuse to openly despise her, and to be done with the Realm. The twitching lip, the scowl, the controlled voice, all evidenced Alaia's intention, as of that moment, to permanently sever the relationship Celeste and Xiomara had encouraged with the faery folk.

Incensed, Nahia's aquamarine eyes flashed warningly. "Don't tell me what to do!"

She caressed the baby's forehead deliberately and lifting his small fist to her lips, she kissed it. With a last withering look at Alaia, calculated to defy and irritate, Nahia flitted out of the window.

CHAPTER 4

FRESH HOPES

Nahia soared over the wall of the Citadel and immediately pitched herself to the ground, the better to feel the speed as she blew across the meadow toward the hills. She shot up the mountainside to the ridge, keeping her angry thoughts at bay by focusing on the terrain rushing at her.

A fiend, am I? Nahia thought heatedly as she exploded over the summit—dust, pebbles and leaves shot in every direction. She lost herself momentarily in the cool mist of the waterfall, but her sea-green aura was soon visible again as she ascended close enough to graze the plunging waters with her fingers.

Nahia cleared the jagged rocks and crossed over to the Cradle of the Pyrenees. She dove into the gnarled gullies and misty woodland on her way to Moon Dancer Lake. "Leave here and never return," Alaia had said, and Nahia sped through, glowering, and grazing branches on her path, not caring about the abrasions they caused. She zigzagged between the shadowy trees, her aura acting like a strobe light, briefly illuminating the creased trunks and undergrowth in bright flashes as she passed.

She sensed the vegetation overhead thinning, signaling her approach to the lakeshore, but she didn't pause. She blazed over the western edge of the lake, rippling the surface with her slipstream. "Can't tell me what to do," she hissed.

Nahia charged toward the dark forest ready to plunge into it, but a silver light flickered from the branches ahead and she halted abruptly, mere feet from the shadowy pines.

"Oh good—you are back," Sendoa said casually, gliding off the bough where he'd been waiting for her. "I was starting to worry—wondered if I should go looking for you."

"No need," Nahia replied feeling a little dizzy from the sudden stop.

"So, how did it go?"

Even though she knew how foolish it had been to expect gratitude, Nahia couldn't help herself. "There were no thanks for the return of the child, I'll tell you that!" With that off her chest, she launched huffily into the crux of it: "Xiomara wasn't even there, only Alaia lurking in a corner. Do you know what she said to me?"

Sendoa shook his head.

"She told me *never* to return, can you believe it? I only kept the baby for *one* day!"

Sendoa gave her a knowing look. "How could you expect otherwise? You made her feel like an outcast all her life, and then you steal her first-born son. Why would she be forgiving of you, much less appreciative?"

Nahia drifted backward a few feet so as to properly glare at Sendoa; she put her hands on her hips and set off: "*I* made her feel like an outcast? I think she did it all by herself. Alaia has always hated everything to do with me. She could *never* be one of us like the rest of her family and she knows that. Sometimes I think she goes out of her way to make herself different. She knows she's not coordinated enough to play our games, her voice is not sweet enough to learn our songs, her hands are not soft enough, her hair is not silky enough, and her eyes are not expressive enough. Her shortcomings are endless! Yet her mother and uncles fit right in with the Faerie Court—how can that be? They are accepted, welcomed and enjoyed by us. It was *she* who chose to focus her attention on ignoring the faery world and see only the human dimension she belongs in, likely because she has nothing to contribute here."

"But, Nahia, you are older than she is, and I would hope wiser. You should have recognized all those shortcomings and instead of punishing her for them, you should have looked for something worthy of praise."

There was a little too much compassion and common sense in Sendoa's argument for Nahia's liking, but she wasn't ready to make any admissions. Why was it so difficult to forgive Alaia for not having faery-like qualities? So what if the girl had instead applied herself to lessons taught by human tutors? So what if she had a great head for business, as Xiomara often said. In fact, despite her young age Alaia had eagerly taken on a great many household decisions her mother and uncles simply had no head for.

"What is that to me anyway—" Nahia blustered to a grinning Sendoa who seemed to know what she wouldn't voice. "The nerve of her! Telling *me* not to ever return?"

"Yes—that is sort of final. I do wonder what Xiomara thinks about it."

They glided toward the forest, side by side, discussing the subject more calmly. By the time they arrived at the ivy-covered mound (just outside the Aspen Grove, which was mercifully silent), Nahia had decided she would speak with Xiomara the very next day. "No point in delaying clarifications," she said, wishing Sendoa a good night.

Whether Sendoa had a soothing effect on her or her reasoning was really on target, Nahia slept soundly through the night, convinced all would be straightened out in the morning.

At the break of dawn, however, a discreet knock at Nahia's door woke her. She opened one eye, then the other, and looked around her chamber, thinking perhaps she'd imagined it. But the soft knock reached her ears again.

"Come in," she called, drawing the silk coverlet to her chest as she sat up on her soft bed-nest, whose gnarled base was threaded thick with sweet honeysuckle.

In glided Oihana's chambermaid decked in the required lilac livery, and she bobbed mid-air, curtseying. "Good morning, my sapling," she sang, vanishing the night screen with a well-practiced upward glance; natural daylight dropped in from the skylight.

"Morning, Zuzen—" Nahia yawned, rubbing her eyes. In the light, her room looked like an underwater green and blue crater at high noon. "Is something the matter?"

"Afraid so—your mother sends for you—the Aspen Grove is speaking once again."

"Oh?" Nahia said, rising out of her nest and shedding her nightdress as she floated to her room's spring for a quick dip. "It is not Alaia again, is it?"

"No my sapling, it is Madame Xiomara and she requests an audience with you and the Faery Queen."

Nahia plunked into the water like one of those pebbles she so much enjoyed tossing into the pond by Paloma's Hall of Glamour. She came out spouting water from her mouth and smoothing her hair away from her face. "Well, that is lucky then," Nahia said, wrinkling her nose—she'd been looking forward to returning to Santillán as soon as possible, because Alaia had told her *not* to. "I meant to speak with her today at the Citadel."

"Sendoa has already gone to fetch her," Zuzen said, patting Nahia down with a bath sheet, "so let's get you fed and over to the Tablinum."

What an ominous location for a meeting, thought Nahia with a raised brow, as she followed Zuzen's lead.

25

The Tablinum was an airy circular chamber, long ago designed by Oihana to promote creative discussion and encourage decision-making. Guests at the Tablinum entered the room and found themselves in a replica of San Sebastián's Bahía de la Concha. Having never seen it, Nahia took everyone's word the likeness was remarkable indeed and trusted she would see it for herself someday. Monte Urgull rose to the left of the bay and Monte Igueldo opposite of it. The half-shell beach with its white sands united the two formations—and the city of San Sebastián crept over the hills.

During the day, the enchantment in the Tablinum made the sky-ceiling look like a cloudless summer day in the city of San Sebastián, while in the evening a full moon bathed everything in silver radiance. Against the horizon, breaking the breeze and the shallow waves, stood the rounded mass of the island of Santa Clara, with its distinctive brambly appearance.

Nahia paused in the passageway leading to the Tablinum. She squinted in the direction of the door and heard her mother's and Xiomara's voices already there. Struck anew by the solemnity of Oihana's chosen meeting place, something writhed uncomfortably in Nahia's belly. She proceeded anyway. *Really, what could happen?*

After an hour's discussion, Nahia had found out. She numbly watched Sendoa emerge from the passageway to escort Xiomara out of the Tablinum and take her back to Santillán. She could feel Oihana's steady glance on her but was too dazed to look at her mother.

"Nahia, darling," Oihana said at length, "it is not completely your fault."

Nahia looked up, "Isn't it?"

"The animosity has been mutual all along, we knew that. Alaia had been waiting to act at the right moment, with the right excuse."

"But, mother, never to set foot in Santillán? How can Xiomara have agreed?"

"Perhaps when you have a child of your own you will understand what lengths one is willing to go to for them—" Oihana replied. "Alaia is acting on what she thinks is best for Calisto, and Xiomara acts on what is best for her daughter."

Nahia couldn't decide what bothered her most—that it had happened so unexpectedly (not two hours before she'd been getting out of bed with great expectations) or that it had been so out of her control. The more she thought about it, the more she realized that not only had she been told what to do and what would come to pass, but that all had been done without her having a say. To add insult to injury, as Nahia headed out of the Tablinum,

Oihana seemed to think it necessary to *formally* forbid her, Nahia, to go into the Citadel in Santillán.

And so began the new dynamic between Celeste's descendants and the Faerie Court. For two decades the only contact with Celeste's family was at the Realm. Xiomara and her brothers, never Alaia or Calisto, joined her for changes of season. Nahia anticipated each visit as intensely as she bemoaned them when they were over.

In 1906, Xiomara died, and Alaia dealt another horrible blow to Nahia; she refused to allow the faery folk to attend Xiomara's burial ceremony. This decision sent a clear message to the Faery Queen, who in turn, in an unprecedented display of injured pride, forbade all further communication or contact with the humans. As one, the faery troop of the Western Pyrenees disconnected themselves from the Santillán-St. Michel family, after eighty-seven years of being bound to one another.

Nahia could not agree with the ruling. She thought it beyond unfair and, as a result, hated Alaia more fervently than ever. She sat quite still on a bough of the Great Oak by the pond, above Paloma's grave, brooding—knowing her beloved Xiomara's funeral was happening at that very moment in Santillán, and she wasn't there to pay her last respects.

As dusk seeped through the canopy, Nahia rose from the branch, cloaked in her glittering sea-green aura. She floated there for a few seconds—brow furrowed. Then, all in a moment, without a sound, she darted purposefully through the trees. Within seconds she was skimming over Moon Dancer Lake. She bounded over the waterfall and with vengeance in her heart, she charged the walls of the Citadel.

Nahia broke into Xiomara's chamber through an open window, not bothering to be subtle; in fact, she hoped to be detected. The glittering orb hurtled into the room and hit the floor hard, instantly disgorging a version of Nahia at full human height amid sparkling dust, which dissipated as quickly as it had appeared.

Nahia stood looking at the familiar surroundings lighted by a dim bulb above the closed door; it gave the room a forlorn appearance. *Perfumed candles should be burned here to honor Xiomara's inner light*, Nahia thought, convinced such kindness would never occur to Alaia.

How many times had she been there before, talking with Xiomara until the early morning hours? Nahia's chest felt constricted all of a sudden, her sight blurred with tears. She spotted the trunk at the foot of Xiomara's bed, and wiping her eyes with an angry swipe, she opened it, digging through blankets and linens to the bottom, until with a fumbling hand, she found what she was looking for.

Nahia pulled out Xiomara's book, the one entitled *Faery Sight*, which contained their history. She pressed it to her chest, "Alaia will die one day," she muttered bitterly, "and I will give this to the one through whom the family can be reunited again."

The door to the room burst open unexpectedly and Nahia whirled toward it, startled though ready to face Alaia, for surely it was she.

It was not. A man stood there, his hand on the door handle. He stared at Nahia, who was rooted to the spot, the book clutched to her wildly beating heart. For a few seconds she thought she was looking at Etienne, magically restored not only to life but to his youth as well.

"Who are you?" he said with a slight frown, and Nahia knew at once—twenty years before, a baby she'd held in her arms had had the same expression. As the initial shock wore off, the differences between Etienne and his great-grandson became more evident.

Calisto, thought the faery, and the beating of her heart intensified, causing her aura to again emit sparks like stardust around her. Through it, she stared stupidly into his ash-colored eyes, unable to utter a single word, though a hundred thoughts raced through her mind. His frown deepened and he took a step toward her. "Who are you?" he repeated.

Nahia opened her mouth to speak but Alaia's voice was heard instead, as she came into the room behind her son. In a complete state of agitation, Nahia shrank, book and all, and flashed out of the window. Whether she'd reacted out of shock, cowardice, or panic, Nahia did not know. But she wasn't upset about it, nor was she fazed by having arrived at Moon Dancer Lake with no recollection of her flight—her head was full of Calisto.

She drifted distractedly over the water, coming out of her shock, trying to unravel her thoughts and feelings. Certainly, the intervening twenty years had turned him into a vision, redefining all Nahia's ideas of masculine beauty. But now there was a deeper pull, drawing her inexorably to Calisto; he was a destiny she could not refuse or resist.

Once again her mother's admonitions came to mind, but Nahia would not allow her thoughts to be derailed. "He's been his mother's treasure long enough," she declared, watching her reflection on the water as she drifted over it. *He is a grown man now*, Nahia thought at length, *and Alaia can't tell me what to do.*

She would present herself to him, in spite of Alaia's expressed command, and let him choose whether or not he'd like to know her. The thought cheered her. She paused over the water and thought everything around her looked different somehow. A smile played on her lips, recalling the pleasurable surprise it had been to see Calisto. She laughed out loud thinking of her stupid aura becoming a whirlwind of glitter, likely obscuring her face. He probably thought her an apparition or a ghost, as so many humans were fond of sighting. Certainly Alaia would never have spoken to him about faeries.

Humming to herself, Nahia flitted through the forest and the Arboretum, back to Handi Park. Of course, she would not tell her mother yet, but she *would* return to Santillán, and she would find a way to see Calisto again. Their acquaintance would begin right away and in secret.

The very next afternoon, determined to make a good, if not unforgettable, impression on Calisto, Nahia turned her wardrobe inside out looking for just the right garment. Her head seemed to rattle continuously with opening statements she might use, but she couldn't decide on any one phrase. Adding to her distress, Sendoa seemed to suspect something, and he kept springing questions at the oddest moments, hoping to surprise her into replying with the truth.

With one thing and another, it took her two days to feel sufficiently prepared. She had settled on an emerald sheath dress she thought would look wonderful with her forest-green hooded cloak.

Nahia had just returned the roll of yellow fabric to Usoa's loom shop (as a new dress needn't be made) and was about to enter her room again when Sendoa confronted her. "You are going to Santillán—aren't you?"

Nahia pursed her lips, refusing to answer. He'd found her out. Sendoa smirked and nodded curtly as she brushed past him, which further irritated her.

Feeling wrong-footed early the next morning, for she had to sneak out of Handi Park to avoid questions, Nahia set off to the Citadel. The fluttering anticipation in her belly only unnerved her more. At least the shades of green she'd layered on herself were quite becoming. As for her opening speech, "I am Nahia," sounded more and more pompous every time she said it, and "Would you believe we are destined for one another?" felt more and more awkward, but she couldn't think of anything more suited to this important introduction—her very life felt as if it hung on its success.

With a frustrated groan, Nahia swooped over the waterfall and down into the valley. The Citadel walls were already in her line of sight. Her heart beat in her throat making it hard to breathe. *I'll let myself be surprised with whatever comes out of my mouth*, she thought nervously; in her current state, she didn't really have a choice.

Nahia opted for Xiomara's bedroom window again. She shifted to human height instantly upon entering and caught a glimpse of herself in the full-length mirror beside a wardrobe; her reflection pleased her. With a rush of nerves, she noticed the bedroom door was open and realized she hadn't really thought what to do if she ran into any of the family members. She had assumed she would find Calisto by himself.

The sound of women speaking reached Nahia inside Xiomara's room. She recognized Alaia's voice at once and assumed the other belonged to a maid; her tone was that of someone giving testimony and it put Nahia on alert.

"Two carriages left this morning?" Alaia repeated what the maid had said as if she didn't believe a word of it.

"Yes ma'am. The three gentlemen were in one and the other carried some trunks," replied the maid.

Nahia dared not credit her ears: *Calisto, gone—Exteban and Bastien too?*

As the conversation down the passage continued, it became a painful certainty. The men had left the ancestral lands, refusing to remain under the dark umbrella Alaia had opened over them. Nahia was sure of it. Xiomara hadn't been buried two days and they all had dispersed. To the faery, the news was bittersweet—Alaia deserved her share, but Nahia's plans had once again been dashed without her having a say.

She smiled ironically—it turned out Xiomara, a human, had been the light, the living force holding them together all those years, not the Faery Queen or even the Faery Princess. Nonplussed, for Nahia had been convinced she was at the heart of their relationship, her thoughts spiraled down to old beliefs. Had the family spent more time with *her*, they would've never considered leaving Santillán, unless perhaps to live full time in the Faerie Realm.

In the sitting room at the end of the passage, the maid had stopped talking and although Nahia could not see her, she imagined Alaia sitting on one of the upholstered chairs facing the windows, staring fixedly at the lonely years stretching before her.

Yes, Nahia thought, *Alaia deserves to be abandoned, but not me.*

The unkind thought lingered long enough to guilt Nahia into feeling a twinge of pity for Alaia, but she watered it down and lost it altogether in shifting back to faery height. She bobbed midair for an instant, taking in the furnishings, the hangings on the walls, all the memories held in the familiar place, and she wondered if she'd ever come back—would there be a reason to?

Nahia shrugged this off too as Calisto's face and form, the way he'd appeared to her two days before, filled the doorway, taking her breath away.

Nahia turned from the rousing vision and flitted out of the room the same way she'd come in, muttering, "Anyway, who says this is the end? He will be back . . . ."

With a backward glance at the window, willing it to be with every fiber of her being, she added, "He *will* come back."

CHAPTER 5
A FAERY'S FIRST KISS

Nahia returned to Handi Park feeling as wrong-footed as when she'd left; the sense of loss would not soon leave the Faery Princess. Throughout the rest of the day, hardly an hour went by she didn't think about Calisto. She went about her daily routine in a distracted fashion; the few seconds she'd seen him had been an assault to her senses. His ash-colored eyes glinted in her mind in stormy flashes. And the sound of his voice echoed in her head. "Who are you?" he had asked, twice! Nahia deluded herself into believing she'd detected longing in his question—desire too—and he might have even recognized a touch of fate as well. Her heart leapt at the thought. A burning desire overtook Nahia; she must find Calisto right away and substantiate herself in his present awareness. Nothing else would satisfy her.

The first seven days passed in feverish musings that failed to yield a concrete plan, and Nahia began to feel anxious. She stole out of Handi Park one morning after breakfast, with a large cup of tea, being careful not to spill as she glided to the pond. She perched herself on a branch of the mighty oak above Paloma's grave in order to brood in peace.

As water trickled merrily over the boulders damming the pond, and the early sunshine seeped through the canopy spreading a misty blanket over the ground, Nahia focused on the practical aspects of her predicament. For instance, how long did Calisto mean to stay away? A few months might be fine, but what if he had no intention of returning? What if, before she could find him, three or four decades passed in that wretched human dimension and he became an old man? Would she still feel they were destined to be with one another?

She knew she must find Calisto soon and bring him into the Realm, where they could exist on the same plane. Setting her cup on the wide branch, Nahia drew up her legs and hugged them. With a troubled sigh she rested her chin on her knees and stared unblinking at the misty pond. She would have to appeal to the Keeper of the Forest, the magnificent unicorn, Basajaun—last of his kind, through whose magic, the Realm, Handi Park, and the faeries in it, were allowed to exist hidden from the human world. She was fairly certain only Basajaun could allow Calisto into the Faerie Dimension, the way he'd once done with Paloma and Celeste.

Although there was still a lot for Nahia to learn, she knew well enough it was because of Basajaun's vital magic that the water in Moon Dancer Lake was warm throughout the entire year in spite of the elevation, which would result in glacial temperatures anywhere else on the planet. And their Arboretum was a lush garden where soft tropical species thrived alongside hardy alpine varieties. Most importantly, Basajaun had devised how time would be accounted for in the Realm—which wasn't a question of time passing at all; it was rather a matter of existing in a dimension with different, magical rules.

As a young faery, Nahia had been told the story of how Basajaun one day combined the individual nature of every living thing around them to make a collective soul for the Realm. Nahia's imagination had immediately conjured visions of the beautiful unicorn drawing streamers of misty light from every creature. She saw him twist those in an upward swirl until they touched the sky, and then he bid them open up like a glittering umbrella over the Realm to encapsulate the brand-new collective soul.

However Nahia chose to picture it then, the result had been a true fusion of individuals where the experience of one impacted the whole. Longevity was easily the best evidence of how Basajaun's magic worked because the life expectancy of all had been averaged into one. Since the Realm included such things as mountains, trees, and bodies of water, the resulting lifespan of the inhabitants had lengthened significantly.

Nahia sipped her tea and shook her head, remembering she'd once tried to explain it all to a very inquisitive Xiomara. "We all reside permanently in the light," Nahia had said to the fifteen-year-old girl, motioning toward the sun, as that was the biggest light within sight and because Nahia still wasn't quite clear herself on that point. "From there, we drop into this planet to learn the lessons the body can teach, and the length of our stay is determined by how our bodies are put together.

"If the structure of a body makes it prone to disease, then its life will be shorter than a body whose constitution is sturdy."

Eyes wide with dawning wonder, Xiomara had nodded and remarked, "That's why it's so important to make the right choices—to have more time."

"Exactly. Each body is like its own time pod—and not just bodies like ours, there are innumerable time pods on the planet: each human, each animal, a rock, the mountains, trees, the ocean, they all exist here as their own time capsule."

Here, Xiomara had tilted her head looking confused, and Nahia hastened to rattle off more of the lessons given her by Oihana. "Time isn't something that passes us by, nor is it something we move through as if over a never-ending path. We carry our own time inside. My mother says it is written in our blood," she added importantly.

"But then, can we know how long we have?"

"Not down to a day or a moment, only a general idea, and always allowing for accidents, deliberate harm, and choices," Nahia trailed off, frowning vaguely. But then she remembered herself and went on to say, "That's the way it is everywhere on earth, but here in the Realm, things are different. The Keeper of the Forest has taken all the time pods and magically bound us. Even though our time is still measured in days and years, the limited time we were born with has been magically re-written—we live so much longer in the Realm because we are one with the mountains and trees."

Contrary to Nahia's expectation, Xiomara hadn't been tempted by such fantastic revelations. Neither had Celeste for that matter, and the faery couldn't understand why. Lost in layers of recollections and lessons, Nahia absently brought the cup to her lips again and pondered whether or not the structure of Xiomara's body or Calisto's would enable them to live in the Realm. Was their structure different than hers? She suspected that it was, and that's why Basajaun's magic would be necessary to change them.

Nahia gulped down the last of her lavender and chamomile infusion. She frowned at its failure to relax her or light up her mind with answers and muttered, "I'll try linden flower tomorrow."

"So are you going to tell me what's troubling you?" Sendoa intruded, causing her to drop the empty cup into the mounds of morning glory at the foot of the tree.

Nahia twisted round to look at him. "Nothing's troubling me," she lied.

Sendoa didn't look convinced, and Nahia bristled.

"I mean it," she insisted, flouncing off the branch and joining him.

Together they set off over the elderberry lane. "You think you know me so well, but really, you mostly imagine things going on with me."

Sendoa ignored her remark. "Seven days ago you went to Santillán—what did you do? You've been different since you came back."

Nahia scowled. "Don't you have anything better to do than watch what I'm doing every minute of the day?"

Sendoa laughed good-naturedly, "Nothing as entertaining."

Nahia looked away but Sendoa grabbed her hand and squeezed it. "Just tell me. No good keeping things shut up—it is so much better to air them out."

Sendoa was right, she needed to release her anxiety more than she knew and the words rushed out of her. "Exteban and Bastien have gone from the ancestral lands, and they've taken Calisto with them. They abandoned Alaia; left *her* alone but didn't bother to tell me, I mean, *us*, anything about it either."

"And no one knows where they've gone?" Sendoa asked seriously.

Nahia shook her head, releasing his hand, "Why would they not say? I thought they valued me, I mean *us*, more than that."

"It is certainly out of character for Exteban and Bastien, but what do you care about Calisto?" Sendoa asked craftily. Nahia turned away again but he persisted.

"What?" Nahia said, annoyed.

"You've not been to see Calisto, have you?"

"Just once—I didn't even talk to him." Nahia groaned defensively, still trying to avoid Sendoa's glance, fearing he would see straight into her heart. But whom was she kidding? He must have heard it in her voice.

Sendoa put his hand on her shoulder. "Look at me," he said.

Nahia held her breath, but did as he asked. Momentarily distracted by the muscle jumping in Sendoa's jaw, Nahia forgot her fears and wondered why he should look as angry as he did. Sendoa withdrew his hand from her shoulder, almost shoving her away, which made Nahia wince.

"Your mother forbade it," he said sternly.

"Yes, but I didn't agree with her ruling," Nahia shrugged.

"So now you are choosing which rules to follow, are you?" Sendoa glowered, bobbing midair in front of her.

"Since when do you care about that? Do I need to remind you, you've been right beside me during most of my rulebreaking?" she fired back and it was his turn to look away, momentarily silenced. Ignoring his confusion, Nahia squared her shoulders and pressed on, glimpsing for the first time the beginning of a plan and clinging to it. "I'm going to San Sebastián," she declared. "I will find where Calisto's got himself to, and summon him back to me."

Sendoa looked at Nahia with something akin to pity, and it irked her. She'd been about to amend her last statement to say she would summon Calisto back to the *troop*, but decided against it.

The muscle twitched again in Sendoa's jaw and a thought streaked across her mind; Sendoa wasn't angry about her rule breaking, he was jealous! She pressed her lips together and watched her friend steadily. He held her gaze but before she could utter a word; he muttered, "I will go with you."

Nahia blinked disconcerted. "You really mean it?"

"I've never been to San Sebastián, and you're bound to get into even more trouble if you go by yourself," he said, recovering his good humor.

Of course he is not *jealous*, Nahia thought, relieved. *He is Sendoa, my dearest friend and accomplice.*

If she'd been told that day eight years would pass before she'd get even a hint of Calisto's whereabouts, Nahia would not have believed it possible to endure. Thus, blissfully ignorant, she spent each day filled with hope, pining, and plotting, blindly trusting tomorrow, or the next day would bring Calisto back to her, while down at the Citadel, Alaia's mind and body became eight years older and her heart eight shades darker in her isolation.

Nahia exerted her powers far and wide searching for Calisto. At the height of desperation, she started fishing for at least traces of his thoughts from others, but she got nothing. She berated herself, questioning her powers, and at last came to the disappointing conclusion her range of influence must have its limits. She cursed herself for having been so busy abducting him she never gave him a Cradle Gift. Why did she not think to give him something she could use now? But even if it had occurred to her, she only had the one chance. What would a helpful gift have been?

Every night Nahia would cast her dreams blindly to the stars, hoping they would catch up with him wherever he might be. She woke in the mornings wishing him a good day and fell asleep at night with his name on her lips.

True to his word, Sendoa had gone with her to San Sebastián at the beginning of the eight-year stretch. There they found out Calisto had originally sailed on a ship bound for England, and Nahia thought it reasonable he might one day come back the same way. She started going to San Sebastián, with or without Sendoa, to stare at the ocean and examine every ship entering the Bay of Biscay, determined to be first to spot his return.

Sometimes she would venture out to the island of Santa Clara, even spend the night there, fearful a ship might sneak in while she slept in Handi Park. She would set up camp on the west side of the island. There, she would cast tendrils of energy like fishing lines into the ocean, and once anchored, she would put herself in a well-rehearsed lucid dream state.

Nahia's obsessive devotion (she'd been reduced to scrying the thoughts of passing sailors and tourists) was rewarded on a starlit spring night on the eighth year of her vigil. She picked up a fuzzy image of him, secondhand, from someone onboard. He was homeward bound on a yacht, and what a satisfaction to have persevered.

Calisto had crossed the English Channel days before and was now sailing within sight of the shores of France, on his way home. From the fragments of conversation she heard, Nahia gathered the vessel would arrive in a leisurely seven days' time.

Unbeknownst to Calisto, the faery's thoughts touched him with sparkling feelers made up of her crackling energy. Nahia seized on anything she could to fix the sight of him and his surroundings in her mind, establishing the necessary connection between them. Not until she felt securely anchored did Nahia rise from her position on the topmost stone she'd piled at Santa Clara's summit (the better to meditate), and hovered there momentarily, her body and mind trained due north, up the coast of France.

With a sigh of relief and a surge of excitement for the next stage of her plan, Nahia bounded back to Handi Park. Inspired far beyond anything she'd accomplished to date, and with so little time before twenty-eight-year-old Calisto arrived, Nahia entered into her potions and conjuring with feverish zeal. She thanked the heavens for the auspicious timing of her discovery, which would enable her to do her work during the cycle of the waxing moon, when her energies peaked.

During the day, Nahia endured Sendoa's suspicious glances and laughed off his questions: "What has happened? You're not going to San Sebastián today? You are up to something, admit it." She was so busy hiding her anticipation she failed to notice Oihana had begun to watch her with curious interest, too.

At night, when all was quiet in Handi Park's lantern lit passageways, Nahia would rise from her nest and slip unseen to the Celestial Observatory, where the second part of her plan began to unfold. Bathed in the soothing bluish light coming through a skylight, Nahia sat on sapphire pavers beside the reflection well, and with extraordinary singleness of mind, she cast herself into Calisto's dreams. Thanks to the connection already established between them, the faery had at last hit upon the perfect gift—Lucid Dreaming—and she bestowed it upon him. She grinned, thoroughly reconciled with herself, as this was so much more helpful than any Cradle Gift she could have given him as an infant.

By the end of the fifth day, she had finished mixing the complicated concoction for stabilizing the shape-shift she wanted to attempt. It was safely maturing by moonlight, on a topmost branch of Paloma's Oak. With a little luck, Calisto's ship would dock on the eve of the full moon.

Nahia continued to sing to him in dreams. She invaded his privacy in ways the Faery Queen would have considered unlawful; she built visions exactly as she wanted him to see. She spoke to him of her longing in such a way that Calisto couldn't distinguish whose it was. And on the last night, she fed him a dream in which she appeared adrift on the ocean and near to death. She hinted that was the likely reason her subconscious mind had been able to reach him, and told him that her near-lifeless body would land at Santa Clara by morning.

Well before sunup, as Nahia threw a cloak over herself; a sense of wrongdoing swooped down on her, whipping her heart into an unbearable gallop. What would her mother think? Everyone would soon realize the Faery Princess had gone, and only Sendoa would have an inkling as to where. Would he tell? Would he come after her?

Nahia tried to shrug off the dreadful feeling but it came out like a spasm. There was no turning back. She opened the door to her room and stepped into the lantern-lit passage.

"Stealing away, like a thief in the night."

Sendoa's whisper startled her badly. Nahia froze with her hand still on the door handle she'd meant to close without a sound. Steeling herself with a deep breath, she turned to face him—he would not stop her, not now. Nahia opened her mouth to speak but he gave her a quelling look.

"I'm not going to stop you, if that is what you're afraid of. But I won't let you leave without this—" Sendoa advanced on her so suddenly Nahia could not react. Before she realized what was happening, he grabbed her face in both his hands and kissed her roughly on the mouth.

Even more surprising, in view of where she was headed, was that Nahia closed her eyes and responded with matching intensity.

CHAPTER 6

A HUMAN'S FIRST KISS

Nahia's brows arched in wonder even though her eyes remained closed while Sendoa's lips covered hers. How could she account for this?

He pulled away. She could still feel his breath on her face as her eyelids fluttered open and she looked at him dreamily, but the smirk on his face confused her, and Nahia frowned.

"You are out of your mind if you think I'll let you waste your first kiss on a human," Sendoa said. "Yes, I know what you're up to."

The dreamy look slipped off Nahia's face completely. Her nostrils flared and she glared at him. She hadn't realized she'd started down the exact same path Amets had! What if she'd given her first kiss to a human and lost her heart to him? And when Calisto died, he would have taken her heart with him. Did she now have to thank Sendoa for anticipating it? She might, if only she wasn't so irked. Still, why did he kiss her with such intensity? And why did *she* respond? Had she misunderstood his intensity? Did she even *want* Sendoa to have meant it?

"Fine! Thank you for your foresight," she blustered. Sendoa winked at her.

Perplexed, and beset by other grating sensations, Nahia glided down the passageway toward the atrium without a backward glance. Her plan was fully formed and its execution would not be delayed, not even to decipher Sendoa's possible motives or feelings. She had already decided that persuading Basajaun and her mother to accept and admit Calisto into the Realm was out of the question. Instead, she would adopt human form to meet him, and when she could offer proof of Calisto's love to Oihana, she would reveal her faery nature to him. Only then would she begin the tricky task of easing him into the Realm.

Nahia exited Handi Park and took to the inky sky above the treetops—she dipped briefly to retrieve the potion from its hiding place on a topmost branch of the Oak and immediately rose again seeking a clear line of sight. She wanted Sendoa's smirk out of her thoughts, but the heat of his lips stayed with her until the glittering outskirts of San Sebastián came into view.

"Stop it!" she groaned, skimming the dark terrain below to distract herself with a sense of speed. She blew past the outskirts and flashed between buildings, following the narrow streets to San Sebastián's distinctive seaside promenade, Paseo de la Concha. She dashed over the narrow strip of sandy beach and reached her target in the middle of the bay: Santa Clara Island.

Nahia landed on the summit beside her pile of stones. She grounded herself to take stock of Calisto's position, and of the time she had before he arrived. He was so close, she fancied catching his scent in the breeze. With renewed faith, she pulled the vial out of a fold in her cloak and briefly admired her glittering handiwork. In two gulps she drank down the potion meant to help her sustain human form long-term.

As soon as she felt the liquid spread inside of her, Nahia focused on helping the shape-shift. The seagull that had been watching her attentively for some time gave an outraged squawk, spread its wings, and soared away the instant Nahia shot up from ten inches tall to her petite human height of five feet four inches.

Her turquoise streaks were gone, and Nahia was glad of it, as during her visits to San Sebastián she hadn't seen a single female sporting such hair color. Plain golden waves would have to do.

With a bitter sense of loss, Nahia also realized that her sea-green aura could not glow when in human form. More than Sendoa's kiss, this made Nahia think about the extraordinary decision she'd made. But there was simply *no* turning back. *And anyway*, she thought, *humans don't walk around with glowing auras.*

There were two, maybe three hours before Calisto's ship docked. Already the sky was lightening in the east. Nahia closed her eyes and took three steeling breaths; when she opened them again she felt ready to act.

She descended to the western shore of the island and picked the spot for her fake landing, shielded from the city and with the open sea before her. Nahia conjured a makeshift raft out of driftwood—it looked convincingly like a chunk ripped from the deck of a boat. She'd altered her cloak and gown so they'd appear ragged. When they were sufficiently torn and filthy to offer the impression of having survived a shipwreck, Nahia submerged herself in the cold water.

Shivering head to foot, she walked back to the raft and draped herself over it. *This bit of reality in the plan will lend credibility to my appearance*, she told herself through chattering teeth. By the time Calisto found her, she would be very cold, exhausted and thoroughly sore.

The yacht ought to have docked, thought Nahia, failing to find a comfortable spot on the raft. Her feverish anxiety peaked, certain he must be on his way. She imagined their two beating hearts coming together at last and hammering inside her own chest.

Trampling sounds reached her and she forgot to breathe. The earth beneath her shuddered with rushed footsteps. Someone knelt beside her, panting, and presumably staring at her. It occurred to Nahia she might look too lifeless; so she let out a timely moan denoting, she hoped, pain and relief.

He gasped and sprang into action upon hearing it; he slid his hand behind her neck and helped her to a sitting position. "For a moment I feared you were dead!"

After a few fluttering attempts, Nahia opened her eyes and, rapture! She beheld the object of her obsession, mere inches from her own face. "You came for me," she said tremulously.

"Here," he said, offering his canteen, which Nahia accepted and took two sips of water. She settled her weight back on his arm, almost snuggled against his chest, and listened to his story, which he rushed to tell, words tumbling out and over one another, impressing upon her his gleeful disbelief. "I landed in San Sebastián near seven in the morning, and like a man possessed I bounded off deck, and jumped into a motorboat, refusing assistance. I sped here to find you, cursing the size of the island because it might have prevented me from finding you in time. But I felt you guiding me like an angel—is that strange?"

"Not at all," Nahia said weakly. "I *did* guide you. I brought you to me because you were my only hope."

"All these days we've talked in dreams, you never once told me your name." Calisto held her close and brushed the blond locks from her cheek.

"Anahí," replied the faery; her lips grazed his as she spoke her made-up name. *Made up just for him*, she thought.

Calisto drew back and touched his mouth. Apparently he couldn't tell if he'd just been kissed or if it had been an accident. "How real you have been in my dreams! I feel I've known you all my life and yet this is the first time we've laid eyes on one another."

Nahia stirred uneasily. Had she ruined everything by being too bold, too familiar? "I feel the same way," she replied demurely. "We might even be connected since another life."

"Yes." he agreed with the entranced look of someone grasping a revelation.

Liar. The word popped into Nahia's guilt-ridden mind as if an outside force had aimed it at her and she shifted uncomfortably.

Meanwhile, Calisto seemed to have worked through his astonishment and disbelief; not bothering with even a furtive glance at their surroundings, he gathered Nahia to him and kissed her, erasing her concerns and convincing her anew that she'd been right all along.

CHAPTER 7

UNSETTLED

Calisto gallantly took off his coat and put it over her shoulders. Nahia was glad of it, as it protected her from the cold, and it concealed the bare flesh visible through her torn clothes. They set off on the tortuous path back to where he'd left the boat. Calisto half supported, half carried her over the rough terrain.

"Thank you," she murmured, feeling both safe and exhilarated in his arms.

"I have you now—thank God," he said, his eyes trained on the sloping ground as if looking for the easiest path. He fussed over her, asking time and again how she was, apparently unconvinced by her reassurances.

Amid tender exchanges, which Nahia took to heart and treasured, he guided her to the San Sebastián-facing shore of the island. She hoped he'd dismiss the rapid breathing and trembling as symptoms of her condition; after all, she was supposed to have been drifting at sea—she could very well be suffering from a feverish delirium—she was indeed feverish and delirious! "I'm sure I don't have a respiratory condition," Nahia rebuked his most recent assessment while he lifted her in his arms as if she weighed nothing and deposited her on the cross plank inside the motorboat.

"Just the same, as soon as we get to my house, I will have the doctor look in on you." He pulled the line he'd tied around a shrub, threw it into the tiny boat, and climbed in. He pushed off with an oar, started the engine, and they set off toward the mainland.

"You live in town, then?"

"I used to live in our family estate in Santillán until I left eight years ago, but we do have a house in San Sebastián where I plan to take you."

Nahia thanked her stars Calisto didn't intend to take her to his mother.

She sat across from him, watching him maneuver the boat toward the dock and had to ask, "You've been gone all this time and just now coming back?"

He took a swift glance at her and turned back to navigating the harbor. "I was twenty years old and had never seen anything but Santillán," Calisto said and Nahia thought she understood. "It was a selfish thing to do, especially since I've been gone so long—other than a handful of letters, I've left my mother to herself all these years."

Nahia's brow creased. *So he wrote to Alaia. Of course he'd write to his mother.* It was more than Exteban or Bastien had done for Nahia, though, where were they to address letters to her if they'd even written any?

"But you are back now," she said as Calisto cut the engine.

"I am, and here we are," he beamed.

He helped her out of the boat, bundled her as best as he could in his coat, and hailed a hansom to take them to the Santillán family house in town; a three-story building beside a fancy theater where Celeste, and Xiomara after her, had exposed their children to the cultural delights of the season.

On some of her latest excursions into town, Nahia and Sendoa had glimpsed the house from the outside, and on one occasion they had even ventured into the fenced garden, whose tall walls kept out the noise and bustle of the street beyond. Once in, they'd found themselves in a secluded forest-like setting that reminded Nahia of the Arboretum back at the Realm.

But on this all-important day, Calisto brought her to the front of the house, where a wave of nostalgia washed over the faery when she saw an elegant brass plaque fixed to the right of the door. It read; *Mansión María Celeste, Established 1849.* Exteban had been barely ten years old when Celeste and Etienne purchased the property and began construction.

"Good morning, Irene," Calisto said to the surprised housekeeper who opened the door. Nahia remembered herself and returned to the moment where a charged silence began to tick.

Irene, the housekeeper, looked bewildered, her eyes moving from Calisto's tense face to the lady's pale one. Nahia wobbled on Calisto's arm, aware of the scrutiny. How to convince Irene all was well in spite of the questionable circumstances? A master returned after an eight-year absence, an unknown woman on his arm, obviously in distress.

But Nahia soon found she needn't have worried; the effect of Calisto's unexpected return was enough to make Irene overlook even the large coat that did not cover Nahia's bare legs and feet.

"*Niño*, Calisto!" Irene cried as her eyes swiveled gaily between them. "We didn't know to expect you—it has been so long!"

"And I am sorry about that—the return was almost as unexpected as the departure," he replied, patting Irene's shoulder kindly while drawing Nahia slightly closer to him for Irene to notice. "This is my dear friend, Anahí. She has survived a terrible ordeal that killed others in her party and it was divine providence I found her." Calisto's voice trembled with emotion as he said the last and Irene's slight frown cleared right away.

From her place in the crook of his brawny arm, Nahia's eyes pooled with tears agreeing inwardly she'd indeed gone through a great ordeal. Feeling extra vulnerable, she wedged herself tighter against Calisto.

Irene clucked her tongue and shook her head as she considered Nahia; then without further ado she offered, "The guest room is ready, and I will run a bath for her, shall I?"

"Thank you, Irene," Calisto said, "and in the meantime I will have Jordi get the physician."

"Thank you both so much," Nahia murmured, squeezing Calisto's arm before taking the hand Irene held out to her.

The two women set off down a wide central hallway; apparently the guest room was on the main floor and not upstairs where Nahia imagined the family rooms must be. She wanted to crane her neck and peek in every direction to satisfy her curiosity, but she thought better of it. Instead, she caught as much as she could out of the corner of her eye: a couple of archways leading to the formal dining hall and what looked like a sitting room, and a closed swinging door through which Nahia assumed must be the kitchen. Eventually they turned left, and the sound of Calisto's voice faded away.

"Who is Jordi?" Nahia asked.

"He is the butler," Irene replied.

"So it's just you and Jordi living here when the family is away?"

"Yes, Miss. We make sure the house is ready at every moment in case someone should come. This is the longest time we have been left on our own, but Ms. Alaia takes care of us. She is niño Calisto's mother."

Nahia experienced a little shock on hearing the name unexpectedly, but she glossed it over. "Calisto's mother doesn't live here then?"

"Oh no, Miss. Ms. Alaia lives in the country, a good three or four hours from here."

Irene opened the door to an airy room painted in soft lilac tones, which immediately put Nahia in mind of Oihana's chamber in Handi Park. Still early in the first morning of her new life and already the two mothers had cropped up twice. Nahia shuddered.

Irene clucked her tongue again and patted Nahia's hand as she guided her into the room. Nahia was pleased to see the French doors opposite opened to the back garden. She could see a small table and two chairs set right outside on the flagstones, under the shade of many trees. After pointing out where the bathroom was and opening the wardrobe to show her it contained some basic men's and women's clothing and undergarments, kept there for any eventuality, Irene left Nahia in her new room.

In under an hour, Nahia had bathed and selected something suitable to wear. She would have to remedy the wardrobe situation soon. Before going to search for Calisto, who in any case hadn't come looking for her, she stepped out into her private patio. She stood on the flagstones, eyes closed, head tilted toward the sunlight filtering through the trees. *This is not a dream,* she thought buoyantly and had to hug herself to contain the unexpected impulse to soar, which she could not indulge.

Nahia opened her eyes and scowled at the garden around her, another stab of reality forcing her to fully appreciate what it would cost her to keep up her disguise. No Glamour, no flying, no diminutive size. The slight breeze made the leaves shiver on the trees and some of them glinted in the sunlight—a flash of silver. Unbidden came the recollection of Sendoa's hands, the crush of his lips over hers, and his gravelly voice like a threat and a promise all in one: "I won't let you waste your first kiss on a human."

"The stars help me!" Nahia muttered her mother's exclamation of choice without meaning to. She rolled her eyes, irritated with herself. *Be done with the past and be present.*

A soft knock on the door startled her. *Calisto,* she thought, relieved, as she hastened to open it. She did her best to tuck Sendoa away in a corner of her mind where she could watch him—keep him from jumping out at her at odd moments.

"The doctor is here," Calisto said, looking at her with hunger in his eyes, which pleased Nahia immensely. She sighed, repeating to herself there would be no changing her mind now—she turned her back on Sendoa, reconciled to the duplicitous life she'd sentenced herself to.

"Just a little dehydrated," the doctor, declared after a perfunctory examination. "She will recover in no time."

"Thank you, my friend," Calisto said, shaking the doctor's hand.

"Don't mention it. This is a healthy young lady you have here," he said, arranging his instruments back in his bag.

Nahia straightened her blouse and rolled down her sleeves, wondering what the cold device, pressed to her chest and then to her back, had told the doctor. Her faery heart must beat the same as a human's, she reasoned, or he would've mentioned otherwise. "If I am dehydrated, should I bathe or drink to remedy that?" she said, thinking back to the Realm and their healing methods.

The doctor's brow creased, but his glance was amused. Calisto's eyes twinkled at her, "We'll have pitchers of water at every table you pass so you can take sips until you've recovered."

Nahia flushed, realizing her mistake. But in the Realm she *could* bathe to absorb water through her skin—did that not work in the human dimension? Fussing with her sleeves she stammered, "Of course. Thank you very much."

Calisto accompanied the doctor to the door and returned to her side. "Thank you for letting him examine you. I was so worried, and his opinion has really eased my mind."

Nahia stopped herself from rolling her eyes. She had repeatedly insisted that nothing was wrong with her, to no avail. If only she could have explained to him about the fluid dialog between a faery and her body and how it alerted her of any malfunction. Still, Calisto's obvious relief and his words *did* move Nahia. She put her arms around his waist, pressed her ear to his chest and murmured, "I was happy to do it. I won't have you fretting over me."

By the end of her first day in the human dimension, Nahia had a decent clue what her new life would look like, and since it included Calisto's company, she was over the moon about it all.

Although anticipated, it caused Nahia a twinge of jealousy when on the fourth day after their arrival he announced he would go to Santillán to see his mother. "How long will you be gone?" she asked, trying to keep a sulky note from her voice.

He grazed her cheek with his fingers and pulled her into his arms. "Only two days, but I can't delay seeing her any longer. I communicated to her my return and I know she's been expecting me every day since."

"Of course," Nahia conceded. "Don't make her wait any longer, but do come back to me as soon as you can."

Nahia walked him to the front door of the mansion and with Irene, and Jordi on either side of her, she waved goodbye and blew him a kiss as the hired post chaise set off. From that moment on, Nahia had not a moment to waste.

She couldn't believe her luck—Calisto would be away during the full moon. *And that isn't until tomorrow night*, she thought cheerfully.

"Irene," she called to the housekeeper, who was ducking into the kitchen through the swinging door, but she pivoted immediately and Nahia rattled off, "May I help you today? I want to learn about the cooking and how things work here—even how I should dress and what people do in this town."

"Of course, I will show you how to make niño Calisto's favorite dishes," Irene offered and Nahia clapped her hands, thrilled.

"Thank you so much!" she gushed, putting her arm around Irene and walking into the kitchen, ready for a full day of discovering all the practical things she needed to be aware of to play her part.

To smooth her entrance into San Sebastián society, Nahia had taken the precaution of bringing a bit of wealth from Handi Park. She had shrunk a small fortune in gems plus Xiomara's precious book, *Faery Sight* and placed them in a leather sack she strapped to her body, so its contents would survive the shipwreck.

She hadn't mentioned the book to Calisto, but she did tell him about the jewels, "They are all I possess in the world—a bequest from my dead parents," she had said, repeating inwardly she, by no means, wished her mother dead with such a story—it was only a casual lie to support her temporary fabrication. In fact, she meant to tell him about their one-day history together, which was why she'd taken the trouble to bring the book along. But the time had to be right for that.

In her bed that night, she could feel the emptiness of the house above her. Calisto wasn't there. She drew the covers up to her chin, eyes swiveling from one corner of the ceiling to the other, listening to the house settle. The trees outside the French doors quivered in the breeze and she shuddered. "Stop it. Nothing darker than night is going on here."

Refusing to turn on even a night-light, Nahia put her hands on the back of her head and grinned at the ceiling. Such wonderful things she'd learned from Irene: food, fashion, and ladies groups—she couldn't wait for him to return. She would surprise him with his favorite empanadas de manzana, the sweet apple pastries which, according to Irene, he could eat until he made himself sick.

Xiomara had loved anything made with apples too, Nahia remembered, and right away *Faery Sight* popped into her head. She got out of bed and grabbed the book out of the drawer where she'd hidden it temporarily, thinking it was time she put it somewhere safer so Irene wouldn't get her hands on it by accident.

She tried to restore it to its normal size but failed and all her happy thoughts blew out like a candle. *My Glamour is gone!* she thought, terror stricken. "Not even such a simple shape-shift as this?" she hissed, staring at the tiny book as if it was guilty of a crime. "How will I reduce my height and fly to the Realm for the full moon tomorrow night?"

Nahia wrapped the book in the camisole again and tucked it at the bottom of the drawer. *Maybe the full moon will give me the little bit of strength I need*, she thought, beginning to simultaneously dread and anticipate the next day.

She woke up grainy-eyed to a room lit up by late morning sun feeling as if she hadn't slept a wink. She ambled to the kitchen and sat gloomily at the table.

"You didn't sleep well?" Irene said, placing a cup of tea in front of Nahia.

"Thank you," Nahia yawned, shaking her head. "But I feel fine. I think I just miss him."

"Come to the market with me today. The fresh air will do you good," Irene, offered kindly, and Nahia agreed, welcoming distractions in any form they might come.

The two women spent the entire morning and part of the afternoon walking about San Sebastián, so by the time they returned to the mansion, Nahia was exhausted.

"Today has been wonderful! Sleep will not elude me tonight, no matter how much I miss Calisto," Nahia smiled drowsily.

"I will prepare a nice bowl of soup for you because if you go to bed now, on an empty stomach, you will wake up hungry by three in the morning."

"Thank you Irene—you are so good to me."

Nahia bathed while Irene cooked, and by the time she'd put on her nightgown, Irene was at the door.

"So this is gazpachuelo?" Nahia asked, sitting on the bed with the tray on her lap and a spoonful of soup ready to go in her mouth.

Irene nodded, as she walked around the bed smoothing the covers around Nahia. "Creamy fish stock with potatoes and some of the shrimp we bought today."

"Simply delicious!"

They chatted agreeably until Nahia finished her soup. "You really are too good to me."

"You get a good night's sleep so you will be all better tomorrow when niño Calisto returns," Irene said, crumpling the napkin and putting it in the empty bowl.

"I will. Thank you." Nahia called after Irene as she left the room closing the door behind her.

It was well after dusk, and surely the moon was about to come out.

Nahia rose out of bed and opened the French doors to her patio. She stood on the flagstones looking at the sky. Yes, moonlight was already lightening the horizon in the east. She closed her eyes and made a silent wish: do not let Irene return to my room to find me gone.

Scavenging her body for every last bit of energy, cleansing herself of all destructive doubt, Nahia harnessed her dwindling Glamour and with it commanded her cells to shrink. Refusing to admit even a hint of insecurity to enter her mind, she succeeded, and opened her eyes having already lifted off the ground. Sparing one last glance to her shadowy chamber, Nahia took to the sky and headed east toward the mountains—home.

This was her first of many visits to come, for she could not keep up her disguise lest she stole the Glamour necessary to sustain it. The restorative full moon and the troop's traditional reveling during the monthly feast secured Nahia's purpose. As she approached Moon Dancer Lake and to avoid detection by the troop already assembled on the shore, she commanded her already dim aura to burn out. She wedged herself between the branches of her favorite blue spruce and she watched Oihana preside over the festivities, all the while drawing into herself the Glamour she needed.

Reduced to thieving, Nahia thought bitterly, resisting, to the point of experiencing physical pain, the desire to tell her mother she was there. As the troop began to thin out near midnight, Nahia had to accept she lacked the courage. Oihana was among the last to leave, and only when her mother was gone did Nahia return to San Sebastián.

She'd left the French doors open, but nothing seemed to be disturbed in her room and obviously Irene hadn't come in looking for her. Before she settled in bed for the night, Nahia retrieved the book once more and restored it to its normal size. On her way to the attic, where she had decided *Faery Sight*'s new hiding place would be, she picked up Calisto's nightshirt from under his pillow.

Nahia transmuted it into a sheet of parchment and imbued it with Glamour as she scribbled, *To read beyond this page, is to agree to complete and utter secrecy, You are the only person these pages were written for. Before you proceed, we ask you now for proof. Bear in mind identities are hallowed, thus the names contained herein have the power to extinguish life, or at the very least, wreak misery on every instant of your existence.* She held the sheet at arm's length to admire her handiwork and was satisfied the charm would prevent anyone reading it, unless they shared in Celeste's family blood. She stuck it at the beginning of the book and deposited it in the dustiest corner of the attic. She returned to her bed exhausted from lack of sleep yet revived with Glamour at a cellular level, and she slept soundly for the next nine hours.

Nahia awoke in the morning refreshed and exhilarated. In the kitchen with Irene, she hummed blissfully while she made enough empanadas to make Calisto ill. Thankfully he had enough sense not to eat all of them in one sitting.

It had been a fortnight since Calisto's weekly visits to his mother had begun and Nahia was in two minds about them; she resented his disappearing one to two days at a time, but she felt thoroughly encouraged on his return, for he acted as if he hadn't enjoyed a single moment they'd been apart.

"I won't be going to Santillán this coming weekend," he said one morning over breakfast.

"Oh?" Nahia set her cup down and looked at him steadily. They'd been living separately under the same roof a little over three weeks, and she had begun to wonder what his intentions might be. Irene had hinted a while back their situation wasn't quite proper, and she wanted everything to be on the up-and-up between them. "Will she mind much?"

"She's not pleased, but I'm sure it's more because of what I mean to do than her mourning my absence," he said with a wry grin.

Nahia inched to the edge of her chair; she put her elbows on the table and rested her chin on her fists. "And what is it you mean to do?"

"She worries I know nothing about you," he chuckled lightheartedly. "What kind of person washes ashore, suffers partial memory loss, and no one in the wide world claims her? What is her ancestry?"

Nahia bit the inside of her lip; it was all she could do to keep her temper in check as Calisto recounted the recent conversation on the subject. How she longed to set Alaia straight on her royal lineage. But that would be folly; her faery ancestry would never impress that woman.

"As if I cared anything about that!" he went on fervently. "I've run out of words to express to her how much I adore you, how refreshing everything about you is, as if you've dropped into my life from another world."

Nahia visibly shook at his last declaration; she put her hands on her lap and squeezed the tops of her legs. *Had he said those words to Alaia?* "You exaggerate," she murmured. "Surely you've made her distrust me already."

Calisto pushed his chair back and came around the table. He knelt beside her and clasped her hand in his. "If I have, I don't care. Anahí, say you'll be my wife!"

Her heart leapt to her throat. A subconscious flash of energy drew the chair out from under her and Nahia dropped to her knees in front of Calisto. "I will, with all my heart, I will!"

A charged kiss sealed his ardent proposal and her devoted acceptance. They emerged from it after long blissful moments, only because the discomfort of kneeling on the hard floor demanded it.

Finding no reason to delay, and as they both preferred an intimate ceremony, the couple began wedding preparations. They meant to become man and wife in seven days' time.

"She will not come," Calisto said upon finishing a call to his mother later that evening.

Nahia assumed a somber posture, though inwardly she was glad, for she was in no hurry to meet Alaia face to face and risk being recognized. "Did she give a reason?"

Calisto, who kept nothing from his future bride, replied, "Mother wants us to pay our respects in Santillán, where she is the lady of the house, as opposed to here . . . ."

"I see—" Nahia waved away the need for him to finish the sentence. "You're not to worry about it; we will plan a trip to Santillán right after the wedding."

Calisto nodded distractedly as if weighing his mother's displeasure against Nahia's wishes. "She won't like us waiting until after the fact. She will feel snubbed, but we can change her mind, can't we?"

"Of course we can," Nahia said, relieved the dreaded meeting had been averted. Best to leave Alaia entrenched at the Citadel in Santillán for now. Nahia would meet her when she was good and ready, not when Alaia said.

On a sunny April morning, a little over a month from when she had entered the human dimension, Nahia became Calisto's wife before a justice of the peace and two witnesses. Afterward, they returned to Mansión María Celeste, where they enjoyed a delicious meal and wedding cake, prepared by Irene. In their absence, she had moved all of Nahia's things to the third floor of the mansion, into Calisto's quarters where they spent their wedding night.

Promptly the next day, Calisto and Nahia set sail along the Bay of Biscay. Their honeymoon included nightly stops in coastal towns they leisurely explored over a period of two weeks. Of course, no one expected them to be available during that time, but even when their trip ended, Nahia did not keep her word to arrange a trip to Santillán.

Within a week of their return, the full moon came again and Nahia was pressed for an excuse to leave. She waited until the last moment, weighing how deeply Calisto slept. Could she sneak away for a couple of hours without him noticing? She lamented she hadn't established many friendships yet, or joined a Ladies' Society. *I must set that up as soon as possible*, Nahia thought, frustrated that such a solution could do nothing for her at the moment.

In the end, she took a measured chance by sprinkling Calisto's dinner with ground valerian root. It acted quickly and by ten in the evening he couldn't keep his eyes open. Nahia seized the moment; there would be no lingering and she must return as soon as the troop began to thin near midnight.

Several hours later, a little dizzy from flying so fast, and wondering if she'd imbibed sufficient Glamour to last through the next lunar cycle, Nahia climbed into bed, glad to see Calisto continued to sleep soundly. *Tomorrow I will make arrangements to join a ladies' club*, she resolved, not the least bit inclined to resort to drugging her husband again. She snuggled close to him and fell fast asleep.

In the morning, with Irene's help and while Calisto reviewed Santillán's production reports sent to him by Alaia, Nahia identified and contacted the most suitable Ladies' Society she could find and became a member.

"Look, how exciting this is!" Nahia entered Calisto's study, brandishing a sheet of paper where she'd written some of the events she would participate in.

"So you are a humanitarian," he said, pleased with the list.

"But there is entertainment as well, and retreats," she said shiftily. "I'm looking forward to making friends."

"As you should," he said, returning to his work.

Nahia hesitated at the door. Although the moment seemed ripe to ask how Santillán's performance was coming along, and whether or not he would soon resume his visits, she didn't say a word lest she remind him of her promise to plan a trip to meet his mother.

Instead, she allowed the silent conflict between her and Alaia to go on for several weeks; each in their own fortress over two hundred kilometers apart, learning of each other's strategies through Calisto's communications.

In San Sebastián, like in Santillán, excuses succeeded one another with almost comical regularity; the new wife and the mother-in-law rejected each other's invitations on account of unavoidable social engagements in town, planting season in the country, plans to expand the María Celeste, measures to prepare for the year's harvest.

On and on it went until Alaia opted for a declining health tactic. At last, Nahia felt in danger of having to give in. Resigned, she was about to set the date when a definitive circumstance presented itself enabling Nahia to again duck the dreaded visit.

"I know what this is," Calisto beamed, helping Nahia back into their bed. The sun hadn't come up yet.

"I'm glad you do," Nahia groaned, dropping back onto her pillow as if she couldn't hold herself upright a moment longer. "Tell me what you think it is—I do believe we might have to call your doctor back. I thought it was the roast chicken we ate, but seriously, it has been two days now."

Calisto scooted close to her; he placed his hand on her belly and kissed her on the cheek. "I believe we're going to be parents."

Nahia's eyes snapped open. She rolled over on her side and goggled at him. "You mean there is a baby inside me?"

"Mm-hmm," he beamed. "We will have the doctor look you over, but I am certain you are pregnant."

By the time they got out of bed a couple of hours later, Nahia was convinced of her condition, she didn't need a doctor's word to confirm it, but Jordi was nevertheless sent to fetch him while Irene prepared breakfast in a state of infectious elation.

Having confirmed Nahia was with child, the doctor left and Calisto immediately phoned his mother to give her the news. Nahia congratulated herself on the timing of the pregnancy; no one could blame her now if her condition was too delicate to travel long distances.

"My mother is thrilled," Calisto said, coming out of the study. "She's coming to San Sebastián as soon as she can arrange it."

Alaia's giving in right away gave Nahia pause and for a moment she thought it a grave backfire. Perplexed, she said, "What a surprise."

Calisto, who had observed the progressing feud between the two women in his life, more baffled than irritated, remarked, "I really didn't think my mother would end up bending."

Nahia considered her husband's words from the perspective of a past Calisto didn't know existed, and it pleased her to detect in him traces of the same disapproval she harbored against Alaia. *He might be his mother's treasure, but he isn't blind to her faults*, thought Nahia, oblivious to how similar her own were to Alaia's.

"It will be lovely to meet her at last," Nahia said, trying not to sound forced. "When will she come?"

"Not for another two weeks."

At least it won't be tomorrow, Nahia thought sourly. "That should give us plenty of time to prepare."

Nahia already thought of the mansion in San Sebastián as her own and Alaia's visit presented a real threat to her sense of ownership. It bred mistrust along with visions of the wretched woman, storming into the María Celeste, bent on asserting herself as lady of Nahia's house. For days she indulged in and derived a twisted pleasure from imaginary confrontations in which she always came out victorious. Still, no faery or human had ever been as happy or as confused over a pregnancy as Nahia. Placing her hands over her flat belly, she consoled herself that there was still time before she'd have to see Alaia again.

Meanwhile, her mind turned to dwell on the hurtful silence stretching between her and her own mother. Alaia's impending visit had filled Nahia with a horrible sense of betrayal to Oihana. That Alaia, before the Faery Queen, would see Nahia in her current state and—the stars forbid it— actually see the newborn child when it came, made the Faery Princess writhe with disgust.

The days sped by inconsiderately until Alaia's dreaded first visit was upon her; she was to arrive by lunchtime. Nahia kept to her room; her belly ached more out of nerves than morning sickness and Calisto indulged her. But as soon as she heard the bustle downstairs signaling the arrival, Nahia got out of bed and stood in front of the mirror for a moment; even though the turquoise streaks in her hair were gone, the rest of her looked as it always had. "She will recognize me for sure," she whispered, but spun on her heel and went to face the enemy anyway.

Nahia heard the grating voice before she saw Alaia and was forcibly reminded of the long ago passage of shame through the Aspen Grove.

"Glad to see not much has changed, although didn't we have that set of ceramic vases in the dining hall?"

Nahia's lip twitched.

"Anahí thought of making better use of the pots by filling them with plants. She loves horticulture, and the lighting here in the foyer really is so much better for them."

"I planted three varieties of passiflora," Nahia said steadily. Alaia's already raised brow climbed higher toward her hairline. As naturally as she could, Nahia advanced toward her and embraced her mother-in-law. "I am so pleased to meet you at last."

"Likewise," Alaia said, and Nahia felt a couple of awkward pats on her shoulder blade.

She backed away with a polite smile and took her place beside her husband. "I hope your journey wasn't tiring."

"Not anything out of the ordinary."

"If you'd like to freshen up, Irene and I have the guest bedroom all ready for you," Nahia said, motioning down the hall.

"The guest bedroom, is it?" Alaia said to Calisto.

"We thought you'd be more comfortable there, and you'll appreciate the privacy."

"As will the two of you, I'm sure, since I won't be in my usual chamber upstairs."

A frown darkened Nahia's expression. *Will she really behave like this during the whole visit?* "How long will we have the pleasure of your company?" she asked outright.

Slowly, Alaia turned and squinted at her new daughter-in-law. "I must return to Santillán on Friday," she said, looking Nahia up and down as if she might see through clothing and skin and uncover something hideous.

The faery in disguise thanked her stars—*only four days.* "I trust next time it will be a longer stay," she said, and then to Calisto, "I think Jordi already brought her things around. Let's let her freshen up, and in the meantime, I will see to our lunch."

Calisto offered his arm to his mother and they set off toward the guest bedroom. Nahia watched them; tense though the encounter had been, Alaia hadn't recognized her.

With that concern out of the way, Nahia found she could feel a little sorry for Alaia in her condition as a human; surely the woman's vision was failing already, she was in her fifties. And on top of age, Alaia had hardly had any contact with the faery folk throughout her life, so really, why would Nahia's features have been fresh in her mind?

Cheerfully, she went into the kitchen to assist Irene with the luncheon; she could take on Alaia for four days, and then she and her ill humors would be gone again. Nahia wondered fiendishly what other piece of furniture or decoration she might relocate to antagonize her but decided against it, for Calisto's sake.

CHAPTER 8

⊕FFSPRING

As Nahia's belly grew, her courage shriveled. She allowed the days to pass in silence, knowing each one divided her more from her mother, her home, and her legacy. And even worse, the longer Calisto remained ignorant of the truth, the more the idea of incorporating him to the Realm became a watered-down notion in her mind.

The strain of her duplicity had begun to wear on Nahia. She couldn't fool herself much longer—the odds of gaining Oihana's acceptance were heavily stacked against her. She regretted more than ever she hadn't said goodbye or sent word of her whereabouts.

Nahia trusted that Sendoa would have been questioned and knew that he would have revealed to Oihana the bulk of her intentions, which only increased her discomfort. She could feel the Faery Queen's disapproval reaching from a distance; her daughter had crossed over to the human dimension, chasing after a man, and had been reduced to sneaking into the Realm at the full moon to steal Glamour. Nahia longed to put an end to it but didn't know how. She suspected the arrival of a baby could go a long way in softening up a grandmother, yet she feared Oihana's reaction more than she had feared being recognized by Alaia.

Nahia knew she had to be the one to initiate contact with Oihana; she must ask her forgiveness—admit she'd done wrong—yet she continued to let time spend itself, and allowed the bouts of depression plaguing her since she discovered she was pregnant become more pronounced.

Maybe the Glamour she sucked up once a month wasn't enough for two bodies. Maybe she craved the attention of her kind at a time when she didn't know what to expect. Was it normal for her to be gaining so much weight?

She had heard about twins and wondered if it happened only to humans; she didn't know a single faery that had had them. Had she been human too long? Could she still call herself a faery if she spent most of her time at human height and in the human dimension to boot? And had her dream patterns really changed that much, or was she tuning into her baby's dreams? What would the baby be—human? Faery? Both?

Oihana would know.

Dispirited by her own circumstances, Nahia focused on easing Calisto's mind instead. He had been watching her with increased concern, particularly after Alaia's departure. Oblivious to Nahia's fears, he seemed more anxious about smoothing out his mother's adverse reaction to meeting his wife. Alaia had been rude and cold several times during her visit, which had created a great deal of stress for him.

"Your Mama loves you very much and it's to be expected she should dislike any woman who comes into your life," Nahia remarked, suspecting Alaia's visit to San Sebastián had been in part to see if anything could be done to break them up. Calisto nodded unconvinced.

Oihana had once told Nahia to wait until she had a child of her own to understand how a mother behaves. She could almost see it now.

Prompted by the recollection and possibly softened by it, she carefully added, "Something in your mother's eyes makes me think her life must've been full of heartache."

Calisto seemed to ponder the remark. "That may be. But I also think she didn't recover very well from my leaving her all those years ago—her uncles too. We left her alone to care for my father, whose health had always been a problem, and I'm deeply sorry I didn't bother to keep contact to at least have come to her when he died."

"I can see how that would make her feel angry and betrayed," Nahia agreed, "and then, just when she thought you had come back to her, I am in your life."

Calisto grimaced. "Exteban and Bastien have yet to return—I don't know if they ever will. Besides me, they are the only family she has."

If he only knew, the two men had detached themselves from the Realm too after so many years of being a family. Nahia was to be pitied also, possibly more than Alaia.

As if to harden her heart, the insulting memory of the hissing Aspen Grove flashed in her mind again. "You fiend—give me back my son!" and then Alaia's own voice thick with rage, her face a mask of loathing: "Leave here and *never* return."

There was nothing Nahia could do about it; Alaia was a prickly, controlling person everyone tried to avoid, including what little family she had. But Nahia waved away all those thoughts and driven by her desire to please Calisto, she hinted hopefully, "But now, a baby is coming."

As soon as the words came out, she wished them unsaid. How would Calisto react? He would never see the part of his mother Nahia had: the unyielding woman, who would not give even her beloved son the satisfaction of accepting his wife and child.

Calisto kissed her. He placed his hand over her belly and gathered her to him. "You're right, this will do wonders for my mother."

Nahia kissed him back but did not comment. She snuggled close to him, fully regretting her suggestion that the arrival of her baby might soothe Alaia's loneliness. *Why did I even hint at such a possibility?* What she really wanted was to keep Calisto and leave Alaia to herself, with no son and no grandchild.

The disgraceful, naked truth flapped in her mind like the tattered sails of a ghost ship. "You are older than her, and I would hope wiser—" Sendoa's words came to her as if Calisto had uttered them, and Nahia's insides twisted with guilt.

"Are you all right?" Calisto kissed her forehead.

Tears welled in her eyes and she spoke without thinking. "I want to see my mother. I want my family."

"Of course you do." Calisto covered her face with kisses and dried her tears. He lifted her chin and smiled at her blotchy face. "I cannot make you forget you are orphaned, but I will convince you that you are not alone. I am your family now, and so is my mother. You are new to her and she has been alone for too long, so it is too soon to ask for a loving reaction from her, but she will come around, especially because there is a baby on the way. You'll see. We will make a wonderful family, the four of us, and however many children come after this one."

Nahia allowed him to kiss her again, her chest painfully constricted. *This cannot be!* "I don't feel well—I think I need to lie down for a few minutes."

"Yes, of course," he stood up directly and held out his hands to her. Nahia accepted the help and together they walked to their room where he fussed over her, removing her shoes, arranging pillows and bedcovers to make her comfortable.

Nahia closed her eyes until she heard him tiptoe out of the room, only then she opened them to stare blankly at the door Calisto had just closed. It was becoming too much, all the sneaking around—lying to Calisto as to where and why she had to leave once a month, and the silence between her and Oihana. The detachment from the Realm and from Sendoa. She glowered at the corner of her mind where she'd put him and cursed him mutely for making her so dependent—she missed the way he listened and how he seemed to know her as no one else did, as Calisto never would. She was lying to Alaia too, but that didn't worry her nearly as much as having offered to do a kindness for her—*what got into me to suggest the birth of my baby might make amends?*

Nahia rolled over on her back, slamming her fists on either side of her body. Disappointment, regret, shame, all of those sensations snaked inside her and she knew she had brought it all on herself by being so reckless. She folded the pillow over her face to stifle a groan. Nahia couldn't tell if it was Oihana's reasoning or her own, but then and there, it became clear nothing good could come from her marriage to Calisto—her selfish plan was bound to crumble under the weight of compounded lies; no matter how many she told, they would never add up to a truth.

Her dispiriting thoughts seemed to halt midair as the crux of her situation streaked across her mind. *He's never known me,* Nahia, *he's only known Anahí.* She let go of the pillow over her face and stared at the ceiling. *What made me think I needed to be someone else to conquer him? Why would he not love me as Nahia?*

A discreet knock at the door stopped her from answering her own questions, and she thought, *Just as well.* Irene came in with a tea tray.

"Remember, niña Anahí, the architect you wanted to see will be here this afternoon." Irene breezed by to place the tray on the round table by the fireplace. She poured hot water into the strainer and teacup to steep Nahia's chamomile.

Nahia sat up eagerly. "You are right, I'd forgotten about it!" She went to sit at the table, glad for the timely distraction. At least she wouldn't be able to stew in her lies while discussing the fabulous addition of a fourth floor to her home. She meant to re-create Paloma's pond up there, complete with vegetation and a trickling creek.

She removed the mesh strainer and as she blew on the steaming cup, it occurred to her the full moon was close at hand. *Why didn't I think of it before?* Her recent doubts and anxiety were likely due to the dwindling Glamour inside of her. All would be right with the world in three days' time. *And really, keeping a detail here and there, which is what I'm doing,* is not *the same as lying to him.* Reconciled with herself, she sipped her chamomile. Nahia had hit on the perfect enabler for her procrastination.

In the coming weeks, whenever she fell into dejection over her duplicity, she counted the days until the full moon and quieted her ill humors with a satisfactory thought—only seven days to go, or five, or two. Also, her first meeting with the architect had been productive to the point a crew had been chosen in the days following and construction had begun.

Even her overnight absences once a month became second nature for her to disguise, thanks to the ladies' club she had joined; to them she attributed her monthly disappearances. She told Calisto that, besides regular meetings, the ladies had a traditional retreat of sorts, which they took turns hosting at their homes. There were over fifteen ladies in the club, and with Nahia being one of the newest members, her turn would not come up for quite some time. But in the interest of backing up her story, Nahia had indeed hosted a dinner or two to show Calisto the ladies did exist.

"I'm well enough to go, darling," Nahia said impatiently one day in December. She pressed her lips into a thin line to keep from uttering grumpier remarks. She reminded herself that by nightfall, she would have had her fill of Glamour and her temper would stabilize again.

Calisto frowned at her very swollen belly. Nahia clucked her tongue and went to him, leaving her half-packed satchel on the bed. "There is nothing to worry about, love. It isn't more than a thirty-minute carriage ride and the doctor said, just last week, he's never seen a healthier first-time mother."

"Still, I would rather have you where I can see you—we are so close to the date," Calisto said mulishly.

"It is over eight weeks away," Nahia smiled, attempting to dilute her irritation, "and I will be back in the morning. Truly, I feel perfectly fine. I won't be straining myself in any way, and I will be with plenty of women who will be glad to assist if I need it."

"I suppose you're right," he said, pulling her to him and kissing her lips, "and you will call me if anything should happen."

"Of course I will," Nahia replied, giving him a quick peck on the cheek and returning to her packing. She could feel Calisto's eyes on her but she would not humor him with renewed assurances.

"I will leave you to it, then," Calisto said at length.

"Thank you—I will be out shortly so we can have lunch together."

Between lunch and the moment the carriage dropped her off at an old post in Biriatou, France, not twenty miles from San Sebastián, Nahia mulled over the fact the birth of the baby was indeed close at hand, and she would need assistance from someone other than a human doctor. As she snuggled in her cloak and walked to the nearby copse, under the cover of which she would shape-shift, Nahia made up her mind to make her presence known to a faery and strike a deal that very night.

Probably because the baby was nearing full term, Nahia felt a definite shudder in her womb the moment she shifted to faery height, satchel and all. She bobbed momentarily between the trees, cradling her belly, wondering if it was as pleasant an experience to the baby as it was for her. Nahia reasoned it must be, otherwise for sure she'd feel cramps and discomfort. She rose above the treetops and instinctively turned east, toward Wizard's Pass.

Even through her aura, which regulated her body temperature regardless of conditions outside, Nahia felt the cold spray of the waterfall as she flew over it on her way to Moon Dancer Lake. It was a clear night, no rain or snow, but she was still glad to break the dimensional barrier and enter the controlled climate of the Realm, where if it snowed, it was only overnight, so as to afford them an enchanted silver paradise to last until midday before melting away entirely.

By dusk, Nahia was safely hidden in her blue spruce near the shore, waiting for the troop to arrive, her belly all aflutter. Within the hour, the moon had risen and the festivities were under way. Nahia had drawn from the faery circle, where Oihana presided, as much Glamour as she dared, when one of the faeries, old Usoa, detached herself from the outer circle and came to rest beneath the branches of Nahia's tree.

"Usoa." Though quiet, her whisper startled the old faery. "No—no, don't be alarmed, it is just me. Nahia." A huge weight lifted the moment she said the words—how lighthearted she felt having made contact.

"Sweet sapling!" Usoa cried; her eyes immediately traveled to Nahia's bulging belly beneath the cloak. "Oh, we have missed you so."

"I've missed you too! But I beg your discretion," Nahia implored, cradling her belly, "and I beg your help."

"Yes, of course."

When the particulars had been explained and promises had been extracted, Nahia blinked away the tears and embraced the old faery affectionately. "Thank you—I will never forget your kindness."

"How will I know when the time comes?"

Nahia coiled a lock of hair several times round her finger and detached it with a light tug. She did the same with Usoa's silver hair. She twisted both locks into a single braid that she cut in half, and handed a piece to the old faery, "Here, you keep this one and I'll have the other. When the time comes, I'll make a fist over it and summon you to me."

"I understand, and I will be there at once," Usoa promised.

And so it was, one stormy night in February 1915, braving the terrific lightning show, the wind, and the rain, Usoa entered Nahia's home in San Sebastián to assist in the eagerly awaited birth.

Disregarding Nahia's declaration that she felt more at ease with just her chosen midwife, Calisto had not rested until she allowed the family doctor to be present too.

From the moment he walked in, Nahia and Usoa were forced to come up with reasons to shuffle him out of the room time and again. Luckily the storm cut power to multiple sections of town, the María Celeste included, which went a long way in their efforts to veil the fact that Nahia's body shimmered in and out of sight while in the throes of labor.

"No use crying out, child," Usoa told her. "You'll only deplete your energy."

Nahia heeded the old faery's advice; she groaned and panted but would not cry out, until with one final, body-splitting effort, the baby arrived. Into a candlelit world she came, amid bolts of lightning.

Nahia looked down on the infant Usoa placed on her chest—mother and daughter were still connected. "Zorione," she sighed, which in the Basque language means *happiness.*

"You have done very well," the doctor smiled kindly, as he severed the cord. "I will fetch Calisto, as I'm sure he is anxious to see you both."

The two faeries exchanged a worried glance as he went out of the room, certain he had once, maybe twice seen Nahia flicker between mass and mist.

"If anything," Usoa whispered, sitting on the bed and cooling Nahia's forehead with a damp cloth while the baby dozed in her arms, "I think the lightning storm outside might have confused him enough to account for it."

Nahia nodded weakly as her glance rose to Calisto, who at that moment entered the room and was at her side in two strides. He clasped her hand and kissed it. "I am so proud of you!"

"She was so brave," Usoa said, patting Nahia's other hand. "Such a beautiful lady she is, and how exquisite the gift of this child to both of you."

Nahia's heart beat faster, flooded with love, and in the dim light of the candles, she glowed. Calisto, who already considered his wife a radiant creature, thought nothing of it.

CHAPTER 9

AMBUSHED

As it transpired, not only had the doctor seen the new mother's peculiar behavior, he had also shared his observations with Calisto.

"He congratulated your husband—of course he would, with two such beautiful saplings in his life," Usoa whispered to Nahia, "but before he left he said, thoughtful like, that he'd never seen such a powerful electric storm; he swore you too were made of lightning flashes."

"And what did Calisto say?" Nahia propped herself on her elbows and groaned in discomfort. Zorione slept in the bedside cradle, undisturbed.

"He only laughed good-naturedly, and he agreed the lightning was as bad as he'd ever seen. He said between thunder and candles he wasn't surprised the doctor might have seen what he said, or worse."

Nahia relaxed back onto her pillows. "That's good, but did he look convinced?"

Usoa tilted her head and pulled a face. "I was listening from the end of the hall and I couldn't make out his expression, but yes, I think yes, he sounded convinced."

Just in case, the two faeries decided that Nahia should casually remark to Calisto about the frightful lightning storm and how it had played tricks on her, she too would swear the room had blinked in and out of sight to discredit the doctor.

Usoa stayed a full day after the birth, but beyond it there was no excuse; mother and child were strong and healthy, so the old faery returned to Handi Park, leaving Nahia to settle into her new family. She and Calisto had made a child who was half of each of her parents but looked like an individual. Nahia couldn't understand it—which half of herself had she lost to Zorione? *Had* she lost half of herself? Or was the baby more of a third heart, linking and separating her parents at the same time?

Unfailingly, Calisto doted over his daughter, and if Zorione was the apple of his eye, Nahia was over the moon with her. As days succeeded one another in blissful domesticity, she became preoccupied with the need to put a charm on Zorione, something to last through the ages, something to commemorate the ultimate fusion of faery and human nature.

With the memory of Celeste heavy in her mind, Nahia set to work and went through multiple drafts of a document she meant to imbue with a binding charm. It took her several weeks to complete it, and only after re-reading a tenth version of it did Nahia grin, satisfied. She went to work on the next requirement—a powerful potion whose main ingredients were her own blood, thickened by ashes she obtained by burning a lock of Zorione's hair.

She used the concoction as ink to handwrite the parchment detailing in beautiful calligraphy all the possessions and family heirlooms of the Santillán-St. Michel clan, which should be transferred to a direct female descendant of Celeste Santillán—because only a matriarchal tribe has full certainty of their lineage.

Alaia could have no objections to the clan being defined, as beginning with Celeste and Etienne, and Nahia was not about to reveal her real motivation, that her link to Celeste as a birth sister had been reinforced by the fusion of their blood in a common descendant.

"I hardly think we need to burden your mother with this—at least not until she comes for Zorione's christening," Nahia said one afternoon while they were gathered in their private sitting room. She held up their six-month-old baby and nibbled on her belly to make her laugh, which Zorione did.

Calisto gazed dreamily at them. "You're right. I see no harm in it, and I can't think of a single reason why my mother would disapprove."

Nahia sent for the family solicitor the next day. She brought forth the document to be legalized, and she signed it in his presence. Calisto signed immediately after, overlooking the peculiar color and texture of the writing, and oblivious to Nahia's bizarre wording (*blood* was a pervasive term throughout the holographic will) that bound his female descendants, at a genetic level, to a faery clan he didn't even know existed.

Zorione's christening went off without a hitch; Nahia had relied mostly on Irene's guidance for the event, as she had no knowledge of religious traditions. That evening, after putting the baby to bed, Nahia went back downstairs to join Calisto and Alaia in a nightcap. The faery experienced a flush of dread upon seeing her husband and his mother bent over the writing table, where he had spread a document. She recognized it right away.

Nahia cleared her throat and entered the study, reminding herself her next visit to the Realm was four days away, and Alaia couldn't have any possible objection to the will, especially with it bearing Calisto's signature. She smiled, hoping to clear her expression. "She is sound asleep."

Alaia's eyes swiveled up from the paper to Nahia's face and then back.

"She didn't give you any trouble?" Calisto said as he approached Nahia and put his arm around her waist.

"No trouble at all," Nahia said lightly, her eyes on Alaia. "I see you've shown your mother the provision we've made for her granddaughter."

"This is a very interesting document," Alaia remarked coldly.

"You mean because it is handwritten?"

"Among other things—"

"It is perfectly legal, I assure you. I'm told it is called a holographic will," Nahia offered, preferring not to make assumptions as to a hidden meaning in Alaia's tone or her sharp, suspicious glances. "And it was far less expensive to have it witnessed by a law firm than having it entirely drawn up by them."

"Very prudent of you," Alaia said, unable to hide the mistrust in her voice, which made Calisto frown at her.

"Mother, don't you agree this shows a loving foresight on our part, to take measures to secure Zorione's future?"

Alaia's eyes briefly narrowed toward Nahia but shifted back to her son as she said, "Of course. You are both responsible individuals and you have her best interest at heart. Yes, I approve."

Nahia wasn't convinced, but really, what could Alaia suspect? Certainly not her true identity. With a twinge of disappointment, Nahia acknowledged Zorione showed no signs of having inherited faery traits; her dark blond hair didn't have any streaks to match the slate-blue color of her eyes, and that she knew of, Zorione hadn't done any involuntary shape-shifting, asleep or otherwise.

If there was no Glamour in her baby, then the more justified she felt in having a holographic will. She wasn't trying to take anything from Calisto or from Zorione; in fact, Nahia was making sure nothing, ever, was taken from Zorione or from her female descendants for centuries to come.

All the reasoning combined made so much sense to Nahia that she never thought trouble was afoot when Alaia extended her stay from the initial week to a whole month. She even thought it convenient—Alaia would be with

Calisto and Zorione while Nahia attended her upcoming retreat with the Ladies' Society. On the whole, with Alaia's visits being few and far between, Nahia could almost envision coexisting with her mother-in-law.

It was late September by the time Alaia returned to Santillán and left them to themselves. Nahia breathed a sigh of relief as they entered the fall of 1915, glad for the absence of her watchful mother-in-law as much as for the cooler temperatures. Addition of the fourth floor was well underway, per Nahia's vision, with an expected completion date of December, just in time for a grand New Year's Eve celebration.

Anticipation of the event kept Nahia in a state of distraction until one night, while Irene cleared the dinner things, she detected something amiss with Calisto. Zorione sat on a high chair beside Nahia, nibbling on slices of pear.

"Thank you," Nahia said kindly to a retreating Irene. She shifted in her seat to properly look at Calisto, realizing he hadn't glanced in her direction during the entire meal. The more she searched her memory, the more evidence she found that since Alaia's departure, Calisto had been avoiding her.

"Darling—"

Despite Nahia's affectionate tone, Calisto flinched and busied himself picking up what the baby had dropped from her bowl. "Mm-hmm?"

"Why won't you look at me?"

"I'm looking at you," Calisto replied defiantly. His ash-colored eyes briefly flashed on her before returning to the baby.

Nahia shrank a little, "What's wrong? Are you angry with me?"

"Nothing's wrong," he said, seeming to let his guard down momentarily. He ran his fingers through his hair in a tired fashion. "I just have a lot on my mind."

"Won't you tell me what's troubling you?" Nahia pressed, thinking it might have something to do with the performance of the Santillán estate, which he and Alaia had discussed at length during her stay. Maybe Alaia was getting ready to pass more responsibility on to him.

Just when Calisto's lack of response began to make Nahia feel scrutinized, he said, "My mother told me some things while she was here—"

Nahia's expression cleared. *Yes, it's about the estate.* "She asked for your help managing Santillán, didn't she?"

Calisto tilted his head and the corner of his mouth twitched upward. For a brief moment, Nahia thought she'd guessed wrong, but he nodded, confirming her suggestion, so she dismissed her own lingering doubts. *The full moon comes in seven days*, she recited inwardly. Until then, she anticipated increased paranoia and braced herself to downplay bouts of mistrust.

Indeed, for the next week Nahia had to make a conscious effort to keep from inflating her reaction every time she felt shunned by Calisto. She told herself it was all in her mind, and all would be well as soon as she replenished the fading Glamour inside of her.

Nahia had been in the habit of reminding Calisto, three days prior, of her overnight retreat with her ladies' club. This time, because of his attitude toward her, she hadn't been able to summon the courage to mention it. The day of the full moon, as she packed her overnight satchel, she nearly jumped out of her skin upon sensing something wrong. She turned abruptly and saw Calisto, mutely staring at her from the door. Her eyes filled with tears, unable to identify the emotion behind his glare but overwhelmed by it nevertheless—was it anger? Disappointment? Contempt?

She rushed to him, put her arms around his neck, and cried out, "I love you!"

It seemed Calisto would not hug her back and Nahia squeezed him tighter, sobbing and feeling rejected. She heard a groan escape his chest, as if he'd lost a silent battle.

He buried his face in her neck. "I love you too," he said hoarsely, and she sighed, relieved. "Don't go—stay with me tonight," he pleaded, kissing her.

Nahia tensed in his arms. Did he know what he was asking? Or was he attempting to mend their relationship? She hated to leave him, but skipping her visit to the Realm was unthinkable.

She extricated herself from his arms with a watery sniff. Holding his face in her hands, she gave him a long kiss on the lips, putting her whole heart into it. When they broke apart, she whispered to him, "I will be back early tomorrow."

Calisto's eyes hardened and his jaw set. "Fine."

He left the room, and Nahia didn't see him again until she went into his study to say goodbye. He was on a call, but she was sure he'd picked up the receiver only seconds before she entered. Nahia blew him a kiss from the door and he held up his hand in dismissive acknowledgment.

Thoroughly preoccupied by the cold mode of her departure, Nahia was oblivious to the journey. Next thing she knew, the carriage had stopped in Biriatou. She alighted onto the worn, leaf-strewn planks of the deserted station and paid her fare.

The chilly October air dispelled Nahia's haze, and the sight of the lofty

Pyrenees on the eastern horizon filled her with anticipation. Clutching the overnight bag to her chest, she traversed the small clearing and entered the copse.

Nahia shape-shifted and bobbed between the trees, frowning. She ran her fingers down her throat and up again, wondering why she felt so short of breath. Even as she floated there her anticipation turned into trepidation. "Calisto," she said irritably, resenting him for the stress he'd heaped on her with his attitude.

She soared above the trees in her sparkling turquoise orb and shot across the darkening sky knowing she would soon be among her kin. Even if they didn't know it, she'd be able to feel them and that was enough.

I, a Faery Princess, have grown accustomed to scraps, she thought ruefully as she bounded over the waterfall.

Hiding between the branches of her favorite blue spruce, Nahia watched the troop drop from the air or amble out of the forest and onto the shore of Moon Dancer Lake. Soon Oihana would be there too. The intense fluttering in Nahia's belly reverberated through her limbs, filling her with a prickly anxiety she couldn't remember experiencing before. For some reason she kept exhaling and forgetting to inhale afterward until she made herself lightheaded. *What is wrong with me?*

Through the branches, Nahia spied her mother; the light of the moon splintered the violet glow of Oihana's aura, infusing it with silver sparks, making her look as regal as ever. She thought she detected traces of her mother's lilac scent in the air and Nahia closed her eyes to dissipate the wave of emotion swooping down on her.

From the shore, the murmur of faery voices welcoming their queen grew into a joyful song. Oihana landed in their midst becoming suffused in sound and light. Nahia felt the pull from the faery ring and did not resist. The cloak fell from her shoulders; she floated off her branch toward the outer circle—she could already feel the crackling energy created by the troop's hearts beating as one and the fused voices of her family chanting in unison, not thirty feet from her.

She glided, her gaze fixed on the dome of light encasing the troop. A slight pressure across her chest stopped her trance-like progress. At first, it didn't register with Nahia; she moved to the side to bypass it, but there was no end to the thin barrier. She tried pushing it out of the way like a branch, but it would not budge. Nahia stared, puzzled—she ran her fingers over it; two taut ropes.

A rustling sound made her whirl toward it in alarm. Once again, what she saw didn't register right away—how could it? A pair of enormous hands detached the ends of the ropes and deftly tied a knot, pinning Nahia's arms to her sides.

Now she was fully awake but couldn't yet comprehend what she was seeing. Concealed in the underbrush, at her full human height, Alaia glowered at her—a satisfied snarl disfiguring her face. A series of sputtering thoughts cluttered Nahia's mind. *How? Impossible!*

For the world, Nahia would not alert the troop to her presence. In silence, she struggled fruitlessly against the ropes until enraged; she shut her eyes tight and concentrated on burning them off. But that too failed.

Alaia taunted her, shaking her head and clucking her tongue. Bewildered, Nahia squirmed and wrestled against the indestructible bonds. Struggling to remain clearheaded, she squinted at them in the dappled moonlight and saw with a jolt they were not ropes at all; they were two braids.

Understanding hit Nahia like a brick over the head. Angry tears stung her eyes, and she blinked them away, grinding her teeth and staring at the shorn ends of Alaia's hair.

She grabbed Nahia by the waist and thrust her unceremoniously into a birdcage, whose bars Nahia quickly felt were made of iron. She slumped down in the center, careful not to let the metal touch her skin lest it burn her. *Maybe I should let it*, Nahia thought bitterly, *I deserve to be branded for underestimating her.*

Alaia raised the cage to eye level and looked triumphantly at the trapped faery. "And I half thought you had lied about not harming us, *not even a hair on our heads.*"

Safe and oblivious in a dome of colorful light, the troop sang on, their precious energy spilling in rivulets while Nahia was stealthily whisked away, her own energy vacating in a steady trickle.

CHAPTER 10

EXPOSED

Alaia traipsed through gullies and climbed slopes, carelessly swinging the cage at her side. The faery braced herself the best she could with the palms of her hands, keeping to the center of the cage, away from the heat emitted by the iron bars. She inwardly cursed Alaia's newfound strength—she had thought her infirm at her age, and yet the woman had pulled this off. If only she could've had some energy from the faery ring. What Nahia had imbibed through her skin upon entering the Realm couldn't possibly see her through this—she already felt drained.

Nahia could tell they were approaching Wizard's Pass; the air had grown cooler and she could hear the distant roar of the waterfall. It never occurred to her Alaia would know anything about faery lore, like how lethal iron is to faeries, or the moon's relevance to their lives. But Alaia had always been a good scholar. *Of course she would listen, in that sneaky way of hers, and learn anything that could be turned into a weapon later,* Nahia thought darkly.

"I knew it the moment Calisto told me what the doctor had seen the night Zorione was born."

Nahia's ears pricked alertly: so Calisto had told his mother. But did Nahia feel betrayed by her husband? Or disappointed in herself for not being more cautious? Or—Nahia sat up straighter and squinted through the bars—was she glad the game was up at last?

"So you figured out my next move, all on your own?"

"I went back to Santillán fully expecting you to return home on the night of the full moon," Alaia gloated, "and I would be waiting for you."

Nahia balled her hands into fists. Of course she'd know about Wizard's Pass, and as a descendant of Celeste, the gift of Faery Sight had been bestowed upon her. *Why didn't I ever think to revoke it?* Grudgingly, Nahia admitted the woman had been cunning beyond her humanity.

They descended the cliffside using Celeste's steps toward the passage behind the waterfall. The constant jostling of the cage had the merit of stopping Nahia from indulging in punishing thoughts; she didn't want to brand her porcelain skin with the iron bars. But as soon as they entered the passage, a dispiriting thought darkened her mind: *Surely Alaia is taking me to San Sebastián—to Calisto.*

Behind the curtain of water, the faery became drenched in seconds but did not care. In four hours' time, Calisto would see her for what she was, and there was nothing she could do to prevent it. She imagined the self-righteous look on Alaia's face returning triumphant to San Sebastián, with the trapped faery on display for her son to behold. Nahia's insides churned with suppressed rage.

Alaia had a carriage waiting for her on the other side of the waterfall. The driver could see nothing of Nahia, and obviously the appearance of a soaked woman holding an empty cage didn't spark his curiosity. Nahia imagined he'd been well paid to meet Alaia there at the appointed time.

Not that it mattered.

Near four o'clock in the morning, they arrived in San Sebastián, and by then, their clothes had dried and Nahia, who had been preparing her defense, felt so weakened that she feared she might not be able to say a word. Because of the iron and the fact she never partook of the inner circle's energy, Nahia's reserves had been drained. Even her aura, normally four inches all around her, clung to her skin now, thin as a mere outline.

Alaia knocked on the door with her fist, and Calisto himself came to open it. She pushed through, ignoring her son's flabbergasted expression. "What is this?"

Alaia strode haughtily into the dining room, forcing Calisto to follow her.

"Mother! What is this?" he insisted, but she did not respond until she had slammed the cage on the table.

Unable to brace herself since her arms were still pinned to her sides, Nahia toppled from her sitting position and brushed the iron bars. Although she recoiled immediately, she still got a welt across her shoulder blades where the iron burned her flesh. Gasping, she wormed back toward the center of the cage, where she remained in a fetal position; the sense of being served up as a main course overrode the angry throb on her back.

Alaia turned to her son, stepping away from the cage to allow him full view of its contents. Nahia's aquamarine eyes were fixed on her husband. Lying there, too weak to move or even speak, she wished she could close her eyes but could not make herself do it. The sight of Calisto becoming unhinged transfixed her, and she breathed in quick, panting spurts, feeling dizzy, exposed.

His eyes, beneath the creased brows, seemed to pop out of their sockets, yet he would not approach the cage. "What is this—" he said for the third time. "Is it a bird? Is it wounded? Why?"

"I didn't want you to *ever* have to hear or see this—" Alaia said in a superior tone, and Nahia was suddenly glad she couldn't see the hateful woman; she continued to watch the changes on her husband's face. "This is no bird," Alaia went on, Calisto's eyes swiveled madly between his mother and her. "This is a conniving, thieving, heartless shape-shifter—"

Nahia stopped breathing, momentarily leveled by the disgust with which Alaia spat out the words. Things were so much worse than she could've imagined.

"Shape-shifter?" Calisto echoed, perplexed.

"I'm sure she will speak soon enough, and I'm sure she will try to convince you she is so much more than you see here."

"Mother—I don't understand. What do you mean, shape-shifter? Who is this?"

"She will tell you she is a faery, and that she is your wife. But I tell you, she is no more than an impostor, a lying female of her species."

Calisto's hands went to the sides of his head, where, for a moment, it seemed he would rip out clumps of hair in desperation. In two strides he was at the table, peering through the bars at the panting shape of the faery within. As he looked on, the thin sea-green aura disappeared with a feeble flash. Startled, Calisto drew back.

"There is a place high up in the Pyrenees where this creature lives with others of her kind. They try to imitate the human ways, but they are frivolous, selfish, and malicious beings—why, this very one, this treacherous fiend, abducted *you*—plucked you from your home when you were but a day old, betraying the alleged relationship between them and our family!"

Nahia groaned inaudibly, her mental and physical pain fusing into one excruciating ache.

"Alleged relationship?"

"Some made-up story involving your great-grandmother, Celeste. It should all have ended with her. But somehow my own mother and even my uncles were duped into continued contact with them. But when I had you, I knew I would put an end to that disgusting connection. I demanded she return you to me, and thank God her mother made her, so there wasn't enough time for her to harm you, or to influence you with their errant ways."

"Abducted—errant ways . . . . Stop! What are you saying?" Calisto lashed out. "Have you lost your mind? Did you say faery?"

"Perhaps I should have warned you about them, instead of keeping you ignorant. But what's done is done, and it was for the best. Now I'm doing what I think is best once again, and you must see this thing for what she really is—self-indulgent to the point of sinfulness, with no morals to speak of. Their kind justifies their decadent behavior, claiming they are one with nature, when what they really do is to allow themselves to behave like animals—with no brainpower or skills beyond their basic instincts.

"Sure, they can dazzle you with tricks like shape-shifting and surround themselves in pretty lights, but then a peacock can astonish you with the beauty of its feathers. A wolf can impress you with its confidence and strength, a swarm of fireflies can mystify you momentarily. But can you attribute human intelligence or a soul to any of them? Certainly not on the merit of feathers, brute strength, or their ability to glow—son, you are smarter than that!"

Calisto shook his head absently. "So faeries exist," he said slowly, and a fleeting fancy struck Nahia, as it had years ago, that he might have at least a subconscious recollection of the day he'd spent with her at the Realm. But he went on, neither confirming nor denying anything.

"And you say I've been tricked into an interspecies marriage?" His voice hardened as he turned from his mother and his eyes fell on Nahia. She felt the weight of it like an anvil.

If at any point he'd wavered on believing his mother, Nahia's silence settled it. There would be no forthcoming explanation or rebuttal from the faery.

"Don't feel foolish, my son. Not many people can resist or see through the charm they can wield."

Calisto approached the cage again and stooped, trying to catch the pathetic creature's eye, "Is this true—are you really Anahí? *My* Anahí?"

His poignant whisper fell in Nahia's ear, but she hesitated, wondering if the question had come from a place of hope rather than a sense of impending doom. Whatever the case, the faery chose not to speak, forfeiting her chance to sway Calisto in her favor. She looked at him glassy-eyed, numb with pain and reluctant to take further risks. If she tried and failed to convince him of her love, it would be over.

"Her name is not even Anahí," Alaia said frostily.

Calisto's heavenward glance seemed to say *This is the last straw.* When he refocused on Nahia, it was as if willing her to somehow respond.

She looked away, defeated, which was enough of an admission for Calisto to straighten up and turn his back on her.

"Her name is Nahia," Alaia supplied helpfully. The faery grimaced, noting the tone of relish and the skipping over her royal title. *Just as well,* Nahia thought dismayed, *since it won't make any difference.*

The faery shuddered, curled up in a ball in the center of the iron cage, tangled in Alaia's hair, convinced she was being gradually poisoned by it. Nahia had no fight or Glamour left in her. She began to seriously ponder how quick the end might claim her when she heard Zorione's distant cry. The baby was waking somewhere upstairs, alone.

Nahia sat bolt upright; her pain forgotten, faintness gone, "Bring my child to me!" she cried unexpectedly, her voice cracking from lack of use.

Calisto jerked toward the sound of it, watching her thrash on the cage floor. His gaze was so intense that she could plainly see his struggle to decide if she was really his wife.

"Bring her to me!" Nahia insisted, and for an instant it seemed Calisto would do as she asked, but Alaia let loose a grating cackle.

"He will do no such thing," Alaia sneered. "I brought you here, faery, to show him what you are. Now he has seen you, and he knows the truth. I'm going to do what I should have done years ago."

Nahia didn't care to consider what that might be; all she wanted was Zorione.

The baby began to cry in earnest, unaccustomed to being ignored. Nahia's desperation boiled over. She threw herself toward the bars hoping she might topple the cage causing it to break open—instead, the iron branded her skin and Nahia screamed, "Zorione!" She scrambled onto her knees. "She's crying for me—she needs me!"

Alarmed, Calisto stuck his fingers through the bars, his face twisted in anguish as he nudged her off to keep her from inflicting more burns. Nahia fell over, winded and pleading, "Give her to me . . . ."

He headed upstairs for the baby but Alaia stopped him with a vise-like claw at his elbow. "I *said*, you will do *no* such thing."

Outraged, Calisto shook his arm loose from his mother's grasp and rounded on her, "Whatever you have said, this . . ." his eyes flashed guiltily toward Nahia, "—*she* is the mother of my daughter—"

Nahia felt the sting of tears as she squinted at her husband and couldn't choke down the hopeful moan escaping her. "Please—"

"You are not in your right mind—you are still under her influence," Alaia shot back.

"For god's sake, Mother!" Infected by Nahia's anguish, Calisto shoved past Alaia toward the staircase. He took the steps two at a time, ignoring the string of accusations his mother flung after him.

"You're not this blind, Calisto, you must reject her power over you. She's a liar—a right fraud who must be destroyed!"

Calisto returned holding a sobbing, stuffy-nosed Zorione to his chest. "Enough!" he lashed out at his mother, causing her to back off, if only for a moment.

Nahia again sat up, eagerly watching the sniffling baby rub her eyes with a chubby fist. Her heart constricted upon seeing the pouting mouth and flushed cheeks. Nahia pressed up against the bars, longing to hold her. Her skin made a hissing sound and a thin wisp of smoke rose from the new blistering welt, this one from shoulder to elbow, but Nahia didn't care.

Holding the baby so his wife could see her, Calisto once again prompted Nahia to scoot away from the iron. Zorione peered interestedly at the cage and its contents.

Then the earth shook without warning.

Alaia had ripped the cage off the table and Nahia crashed against the bars, which scored her back with gridiron marks.

"Never again will you interfere in our lives." Alaia cried, sweeping out of the dining room; the cage swung like a purse at her side. Nahia rolled around, ineffectively shrinking from each painful contact with the bars.

Zorione cried. Calisto roared, "STOP," but Alaia would not listen. Puzzled, Nahia felt herself being hauled upstairs—she'd been expecting Alaia to carry her *out* of the house.

A cold wave of fear washed over the faery when she understood Alaia's intention. They were on the temporary, rickety stairs leading to the fourth floor, which was under construction and had no doors or windows yet. Amid Zorione's screams and Calisto's swearing, Nahia's gasp went unnoticed. She was going to be *thrown* out of the house.

Alaia teetered on the edge of a doorless opening on the wall, holding the heavy cage aloft with a trembling arm. "Never again!" Alaia screeched as she swayed back, a mighty forward heave followed by the sharp releasing of the cage. Nahia screamed as she hurtled into the vacant violet sky.

As if hitting an invisible cushion, the cage stopped abruptly and bobbed midair. Despite her confusion, Nahia managed to worm away from the bars to prevent more burns, although a strip of heat still throbbed near her cheek. In the instant's reprieve, Nahia panted, knowing she could not take much more.

A soft breeze caressed her and the scent of lilac entered her lungs, like a healing balm. "My mother! Here?"

If not a delusion, Nahia could not account for it—could her mind be granting her a dying wish? Swells of gratitude, shame, and relief built up inside of her.

It was not a hallucination; her throat tightened and her heart beat fast. She saw Oihana lower the hand she'd held up to freeze the trajectory of the cage and she passed by Nahia, seeming to have eyes only for Alaia. Unable to tear her gaze away from the formidable Faery Queen, whose aura blazed with steely determination and restrained ferocity, Nahia dared to hope.

Seeming to sense the arrival of a force to be reckoned with, Nahia saw Calisto shield the baby in his arms and back away. Alaia stood her ground defiantly, attempting to block the opening by standing in the center of it; a pointless exercise, since Oihana charged with such power as to demolish the walls on either side of her—Alaia flew backwards and landed gracelessly a good six feet away on the debris-strewn floor.

Oihana shifted to human height so fast it seemed she'd disappeared and reappeared in a fraction of a second. The cage, with Nahia in it, continued to float three feet outside the hole in the building, where Oihana had left her. She experienced an upsurge of pride for her mother.

When the dust and splinters from the shattered walls settled, Alaia scrambled to a shaky standing position, possibly with renewed intentions to fight. The Faery Queen did not condescend to look at the woman, and instead, with a blast of power that electrified the air around the entire block, she pitched Alaia toward a wall, against which she slumped, unconscious at last.

Indifferent to her dilemma, Oihana breezed by Alaia and stood eye to eye with Calisto. His first reaction, Nahia saw, was a half turn to shield Zorione, but then with a jerky movement and no exchange of words Nahia could hear, he handed the baby to Oihana. Zorione did not squeak; eyes wide, she allowed herself to be transferred from her father's arms to her grandmother's.

With the baby perched on her hip, Oihana glided out of the large hole she'd created. A graceful, fanning motion of her fingers preceded the undoing of the braided bonds. Nahia let out a pathetic moan as Oihana did a double shape-shift, changing herself and the baby to faery height for the journey home. She scooped up Nahia the instant the cage disintegrated around her.

With the baby on one side and Nahia on the other, the Faery Queen left the María Celeste without a backward glance toward the still cataleptic Alaia, or to Calisto.

The outskirts of San Sebastián rolled back beneath them as they flew in silence. Nahia felt Oihana make a slight northeast shift in course and heard her say, "I love you."

Nahia laid her head on her mother's shoulder. She looked at the slender neck, the amethyst eyes fixed on the Pyrenees outlined in the horizon, and she breathed in Oihana's scent, letting relief and gratitude erase all traces of her shame. Ripples of peace and exhaustion warmed her from the inside out. Nahia squinted at the sun rising behind the mountains in the east, and the corners of her mouth twitched upward. On the brink of sleep she at last said, "Please forgive me."

"There is nothing to forgive," Oihana replied. "I know why you did what you did—if I was angry it was because I lamented the fact that history *does* repeat itself."

Sleepily, Nahia listened to the words as if funneled into her ear through a long, winding pipe causing her to miss her mother's hint. Zorione's gurgling sounds of pleasure mingled with Oihana's voice added to Nahia's sense of safety. She was going home. All was well.

CHAPTER II

GOOD RIDDANCE

The cool mist and the swooping sensation in her belly told Nahia they had bounded over the waterfall, but it was the eerie quivering of the air, followed by a cracking clap of thunder that lifted her drowsy exhaustion. She opened her eyes. "What was that?"

"Celeste's access to Wizard's Pass is no more."

Nahia shuddered. Her mother's dispassionate tone intimidated her as much as the controlled fury that had caused her to act; the Faery Queen had exerted her formidable power and demolished the long-ago designed stairs, sealing away the Faerie Realm from those who knew of it and sought to harm them.

Not twelve hours ago Alaia had dragged Nahia through there, triggering a series of injurious events and causing more than just bodily harm. Nahia had been forced to reexamine her current feelings. Her brows knitted with worrisome ideas streaking across her mind. Why wasn't she more upset about leaving Calisto behind? And what had Oihana meant when she said history repeated itself?

Wide awake, Nahia faced the wind and shook her blond curls, glad to see her turquoise streaks had returned. A rosy mist floated over Moon Dancer Lake—earth and sky inverted. The forest lay dark beyond it. Nahia reached across her mother's chest and squeezed Zorione's plump fist; linking the three generations and basking in the feeling of harmony it gave her.

They sped across the silent Aspen Grove and dove into the ivy-covered dome, which concealed the access shaft to Handi Park. A random memory of Celeste comparing Handi Park's entrance to a deep bird's nest made Nahia grin.

It seemed the prolonged absence had sharpened Nahia's appreciation of her home—she looked eagerly about, recognizing and rediscovering it all. They entered the shaft straight into the dome of the atrium where an entire root system, like a leafless version of the tangled mess outside, curled itself on the rounded ceiling.

They blew by the suspended bridge stretching across the diameter of the dome and descended through the center of ten stories of exhibition stands. "Grandmamma's Trade Center," Nahia told Zorione in an effort to reattach to the traditions she'd forsaken. The baby didn't respond but continued to look around, thoroughly engrossed. Oihana smiled.

Nahia remembered the annual harvest fairs, the stands, a riot of color and sound. It was impossible to count how many days she'd spent spiraling the ten stories to the bottom and back up again, ferreting through the treasures on display and listening to the tales told by exotic faeries who came from faraway continents.

When their motion shifted from vertical to horizontal, Nahia felt a slight compression; the tune she'd been humming fluttered and Zorione's head tilted against Oihana's shoulder. They had reached the circular receiving hall, where a bubbling spring in its rectangular pool radiated a bluish light. The twenty-one doorways to Handi Park, each about two feet in height and all marked with different-colored lanterns, surrounded them. Oihana hedged the doorways, which Nahia knew led to such places as old Usoa's Chamber of Looms and Weaving, the Caldera, the Celestial Observatory, and the entire urban sprawl of faery dwellings.

The doorway marked with the royal amethyst lantern swung open before them. Nahia hummed contentedly as they passed, proud of her mother's remarkable abilities, not only in the small displays, but the grand ones as well. Nahia had already committed to memory every bit of her mother's astounding confrontation with Alaia and Calisto and had made mental notes to improve her own skills.

"Well, well, well—"

Oihana paused and Zorione turned her head toward the throaty voice. Nahia's humming ceased and her lip curled as her gaze fell on the stunning faery, languidly leaning against a wall and staring at them.

"Hello, cousin," Nahia said sharply.

"Ederne, you are up early," Oihana observed as she and Nahia alighted on the pebbled floor, Zorione remained secure in her grandmother's arms.

Ederne pushed off the wall and approached the royal trio, her eyes on

Nahia. "I sensed something wasn't right—I knew you wouldn't hesitate in coming back, because you are shameless and entitled." She rounded on Oihana to continue. "But I can't believe *you* would take her back—*no*—that you would go fetch her yourself and bring her back? I wouldn't have thought it."

"What's it to you?" Nahia stepped in front of Oihana, feeling instinctively protective of her baby and her mother.

Ederne sneered, "I can only hope she's brought you back to judge you here. I do hope you will be properly banished. I'm sure the council will demand it."

Nahia squinted at her cousin, and as she had many a time before, she pondered how someone so beautiful on the outside—for her red hair, fiery eyes, figure, and voice, made Ederne one of the most perfect of their species—could be so rotten inside. Vanity and a desire to control consumed Ederne; she could not love and could not comprehend tolerance. Nahia had long ago learned her cousin simply couldn't understand the concept of a greater good, as it was inconveniently outside the scope of her own person.

"No doubt you've been busy instigating the council to get me exiled, or at least forbid my return," Nahia said, understanding that her cousin's hopes hadn't changed since they were children.

"This is not any of your concern, Ederne," Oihana said dismissively, coming to stand beside her daughter. Zorione stared, fascinated by the cascading red locks.

"Not my concern?" Ederne said with a raised brow. "You allow a member of the royal family to violate the rules of the Realm—what kind of example is that for the rest of us?"

Nahia felt a twinge of guilt and unexpected concern; did Ederne know what she had been up to? Who she was, even now, married to? And if she did, what angle would she find to inflict harm on them?

"Like the rest of us, the Faery Princess is allowed to make mistakes and repair them," Oihana said, emphasizing Nahia's title and rank.

"Don't try to pass it off as a minor mistake, Aunt," Ederne scowled. "Nahia hasn't just grown the wrong flowers in the Arboretum, or put one too many eggs in her flan—she ran off with some human, and her slumming has produced a half-breed," she spat, jutting her chin toward Zorione; the baby's brow crinkled as if she'd been flicked on the forehead.

Some human, Nahia repeated inwardly. *Can it be she doesn't know the human in question is a descendant of Celeste's?* Nahia made her expression as blank as she could to suppress outward signs of satisfaction. *I won't be making* that *clarification, and if Alaia breaking our ties all those years ago prevented Ederne making a connection today, I'm thankful.*

"Her royal legacy should be denied, at the very least."

And there it is, Nahia thought. Ederne would not give up her dream to rule the Realm one day, and the quickest way would be if Nahia were out of the picture.

"As I said, this is no concern of yours—it is for me and the Faerie Council to decide. But rest easy, your view is noted," Oihana said, breezing by Ederne. Nahia followed in her mother's wake looking slantwise at her cousin's pursed lips and smoldering stare.

Once inside her chamber, still done in shades of green and blue, just as she'd left it, Oihana handed Nahia the baby. She said, "I will be meeting with the council today, and in three days' time I expect we will have reached a consensus."

Nahia blanched, fearing for the first time what the consequences of her actions might be. Ederne couldn't be right—they wouldn't exile the Faery Princess, would they?

Oihana grazed her daughter's cheek and smiled. "No use worrying."

Nahia bounced the baby unnecessarily. "You don't think it'll be like Ederne said, do you?"

"I don't believe it will be as bad as your cousin hopes," Oihana intimated and left her daughter and granddaughter to settle in.

Nahia put the baby in their nest and left Zorione to stretch contentedly on the down mattress while she discarded her tattered clothing. She bathed quickly and came out perfumed and feeling revived. In front of the mirror, Nahia examined the various burn marks left by the iron bars. She pulled a face and resignedly took the jar with the Comfrey salve; she began applying it to all her welts while humming the incantation to accelerate the healing process.

"They'll all be gone by nightfall," she sang to Zorione, who had begun to fuss. She picked her up, and hearing a knock on the door, she turned toward it.

Zuzen floated in without waiting for a response, preceded by a tray with Nahia's breakfast and a bottle for Zorione.

As Nahia poured water for her chamomile, the doorway filled with a very recognizable silhouette. She appreciated instantly how much she had missed him during the nineteen months her adventure had lasted. For a moment, all she could think of was the intensity of the kiss he'd given her the last time they saw each other, and she blushed. The cup overflowed; she stopped pouring and set down the teapot with a clatter.

Sendoa's eyes traveled from her to the baby feeding contentedly in Zuzen's arms and Nahia blushed harder. She stifled a groan—he hadn't said anything but she sensed accusation in his stance and in his looks.

Flustered, Nahia gulped hot water and frowned at it, surprised at its lack of taste; she'd forgotten the strainer with the tea leaves. Irritated, she set down the cup and gave Sendoa a challenging look.

"Glad to have you back," he said, shifting back to his usual good humor.

After that, it was as if they'd never been apart. Over the next three days, Sendoa kept by her side to calm her nerves until the council made their decision. Nahia noticed he was more attentive to Zorione than he might be to any other child, and was both gratified and puzzled by his tendency to dismiss the father while pointedly considering her the only parent.

Very early on the third day, Zuzen came to fetch Nahia. She left Zorione asleep in their nest and followed Zuzen to the Tablinum. As they approached, Nahia could hear Ederne's throaty voice within, rising with displeasure.

"After such a selfish, disloyal act, Nahia should have been disowned and stripped of her royal legacy. We have no hope of progressing or of becoming a force to be reckoned with, if spineless governing such as this is our trademark."

Nahia paused; she and Zuzen exchanged anxious looks. Sendoa glided over to them—he'd been awaiting the outcome outside the Tablinum.

"When has our aim been to be a force to be reckoned with?" a familiar voice interjected calmly. Nahia recognized old Usoa. "Our contribution to the Faerie Dimension has always been trade and development. We are not hostile, we never have been."

"That is why we are wide open to an attack. Is that what you want? To be taken over by another troop, a more prepared group who will impose their practices on us?" Ederne said.

Nahia couldn't believe her cousin's reach—that she would talk to the council as if she knew anything. Could it be no one saw through Ederne and what her intentions were? She shook off Sendoa's hand, which he'd placed on her shoulder to soothe or detain her, she couldn't be sure.

Nahia didn't knock, but did not throw the door open either; she glided in, swiftly appraising the situation. Ederne had taken position at the foot of a table, which sat on the sandy replica of the Bahía de la Concha. The rest of the council occupied the remaining seats, with Oihana at the head.

"Why don't you just say *you* want to take over, *you* feel more prepared than everyone here, and *you* will impose your practices on us," said the Faery

Princess with a steady voice though a hostile vibration buzzed inside of her. "That way, we can talk about it openly, at last."

Ederne whirled toward her; a red ring smoldered in her eyes as she glowered at Nahia and at Sendoa, who had followed her in. She pursed her lips and swept the room in a quick glance, seeming to weigh her response. "I am certainly more prepared than you ever hope to be. In my view, your fickle loyalties make you unfit to take over when—" she let the sentence hang incomplete, but the languid tilt of the head in Oihana's direction made Ederne's meaning clear. Frowns and headshakes broke out around the table, as the six council members obviously disagreed.

"And you think you are next in line?" Nahia challenged, knowing something her cousin didn't.

Ederne shrugged pompously. "Of course."

"My fickle loyalty, as you call it, might be assessed otherwise by the council and will not interfere with succession, while you have disqualified *yourself,* displaying your ignorance of even our most basic traditions and teachings."

Ederne frowned, caught off guard; her eyes flashed red again. Nahia smirked and proceeded to enlighten her. "You are the daughter of my mother's *brother.* Your blood does not flow directly from the royal, matriarchal source." Nahia let her words sink in, watching the crease deepen between Ederne's brows.

Her expression cleared soon enough though, and it was Nahia's turn to pause on seeing the chilling sneer on Ederne's face. Had she just read her cousin's mind, or had she merely pieced together her reasoning? Whatever the case, elimination of the Faery Queen and of the Faery Princess would suffice to clear Ederne's path—her sneer declared it so.

Far from deterred, Nahia wondered if Zorione, in her condition of half-breed, as Ederne called it, could inherit the Faerie Realm should she and Oihana go into the light?

"We learn something every day, don't we?" Ederne said haughtily; her scornful glance paused on each of the council members and Oihana before returning to Nahia. "The time has come for me to leave this stagnant, corrupt hole in the earth. I refuse to submit to your unfair, narrow-minded practices."

"You are my niece, and you will always be welcome here," Oihana said, rising from her seat. "This is not the first time you have left us, and I trust your next return will bring about an understanding between us."

"Ha!" Ederne shoved past Nahia. "There won't be a next time," she said, looking over her shoulder as she left the Tablinum.

No goodbye had ever sounded more ominous to Nahia, or untrue. She felt certain Ederne would rally and charge again—it was just a matter of time.

CHAPTER 12
AN ASTRAL VISIT

"You are not banished, or disowned—" Oihana's voice called Nahia to attention and to the realization some form of punishment was still pending. "I'm sure you figured that out when you came in."

Nahia nodded stiffly. Sendoa pulled out a chair for her and she sat down looking distracted; he remained at her side.

"I do not agree wholeheartedly with Ederne, but she made some valid points." Oihana shook her head when it seemed Nahia would speak, and the Faery Princess backed down. "You behaved impetuously. It was a selfish thing to do, and it exposed us to humanity, in spite of all the precautions we take to exist in secret."

Nahia felt certain all eyes were on her, she kept hers fixed on the lacquered surface of the table. She bit the inside of her lip as her mother enumerated the mistakes, which seemed more horrible when viewed through a haze of shame. Under the table, she began bouncing her knee.

"You disappeared without a word to your mother." Nahia shuddered, aware of Oihana's deliberate formal address. "And began a campaign of deceit with a man you supposedly loved."

Nahia looked up and two fat teardrops rolled down her cheeks.

"If you can lie to someone you love, then you *do not* love them," Oihana declared.

Nahia wiped her tears with the back of her hand and sniffed. She resumed staring at the table and began scoring the tops of her thighs with her nails instead of bouncing her knee.

"Nothing good could come from that union—two such different worlds could never unite if the essential element of truth is withheld—can you see it now?"

"I did love him—I *do*. I love him," Nahia sobbed. She looked up in time to see old Usoa nodding wisely. At least *she* believed Nahia.

"You will speak to him truthfully," Oihana went on businesslike, "and as parents to Zorione, you will both decide what is best for her, no matter what sacrifice that implies to either of you."

Nahia understood this might mean giving up her child, but she assented meekly in spite of the cold dread suddenly gripping her heart.

The session closed with Oihana stating that the particulars of the execution were left to Nahia's discretion, but she was expected to complete the task sooner rather than later.

Two weeks after her return to the Realm, Nahia still hadn't taken any action. Instead she'd been showing off her baby to the residents of Handi Park and glorying in their admiration. Zorione received the attention with endearing alertness, always touching the faces of anyone who came within reach of her chubby little hands.

Early one afternoon, Nahia sat across from Sendoa in her favorite corner of the royal garden in Handi Park. Sunbeams filtered from the top, infusing everything with a misty light whose warmth prompted the gardenias to release their scent. "I'm better off talking to Calisto when the waxing moon begins. It's only three days away, and that's when creative energy is most favorable," Nahia said defensively.

Sendoa's eyes laughed at her. "By all means, continue to delay—how else can you flaunt your powers of procrastination?"

Nahia looked at him narrowly and replied with as dismissive a tone as she could, "The auspiciousness of the crescent moon is a fact. How can you call it procrastination when I have no control over the lunar cycles?"

Sendoa arched his brows, grinning. "Will you go to San Sebastián then, or will you summon him through dreams?"

"I have to go to him as a faery. But I will let him know beforehand, in a dream."

Sendoa nodded. "Good thinking. A forewarning is like an appointment, and it will be a sign of respect I'm sure he will appreciate. What about the baby, will you take her?"

"She will stay here," Nahia said at once, glancing quickly at Zorione, who was crawling on the moss-covered ground and pressing the palms of her hands by turns on different lumps. After an instant's thought, Nahia softened her reply. "It will be better if our first conversation is without distractions, but I will reassure him I have no intention of keeping *him* from Zorione."

That very night, after putting her daughter down for the night, Nahia went to the Celestial Observatory. She loved the bluish light in there because of the instant soothing effect it had on her. The sapphire glass tiles on the floor and on the walls gleamed like moonlit water. In the center of the room stood the reflection well, whose base had been crafted out of clear glass blocks.

Sitting beneath the shaft of the petrified tree, Nahia ran her fingers over the glistening rim, gazing at the tranquil water reflecting the fragment of sky above. Oihana had taught her and Celeste about the moon and the stars and the very real impact they had over everything and everyone.

Nahia sat in meditative position, eyes closed, face upturned to the sky. Her concentration became so intense, she saw herself rise through the tree shaft and break out into the open. Devoid of physical mass, she launched her spirit, unhindered, through the starry night.

Nahia followed the Urumea River as it snaked into the city of San Sebastián and to the bridge closest to the María Celeste. She paused outside the mansion, wistfully eyeing the place she had called home not three weeks ago. Her eyes took in the incomplete framework and walls of the fourth floor she'd been so excited about (back in the Celestial Observatory, Nahia sighed longingly). Only one light shone from a third-floor window—it was their room.

Overcome with an intense desire to see him, she willed herself without further delay and was at his side. He sat at the desk, elbow on the table and chin supported on the palm of his hand, staring into space.

"Calisto," Nahia whispered into his mind and he closed his eyes.

"I've missed you so," he said, and she thought he sounded relieved.

Nahia placed an invisible hand on his shoulder. Seeming to feel the energy there, Calisto turned toward it acknowledging her presence, which gave a flimsy substance to her projected self. Nahia stepped onto the desk and stood, ten inches tall, in front of him. Flushed with pleasure over his words and the way he looked at her, with mingled wonder and devotion, she declared she'd missed him too.

"And how is our baby?"

"She is doing wonderfully—she has charmed everyone with her beauty and sweet disposition," Nahia gushed, starry-eyed and careless as to how

Calisto might receive the report; it didn't occur to her that he might want to hear their child had missed him.

Calisto nodded, his expression guarded. "Why did you lie to me?" he said heavily, and in that moment, all that weighed on his mind became apparent to Nahia. But he didn't give her a chance to acknowledge it, he simply blurted out the rest of what had been troubling him. "I've been wracking my brain trying to cope with what I've learned. It kills me to know the person I loved doesn't exist—not only was she a fabrication, she was a different species."

Nahia's delight on seeing him slipped off her face like a melting wax mask. "Anahí was *mostly* me! And I loved you as her *and* as me," she cried, watching him intently to anticipate his reaction, "I love you still!"

Calisto clicked his tongue, "Nahia, is it?" The Faery Princess assented. "My mother says you have always hated her. Is that true?"

Nahia gulped, "Did she tell you how *she* felt about me, how she treated me?"

"She says you excluded her and made her look bad in front of my grandmother and her uncles. She says you took me away from her when I was a baby, out of spite, and that you married me to avenge the humiliation she put you through when you had to give me back."

Nahia stifled a groan. How unbearable to have her offenses recited back to her like this. "Alaia never wanted to participate. She was jealous of how easy it was for Xiomara and her brothers to fit in while she was so awkward and grave—and I kept you for a mere day!" Nahia flushed, remembering Oihana's warning she was to speak the truth. But how could she tell Calisto she had meant to raise him in the Faerie Realm and would probably have done so, had Xiomara and Oihana not interfered.

"But you've kept Zorione nearly three weeks now. Do you mean to keep her for good?"

Nahia slumped. *This is where procrastination has led me,* she thought. *Had I acted right away, Calisto wouldn't have had time to brood over his questions and feelings. But I left him on his own for three weeks—of course he would blow up.*

"I'm sorry to say it, but your mother has always been hostile toward me and my kind. I know she relishes filling your head with garish faery tales—"

Calisto let out an involuntary chuckle and Nahia paused, nonplussed.

"But you *are* a faery," he said with the first hint of humor Nahia had heard in a long time. "What else would you call a story about you and your kind?"

Nahia grinned sheepishly, "Come to the Realm—let's you and I talk."

"How do I get there?"

"I will come for you early in the morning," she said, grazing his stubbly jawline with her fingers.

"I will be waiting."

The vision conjured for Calisto refracted when Nahia opened her eyes in the Celestial Observatory. She stretched and rose from the rim of the reflection well, mulling over how her feelings had shifted along with his mood; she'd started out breathless, then become defensive, frustrated, confused, and finally elated when it seemed Calisto didn't hate her after all.

She drifted back to her room, where Zorione continued to sleep soundly. She got into her nest, beside the baby, and fell asleep with a smile on her face—she would see Calisto in the morning.

CHAPTER 13

TOGETHER AT LAST

Somewhere, a baby cried. Nahia looked but couldn't find him in the gloom. *Calisto.* Where had she put him? Her movements were sluggish and her vision limited. *He's hungry—that sounds like a hungry cry.* Rather impatiently, she tried to hurry her steps and had a shock, realizing she wasn't even on her feet.

Her eyes popped open. Nahia sat up in her nest, Zorione fussing beside her. She picked up the baby. "I'm sorry, I was sleeping so soundly," she yawned. "Are you hungry, my love? Let's get Zuzen, shall we?"

But she didn't have to leave the room; before Nahia even swung her legs out of the nest Zuzen breezed in with a breakfast tray. "Good morning," Nahia sang, handing the baby to Zuzen as soon as she had set down the tray. "How attuned you are to Zorione's schedule, and how grateful I am to you for it, especially today—I must go to town and fetch Calisto."

In a flurry of agitation, Nahia bathed while Zuzen fed the baby and made suggestions as to what Nahia should wear. She dressed quickly, and after a bite of her blueberry scone, which she washed down with two gulps of chamomile, Nahia kissed her daughter's forehead. "I'll be back shortly, with Papa," she said, wrapping herself in a blue cloak.

Nahia flitted out of her chamber and took a shortcut through the skylight in the Celestial Observatory. She soared above the canopy and flashed west, over the mountains, hills, and valleys and to the coast. Within sight of the María Celeste, Nahia spied Calisto in her favorite spot in the back garden, searching the sky. She halted midflight, warmed by his thoughtful state, fancying he awaited the reunion as intensely as she did. Heart thumping, she descended into the garden. Nahia's glittering aura caught his eye as she ducked into the shade of the trees and landed on the lip of the birdbath. He hurried to the stone bench beside it and sat down so they could be at eye level.

Nahia stifled a nervous giggle and said in a quivering voice, "Good morning."

"I was worried you wouldn't come—but here you are," he said, clearly relieved.

The Faery Princess frowned, a little unsettled. Was the trust between them really so damaged that he could not believe what she'd said the night before? Nahia humphed, determined to have him forgive and believe in her again. "You feel you will have to start over with me, and I understand. But by the end of today you will see past my height and realize I am the same person you knew in Anahí."

"Just your height?" Calisto grinned. "Isn't there so much more? What about your age? If I'm to believe my mother, you are a cradle-snatcher. Are you really a hundred years old?"

Nahia's aura flickered. Was there no end to Alaia's insidious meddling?

"As measured in this dimension," she said, struggling to keep traces of irritation and superiority out of her voice, "I will be ninety-six this year."

"Whew!"

Nahia's brow went up sharply; half scolding him, half justifying herself, "I see what you are feeling: you've not turned thirty and yet already seventy years separate us." An unexpected recollection of Celeste's withered body inside the coffin washed over her—Celeste had been only sixty-three in human years when she died. What would she have looked like had she lived to be Nahia's age? She rolled back to the present and erupted with, "What a punishment! To attain wisdom and experience that set you at the prime of your intellectual ability and not having a better use for it than dealing with a decrepit body."

Calisto, who'd been leaning toward her as if to catch her every word, shrank back alarmed and Nahia had to change tack. "I admit, if given the choice *I* would pick my way over and over—and I can't understand why your family picks the human way every time."

"You mean, we've had a choice?"

Nahia nodded, "Every one of you, since your great-grandmother, Celeste. And now it's your turn—I want to take you with me. I want to give you that choice."

After brief consideration, he said, "What do I do?"

"You just enjoy yourself. This is everyone's favorite part," Nahia assured him, "I will reduce your height and disperse your weight so you can fly with me—I warn you, I'm very fast."

Calisto seemed worried and opened his mouth, perhaps to express some lingering concern, but Nahia had done with the conversation. She pinched her eyes closed and opened her hands toward him, determined to astonish him with her skill. She drew height and weight simultaneously from him.

A growl caught in his throat and Nahia smirked, thinking that must've been the moment he unraveled through his navel, as if the top and bottom of him had leaped and dived all at once into his core.

Her eyes snapped open in time to see him double over as if he might prevent the shape-shift that had already happened. With his weight only mostly dispersed, Calisto hovered midair, looking stunned. In the split second it would've taken for him to drop, Nahia grabbed his wrist and soared over the garden of the María Celeste. A sharp eastward shift in her flight pattern and they were on their way to the distant Pyrenees.

Shaken, Calisto let out a roar that soon changed to exhilarated laughter as the sea of clay-tiled roofs rushed beneath them, giving way to rolling hills blanketed in fiery fall vegetation. Encouraged by his reaction, Nahia tackled a vertical ascent flush with a rock wall and after that, a waterfall, forests, Moon Dancer Lake, and the Arboretum, all passed in flashes beneath or around them. Calisto hardly had an instant to exclaim over it all.

Nahia had never flown this fast, but she wanted to impress her husband and thought, correctly, he would enjoy the thrill. The ivy-covered mound came into view and Nahia, in full command of herself, didn't bother to slow down. With extraordinary skill she dove in and they were swept, as if by a mighty current, into the shaft, only to be disgorged seconds later into the circular receiving hall.

Nahia halted with a bounce, mere inches from the ground.

"Whoooaaa!" Calisto laughed, letting go of Nahia's hand, which caused him to immediately drop to the pebble-encrusted floor.

Nahia alighted gracefully in front of him. On tiptoes, she put her arms around his neck and kissed him. "Welcome," she whispered. "Let's go find our daughter, shall we?"

"I can't wait to see her. I've missed her—*both* of you, so much."

They found the baby in the Tablinum, where Zuzen had taken her to play on the sand.

"Papa," Zorione said holding up her arms, and once he'd scooped her up, Calisto did not put her down the rest of the day.

Nahia became the perfect hostess, she answered his questions patiently and introduced him to everyone they met. They toured the inside of Handi Park, and in the afternoon, they explored the Arboretum and Paloma's Grotto. It took no leap of the imagination for Nahia to see him living in the Realm—he could not fail to see how idyllic their existence would be. Yet the day came to a close, and baffled by his reluctance to announce, then and there, that Handi Park was his new home, Nahia had to take her husband back to San Sebastián.

She returned from escorting him just in time to take the sleeping Zorione from Zuzen's arms, kiss her, and deposit her in their nest. Nahia reclined beside the baby and began rubbing her back distractedly while she mulled over the events of the day. She was in two minds about the outcome: Calisto had thoroughly enjoyed himself—his delight on seeing Zorione again had been genuine. His renewed devotion to Nahia had been palpable—yet he asked her to take him back.

Nahia had fully anticipated Calisto being under her power, unable to refuse her. She had counted on the overwhelming effect of sights and sensations in the Realm to render him pliable; and by all accounts that was exactly what happened, so where had she gone wrong?

A soft knock on the door distracted her, but rather than getting up or disturbing the baby's sleep, Nahia glanced in the direction of the door and willed it to open. Oihana stepped in, eyes sparkling as she beheld her daughter and granddaughter. Nahia's aura glittered in response; she could feel her mother's love, and mingled with it was the emphasized sense of welcome—all was forgiven.

"I love you, Mother," Nahia whispered.

"I love you too," Oihana said, kissing her forehead. "How was your visit?"

"There was an unexpected setback," she replied. "I was so convinced Calisto would stay with us, but he is worried about Alaia—he says she's been taken ill."

Oihana tilted her head; a slight crinkle above her nose suggested a degree of concern. "Do you suppose our latest encounter caused it?"

"I shouldn't think so," Nahia said indifferently. "If anything, Alaia is sulking and trying to keep Calisto from doing something *she* would consider rash."

Oihana listened in tense silence, as if holding back a remark.

Nahia understood her too well. "I'm not being unfeeling, Mother. Calisto said it himself: it is no more than a cold brought on by the change of season—he only worries about it because she is getting older, and even a trifling thing can turn to something serious if not properly examined."

"Well, you can't blame him, and it is rather compassionate of him to care for his mother like that—it bodes well for how he might care for you and Zorione in the future."

Nahia pursed her lips but didn't comment; she thought it would likely fall on her to care for him, especially if, like the rest of his family, Calisto chose to live in the human dimension.

"So you've taken him home tonight, but does he plan to come back? What about my granddaughter?" Oihana said, caressing the baby's hair.

"He was reluctant to make plans," Nahia admitted, "at least until his mother is on the mend or recovered from her sniffles. I really hope she will not drag it out until next spring."

Oihana shook her head and clucked her tongue. "Nahia!"

"But it's true—I wouldn't put it past Alaia to exaggerate every cough and sneeze to make it seem like some horrible, infectious disease, just to keep Calisto at her bedside or constantly fetching her medicine."

"You are incorrigible—"

Nahia caught herself halfway rolling her eyes, remembering how much her mother disliked the habit. "I suppose the good news is he has agreed to leave Zorione here until Alaia's condition is sorted out."

"That makes sense. I expect he will be traveling a great deal between San Sebastián and—or do you think he will move to the Citadel in Santillán?"

"I hadn't thought about that. But I suspect she wouldn't want him to, because if he does, he will be able to judge how much she's faking."

Oihana's frown deepened and Nahia pulled a face.

"I will leave you to your thoughts now, and I wish you pleasant dreams." Oihana kissed her goodnight and caressed Zorione's cheek.

"You too, and I love you," Nahia called after her.

Heeding her own advice, or rather, taking her own suspicions seriously, Nahia decided it would be wiser to tether herself to Calisto as she had months before, when their affair had started. The very next evening, after his departure from the Realm, Nahia began nightly sessions with him through the gift of Lucid Dreaming she'd given him. The arrangement did not come close to the life Nahia had envisioned with Calisto and Zorione, but it was better than nothing.

Daily, she told herself things would change and that Calisto would soon be with them, all day, every day. Night after night, she talked with him in dreams and brought Zorione to see him. She did fairly well hiding her annoyance over his extended absence and was secretly glad every time Zorione cried and carried on when it was time to say goodbye. She hoped he felt guilty about not being with his wife and daughter.

"And how is family life going?" Sendoa asked one morning.

Nahia glared at him—she wished she hadn't bragged so much to him about how quick and effective she was going to be against Alaia's influence.

"We are living in a dream," Nahia said wryly, "but I will have him with me soon, the Spring Equinox is around the bend—so yes, five months is a lot longer than I planned, but I'm working on it."

"I didn't mean to point out your failed calculations so much as highlight how spot-on your suspicions about Alaia were," Sendoa said, sobering up. "I think it's time you give her credit, and maybe then you can begin dealing with her at the level she deserves."

She looked at him momentarily disconcerted. "And what is it she deserves, according to you?"

"Just try to understand her. Alaia's plight is no different than yours. Your attitudes and reactions are different, but love for your children is at the heart of it."

Nahia was not about to admit to Sendoa he might have a point; instead, irritated by his insight and wisdom she redirected the conversation. "You really are insufferable. Tell me again how old you are?"

Sendoa chuckled. "I'm only seventy years older than you, but I've made good use of each one and made it my business to observe and learn."

"Pshaw! I would never describe you as a mere *observer*—your nose, and the rest of you, is always stuck in the middle of everything. As for you learning anything, that is a laughable notion; it is more likely you get hit by random insights, though I will allow you have a knack for bringing them up at the right time."

Sendoa laughed out loud, and the corners of Nahia's mouth twitched upward in a reluctant grin.

Like Nahia's good humor, spring came and went, summer came and went, and still Calisto remained in the human dimension. It wasn't until the fall of 1916 that a drastic change occurred and it filled Nahia with dismay.

She had opted for early-morning visits with Calisto, to place herself in his mind at the start of his day. The strategy had proved valuable until one morning she couldn't locate him—apparently he was awake. Puzzled and somewhat displeased, because it was too early for him to have gone somewhere, Nahia rose from her nest, careful not to wake the baby. She conjured a small light and set it on the slab border of the spring; its gentle glow reflecting on the water warmed the pre-dawn darkness. She sat across from it, letting her eyes rove over the bubble of light and its splintered reflection on the running water. She breathed evenly, until she no longer saw the conjured light or the spring; instead, she scryed the Citadel in Santillán for Calisto, convinced she would find him there.

She found him in his mother's chamber and became sickened by what she saw there. On the bed lay a waxen figure with sunken, staring eyes, gleaming dully as if through a murky film. Calisto, and one of Alaia's maids stood on either side of the bed like mute sentinels. At length, Calisto went to sit on the edge of the bed and Nahia watched him move his hand over his mother's face. The eyes closed and Nahia was glad of it, for the sight of them had shaken her. Then several things happened at once.

Calisto bowed as if in prayer over his mother; Nahia started toward him meaning to at least let her husband feel her consoling presence, but a wraithlike Alaia rose between them. Nahia reeled—indeed, back in her chamber she swayed where she sat at the edge of the spring. Had she ever seen such hatred in Alaia's eyes? Not even when she had abducted her newborn baby. Nahia shrank. Alaia's mute demand couldn't have been clearer. "Leave here and *never* return."

For once, Nahia's natural defiance did not surface. She never knew humans could do such a thing. How could Alaia be dead on the bed and standing in front of her at the same time? Nahia squinted into the venomous glaring eyes of the shade, trying to understand.

Yes. It had to be Alaia's residual energy, which she'd chosen to squander in hating rather than loving. Alaia could have embraced Calisto soothingly, but no, she chose to loathe Nahia to the very end.

The faery stood her ground, reaching back in time for any lessons or related wisdom until she hit upon them. Oihana's own brother, Ederne's father, a known member of the Unseelie Court, had not been able to pass into the light and been swallowed by the darkness that had characterized his life. "He must live his life over," Oihana had once shared with Nahia. "He will be born again as something other than what he was, usually the thing his dark behavior had been aimed at—an animal, a plant, or even a human. It is the only way such a being can learn his lesson."

Nahia stared at the specter with renewed interest, wondering if bad humans could be claimed by the darkness too. And more worrisome, what if Alaia's evil had been so focused on Nahia that she actually came back as a faery?

"*You* be gone, shade!" the cells in Nahia's body clamored, all the way from where she sat in her chamber. Her heartbeat slowed only when Alaia's residual particles had collapsed and sprinkled the floorboards, like so much dust.

Nahia made her presence known to Calisto, who merely closed his eyes in acknowledgment as he continued in a mournful attitude, bent over his mother's body. "I want you home with me and our baby," she injected the thought into his brain, surrounding him with soothing energy. He nodded and Nahia immediately caught a flurry of practical thoughts crowding his mind: burial services, sorting out management of the household and its staff; Irene and Jordi would have to be notified too.

"I will be ready in three days' time," he told her, and Nahia intensified the warmth of her embrace, which wrung tears from his eyes.

CHAPTER 14

ANTICIPATION

Three days later, and true to their extrasensory arrangement, Nahia arrived at the Citadel, exhilarated to at last take Calisto with her to the Realm. She was glad Alaia's body had already been disposed of, and while Calisto packed a light bag, Nahia visited some of the rooms to see for herself if any of Alaia's negativity lingered within the walls of the fortress. She didn't find any. Nahia told herself (and believed) it had all been locked in Alaia's casket, where it could rattle her bones without disturbing anything aboveground.

For several years, Nahia and Calisto led a faery-tale life in Handi Park. He had entered the Realm at age twenty-nine, and she was pleased to see, as they approached Zorione's fifteenth birthday, that her husband's appearance had altered as if only one year had passed. She had Oihana and Basajaun to thank for that.

Their daughter was to attend her first solstice celebration and the girl's excitement had reached cosmic proportions, bolstered by Nahia, who didn't doubt for a moment traces of faery Glamour would surface on that night of nights. The afternoon of, Nahia paused at the door of the chamber where her daughter was getting ready, and listened.

"Do you think I will be able to reduce my height at will? Oh no, no! What I really want starting tonight is to fly, just by thinking it." Zorione chattered while Zuzen combed back her wet hair. "It felt like today would never get here," she went on, eyes closed and a dreamy smile on her lips. "Mama says, never has a baby received so many Cradle Gifts as me. Do you think that will be a problem?"

"I don't see why, my sweet girl," Zuzen replied, deftly braiding the chestnut locks. "While it is true you received many gifts, they were not the kind to affect your faery nature—there was a lot of temperament and physical attribute gifting the day you arrived."

Zorione giggled, "I know. That's why I'm always smiling and why my hair is so long it reaches the backs of my knees."

A sudden disquiet gripped Nahia; what if *no* faery traits emerged? What if she had failed to make an imprint on her own child, or what if Calisto's non-faery nature overrode hers? What if Alaia's resentment and aversion prevailed over her own royal contribution? Nahia could not unsee the specter of her mother-in-law, full of loathing and demanding she stay away from Calisto and presumably, Zorione. Will she be cursed or punished for going against a dying woman's last wish?

Nahia shook herself mentally and bodily. *That won't be,* she thought, marching into the room and kissing Zorione on the forehead. "And don't forget how beautiful you are, my Zori, and how well you sing and paint," Nahia intoned, doing her best to hide the nagging suspicions—*surely, the legacy of a Faery Princess overrides any human contribution*, she pondered moodily, frowning at Zorione's strong jaw, so like Calisto's.

"Your gown for tonight is ready and Usoa is sending it over shortly," Nahia said, caressing her daughter's cheek and wondering what else of Calisto's, or his mother's, lurked in the girl's body.

"Isn't it the most beautiful salmon silk you ever saw?" Zorione beamed.

Nahia laughed out loud, "Salmon do not produce silk."

Zuzen laughed and Zorione pulled a face. "You know what I mean. I just love the orange-pinkish color. And the silk! It feels like a film of warm water over my skin—it's wonderful!"

"Yes, so you must thank Usoa again—she is a genius."

"You know I will. I mean to go to her as soon as I'm dressed so she will be the first to see me, after you and Papa, of course."

"That's my sweet girl," Nahia kissed her again and left her daughter with Zuzen to finish her coif.

At dusk, Nahia and Sendoa sat by the gardenia bushes, speaking sedately with Oihana until at last, Zorione entered the garden, escorted by Calisto. Nahia's heart raced with the sudden wild certainty Zorione's aura might have finally broken through, but then she realized, with a bleak tremor, it was just the color of the dress coupled with the fiery light of the sunset filtering from above.

Calisto twirled Zorione, the better to show her off, and the glow from Oihana's and Nahia's auras intensified to encircle them all. Zorione looked radiant in her simple silk gown, the bodice threaded with tiny glass beads in every shade from yellow to red, flashed becomingly at her slightest movement. Her chestnut hair had been partially braided and twisted to shape elaborate rose blossoms from which loose curls cascaded over her shoulders and down her back.

Sendoa bowed and declared Zorione a vision. Calisto kissed her hand and said, "Hear, hear!"

Nahia felt a knot form in her throat; she wiped the corner of her eye and embraced her daughter directly, careful not to touch the hairdo. Her mind flitted between the present and her very own first solstice celebration, almost a century ago.

"Shall we?" said a glowing Oihana, and everyone expressed their eager assent to be off to Moon Dancer Lake for the festivities.

CHAPTER 15

DISENCHANTED

Shortly after midnight, back in her chamber, Nahia wondered how the giddy anticipation of a few hours before could have fizzled out so. She wore a hard look as she undid the braided rose blossoms in Zorione's hair; she tried to smooth it down but it was so crimped nothing but a wash would fix it.

"I know you blame me. You think I lied to you and misled you, but I truly believed the faery alchemy would happen tonight." Nahia's fingers worked softly in contrast with the roughness in her voice. "For the stars above! You are my daughter and you've lived in the Realm for fifteen years—Celeste was a human and even *she* was able to take in some magic just by living here."

"Maybe it is like Grandmamma said," Zorione sniffled, looking at Nahia in the mirror, her eyes brimming with tears. "My babies will be the ones who get all the Glamour," she blinked and the tears spilled.

Nahia clucked her tongue, exasperated. She embraced her daughter and kissed her. "I wish it weren't so. I hate it when my mother is right!"

"And I hate it when my mother is wrong," Zorione said thickly.

Nahia frowned as she looked in the mirror, mother and daughter cheek to cheek. "I don't like being wrong."

Zorione produced a watery grin. "It's all right. I am disappointed, but not heartbroken," she said matter-of-factly as she reached back and nimbly coiled her hair into a knot. She fixed it at the base of her neck and added, "Wasn't it Usoa who gave me the Cradle Gift of an easy temperament?"

Nahia bit her lip and nodded. "Never you mind, my Zori, we can compensate for just about anything—I will teach you everything I know about potions, and you'll find more Glamour in that than in flying or shape-shifting."

She saw the gamut of happy prospects spreading before them—Nahia would pour into her daughter all the potion-making wisdom she had acquired over the years, and Zorione would eventually surpass her in knowledge of all the herbs and roots in the Realm. For a few shining moments, Nahia saw how it could be, but the look on Zorione's face punctured her buoyant fancy.

The expression spoke of irreversible regret, as if Zorione had made up her mind about something and would not be persuaded otherwise. Nahia raised her brow slowly, suspecting but unwilling to come to a conclusion yet.

"I love you, Mama," Zorione said, and Nahia's heart fluttered, overcome with dread. "Papa and I have been talking too."

Nahia turned from her daughter flushed with anger, jumping to conclusions. It seemed Alaia would get her way. At length, she felt Zorione's tentative touch on her shoulder. Nahia pressed her lips together in an effort to get her temper under control.

"Mama, please. Papa and I decided if some form of power emerged tonight it would prove I belonged here, and he would stay too. But if it didn't—" Zorione let the statement hang in the air. Nahia felt herself on the verge of raging back; how dare they make such a decision without consulting her—did she have *no* say in the matter? She was wife and mother! She was the Faery Princess, next in line to the throne, to become Queen of the Realm of the Western Pyrenees!

Nahia rounded on her daughter. "After me, *you* are next in line to the throne," she said, determined to wreck the hurtful plan she hadn't been invited to shape.

A brief shadow darkened Zorione's expression as if she hadn't considered this, but then to Nahia's consternation, she recognized Alaia's insufferable, practical thinking as it streaked across her daughter's brain and shot out of her mouth.

"But Mama, you and Grandmamma would have to go into the light before that happens. Grandmamma is almost seven hundred years old and she doesn't look anywhere near ready to exit this world, nor do you, thank heavens!" Nahia shook her head stubbornly as Zorione continued to argue, "I might live another sixty years, and Papa and I agree we want to be in San Sebastián, where we are like everyone else."

"Have you seen your father? He's been here these fifteen years and he looks and feels as he would in the passing of a single year in the human dimension. If you go, you will be giving up a lot more than sixty years." Nahia felt a physical ache in her chest but refused to say more; she stared at her daughter through steady aquamarine eyes until Calisto appeared in her peripheral vision. Anger and understanding boiled up inside of her—it was base treachery as much as it was self-defense on their part.

The seconds stretched into minutes, and Nahia still didn't speak; she stumbled through the rubble of her collapsed family until, in her mind, a bitter wind picked up and blew away all traces of their life together in the Realm.

Calisto had come to stand beside their daughter and they reached out to her at the same time. Nahia felt Calisto's hand on her shoulder and Zorione's warm touch on her cheek. She blinked at last and drew in a deep breath. How would she get on *without* these two people in her life every day?

"Mama, please say something."

Calisto squeezed Nahia's shoulder lightly.

"I don't know what to say, sweet girl—" Nahia's voice quivered, which made Calisto pull her to him. She put her arm around his waist, pressing herself against him and pulling Zorione into the embrace. "I don't want us to part," Nahia whispered hopelessly.

Calisto and Zorione left the Realm in the fall of 1930, but not before Nahia had bestowed one more gift on her child, the same one she'd given her husband years before: Lucid Dreaming. Through it, Nahia later found out that Irene, their old housekeeper, had spread a story around town in which Nahia had died mysteriously. Calisto, of course, had remained at the Citadel in Santillán with Zorione until his own mother died and then he had traveled with the baby for several years, deciding to return to San Sebastián only after Zorione had turned fifteen.

To explain otherwise or to tell the truth would have been madness, and Oihana would not have allowed it. Calisto the widower and Zorione the orphan began their life in San Sebastián.

The small family eased into a regular dream connection, with sporadic encounters at the Citadel, which became a natural middle ground for them, just as it had been while Celeste and Etienne lived. The years passed and Nahia watched her daughter develop into a woman. It came as no surprise when the vivid dreams they shared became tinged with romantic longings on Zorione's part. She'd met a Portuguese businessman, and the whirlwind romance they embarked on culminated in a proposal.

In the summer of 1936, after weeks of feverish planning, Nahia attended Zorione's wedding in San Sebastián, in faery form, visible only to her husband

and daughter, as no one else in the congregation had been granted the gift of Faery Sight. Oihana and Sendoa accompanied the mother of the bride; they would not have missed it for the world.

"This marks another level of separation," Nahia grumbled to Sendoa. She hadn't said much on the journey back, and only when she and Sendoa were alone did she speak. "Her life as a married woman begins today, and she won't have time for me. As it was, I only saw her during season changes."

"If your dream connection slows down, don't you withdraw and sulk," Sendoa warned her.

Nahia bristled. "I refuse to impose."

"Well, let's hope Calisto steps in if Zorione gets too sidetracked with her husband to remember her mother. But you'd do well to remember that she is your daughter, and you should let her know you're around even if she doesn't acknowledge you."

Calisto indeed stepped in, and it was a bittersweet experience for Nahia the night Calisto announced they would be grandparents. Unable to help herself, she went to Zorione right away and was received in her dreams with genuine elation. The faery felt even if for one night, the old closeness had been renewed, as if it had never stopped; mother and daughter spoke for hours, telling each other all that had happened in the silence.

Zorione gave birth to twins, a girl and a boy, and during her visit to San Sebastián for the Cradle Gifting, Nahia was quick to remind Calisto and Zorione about the holographic will, and so the children were named accordingly: Mireya and Carlos Santillán.

Nahia returned to Handi Park that night anxious to review her impressions with Sendoa; he'd become a sounding board she could not do without. As they flew over the forest toward Moon Dancer Lake, she dismissed his spirited congratulations on becoming a grandmother and his condescending reassurances of how well the status suited her.

"I'm still younger than you," Nahia said flatly, perching herself on an enormous boulder at the edge of the forest.

Ignoring the scowl on his face as he alighted beside her, she spoke her mind. "Her husband does not know who I am, and she intends to keep it that way. And now, there are children who won't know me either. I will just be someone they see in their dreams," Nahia choked down a moan—the feel of the tiny babies in her arms, blood of her blood, alive and so out of her reach.

"So it was Lucid Dreaming for the twins too?" Sendoa asked kindly.

Nahia nodded. "That's what I've been reduced to! It is the one gift that allows me conscious interaction with all of them."

"And it saves you the effort of coming up with original gifts for each new descendant," Sendoa pointed out helpfully.

"But I liked being creative with my Cradle Gifts," Nahia griped.

"What you like is doing what you want, and this situation, which you created, has limited you."

Nahia protested, "I know I created the situation, but I was managing it fine until they chose to rebel."

"You make it sound like insurrection—you know your choice of words only magnifies the negative," he chided. "The truth is, only your needs were being met; you were willing to ignore their free will and didn't stop to consider their feelings."

Nahia rejoined, eyes flashing angrily, "I mostly thought of *them* when I brought them here. Really! Whose life wouldn't be improved beyond recognition by living here?" Nahia said, looking over Moon Dancer Lake and its white sandy shore, truly wondering how anyone might prefer any other place.

"Obviously, your husband and daughter," Sendoa declared with raised brows. "It is you who believes nothing is better than the Realm because you *are* a faery and you belong here. But they are human, and their dimension calls to them, the way only *home* can."

Nahia's face crumpled and she leaned into Sendoa. "I wanted this to be their home."

He put his arm around her and kissed her forehead. "I know."

The spark of mischief in Nahia's aquamarine eyes flickered and ceased that night. Sendoa told her so a few days later. She glared at him befuddled and he quickly swore the spark had been replaced with a steady, cool fire he recognized as maturity and budding wisdom.

Many years passed, and although she didn't admit it to Sendoa, Nahia often checked her eyes in the looking glass and concluded he was right about the missing spark; events in her life had snuffed it out and she wondered how much duller her eyes would get as life went on.

Nahia thought she'd prepared her heart for it, but when Calisto died in 1953, she couldn't breathe as the newly felt absence slithered into every corner of her spirit and mind. She could count on her husband no longer.

Zorione saw the justice in Nahia's request to at least keep him in death and coordinated an elaborate ceremony in town featuring an empty casket, while Nahia for her part coordinated the transportation of her husband to the Realm. She knew just the place—by the pond, at the foot of the Great Oak, beside Paloma's remains.

That same year, Nahia's feisty granddaughter, sixteen-year-old Mireya, gave birth to a baby girl amid a lively scandal in town, for Mireya would not reveal the father's identity. She named her Catalina Santillán, honoring the holographic will. To further assert her independence, Mireya and her daughter moved into the family's second home in town—Santillán Manor.

Nahia's thoughts often dwelled on that and always concluded her girls were as faery-like as ever she could've hoped. Neither Zorione nor Mireya were bothered by the absence of Catalina's father—they were simply raising the child in the family's bosom, like any matriarchal clan would consider natural.

When Zorione died in 1961, Nahia's world shook. It seemed the relationship ended as quickly as the snapping of fingers.

"It was a terrible mistake!" Nahia raged to Sendoa. "I should never have agreed to be kept a secret—my grandchildren should know that I exist, that I'm not just someone they dream about." Crazy thoughts went through her mind. What if she abducted them all? What if she ignored Oihana's rule of secrecy and Sendoa's angry warnings?

"If you tell, you will be repeating your old mistake," Sendoa lashed out. "All they know is the human dimension—that is their home. Do you really mean to drag them here to something they know nothing about and expect them to be happy? Will you plow through the dreams and desires of a whole new generation, just to satisfy your own self? I don't believe it!"

Nahia tried to pass her trembling as a shrug—she'd never seen Sendoa as livid as this. Glaring at him nevertheless, she rejoined with, "Mireya and Carlos are only twenty-four years old. Carlos will likely leave San Sebastián in search of adventure, but Mireya has eight-year-old Catalina to raise on her own."

"You forget Mireya's father—he's still alive and at home," Sendoa pointed out and continued in a snide tone, "I suppose it's not your concern if he wants his family around, after losing Zori."

A myriad of retorts exploded in Nahia's mind but she choked them down, annoyed that just as Sendoa said, they were all the same arguments she'd employed years before. "So I'm to be forever divided from my family?"

Sendoa's expression softened. "You can watch over them—"

"From afar. In their dreams, right?" Nahia challenged, shrinking from Sendoa when he tried to touch her.

He looked genuinely troubled and it seemed to Nahia he might rethink his advice. Mystified, she realized it hadn't crossed her mind to do what *she* wanted, unless it was with Sendoa's stamp of approval. Did she really value and trust his judgment that much? When had that happened?

The ready response: over the last 140 years.

Nahia's shoulders sagged and this time she didn't need Sendoa to remark on it; she felt her eyes become a degree duller. "I hate experience and wisdom," she muttered.

PART II

1961 T⊕ 1992

Maturity is not an outgrowing, but a growing up: an adult is not a dead child, but a child who survived.

Ursula K. Le Guin

CHAPTER 16
⊕IHANA'S TALE

Six more years piled on, during which Nahia visited Mireya and Carlos every fortnight, in their dreams. Because Catalina's own Cradle Gift would not take effect until her fifteenth birthday, Nahia contented herself with whatever information she could glean from Mireya's dreams.

Zorione had explained to the twins that the woman they dreamed about *was* their grandmother, who had died young and become an angel to watch over them. The notion never failed to amuse Nahia and she looked forward to the same explanation being given to Catalina within the year. *What would Sendoa think about that?* she wondered ruefully—*probably that in the human dimension, angels are in the same realm of "odd" as faeries.*

Such were Nahia's musings one chilly autumn afternoon. She drifted listlessly through the Aspen Grove on her way to Handi Park when a horrific cry rent the air. For a few bewildered seconds Nahia thought the grove had come alive with a distress call—but not one of her descendants knew of that means of communication, and besides, they were all in San Sebastián at the time and not at the Citadel in Santillán.

A silver flash zipped past Nahia and Sendoa was suddenly there—his powerful back to her in a protective stance. On tiptoes to see over his shoulder, Nahia stared wide-eyed as tree limbs and whole trunks were blasted out of the way by something enormous.

For a brief moment everything stopped; the terrible rumble of wood cracking ceased and an eerie whistling sound pressed on her eardrums. It lasted long enough for Nahia to realize that a rolling unknown force hadn't caused the commotion; it was, rather, a concerted strike soon to restart.

In those scant seconds of silence, conjectures tumbled one after the other in Nahia's mind. They came to a sharp halt when she glimpsed the familiar red locks flailing in whirling currents of debris. The blood in her veins seemed to freeze. *Ederne, returned?* And taking aim again!

Instinct took over; rejecting Sendoa's protection, Nahia came around to stand beside him. At the same instant, Oihana alighted on his other side. The three of them faced Ederne, who had concentrated and released a blast so powerful the trees appeared to jump out, roots and all, as the scorching heat passed.

Nahia, Sendoa, and Oihana shot upward and away from the projectile's path.

"Keep her out of Handi Park!" Oihana cried out, focusing her energy to drown out the fires erupting all around. Nahia followed suit—knowing she could not destroy Ederne because she was a blood relation, yet to merely protect and restore was unthinkable. So for every tree Nahia righted, she also made a gash on the ground at Ederne's feet causing her time and again to stumble and change direction, determined to at least complicate her advance while getting herself closer to gag and bind her wretched cousin.

A powerful neigh resonated, and on hearing it, a surge of adrenaline and relief flooded Nahia—they were safe now. The presence of the unicorn, Basajaun, imparted hope and strength to them all.

Three brutish-looking faeries Nahia did not recognize appeared out of nowhere. "She's not alone!" she warned the others.

From Sendoa's palms issued another shower of silver arrows that sent Ederne scurrying for cover and he pressed his advantage, steering her away from the entrance to Handi Park. The Keeper of the Forest entered the fray as Ederne's thugs attempted to shield her. Two faery braves materialized, having answered Oihana's silent call. They took up post on either side of Basajaun and it seemed they had Ederne cornered, while Sendoa focused on her thugs.

Nahia took her chance and pounced from a distance of five feet, but Ederne saw her coming. With a vengeful snarl Ederne raised her hands, body suffused in a red haze of concentrated energy, recklessly discharging her deadly blasts. Nahia wrestled Ederne amid a riot of sound, light, and heat. A tree gouged by one of the blasts began to fall on the grappling cousins. Nahia rolled out of the way a split second before they were flattened by it, dragging Ederne along.

Nahia pinned Ederne and immediately conjured a vine. It coiled itself round her cousin, immobilizing her at once. Nahia rose from the writhing form on the ground to survey the damage. What she saw first were the two faery braves lifting the fallen tree off the still form of the unicorn. Her heart stopped, Nahia stared, but as soon as the weight lifted, the Keeper of the Forest struggled to right himself, and succeeded. Full of concern, Nahia watched him retreat slowly into the grove and out of sight.

"Your mother," Sendoa whispered in her ear, and Nahia whirled, somehow knowing exactly where to look. The second blast discharged by Ederne had hit Oihana. Nahia raced to her and knelt beside the Faery Queen. She could hear Ederne's outraged growls but she ignored them, fully focused on her mother's wounds. The fabric of her dress smoldered, laying bare a raw gash over the ribs and the inside of the arm. Oihana's blood dripped steadily from her wounds.

"Shut up!" Nahia screamed, turning on her cousin whose growling, even through the gag, kept getting louder. "Get her out of my sight," she said to the braves, "take her somewhere outside Handi Park until I can—"

With a mighty exertion, Ederne managed to break the ivy bonds and she hovered triumphantly, eyes flashing from Nahia to the two faery braves and to Sendoa, who had rounded on her as well.

The four of them acted at once, and they all missed.

Nahia gasped the instant Ederne disappeared. "It can't be!" Reluctantly Nahia had to acknowledge her cousin's speed, which was as uncanny as her strength. A few aspen leaves swirled in the spot where Ederne had been. Sendoa and the other two stared as if waiting for Ederne to reappear in full attack mode.

"She won't be back," Nahia said at length, "not for a while anyway."

The two thugs, bound and gagged, lay there grunting and eyeing them warily.

"Take these two beyond the boundaries of the Realm, over the waterfall," Sendoa instructed the braves. Nahia hoped fervently they would drop them from the top and let them break on the rocks at the bottom. But she knew that would not come to pass. Oihana's troop would not destroy, not even a declared enemy.

Nahia and Sendoa exchanged a dark look as they bent over Oihana's trembling body. He lifted her gently and carried her to the royal chamber inside Handi Park, Nahia drifted mutely beside them.

The healer came and went, leaving Oihana with cleaned, dressed wounds; she had stopped the bleeding but did not look hopeful as she bowed out of the room.

Kneeling by the bed, holding her mother's hand, and watching her prone

113

figure in a daze, Nahia recalled Zorione once saying Oihana didn't look anywhere near ready to return to the light—well, the violence done to her this day had certainly made it imminent.

"Some water, please," Oihana said in a raspy voice, propping herself on her elbows. Nahia rose hastily and placed pillows behind her mother so she was in more of a sitting position. She brought back the glass and put it to her mouth. After two sips, Oihana sank back, whimpering against the pillows.

Nahia thought there must be something she could do for her mother's relief, or for a measure of hope at least, but she couldn't stop thinking about the healer's grim expression upon leaving the room. She grabbed Oihana's hand, and as the silence grew, so did Nahia's anxiety.

Say something, Nahia thought in a panic. Could it really be no words would get through the knot in her throat? And there were so many good ones; gratitude, appreciation, how much she loved her, and how excruciating her absence would be—

"Mama," Nahia groaned, dismayed, "tell me what to do; surely together we can fix these," she said, motioning to the dressed wounds.

Oihana shook her head. "Ederne's intent was too dark, and the damage is irreversible."

Nahia resumed kneeling by the bed and she kissed her mother's hand again. "What about a potion, a salve, anything to ease—"

Oihana shook her head again. "You must listen now, my Nahia, as there is much we need to discuss."

Nahia looked into her mother's feverish eyes, grasping the seriousness of the situation; the Faery Queen meant to put her affairs in order. "Should I summon the council?"

"No, my love, this is between you and me."

"I understand," murmured the Faery Princess, dispirited, wondering what sort of ritual was about to take place. To her knowledge, there were no relics to be conferred—Oihana had never worn a crown or carried a scepter, yet no one questioned her because of her regal demeanor, majestic stature, nobility, and wisdom—when Oihana spoke everyone listened.

How do things like that get transferred? Nahia frowned and answered herself, feeling suddenly deficient. *They don't—they must be learned if one is not born with them.*

"I once told you, I feared history repeated itself," Oihana said, catching Nahia off guard.

Her eyes narrowed as she tried to recall when that had been, and suddenly she remembered—Oihana had said it the day she rescued her from Alaia and brought her back home.

"Long ago, like you, I fell in love with a human," the Faery Queen continued, "and I forsook my family over what I thought was true love. I lied to him about my faery nature, and I gave him not one child but three."

Nahia flinched with each declaration, as if pelted with cold raindrops on her bare skin.

"Indeed, when I challenged Alaia and took you and my granddaughter from them, I felt certain you were walking the same path I had in my youth. Only years later, when Zorione and Calisto left us, did I see the marked differences between my choice and its outcome, and yours."

Undecided as to the prevailing emotion, astonishment or curiosity, Nahia squeezed her mother's hand in both of hers and climbed on the bed. "Mama," she murmured, "what did you do?"

"The year was 1542 (Nahia calculated swiftly: Oihana had been 320 years old) when, wishing to distance ourselves from the civil unrest surrounding our home, my mother and a retinue of thirty faeries left Italy to start a new life. My mother, the Faery Queen, chose to settle us on a desolate territory, on the border between France and Spain, where stood an inhospitable mountain called Monte Perdido.

"Accustomed as I was to the proximity of humans back home, it didn't take long for me to begin spying on the small though thriving human village at the foot of the great mountain.

"His name was Antonio San Angelo," Oihana said, her glance on Nahia. "He was an explorer, stationed in Monte Perdido. I persuaded myself in love and soon began visiting him in human form. I steeled my resolve one day and told my mother I meant to embrace a human life with him. She forbade it, of course, but I was beyond the reach of reason. She told me never to return and I promised I would not."

Nahia's tears spilled in silence, already spotting differences in their stories; unlike Nahia, Oihana hadn't lied to her own mother.

"Antonio's hold on me lasted four years, during which I was deceived in him." Nahia's ears pricked at this and her attention intensified; she scooted closer. "We had three children: a son, Nino, and twin daughters, Ibai and Nere. I was so very happy, my Nahia, I really believed my life was charmed. Worse yet, I gloated—I had the best of both worlds—a man who loved me and three beautiful children, and my faery nature too—for I took care to draw from the moon what I needed to nurture it, until one autumn night, curious as to where I disappeared to every full moon, Antonio followed me into Monte Perdido, to a bathing place I thought only I knew of. I disrobed and stood under the moonlight for a few moments before I disappeared before his eyes. I had reduced my height, but as he did not have the gift of Faery Sight, he concluded I'd vanished. Before he could react to having witnessed such artifice, he detected an eerie luminescence, my aura, which prompted him to stay and watch. My ritual concluded, and unaware of his presence I recovered my human height, which meant to his eyes I reappeared as if by magic. He let me return to our home, ignorant of what he'd seen, and there he confronted me in a most violent manner.

"A religious man he was, and to have witnessed such a thing naturally filled him with terror. As if to fuel his superstitious small-mindedness, a cold wind swooped down from Monte Perdido unleashing an electrical storm, which struck fear into his heart and the villagers' too. He dragged me to the town square, along with my girls, and there we met the townsfolk who had come out, crossing themselves, to gawk at the storm and to see what was the matter with Antonio and his woman."

Nahia gasped, heart gripped by fear, so submerged in her mother's tale she fancied seeing it all unfold.

"Antonio accused me of sorcery, said the girls were tainted as well, but he exempted our boy from the stain. He demanded the girls and I be destroyed, and the villagers, incited by lightning and thunder, believed Antonio when he attributed nature's display to my fear and displeasure over being found out. I believed the stars were having their revenge on me for my lie, and I might have accepted my fate, but I would fail my innocent daughters. He and I clashed in public; the girls, barely three years old, screamed as Antonio and I pulled on them bodily."

For the first time since her narrative began, Oihana paused and became downcast. Nahia reached for the glass of water and offered it to her. Oihana drank and looked at her daughter through glittering amethyst eyes. "Thank you, my love," she said, and Nahia assented, pressing a cool cloth to her mother's forehead.

"Lightning struck the thatched roof of a dwelling near the square and a fire started. We were thrown into chaos, the villagers' attention divided between us and the fire, which the wind had already caused to leap onto a second roof. I had hold of Nere, while Antonio had Ibai. Nino cried in the arms of a missionary sister who taught at the school. My girls' cries mingled with the din from the villagers screaming for our death as loudly as for water to quell the fires. But the shriek that came out of me when Antonio slit Ibai's throat drowned them all out, at least to my ears."

Nahia's hand flew to her own mouth, appalled. She searched her mother's face but could not summon Oihana back from the distant past. "He let Ibai's small body drop at his feet, and driven by his ignorant rage, he advanced on us. I held Nere to me, letting my horror, incredulity, and grief alchemize into blinding wrath with every beat of my child's frightened heart.

"I knew what I would do, but Nere must not be there to see it. As if summoned by providence, Eleanor, the keeper of the inn where Antonio and I had resided for years, appeared at my side, begging of me what was happening and why? Near unhinged but with a sudden wild hope, I implored her to take my child far from there. I thrust Nere into Eleanor's arms and told her to go, unable to spare even a final glance, for Antonio was on top of me, dagger in hand. Trusting the confusion to protect my secret, I shifted to faery height and his dagger tore through empty air. He lost his footing.

"I rose above him untouched and commanded every blood vessel in that murderer's body to shut down, I wielded all my strength and I took pleasure in seeing his eyes grow wide with terror when he felt it happen. I watched him until his heart burst," Oihana said coldly, embedding forever more in Nahia's mind the image of a heart pumping blood into sealed arteries. "I looked at Antonio's body, at the blood pouring out of his ears and mouth, and could not fathom ever having loved the man. I turned from him without a backward glance."

Nahia looked at her mother with a mixture of furious pride and overwhelming sorrow for what she had endured. In renewed awe of her, though breathless with emotion, Nahia had to ask, "What happened to them, to Nino and Nere?"

"Eleanor did as I asked her—she escaped from Monte Perdido that very night, taking my Nere with her. Nino, who by all accounts had been tragically *orphaned*, stayed in the village and was kept by the missionary sister. I realized then I would not be able to recover him; to appear back in town would only confirm Antonio's madness and bring a full-scale persecution upon myself. As for Nere, if I established a safe haven, I might be able to go back for her. So with that hopeful plan, I retreated to a location high up in the Pyrenees, but not before entering my small home in the village from which I rescued a blanket that had belonged to my girls. I would track her with Glamour until we met again.

"I brought the blanket back to Handi Park, which was no more than a burrow where I could hide, and I enhanced the fabric in preparation for the final enchantment. When it was ready, I stole into the small dwelling in Pamplona, where Eleanor had taken Nere. I kissed my baby and took a lock of hair, which I used to embroider her name on the blanket. Then I transmuted it into a map-like tapestry imbued with such Glamour as to allow me to *see* her. Such joy I felt when the very next day, I saw it had worked. I followed my child's progress from then on. But my Nere grew up quicker than my efforts to create a safe haven yielded results; she left Pamplona and had moved into France before a band of a dozen traveling faeries wandered into my territory. They accepted my hospitality and stayed with me. With their help, I made real progress, but by the time Handi Park had expanded into a decent living space, and the foundation of our Arboretum had been seeded, Nere had met and married a man she loved.

"As Nere had no knowledge of my existence, I could not justify tearing her from her family, nor could I repeat my own mother's cruelty and discard *her*. So I denied myself the pleasure, and continued as I had been, watching her from afar. And when Nere had her first daughter, Juliette she named her, I visited them, though they never knew it, and I brought another stolen lock of hair."

Nahia sniffed and wiped her eyes impatiently. It filled her with regret to know there had never been a moment's censure on Oihana's part, not when Nahia lied, or when she had stolen Glamour like a thief. Her mother's generous heart had forgiven the instant Nahia made her choice and that only intensified how undeserving she felt.

"I made the tapestry in 1546, Nahia, and I never stopped tracking them—my girls," Oihana sighed. She raised a sluggish hand toward the hanging on the wall opposite the bed. Nahia had always seen it there, thinking it a simplistic design of green and brown between large blotches of blue and sprinkled with something like leaves, without rhyme or reason. She had never understood the content, until now.

Nahia walked over to it and began scanning it in a state of agitation; there were the names of long dead women and their offspring, all of them sharing in the Faery Queen's blood. Nahia noted they were scattered over Spain and France, though largely concentrating on the border between the two countries.

She found Nere on the map, near Marseilles; apparently, that was where she and Eleanor ended up after their flight from Monte Perdido and their short stay in Pamplona. As Nahia ran her fingers over the embroidered name, a flash of heat coursed through her, and a series of visions, wrapped in a golden haze, presented themselves to her. Although Nere was long dead, her lock of hair and Oihana's Glamour had bound the most precious moments of her life to the tapestry for Nahia to glimpse and understand.

She saw Oihana's girls laugh and cry through the years; they loved their men and had their children. Their eyes invariably shone as if with a secret satisfaction, their bodies, lithe or voluptuous, danced to furtive inner melodies. Soft breezes kissed their faces and moved their hair, and Nahia imagined Oihana was that breeze, swooping down on them from afar to love them the only way she could.

There was no mistaking the Faery Queen's genetic spark, traveling from one to the next of them—Nahia traced each name with the tips of her fingers, experiencing the same surge of heat, followed by a brief history, so infused with feeling, Nahia fancied she could discern the driving force of each girl. Nere had been optimistic and carefree, Juliette had been serene and tolerant, Émilie, an unruly wild child. Adèle, Mother Nature incarnate. Camille, Rose, Angèle, Naomi, and then, before she could wonder what she might feel about herself if her name were on this tapestry, she read: PALOMA.

Nahia reeled. This had to be Celeste's mother, so close to San Sebastián. Paloma's name was right where the old citadel of Santillán was located. Dazed and momentarily paralyzed, she stared at the name, taking deep breaths. She could feel Oihana, reclined statue-like behind her on the bed, knowing where on the map she had arrived.

Nahia pressed her finger over Paloma's embroidered name, and yes! A sudden flood of rich images overwhelmed her; Paloma's childhood and adolescence, her wedding day, and eventually Celeste, and Nahia herself, appeared. Through it all, Nahia fancied she felt an extra pulsation of love and joy emanating from Paloma's name that made her suddenly choke down tears.

"Oh, Mama—" Nahia raced back to Oihana and knelt beside her again. "All those years Celeste and I called each other birth sisters because we'd been born on the same night," Nahia cried gleefully. "And you knew all along we really *were* sisters!"

"I cannot tell you what a joy it was for me when that child of mine literally appeared at my doorstep," Oihana said, eyes shining, voice throbbing with emotion. "It was such a gift to have had those few years with her; to me, Paloma was the embodiment of Nere and all the others."

Tears glittered in Nahia's eyes; such hope, joy, and pride as she could hear in her mother's voice and plainly see on her face had to have immense healing power. But Oihana shifted slightly on her pillows and grimaced, reminding Nahia of the bleak nature of her wounds.

Ederne's blasts of energy had been infused with so much rage and hate they would not allow repair of cells or tissues. Just like the trees she could not heal and would have to replant, Nahia found herself wishing she could somehow replant her mother.

"Sendoa is coming—" Oihana whispered.

CHAPTER 17

THE KEEPER'S KEEPER

Nahia's eyes swiveled toward the door, and the soft knock, though expected, caused her to start. She willed it open. Sendoa marched in, silver aura flashing, looking relieved. "He has been found. And I've confirmed it myself, it was not a direct hit, the tree did the damage, so with your assistance, he should recover nicely." He addressed the last to Nahia.

Oihana's eyes turned heavenward. "Thank the stars," she murmured, squeezing her daughter's hand. "Go to him, darling, you know what needs to be done."

"Of course," Nahia said croakily. A wave of frigid water washed over her; the Keeper of the Forest, Basajaun, had been found and *she* was expected to heal him? Only the Faery Queen, who was supposed to live forever, should be trusted with such work! In her mind's eye, Basajaun disappeared slowly into the forest again and Nahia trembled, feeling unequal to the task.

"Shall we?" Sendoa asked, and she assented.

Nahia followed him out of the royal chamber and out of Handi Park, glad to breathe the fresh air, even if it didn't bring her clarity or relief. They flitted through the Aspen Grove into the Arboretum and then into the dusky forest. Soon they arrived at a patch of brushwood Nahia recognized right away as the place where she'd once brought an offering to a doe in exchange for milk to feed a hungry Calisto.

A knot formed in her throat. She took Sendoa's hand as they descended upon the place where she could already see the pearly form on the leaf-strewn ground. Nahia bent over the magnificent animal, pleading nonstop with the universe to be allowed the crucial presence of mind during her first close contact, *ever*, with the Keeper of the Forest.

She placed a tentative hand on the exposed flank, which rose and fell rapidly with his labored breathing. Basajaun nickered, and Nahia replied softly, "Hello." His heart beat in frantic unison with hers. Basajaun raised his head and fixed her with a liquid, black eye—such profound innocence she'd never seen before—he knew no fear or self-pity, only wonder over a predicament he did not understand.

Basajaun tensed beneath her hand. His ears pinned back, he emitted a sudden snort and Nahia's blood turned cold; she reacted instinctively to the unicorn's warning. She rose and hovered protectively on one side of Basajaun. Sendoa did the same on the other side and, back to back, they scanned the undergrowth. Nahia raised her hands and began conjuring a shield to spread over her and Sendoa and over the form of the unicorn. But before she could complete it, the scene became immersed in a red haze.

Breathless, Nahia spun toward the sound of Ederne's triumphant howl and shouted, "*No!*" at the lethal, fiery javelin hurtling through the air. Silver shards erupted over Nahia's head like a meteor shower; Sendoa had aimed them at Ederne.

Nahia fell back unharmed by the force of the javelin. Sendoa's shards had pinned Ederne to a tree, and he pounced on her. Nahia didn't pause to see if he had immobilized her cousin. She whirled toward the unicorn, and a second guttural "Noooo!" escaped her throat—the incomplete shield had not protected Basajaun! Ederne's screaming reached Nahia as if from miles away. She didn't care, Sendoa would see to her, but she, Nahia, had to save the unicorn; he must *not* die.

She closed her eyes the better to see with the palms of her hands; she moved them over the clammy, white pelt to assess the damage despite the dull pain throbbing in her temple. Nahia blamed herself, but was determined to repair the harm done by her slow response.

I will mend him, I will mend him. The chant circled in her brain and flowed to her hands, where the concentrated energy glowed cool blue. Basajaun's body flickered between mass and mist, distracting Nahia from her intent and calling her attention to the eerie silence; she couldn't hear Ederne anymore. *Sendoa must've gagged her*, Nahia thought fleetingly as her chant unraveled. Her conviction faltered, and she had to recognize the futility of her efforts. She could not revitalize the charred cells, and she could not regrow the destroyed tissue. Terror gripped her.

She felt Sendoa's cool hand on her shoulder. "It has stopped," he said, and for a hopeful moment Nahia thought he meant Ederne. But no such good fortune was in store for her. The unicorn's flank no longer moved. Nahia dug her fingers into it, horrified.

Sendoa squeezed her shoulder and Nahia twisted away from his touch. She knew no time could be wasted, but she did not feel ready for what must be done next. If only the shield had been effective. If only her mother were there to take charge. Frustrated, scared, and resentful, she ran her hands over the lifeless body, working herself up. It was imperative she act now—the noble heart had already stopped beating.

Oihana's words rang in her ears: "You know what needs to be done."

A bleak resolve overtook the Faery Princess who assumed human height, the better to go about the ghastly task. With fixed thoughts and a commanding hand, Nahia directed the separation of the membranes holding together the eyes and the heart of the unicorn. All the while, a lilting song flowed out of her:

> *O Basajaun*
> *A comet your passage has been*
> *Fleeting yet magnificent in this life's din,*
> *You leave us with the memory of your light.*
> *And I beg of thee, a gift before you take that final flight.*
> *Your eyes, that your vision may again be carried out*
> *Your heart, that your love may flourish eternal, beyond any doubt*
> *O Basajaun.*

Although there was no bloodshed, for Nahia's skill to alter matter was unmatched, she felt no better than a butcher as she gaped at the glittering organs, floating unnaturally outside their rightful vessel.

Basajaun flickered one last time, and the emptied body disappeared.

This is needed to save the Realm, Nahia kept telling herself, but it didn't ease the revulsion she felt over the coldness of the act. She had defiled a magical creature.

With a hollow feeling inside, Nahia stared at the precious organs for another instant and then, with no other view than finishing the task as quickly as possible, she drew energy from every cell in her body to effect the final transformation. A cool, aquamarine blaze enfolded the eyes and heart of the unicorn and compressed them into three stones. Nahia made a fist over them and tucked them away in her cloak as if hiding evidence of a crime.

Nahia reached back with one hand and rubbed the base of her neck, feeling the toll of the energy expenditure. It was full dark as she turned away from where Basajaun had been. She could easily make out her cousin's form, slumped against a tree trunk, bound in a silver cord and shrouded in a pulsating red haze. Rage coursed anew through Nahia for the atrocities committed by her cousin, by Ederne. *Ignorant, vile Ederne!*

Still at human height, Nahia strode over and towered over her. Ederne's eyes swiveled madly from her face to the place in the cloak where the unicorn's transmuted organs had been placed. She couldn't tell if Ederne knew what the death of the unicorn meant for the Realm, nor what Ederne's thoughts were about what she had seen Nahia do. She didn't care.

"That is nothing to you," Nahia hissed. With none too gentle a swipe, she grabbed her cousin around the waist in one fluid movement. "You have finished us all, you fool," she spat, and still full of rage, Nahia took to the air.

She shot up through branches to the open sky, not caring a thing about twigs and leaves lashing the prisoner. Sendoa caught up with her and took up the post of a silent escort. Nahia didn't know if he meant to help her or keep her in line; could he sense how tempted she was to test the rule about not killing a blood relation?

When Nahia reached the waterfall, she held Ederne by the neck so they were at eye level, glad to see the cuts and scrapes on the beautiful face. "I very much want to squeeze the life out of you," Nahia snarled while in fact compressing Ederne's throat until an angry groan issued from behind the gag. Beside her, Sendoa seemed to tense up but he did not move or speak.

His attitude had a curious, calming effect on Nahia; to know Sendoa wouldn't stop her made her actually reconsider the desire to throttle her cousin. Hastily, before her wrath cooled down, Nahia wound up the arm with which she held Ederne and pitched her over the edge of the waterfall with all her might.

"I banish you," Nahia shouted after her cousin, fervently hoping the wicked creature would crash and die. "Don't ever return!"

A prickle of remorse struck Nahia immediately after. The thought of Alaia bellowing similar words, years before, came to mind, but she shrugged it off, in no mood for contrasts or karmic lessons. She squinted in the dark searching for the small red orb, but it had long disappeared into the roaring waterfall.

"Whew!" Sendoa said, floating beside her in the cool mist. He bumped her shoulder with his. "That was a good throw."

Nahia rounded on him with a reluctant grin, and resumed faery height before she spoke. "She will disperse her weight and land safely, and she's so crafty she'll undo the ties you conjured in no time. I just hope what happened tonight has shaken her enough so she *never* returns."

"That is wishful thinking," Sendoa muttered darkly.

Nahia bit her lip and raised one eyebrow at him. "That may be, but can't I just believe, for now, she *will* stay away and be done with us?" she said, grumpily shifting direction toward Handi Park.

"Should we at least check if she survived?"

"Of course she has! That's the curse of the blood; she is protected from any fatal attempt on my part," Nahia shot back. Hearing and disliking the defensive note in her own voice, she traveled the rest of the way in moody silence, assimilating the harrowing behavior she'd engaged in, aware it had caused an irrevocable change in her. She had mutilated the Keeper of the Forest, yes, for good reason and with great skill, but a mutilation nevertheless. Then she'd given free rein to her anger and roughed up her cousin with full intent to kill or, at the very least, to harm.

Nahia could not mitigate that.

CHAPTER 18

THE WEIGHT OF A WORLD

Heavy hearted, Nahia returned to her mother and was greeted by the dispiriting report that although more attempts to heal Oihana's wounds were made in her absence, they had been fruitless. The Faery Princess again knelt by the bed and held Oihana's hand while she slept. She closed her eyes, as if asking for forgiveness and succumbed to nightmares about what had happened.

Sometime before sunrise Nahia came to; she had crumpled into a heap on the floor by her mother's bed.

"We wax and wane with the moon—" The Faery Queen's frail whisper broke the tomblike silence, startling Nahia.

She righted herself and refocused; how lovely Oihana looked in the delicate glow of the lilac room. "Be at ease, Mama, I *do* know our energy is highest when the moon waxes, and weakest when it wanes," she assured her, troubled by the deathlike pallor of her cheeks.

Unexpectedly, Oihana's body flickered between mass and mist for the first time—the process of returning to the light seemed to be in its last stages. Miserably aware of it and wishing something could be done to restore her life force, Nahia clasped her hand and cried out as soon as Oihana flickered back. "What am I to do?"

Hoarsely, the Faery Queen replied, "Live on."

A desolate moan escaped Nahia's lips. "Mama—I can't take this on," she sobbed, crushed by the weight of responsibility and burying her face on the tousled sheets.

"You did so well, my Nahia," Oihana whispered, placing a tremulous hand on Nahia's head.

The Faery Princess sniffed and sat up. "You mean because of these—" From a fold in her cloak she pulled out the three precious stones. She held them on the palm of her hand for Oihana to see: a large ruby, and two onyxes.

Oihana nodded weakly and closed her eyes. Only the crease between her brows denoted the exertion.

The three precious stones rose from Nahia's palm and floated in front of her for a moment before Oihana fused them into a skillfully set pendant. A silver flash crackled in the air and from it, Oihana conjured a pewter chain, which threaded itself through the ring on top of the newly made pendant.

"You must safeguard Basajaun from now on," Oihana murmured; she had spent nearly all her remaining strength in the effort.

Nahia plucked the chain with its pendant from the air and slipped it over her head. There Basajaun rested, cold and hard over her breast. She bowed her head, fighting off the vision of the Keeper's last moments—the beautiful unicorn, whose magic had kept the Realm alive for centuries, was no more.

Nahia covered the pendant with the palm of her hand and pressed. She fancied feeling a dim whir and told herself it had to be the concentrated living force emanating from the dormant organs.

Oihana's voice brought Nahia out of her distressing reflections.

"Only a natural phenomenon can bring about the birth of a unicorn . . . ."

"I know, Mama, *thundersnow*. But such an event hasn't happened for centuries."

"This is why we cannot pin our hopes on one. Instead, we have this," Oihana said, motioning to the pendant. "When the time comes, you will direct your thoughts, like an arrow toward a target. Remember, my Nahia, love and selflessness are vital for the ritual spell *and* for the potion. The energy *must* originate in your heart—"

Nahia shrank. *Love and selflessness*, those were exactly her weakest qualities. How was she to develop those virtues? Would she know if she'd succeeded when the time came? She uttered a faint protest to hide her inadequacies. "Basajaun hasn't been gone a day, and you must rest. We can discuss how he will be brought back tomorrow . . . ."

"Look above, through the skylight," Oihana exhorted her daughter, undeterred.

Nahia obeyed; she would not diminish her mother's sense of urgency. Her glance swept upward. The Pleiades twinkled at her from the cold, dark heavens. "The seven sisters," she said grimly.

Oihana nodded, "Seven colors of the rainbow, seven notes in a musical scale. Seven is the number of our natural world, my Nahia, and it is also the number of basic energies in our bodies."

"I know, Mama—there are seven seas as well," Nahia added lightly. She already knew the relevance of seven, yet awareness of it and of the rituals and procedures did not change the fact that all Nahia wanted was for the Faery Queen *not* to pass into the light, leaving her alone with the burden.

"To recover from what has been done, the Realm must go dormant for seven cycles of seven years. And because Basajaun was the last of his kind, it will take the same length of time for the magic residing in those stones to be fully strengthened."

Nahia made a fist over the pendant; the unavoidable burden was hers.

"The troop, along with the council, must remain underground in Handi Park, where your combined energies will sustain you. Ederne is sealed off from it, but not from the land above."

"And I must bide my time," Nahia said, reluctantly accepting what her life would become. The next forty-nine years suddenly stretched before her—a lonely road fraught with strain. Even so, her mind leapt toward ways of allowing the troop a degree of freedom from an underground life whenever possible if she kept Ederne away from the dormant Realm.

"Please remember, we haven't a hope of restoring the dimension or bringing forth a new unicorn if this is attempted before the prescribed time," Oihana warned; her body flickered several times in rapid succession, heightening Nahia's misery. "The Keeper of the Forest must be brought back at the end of the seventh seven-year cycle. Only then will the dormant energy in the pendant be ready to inhabit a new magical body."

Nahia frowned. This was new—*a new magical body?* "Which will come from where?"

Oihana pierced Nahia with a feverish glance. "One is coming who will be the necessary sacrifice. This vessel, with the required royal bloodline, will enter our dimension forty-nine years hence."

Nahia's expression darkened; she had never known her mother to use the gift of Future Sight. "You mean it *has* to be one of our descendants?"

"It must be so," Oihana said closing her eyes. Whether she had done it to avoid Nahia's glance or to stop a possible rebuttal, Nahia couldn't tell. "As my immediate successor, it falls to you to prepare, to gather all the elements and be ready at the appointed time to reawaken the Realm."

The distressing effect of her mother's voice, faltering in time with her flickering physical body, kept Nahia in a heightened state of anguish. Yet she couldn't help casting her thoughts to the future—who would the magical vessel be? She saw the faces of her girls, the two who were still living in the human dimension, and she tried to imagine who their offspring might be in the next forty-nine years. Something inside Nahia recoiled; she couldn't see herself handpicking a sacrificial anyone!

"Look at me, Nahia," Oihana said sternly. "*You* are the rightful queen; that is your destiny, no matter the cost."

The Faery Princess blinked away the tears and nodded briskly, hoping to disguise her doubts. She opened her mouth to say, I love you, but Oihana interrupted, "Promise me!"

"Of course, Mama, I promise," Nahia said, troubled by her mother's agitation. Oihana's cool fingers on her cheek drew a strangled "I love you," from Nahia. The phrase still lingered in the air when Oihana exhaled her last breath and vanished in a glittering puff, leaving nothing behind but her distinctive lilac scent.

Nahia filled her lungs with the flowery perfume. Oihana's gown crumpled onto the bed and rested there empty, vacated of her mother's form and presence.

"Farewell, Mama. I love you," sighed Nahia, raising her eyes to the Pleiades. A new chant had begun and it would be with her for forty-nine years. *Bide my time. Keep Basajaun safe until the seventh seven-year cycle is complete. Give Basajaun a new magical body.*

CHAPTER 19

RESTLESS

Through the whole ceremony in which the council recognized Nahia as heiress apparent of the Realm, she felt disconcerted. She attributed the sensation by turns to the death of her mother, or to the fact the binding magic of the Realm was gone. Even when Aintza, head of the council, placed the ivy garland, beaded with colorful crystals, on Nahia's head, she didn't get the closure she sought, maybe because it conferred nothing more than a temporary title—Nahia could not be the true queen until the Realm was restored, and that would not be for another forty-nine years.

When the ceremony ended, Nahia went to her mother's room, as she had been doing each day since Oihana passed. Looking in the mirror, she removed the garland and set it on the table, letting a sense of normalcy wash over her. Catching sight of the tapestry, with her sisters and daughters in it, she turned away from her reflection in the mirror and went to it.

Nahia put her fingers over her own name and the golden haze of her life enveloped her. In a moment fraught with emotion, unlike other experiences to date, a clear understanding overtook Nahia. Oihana had not recorded her girls' personality traits; she had recorded her Cradle Gifts to them!

Nahia's eyes opened to a life-altering reality—she was not stubborn and obstinate, rather she'd received the gifts of tenacity and perseverance. Not selfish and controlling, but caring and protective of others. Not quick tempered, but passionate.

Nahia's heart swelled with radiant hope for her own existence—she would no longer see a set of limiting character flaws; she would instead realize the full potential of her Cradle Gifts. She sniffled and wiped her eyes with the back of her hand, feeling Oihana's presence all around and wanting nothing more than to hold on to the vision her mother had opened up for her, forever.

Time began to pass in the Realm. Dispirited, Nahia saw her troop's numbers drop from over three hundred during Oihana's reign to under fifty after her death. But she couldn't blame them; it was no life to be trapped underground in Handi Park because that was all their combined Glamour could sustain. She let them leave, extracting promises from them to let her know where they settled so she could reach them when the Realm was restored.

In 1972, Nahia and Sendoa descended to Santillán Manor in San Sebastián. They didn't bother to assume human height, trusting their auras to go undetected in the bright summer sunshine. A Cradle Gift was in order for the newest member of the family, Catalina's infant daughter, Alba.

As with the others, Nahia gave her the gift of Lucid Dreaming, which would allow her to share in Alba's life, though not until the girl turned fifteen and the gift took effect. As their visit drew to a close, Nahia kissed the sleeping baby and took the lock of hair she needed for the tapestry. She signaled to Sendoa and they left, unseen by Catalina and the rest of the household.

Barely out of the manor's neighborhood, Nahia sensed a disturbance. Her eyes flashed the question to Sendoa and he agreed—he'd felt it too. Although they hadn't seen her, they knew Ederne had watched them enter and leave the house.

"First time in five years." Sendoa clasped Nahia's hand on impulse.

"Do you think I'm going to give chase?" Nahia smirked giving his hand a squeeze.

"There's no telling what you'll do, but I'm going with you whatever you choose," Sendoa laughed.

"I know it's me she's after—I just don't like having confirmed to her my attachment to Celeste's descendants continues," Nahia said, knowing it would be best to refer to them as Celeste's descendants rather than her own, in case Ederne's hearing had sharpened beyond reason. She also wondered if placing a sentry at Santillán Manor would help or damage the situation—the last thing she wanted was to arouse Ederne's curiosity. Better to let her think it was merely a standard Cradle Gift visit.

"She means to unnerve you, as always," Sendoa pointed out.

"She's good at it."

"So don't do anything stupid," he said, pulling her due east, toward the mountains.

"Why do you suppose the shared blood prevents *me* from harming her, but she could shred me to pieces if she got a hold of me?"

"I think you have that winning combination of blood and royal title that places you above committing base crimes," Sendoa grinned.

As the city of San Sebastián thinned out beneath them and gave way to hills and meadows, the taut energy in the air relaxed, letting Nahia know they'd left Ederne behind.

"Don't worry about them," Sendoa rejoined as they flew over the Arboretum. "If anything is amiss, you will see it in Catalina's dreams."

"You're right."

Determined to avoid Ederne, Nahia was careful not to go near her girls in San Sebastián, not even when Catalina died unexpectedly in 1975, leaving her two-year-old daughter in the care of her husband. Until the girl Alba turned fifteen, Nahia had a difficult time keeping track of her because Mireya had followed her twin brother, Carlos, to Portugal, forsaking her granddaughter.

What Nahia knew of Alba was that she struggled with her father, Fernando Gonzaga, for he was a demanding, traditional man who had no idea how to raise a child. The responsibility had fallen on Soledad, the young housekeeper of Santillán Manor. Nahia had gathered that and other tidbits from Mireya's dreams where Soledad's letters invariably surfaced. Nahia knew if not for Soledad, Alba would have been unhappy beyond recovery.

When she at last turned fifteen, Nahia began visiting Alba in dreams, and loved the child—she was bright and had a smile that could melt anyone's heart, except her father's. Nahia was pleasantly surprised to discover Alba's dreams were all about Mansión María Celeste, her old home, fallen into grave disrepair after decades of abandonment. Somehow, Alba had ferreted *Faery Sight* out of the mansion's attic where Nahia had hidden it and she'd taken it to Santillán Manor for safekeeping.

Nahia and Alba had a standing appointment at the mansion, in their dreams. They cleaned and refurbished, they hung draperies, rolled and unrolled rugs, rearranged furniture, and during one intense Midsummer Eve, Nahia even completed the fourth floor of the building to fuel Alba's obsessive delight. But like her other girls, as Alba became a young lady she lost interest in her girlish pursuits, and when her authoritarian father tried to impose his traditions on her, she rebelled.

"She's leaving the country!" Nahia opened the door Sendoa had knocked on and stormed out of the royal chamber.

"Who?" Sendoa asked, following her on the path to the garden.

"Alba. She's decided to go across the sea to a place called United States."

"That is in the Americas," Sendoa observed, making a whistling sound under his breath.

"I've never traveled that far," Nahia cried feeling thoroughly left behind. "Not even my mother could say she traveled across such a vast ocean. She came from Italy and that's nothing to what Alba proposes to do!"

"Don't forget there are flying machines now. People can get to faraway places in one day. When your mother's troop came, it was likely they were hidden in merchant wagons with all their belongings, and their journey would've taken months."

Nahia pondered this. Why had it never occurred to her to travel the world—had she always been content to stay at home? Satisfied to just hear stories and gape at colorful faery caravans once a year during Oihana's trade festivals? And they hadn't had one of those since Oihana returned to the light. Nahia had never even crossed the channel into Britain, or Gibraltar into Africa. Was she jealous of Alba's adventurous heart?

"I've not been beyond Santillán and San Sebastián—" Nahia complained, and when Sendoa didn't have a ready remark, she indulged in a surge of rebellion. "If I didn't have the responsibility of the Realm, I would've left long ago to see the world. Even Ederne has seen more than me, and I'm heiress apparent to the crown. Is it right others should have broader experiences than me? How am I supposed to rule properly if I haven't seen what is out there?"

Sendoa shook his head patiently. "What is really bothering you? Is it the responsibility? Is it because Alba is leaving? Have you been cooped up too long?"

Nahia turned away from his steady glance and groaned, "Is my mother's way the *only* way?"

Sendoa came around to face her. "It is what works here," he said, looking around the beautiful garden and the dwellings harmoniously squeezed between root systems. "And soon, it will work again aboveground so we can stop living mostly underground," he said, glancing toward the skylights from where natural daylight cascaded on them.

Nahia grimaced. Perhaps Sendoa had a point, but the year was 1989 and there were still over twenty-five years before the *one*, the magical vessel, likely to be Alba's grandchild, would enter the human dimension.

Alba left San Sebastián with her friend Verónica, both overflowing with giddy exhilaration. Through dreams, Nahia got her first view of the world across the great Atlantic Ocean, and her sulky demeanor lessened only with the vivid confirmation that although the ties had stretched, they had not broken. Once again Nahia congratulated herself on her gift giving ability— Lucid Dreaming was the best thing she'd ever come up with.

Within three short years of Alba's departure, a great many things happened: Alba met and married a man she referred to as her *Italian prince*. Verónica married as well, and the two couples left the high-rise city of New York. They set off across the mammoth country to the western side of a mountain range, and they settled in a place called Utah.

There, in July of 1992, the next echelon to be added to Oihana's tapestry came into being.

CHAPTER 20

UNDETERRED

Nahia, who hadn't left Handi Park in several years, was preparing to make her first trip, not just into town, but across the big water to give Alba's baby a Cradle Gift.

As spring came to a close and June approached, Nahia settled on a date to depart—after the solstice celebration. Sendoa would not hear of her traveling such a distance alone, and Nahia, secretly glad, agreed to let him come. She trusted him to keep her from blowing off course, and to be the itinerary keeper. Nahia meant to see every interesting spot between the Western Pyrenees and the Western Rockies. She figured they could travel there in little over a fortnight—a welcome vacation from their underground, slumbering lodgings.

The two friends set off at the end of June amid the troop's wishes for a safe journey, but they had barely made it over the waterfall when Ederne appeared out of nowhere.

"Sentries!" Nahia cried out, looking wildly about. "We've seen neither hide nor hair of her for years, and suddenly on this day, she shows up?"

Sendoa put himself between Nahia and Ederne. Two sentries came forth and Nahia's composure seemed to return.

"Going somewhere?" Ederne sneered.

While Nahia sputtered for a biting retort, Ederne, swifter than ever before, shoved past Sendoa and pounced on her.

The cousins grappled midair for a few seconds until Sendoa recovered and the two sentries reacted. In spite of the commotion, Nahia could tell three other bodies had joined the fray—for sure the same thugs Ederne had with her last time. A searing blaze grazed Nahia's upper arm, pitching her to the ground and causing serious damage to her leg. She ignored it and dived back in, managing to immobilize one of the thugs.

Out of the air, she plucked Sendoa's cry of "Get out of here, NOW!" and she took it to heart, seeing him fully engaged in wrestling Ederne, but not without first immobilizing the other two thugs so as to free the sentries to help Sendoa.

Nahia searched the skies, she saw the sun continuing its rise in the east, so she sped west. Before she even came out of her reactive state and the chant of *Straight line across the ocean*, had eased its strident repetition, Nahia was flying over water—no land in sight.

The shock of what had just happened took hold of her as the pewter water beneath turned a deep blue with frothy brush strokes. *What nerve,* Nahia thought, outraged and shaken. A sob escaped her, a sense of dread and loneliness engulfed her. *And what happened to Sendoa?*

She couldn't tell if she was crying or if the force of the wind blew tears out of her eyes. She repeated to herself, clever and powerful though Ederne was, she could be no match for Sendoa and two sentries.

Nahia looked much the worse for wear. She'd been flying up to ten hours per day, anxious to put more miles between her and Ederne. During the crossing, she had been able to touchdown a handful of times but only for a few hours, when she spotted a ship or floating debris. So it was a great relief when she got her first glimpse of land, glittering with city lights.

In Alba's dreams, Nahia had seen the Statue of Liberty, and that same beacon, visible to her now, became her target. Like a miniscule shooting star, the faery put down on its highest point—the flame. Fascinated, she stared at America's entrance and fancied she felt what Alba and Verónica must've felt when they arrived. To Nahia, the glare of the setting sun seemed to fight a losing battle, all its brilliance absorbed by the twinkling city lights. She stared drowsily at the fiery western horizon and fell asleep, exhausted.

One of Ederne's rogue faeries, with spindly hands and sharp claws, wrestled Nahia to the ground. Infuriating, nimble creature. Whenever she tried to grab him, she was two seconds too late and he fluttered away. Though sluggish, she at last managed to get hold of its ankle—how outrageously thin it was! Nahia could snap it in two. The horrible creature screamed and struggled. It hit Nahia with its head and she wondered how it could poke so.

Nahia would not let go; she shook the ankle forcefully and the screams turned into frightened squawks. The creature pecked at her cheek, forcing

Nahia to protect her face. She let go of it and scrambled to a sitting position, aching from head to foot, and began sliding off her bed. No—not a bed!

Nahia screamed and the seagull that had been poking her with its beak squawked angrily and jumped backwards but would not fly away. Reality came crashing down as she floated above the liberty torch, hand over her chest as if to slow down the beating of her heart. It was an overcast morning and Nahia couldn't tell how high in the sky the sun was, but she sensed it was early.

Mourning Sendoa's absence and pining for his reassuring voice, Nahia descended on a huge, rectangle-shaped Arboretum amid tall buildings. She found food and ate it in silence, with only her worried thoughts for company. By the time the clouds cleared and the sun peeked out, Nahia had had her fill and took off again, feeling grateful that going forward, she would be flying over land, which ensured abundant opportunities to locate food and shelter.

Three days later, she glimpsed the great Rocky Mountains in the western horizon. With renewed zeal she bounded over them, marveling how like her Pyrenees they were. By dusk, tucked safe in a gully that spread down the western face of Mount Ogden, Nahia looked on the city below. Alba was down there, already in the beginning stages of labor. She'd made it just in time. The thought that Sendoa would be proud, silly though it was, warmed her heart.

Nahia kept vigil until the baby was born, at 3:58 in the morning, 21st day of July, 1992. Alba named her Maité, and Nahia heartily approved—in the Basque language of San Sebastián, it meant *lovable*.

Tired, grainy-eyed and sore, Nahia rose from the branch where she'd been crouching and flitted down the mountain; her cloak grazed the scrub oak and sage covering the hillside. With a surge of excitement, she considered this was the first time a descendant of hers was born in a hospital rather than the family home—and she'd traveled half way around the globe to see her. Feeling justified in taking the extra precaution, Nahia pulled the pendant off her neck and stuffed it into a secret fold of her cloak. She also surrounded herself with a protective energy shield meant to alert her of any negative energy around her.

Once inside the nursery, doing her best not to disturb the other infants, Nahia shifted to human height and approached the bassinet containing her fourth great-granddaughter. With a trembling hand, she touched the baby's smooth forehead. Maité's eyes opened. Something wasn't right. No sooner had Nahia made contact than she felt it in her bones, as if she'd walked into a trap. Her confidence in the energy barrier she'd conjured wavered and crumbled as a faint humming drifted into her range of hearing. Nahia's heart jumped to her throat.

With an increased sense of urgency and doing her utmost to ignore her multiple aches and pains, the Cradle Gift of Lucid Dreaming poured out of her and fell on the baby with a shower of fragrant jasmine petals. "Seek the truth in your slumber. Your dreams will take you into the world of others."

Her singsong voice dimmed the humming for a moment and hung in the air as Nahia looked into Maité's small face one last time. The baby's eerily wide-open and seemingly focused eyes disoriented her. The faery reached into the crib and Maité made a tight fist around Nahia's little finger.

Beads of sweat gathered like dew on Nahia's porcelain brow. "Beware of the Beautiful One," she told the baby. The humming became a hiss, closing in around Nahia; she could hear it outside the building, lapping at the walls. She cocked her head to one side, her eyes narrowed. Fear and rage in equal measure overtook her upon hearing the virulent laughter she knew so well.

Nahia's gaze flitted from the open doorway to the four inky corners of the nursery and back to Maité. Heart pounding in her chest, she leaned over the crib to kiss the tiny fist. "If I brought her to you—" Nahia's words were a guilt-ridden moan, "but the Beautiful One won't know the truth; I promise you that much. Her ignorance will be her undoing."

Nahia shape-shifted back to faery height and a cracking noise broke through the droning hiss. Ederne's horrible laughter drowned everything else. Nahia gritted her teeth as her punctured energy barrier began to deflate around her, but a surge of adrenaline wiped out her pain.

With a swift horizontal shift toward the door, Nahia hastened out of the nursery and passed the nurses' station undetected. She found a partially open window at the end of the hall and squeezed out of the narrow gap into the cool predawn air. She propelled herself forward with all her might—so eager to escape, she only fleetingly glimpsed a wall of red vapor materializing in front of her.

As Nahia rushed forward, the thick mist stopped her momentum with bone-cracking force. She plummeted like a rag doll toward the concrete sidewalk four stories below. Nahia twisted in the air and saw the blazing red eyes glare at her falling body with detached contempt. The instant their eyes locked, Nahia saw her cousin lunge downward, as if pulled by a magnetic force, and Nahia felt herself snatched from the grip of death a fraction of a second before hitting the ground.

Still rattled by the collision with the deceptive vapor, and drifting in and out of consciousness, Nahia caught glimpses of Ederne's red locks and her smoldering eyes. As they rocketed into the air, the pressure of gravity pounded on her temples.

"Whatever gift you gave her means nothing. That baby is nothing. She will have no power over me. She is no better than her ancestors."

Nahia tried to collect her wits while Ederne appeared to search the sky for a suitable route. Nahia felt a shift in their direction. East.

Ederne let out a haughty laugh but then leaned in close to nuzzle Nahia's neck. "Do you realize you are now in my debt?"

Nahia gasped. The effects of the collision seemed to be lifting. She needed to fight, but her limbs wouldn't respond.

"For now, however"—the throaty voice went on while prying Nahia's mouth open with her fingers—"a little something for the crossing?"

Nahia heard the hated laughter ringing in her ears and tasted the acrid paste smeared into her mouth. It liquefied on contact.

"No!" Nahia mumbled through fruitless efforts to spit it out, but it was too late. The numbness spread down her throat; her tongue felt like a stuffed flannel cushion. Very soon her limbs would be immobilized. Nahia's eyes took on a marble-like appearance as the potion worked through her. Her turquoise-streaked curls flailed in the wind that snatched tears of rage from her eyes.

"Ederne, stop," Nahia murmured feebly. She fought to keep her eyes from closing while her cousin's laughter clanged in her ears.

Nahia lost the battle against the effects of the strong potion; darkness settled in her heart. Had Ederne escaped Sendoa or defeated him?

Her cousin's flawless face bathed in the sinking moonlight was the last thing Nahia saw before her eyes closed.

CHAPTER 21

A FRIEND IN DEED

Nahia opened her eyes in the inky darkness. Her other senses sharpened and she felt cool packed dirt beneath her, something tight and heavy on her wrist—*shackles?* And the pressing silence hinted at absolute insulation from the outside, or perhaps an underground location. Recent events assembled sluggishly in her mind; she wondered where she was and how long she'd been there—had she even left America? A vague recollection of salty air came back to Nahia, but she couldn't be sure when that had been.

She sat up feeling dizzy; without doors or windows, she couldn't tell if it was day or night. She reached out blindly, accidentally dragging the chain over her leg, which immediately burned her skin. She swung it off. With the tips of her fingers she tested the strap binding her wrist—heat came off of it before she even touched it—iron. That explained why she felt so weak. The part in direct contact with her skin felt like leather, so her wrist was intact.

Careful to keep her limbs away from the harmful metal, she reached out with her free arm and felt a wall. She dragged herself toward it and leaned against it. From there she squinted in every direction until she saw grayish strips of light overhead: a trapdoor. Her chains permitted her to scoot beneath it, and there she breathed easier.

A sense of dread gripped her suddenly—Basajaun. With her unshackled hand, Nahia fumbled over the cloak and sighed with relief when she felt the cool hardness of the pendant, safe within the folds of fabric. Then she was free to think about her predicament. Knowing Ederne, she would have a guard outside, or could she be guarding the prison herself? Nahia decided the easiest way to find out was to be direct.

"You there," she called out and immediately heard scuffling noises aboveground—she had surprised whoever was up there. "Let me out!"

Silence. Then, "Nahia, is that you?"

It was Nahia's turn to be surprised. She hardly knew what she had expected, certainly not that voice. She'd last heard it over a hundred years ago.

"Amets! Where am I—where have *you* been?" she cried, wildly scrambling to her feet but holding on to the wall for support.

"I have been wandering—I've been away," he said in a remote, unsettling voice.

"I know you have, and I've missed you!" Nahia pleaded, thinking he sounded worse than before. He'd been separated from his heart since Celeste died, probably becoming more and more detached from reality every year. "How is it you're up there?"

"I saw Ederne—and I followed her here."

Nahia held her breath, but when he didn't say more, she asked, "Where are we?"

"She put you in here last night," he said. "I didn't know it was you."

"Where am I?"

"In a cave."

Nahia closed her eyes, pressing her lips into a thin line. "Amets—please help me get out."

Silence. She continued to stare at the trapdoor as if she could will it to open. *I could if I wasn't so weakened by these iron chains,* Nahia thought irritably. The trapdoor opened so abruptly, Nahia thought she might have managed it by herself, but then Amets' form darkened the center of the opening and he descended into the gloom.

Neither his aura nor hers could light up in their current state; Amets, because he had lost his heart, and Nahia, because the iron had diminished her life force. Although he was hovering before her, Nahia could see only the warm glow of his amber eyes—two gleaming orbs suspended in the dark.

"Please, help me with this chain on my wrist," Nahia urged.

It seemed to cost him some effort to gather his energy and focus it on the simple task of breaking the strap, but he did it at last. Revived, Nahia grabbed his hand and dragged him upward, out of the cave. She could tell right away that dawn was approaching, but she could not keep her shoulders from drooping in dismay upon seeing the vast open sea before her. "Where are we, Amets?"

He looked at her, puzzled, but did not reply.

Wherever we are, home must be to the east, Nahia thought crossly. Still holding his hand, she took to the air, turning her back on the ocean and wondering if she should try to find food before embarking on what could be a very long journey.

As she rose above the hilltop, the sight that greeted her made her laugh out loud. Bahía de la Concha. Ederne had chosen to trap her in a cave, on the west side of the island of Santa Clara. Exhilarated to find herself so close to home, Nahia sped toward the mountains, dragging Amets along with her. When they had cleared the edge of San Sebastián, she felt him squeeze her hand and she slowed down.

"What is it? Don't you want to come back home with me?" Nahia pressed, but Amets shook his head stubbornly. She stopped, ready to square off with him, but his attention was childishly focused on prying himself loose from her grip. She released his hand deliberately. "Please, dear friend, come home."

The pink blush of dawn had begun spreading from the eastern horizon, and Nahia thought she saw tears glittering in his eyes. Amets shook his head again and drifted away without a word. She watched him until she couldn't see him anymore, then she turned and hurtled toward the cradle of her Western Pyrenees. Her only objective—to reach the safety of Handi Park before Ederne got wind of her escape.

PART III

1992 to 2015

It is during our darkest moments that we must focus to see the light.

Aristotle

CHAPTER 22

CARIBBEAN BOUND

"I was wondering if you'd ever come back." The relief on Sendoa's face and the fact he had obviously raced all the way to Moon Dancer Lake to meet her were at complete odds with his nonchalant greeting.

"I'm glad to see the sentries are doing their job. I assume they alerted you?" Nahia replied casually. Although it disappointed her that their respective attitudes precluded the embrace she had anticipated, she recognized it saved her the discomfort of being touched when she hadn't bathed in days, not to mention that any contact would likely revive all her aches and pains.

"We have been on alert since the day you left."

"But how long have I been gone, how many days?" Nahia asked anxiously.

Sendoa paused over the Arboretum, betraying some concern at last. "It's been eleven days—do you not remember? What's happened to you?"

"Heavens!" Nahia gasped and began reasoning out loud. "It took me six days to get to Maité because I was trying to cover my tracks, in case I was being followed. I could have done it in five, maybe even four and a half. She, of course, would've flown straight back, and maybe I was unconscious in the cave a lot longer than I thought." Too appalled to even consider that Ederne could outstrip her when it came to flight, Nahia reluctantly acknowledged they might be neck and neck.

"She—you mean your cousin? And what cave?" Sendoa frowned, his expression darkening so much it seemed they'd dipped into the cool shadows of the Arboretum.

Nahia motioned for them to continue—getting to her chamber for a bath and decent rest was foremost in her mind. Every detail of the journey poured out as they went, and by the time they had passed the Aspen Grove

147

and descended into the receiving hall in Handi Park, Nahia had given Sendoa a succinct account.

Zuzen, Oihana's old chambermaid, came out of the doorway marked with the amethyst lantern to greet them. "Oh, dear!" she gasped, hand flying to her mouth.

Under Zuzen's stunned gaze, every bruise and burn mark on Nahia's skin flared and cried out a complaint. She tried to smooth down her hair but couldn't get to it; apparently she was wearing a bird's nest for a hat. Her grubby skin clamored for a wash; her cloak and the rest of her filthy clothing should be discarded at once!

"Please, let's take care of me," Nahia exclaimed sweeping by Zuzen, who continued to stand there with her mouth partially open, and dragged her off through the royal doorway to her chamber.

"I will see you as soon as you're finished," Sendoa called after her.

"Yes, but I need to sleep too," Nahia called back, fearing the latter might take a whole week.

With impassive demeanor, Nahia dragged out her recovery from the trip to America, purposely delaying a return to her monotonous underground existence in Handi Park. Sendoa and Zuzen, the only two with the stamina to humor her for any length of time, finally stopped catering to her after four weeks.

Sourly, she returned to managing surveillance shifts, healer schedules, and Handi Park's storerooms. Her only source of excitement consisted in watching Maité's development through Alba's dreams, and wondering grumpily when she might have the opportunity to collect a lock of hair for the tapestry in the royal chamber.

Some days went by so slow that Nahia thought they'd never turn to afternoon or night, much less add up to a week. So it wasn't until the girl's fifteenth birthday finally arrived that Nahia's lethargic attitude lifted at last. With her heart all aflutter, Nahia went into Maité's dreams in 2007, thus beginning a direct connection with the person she knew would one day give birth to the *magical vessel*.

During their very first meeting, Nahia confirmed what she'd begun to suspect while in Alba's dreams; Maité looked a great deal like Celeste, same hair, same golden skin, same height. The only difference was in their eyes; Celeste's had been light brown, like honey and sunshine, while Maité's were stormy gray, like Calisto's.

A little discomfited, the faery went back to her old question; would she ever see *her* imprint in another being? She cataloged her daughters from Zorione all the way to this latest descendant and became disheartened—not one of them looked like her.

Their dream visits increased nevertheless, and with a spark of delight and dawning wonder, Nahia began to notice a bright streak of Glamour working through Maité. "My babies will be the ones who get all the Glamour," Zorione had said long ago, and Nahia was forced to conclude that the legacy must have been dormant indeed in all the others.

Although inconsistently, Maité could produce a trance-like state in others, and her body readily yielded to energy triggers for shape-shifting and flight—Nahia couldn't recall ever flying with any of the others while in a dream state. *Better Glamour than facial expressions or hair color*, Nahia thought gleefully.

She began to wonder at what point she should bring Maité into their family history, as the girl knew nothing about her connection with the Faerie Realm. Neither Alba nor Maité knew Zorione's old story about Nahia being a grandmother who died young. They thought Nahia was just a bizarre, flying woman with turquoise-streaked curls who frequented their recurring dreams.

A bright idea struck Nahia in the summer of 2009—she would stage a treasure hunt and lure Maité to San Sebastián with ingenious clues, so she could begin discovering her heritage.

The plan began to unfold in her mind. Nahia made a fist around precious Basajaun as she considered parting with it. She would miss the magical energy emanating from it—how it had sustained and motivated her in exchange for the safety she provided. But who better to receive it and benefit from it than the person meant to renew the family connection? Who better to keep it safe than Maité, who would be instrumental to Basajaun's return?

The faery gathered the holographic will she had created long ago, when she was Anahí. She removed Basajaun from around her neck and added it to the leftover jewels she had taken from Handi Park long ago to finance her quest to win Calisto. Nahia would have liked to include Xiomara's account of her childhood with Celeste, the book called *Faery Sight*, but did not know where Alba had hidden it after she removed it from the María Celeste.

She placed all the items in an old chest and, indulging in a bout of sentiment, Nahia headed to Santa Clara Island. Since Maité's gray eyes reminded her of Calisto's, what could be more fitting than for the girl to begin her discovery in the same place where Nahia had made her fateful entrance into the human dimension? With the chest safely concealed beneath her cloak,

Nahia descended from the summit and went into the dark cave where she'd once been trapped. The faery grinned. It was perfect. It would be mysterious and challenging for Maité—it would wake her sense of adventure.

She hid the chest in one of the earthen walls. Pleased with her scheming, she went about erasing the traces of Glamour around it so it looked as undisturbed as the other walls, with roots protruding here and there. She floated toward the opened trapdoor, her mind leaping ahead to the day she would see Maité face to face, when a shadow filled the opening above.

"Well, well—I wouldn't have thought it, but you came back, all on your own, after all these years."

Nahia halted midair, hating the position she'd gotten herself into. Her one escape route blocked. She bit down so hard she drew blood from her lip; how did it not occur to her Ederne might be watching? Why did she assume her cousin had lost interest in the location—what a grave misjudgment.

"Get out of my way," Nahia hissed.

Ederne centered herself over the opening. "I don't know how you got out of here last time—likely your manservant, Sendoa, came to your rescue."

"He's not my servant," Nahia snarled while her mind raced, considering and discarding options. She heard it before she saw it and reacted in the nick of time. She leapt out of the way of Ederne's powerful blast, but its force sent her sprawling to the floor of the cave.

Nahia's head hit so hard her vision went dim for a few seconds, enough of a lapse for Ederne to pounce. Before Nahia knew it, her ankles and wrists had been shackled so tight she could feel the heat of the iron through the thin leather lining. Nahia could hear her cousin raging somewhere outside.

"No one gets in or out of here until I return. In a week's time, I will move her myself."

The trapdoor fell releasing a cloud of dust. Nahia shut her eyes, thinking of the grunting replies she'd just heard—they sounded like the trollish thugs who had helped Ederne before.

She cursed herself for not telling Sendoa. How long would it take him to realize something was wrong? And when he did, would it occur to him to look for her in Santa Clara? Nahia tested the shackles and found the two-inch slack a maddening limitation. She rattled her chains listlessly for a few seconds, wondering why her imprisonment would last one week. *Where will she move me—what is she up to?*

A few hours after Ederne's departure, scuffling noises ensued near and over the trapdoor. Nahia sat up taller. Someone was trying to get past the guards, and once again she recognized Amets' voice. Dismayed, she wondered if he had a hope of defeating Ederne's thugs in his condition. While Nahia feared for his well-being, she couldn't help wishing his old power would push through the stupor he lived in and help her out a second time.

The struggle seemed to go on for a few minutes during which Nahia, bewildered, heard the distinct groaning sounds made by bodies engaged in physical battle. When it seemed the grappling had ended, Nahia held her breath hoping and dreading confirmation of who the victor had been. Someone lifted the trapdoor and Nahia squinted at the light. Relief washed over her as Amets descended to her side.

"At first I thought she was up to no good," Amets said as they emerged from the cave.

Out of the corner of her eye Nahia saw he had in fact overpowered Ederne's goons—he'd draped them haphazardly over branches. Nahia looked at Amets askance, wondering if his ability to direct energy had gone bad, as from the looks of it, he had jumped bodily into the fray. "And was she? Up to no good?"

"When she saw me near the house in town, the one called Santillán Manor, and she asked what I was doing there, I told her I was waiting for Celeste to come back—the house has her name on it, you know. You have been there yourself. That's why I know Celeste must be coming back soon."

Nahia stopped midflight over the water; they hadn't even reached Bahía de la Concha. "What was Ederne doing *there?*"

"She visits Celeste's father regularly," Amets said, doing a double take when it turned out Nahia wasn't at his side. He backtracked slowly. "These last two weeks at least."

Nahia couldn't comprehend what she was hearing; it took her a few seconds to understand Amets was referring to Mr. Gonzaga, Alba's father and Maité's grandfather. *What could Ederne want with him?*

"Your cousin still dislikes you, it seems," Amets commented, stopping beside Nahia.

"Why do you think Celeste will be back? Have you seen her?" Nahia asked breathlessly. Could Amets have gained access to Maité somehow? Did he know she was almost a copy of Celeste?

"I haven't seen her yet, but I will when she returns," Amets said dreamily. "Ederne says so—she told me humans far away hold Celeste captive, and she told me I can help speed up her return."

Nahia did some fast thinking while trying to keep up a natural conversation. "And how are you to help Ederne—what has she asked of you?"

"I am to accompany her on a long journey," Amets said importantly. "She spends most of her time as a human, particularly when she visits Celeste's father. She's promised to change me into a human so we can fly on an airplane. We will catch up with Celeste's captors and free her."

Nahia bit her lip. Wild thoughts chased each other in her mind. *How is this to be believed? Amets is not himself, hasn't been for nearly two centuries. Humans don't come back once they've gone into the light.* "This has to be a mixture of Amets' wishful thinking and Ederne's willful deceit," she muttered. *Surely Ederne is trying to return to the Realm and must be surrounding herself with the right individuals—Amets has always been a beloved and respected member of the troop—no question what Ederne's angle is in approaching him. What about the captors she's lied about to Amets? Could Ederne really be referring to Maité's parents? And does she even know Maité and Celeste are so similar in appearance, or is she just fueling Amets' fantasy to make him do—what exactly?*

"And where are you flying to?" Nahia asked, realizing she'd been quiet far too long.

"Ederne called it the Caribbean, and we are flying there on an airplane," he said simply, and then like an afterthought he added, "Tomorrow."

Grasping at straws, Nahia asked, "What else have you seen Ederne do in town?"

"I have mostly seen her with Celeste's father, like they are courting." He seemed to ponder something else, and at length he added, "Once she took him to the old Citadel in Santillán and they went to the waterfall above—it looked like he didn't know it was there."

What are you up to? Nahia wondered with serious misgivings now. How much did Ederne know? And why would she be courting Mr. Gonzaga, unless she thought by marrying him she could become the owner of the Santillán property? *Ha*, thought Nahia, immensely proud of her foresight in writing the holographic will long ago. *Ederne doesn't know only a female descendant of Celeste Santillán has a right to the land.*

But her happy bubble burst when she considered another factor: What if the people Amets referred to as Celeste's captors were indeed Maité's parents—what if Ederne knew about the holographic will, and aimed to eliminate Alba, which would leave only Maité who wasn't yet seventeen—a minor. *And Ederne means to use Amets to bring Maité to San Sebastián, to what? Eliminate her too?*

Nahia swallowed a gasp. "Did they go beyond the waterfall?" she asked, thinking anxiously about Wizard's Pass and hoping Ederne hadn't disclosed it to Mr. Gonzaga. Even with Celeste's stairs destroyed, humans might still discover the passage behind the waterfall.

"No," Amets said, "they trudged around talking about development, and Ederne said something about exclusive rights, which I didn't understand."

Nahia had to acknowledge her cousin's cleverness, distasteful and ruthless though it was. Ederne had not changed, she meant to return to the Realm and become queen, caring nothing about whom she sacrificed to get her way.

Unlike her cousin, Nahia would not dream of using or hurting Amets. To even hint to him that the person he would eventually meet was not Celeste but a descendant of hers would shatter his already unstable mind for no good reason. "Don't mention me to Ederne," Nahia said smoothly. "She won't be pleased to learn you let me out, and if you make her angry, she might not take you with her."

Amets' brow furrowed. "What if she asks?"

"She won't ask until she returns and finds I'm gone. I will make sure the guards you put out of commission won't sound the alarm until she returns. If she asks you anything then you will say you know nothing about Santa Clara."

Amets wagged his head, betraying some uncertainty, but soon his expression cleared and he seemed to approve the plan.

Nahia felt compelled to add, "Just the same, you be careful out there, my dear friend. And keep your eyes open in case Ederne is trying to trick you—you know how she is."

"I remember," he nodded placidly. He put his brawny hand on Nahia's shoulder and added, "I will be careful."

Floating over the bay, Nahia watched Amets dip and rise all the way to the city until she lost sight of him. "Farewell, my friend," she whispered, trusting that when they met again, in the heat of whatever confrontation Ederne cooked up, Amets would be on Nahia's side.

She turned her back on the city and went back to the unconscious guards near the mouth of the cave. Such simpletons they were, Nahia had no trouble erasing from their minds what had happened. They would wake up to undisturbed surroundings and be baffled over having fallen asleep on the job—they might even blame it on the very quiet faery they were guarding.

Nahia chuckled imagining the rage her cousin would experience when she came to move the hostage, wherever she'd intended, and found her guards had been watching an empty prison all along.

While the trollish guards snoozed away, Nahia reached out to Alba in her dreams—it was very early in the morning in America. To her surprise, Alba and her husband, Sósimo, were not in Utah but in the Caribbean, on an island called Guadeloupe, celebrating their anniversary. She calmed herself reasoning that Soledad, the housekeeper, and Mr. Gonzaga, must be aware of Alba's plans, and of course, Mr. Gonzaga would have shared the news with Ederne—if she really was his girlfriend.

Ederne on an airplane couldn't be beaten, Nahia knew it. *So I can't waste a single moment*, she thought fiercely. *I will be right behind her and I will not be late. Whatever madness Ederne has in mind* will *wait until I get there.*

CHAPTER 23

THE EYE OF THE STORM

Anchored to Alba through the Cradle Gift of Lucid Dreaming, Nahia navigated unerringly, and thanks to violently favorable winds she arrived in Guadeloupe in two days' time. Once there, catching the local talk as well as Alba's impressions, Nahia understood she'd been literally blown in with a brutal tropical storm. Flights had been canceled, sail dates had been postponed due to weather, yet Alba and Sósimo were determined to get back home; they had promised a special trip to Maité, whose seventeenth birthday was in less than two weeks.

Nahia vaguely wondered about Amets and Ederne, feeling moderately hopeful their flight had been diverted or canceled, but would not waste time with that. She took her post near Alba and Sósimo—they would need her help if they meant to fly out in such a storm.

Keeping the dear couple within her sights, Nahia bobbed behind them from seaport to airport, fighting intermittent thoughts about Sendoa and the council; she'd disappeared without a word of her plans to anyone. Troubled, she muttered to herself, "It was a *secret* plan, and I did mean to go back to Handi Park as soon as I hid the chest."

Near midnight, Alba and Sósimo had struck a deal with a shady character that piloted a rickety old flying machine. He would take them to the Virgin Islands along with some luggage that had been left behind, surely by tourists in a hurry to leave the island. The pilot assured Alba and Sósimo the storm had passed and was already moving south. Nahia glanced beadily at the palm trees outside; they were blowing sideways. *This does not bode well*, she thought with a raised brow.

The couple would not be persuaded to delay, so Nahia braved the wind and scouted the outside of the craft looking for a safe nook to travel in. She found no such spot, so she clung to a suitcase. The pilot picked it up, oblivious to her presence, and hurled it into the cargo hold behind the passenger seats. While the three people boarded, Nahia remained hidden, trying to ignore her serious misgivings about takeoff and staying airborne afterward. Through the gap between seats, she focused on Alba's outwardly calm profile.

The small airplane climbed, rattling and shaking as if it would snap in two at any moment. Nahia felt a surge of pride for Alba and Sósimo's grit—in spite of the weather and the questionable condition of their vessel, they were determined to get home to their daughter. Nahia hoped the third, more sinister threat looming over them did not become a reality.

They hadn't been in the air more than twenty minutes when it became clear to Nahia Ederne's flight hadn't been canceled as she had hoped. With a dire sense of doom Nahia saw the flashes of silver lightning outside become tinged with red. It was no ordinary storm, and Nahia felt the time had come for her to display some grit too. Alba prayed. Sósimo held tight to her, and Nahia began conjuring a shield to protect them against the impending attack. Not twenty seconds into it the most improbable, unexpected thing happened and broke her concentration.

Inexplicably, Maité appeared before her parents, and Nahia reeled. The protective cool blue shimmer beginning to inflate inside the cabin popped into nonexistence as Nahia pondered the strange phenomenon. Maité must've been dreaming at home; surely Alba's prayers had summoned her, and she responded by projecting her astral body to where her mother was.

The girl's uniqueness hit her anew; yes, Maité had Nahia's blood and Oihana's too, but nature had selected *her* to brightly display the streak of Glamour that had been dormant in other generations.

"It's too late, my love. Please, please always remember how much we love you!" Alba said, her voice quivering with fear and hopelessness.

"I'm sorry, folks. We're going down," the pilot yelled over his shoulder to Alba and Sósimo, unaware of the three additional passengers. For when Maité appeared inside the plane, Amets had materialized too, convinced Maité was Celeste; of course he would be there to protect her. Nahia frowned, momentarily astounded by his presence of mind—to transform mass and pass through the exterior of the plane? She wouldn't have thought it. Perhaps seeing Celeste so unexpectedly had triggered a heroic recovery of his abilities.

"Mom, Dad—wait!" Maité screamed. Her parents were strapped to their seats; she was splayed inside the cabin trying to keep her balance, and trying to free herself from an unexplained person, Amets, who held her tight and seemed to want to drag her toward the door.

"Maité, *despierta!* Wake up!" Alba cried out at the last second. Through the tiny window nearest her, Nahia got a slanted eyeful of the crest of a huge, frothy wave rising to swallow them. Maité obeyed and disappeared instantly.

Nahia imagined the poor girl waking up in her bed, far away, wondering if she'd had a nightmare, and her heart ached for Maité, knowing she would find out soon enough it had been real.

Amets' arms flailed for a moment—Celeste had disappeared, his face was a mask of rage and Nahia knew he'd go after Ederne. Without pausing from her work to disperse the weight of the airplane, Nahia called out to him, "Amets, look at me—get away from here, go back to the Realm and they will help, they will explain what's happening. Remember not to mention me to Ederne."

Amets gave her a tortured look. "You were right, she tricked me. She never liked Celeste and she brought me here to help kill her." He disappeared without reassurance he would do any of what Nahia asked of him. More furious red blasts seemed to light up the night and Nahia thought she saw him bodily attacking Ederne but couldn't be sure.

They hit the water so hard Nahia felt she'd failed to disperse even an ounce of their combined weight. Inside the cabin, Alba, Sósimo, and the pilot scrambled out of their seat belts and strapped on life vests, seemingly unable to credit their good luck.

"We gotta go, gotta go!" the pilot shouted, opening the door and letting in the wind, rain, and sea. "No clue how long this thing will float!"

Leaving all their possessions behind, the three people in their lifejackets flung themselves into the raging water and held on to one another. Nahia braced herself to struggle against the wind and keep them within her sights—until the sea decided to wear itself out. Mercifully, there were no more red flashes, but there was no sign of Amets either.

CHAPTER 24
FINDING A WAY

Nahia fought the gale-force winds. Below, the cluster of three rode the frothy mountain-like swells for interminable hours, until at last the worst of it passed. The winds simmered down to strong gusts, tapering the heaving of the sea and giving all of them a respite. The faery began scouting the area, venturing out only as far as she could without losing sight of her charges. After several attempts, she located a speck of land with some wind-damaged palm trees and a fresh-water spring.

Nahia set out to guide the group; they'd been adrift over twelve hours and she feared they would not survive much longer. She allowed her aura to twinkle before them and just as Nahia had intended, they thought it a lighthouse. With a surge of hope they swam toward it, encouraging one another through the night until exhausted, hungry, and disoriented they reached the shore. Nahia cried tears of relief, envying them the benefit of having each other for company—how she wanted Sendoa by her side!

Over the next several days, the faery left the castaways mostly to themselves. They were motivated enough to find water, food, and shelter so she didn't have to worry about providing it. Instead, she spent as much time as she could in Maité's dreams. For once, Nahia wasn't pleased her conjectures had been so accurate. In less than two weeks, the poor girl's life had become unrecognizable. Ederne's elaborate plan had indeed consisted in seducing Maité's grandfather, Fernando Gonzaga. She expected him to cede title of the property high above the Citadel of Santillán, which included the waterfall portal into the dormant Faerie Realm. When Mr. Gonzaga confessed the land could only be inherited by a female descendant of Celeste Santillán, Ederne, who in human guise called herself Eva, gulped down her anger and without hesitation, incorporated Alba's death into the plan, thus forcing the minor girl, Maité, to come home where her next of kin lived. Once there, Maité's grandfather could legally act on her behalf.

Wedged between the fronds of a palm tree, Nahia stared into space, revolted by her cousin's clever setup; she had Mr. Gonzaga in her power and he would do her bidding.

Refusing to admit defeat and reminding herself Ederne's ignorance would be her undoing, Nahia counted off the points in her favor. Ederne had failed; Alba and Sósimo were alive. Maité's powerful royal blood, her dominant streak of Glamour, and Nahia's gift of Lucid Dreaming made the girl a triple threat. And after seeing him frequently in Maité's dreams, Nahia knew Amets had returned to the Realm to seek help. She could rest assured he would do anything in his power to keep Maité safe.

Nahia produced images of Alba and Sósimo, alive and well, and showed them to Maité to breathe hope into her. But she did not succeed; convinced she'd witnessed the death of her parents, the girl saw them in dreams and thought they must be in heaven. As if to crush Nahia's efforts, the authorities declared Alba and Sósimo missing, which spurred a memorial service at home, complete with burial of two empty coffins, and Mr. Gonzaga's demanding his grandchild be sent to him.

As Ederne had contrived, Maité arrived in San Sebastián, but in two days' time and much to Nahia's glee, Ederne's plan began to go awry. Maité came in contact with two items Alba had treasured as a child and had left hidden in Santillán Manor: a portrait of Celeste, and the book called *Faery Sight*. The discovery sparked enough hope and curiosity in Maité to begin tentatively considering the impossible.

Nahia had to often remind herself it was all new to Maité, therefore she couldn't expect her to act confidently, much less follow directions blindly. Also, grief and all the unanswered questions seemed to dim their communication, which hindered Nahia's efforts to convince Maité she wasn't crazy and that *Faery Sight* wasn't a work of fiction—her great-great-grandmother *had* been raised in the Faerie Realm. Faeries *did* exist!

It took Maité a while to believe and accept, but when she finally did, and at great peril to herself, the girl resolved to take control. Amets had been in her dreams for weeks, luring her back to Celeste's home, until tired of doubting, Maité listened to her heart and followed the clues Xiomara had revealed in *Faery Sight*. She ventured into the unknown via Wizard's Pass and got to the other side, alive. To see Amets in person vindicated Maité beyond her wildest hopes. But the momentous confirmation of the existence of a magical Realm was short-lived, for thither followed Ederne to unleash a vicious attack.

Breathless, Nahia watched the frightful sequence of events, secretly hoping for a glimpse of Sendoa, but he never entered Maité's field of vision— she only had eyes for Amets, who risked his life to protect her and at the last moment whisked her out of the front line. He flew her to Santa Clara and showed her the entrance to a cave where she could hide.

Nahia intoned a song of gratitude and sharpened her focus, determined the sentiment should touch Amets, no matter how far, for soon, the chest, Basajaun, and the original holographic will would be in Maité's hands.

But Ederne would not easily give up her prey; she had followed Amets and minutes after he landed, she descended upon them, decrying him as a traitor. The moment's indecision to enter the cave cost Amets his life; Ederne struck him down.

Nahia's grief-stricken cry, far away in her palm tree, drowned out Ederne's raging scream of "She has escaped!"

Nahia's sorrow echoed in Maité—Amets could not be dead!

Wiping the tears with the back of her hand and wishing she could be ignorant of Maité's predicament, like Alba and Sósimo were, Nahia held her breath, seeing the girl trapped inside the same cave she'd been imprisoned in twice before. Yet, in a few short seconds, Nahia was again in awe of Maité's innate powers; Ederne attacked but she blocked with the sheer power of her mind—the girl imagined a concrete wall rising to protect her, and it did!

From then on, Maité's confidence increased. Nahia grinned, privy to the contrasting feelings making the girl believe in herself: her worst fear and her dearest wish had come to pass. The moment fantasy and reality became equally true in her brand-new world, her spirits soared above self-doubt.

Maité began to see her gift of Lucid Dreaming as a tool and as the weapon Nahia had intended. She tapped into the power of her mind; she combined her education with her instinctive wisdom and applied it. During the final confrontation, instead of destroying Ederne, Maité chose to erase all the traces of Glamour in her. She succeeded by imagining the brilliant faery cells like beacons in a DNA strand; she targeted each one with intense focus and fractured them into nonexistence. Maité stopped only when Ederne sagged, looking broken and incomplete at a cellular level. Astounded, Nahia recognized Oihana's legacy in Maité's chosen way to finish Ederne: to create and nurture, never to kill.

From thousands of miles away, Nahia shared in Maité's triumph and secretly delighted in the other surprise still in store for the brave girl. Her parents would soon return from the dead, and her happiness would be complete, for she had reconciled with her grandfather, and in San Sebastián she had found David, the love of her life.

As for her horrible cousin, already Nahia felt the world was a better place—what harm could come from one such as Ederne, relieved of her faery powers and condemned to live out the rest of her life as a human?

CHAPTER 25

UNEXPECTED BY THE SEA

Having eyes and ears intent in two so distant parts of the world began to take a toll on Nahia. Fortunately, the sleepless hours and grueling energy expenditures, necessary to monitor Maité's progress and provide critical information in a timely manner, were at last behind her. Now Nahia could redouble her efforts to get Alba and Sósimo rescued, which would command her attention every waking moment and involve a great deal of physical exertion.

Not until two days after Ederne began her existence as a human did Nahia's efforts at last pay off.

As it had become her custom most afternoons, Nahia again ventured a few miles out to sea from the castaways' island, hoping to find and attract help. Shortly before dusk she spotted a deep-sea fishing boat seeming to have engine trouble. She again passed herself as a distant lighthouse, and soon the boat began drifting toward the elusive light. By nightfall, the boat with its crew and passengers had arrived at the island.

The next day Alba, Sósimo, and the pilot boarded the repaired vessel and left the place they'd called home over the last three weeks. As it afforded abundant hiding places, Nahia boarded too, and within five hours they arrived in St. Thomas in the U.S. Virgin Islands. Nahia was immensely gratified to hear Mr. Gonzaga had arranged for his daughter to bypass Utah altogether, as Alba and Sósimo were expected in San Sebastián, to reunite with their daughter.

Nahia hung around while her three charges were interviewed about their adventure, and she followed when they were ushered to a hotel where they were properly fed. Undetected, Nahia sniffed, sampled, and helped herself to the flavorful food in platters on the table, listening to humans talk about emergency documents being transacted for the two who would travel that night.

Alba, Sósimo, and the pilot were presented with a change of clothes, and it hit Nahia she hadn't changed in eighteen days—none of them had. She was in tatters so she flitted to the gift shop in the hotel lobby and picked out a blue dress she liked. "If they'd known there was a fourth survivor, they would've given me clothes too," she told herself, rolling the dress and holding it to her chest as she returned to her group.

They were shown to a couple of clean, airy rooms overlooking the bay. Alba and Sósimo cleaned up in record time, clearly wanting nothing more than to sleep on a bed. Nahia didn't have to wait long; she heard the breathing pattern of deep sleep and assumed human height. She bathed quietly, relishing the fresh water and soap after days and days of her skin being cured in salt. She put on her new dress before resuming faery height.

Standing on the bathroom counter, Nahia inspected her appearance and liked what the prolonged exposure to the sun had done. Her skin's creamy porcelain look had been replaced with a golden sheen—it reminded her of Celeste's skin, and of Maité's. She looked critically at her reflection and decided her tan made her aquamarine eyes stand out more. "He'd like it," Nahia whispered, thinking of Sendoa.

Overall pleased, clean-smelling, and properly dressed, Nahia curled up on a cushioned chair on the veranda and fell asleep while the breeze dried her turquoise-streaked curls. By nightfall, with a mixture of sensations cluttering her heart Nahia followed Alba and Sósimo to the airport, and watched them board, momentarily overwhelmed by a wild impulse to sneak into the plane and go back home with them. But at the crucial moment, she didn't act.

Bobbing above the tarmac, Nahia squinted at the night sky—the lights of Alba's airplane were already lost in the stars and the faery was alone. In approximately twelve hours, her girls would reunite after a nightmarish separation in which Maité had become an orphan, and had traveled across the ocean to discover she'd been manipulated by magical relations she never knew she had!

The revealing thought had streaked across Maité's mind when, in dreams, Nahia tried to explain about Ederne. "No better than the average pettiness of humans," had been Maité's thought about the feuding cousins, and Nahia, although stung, had to acknowledge she'd contributed to the unfavorable impression made by the Faerie Realm. She squirmed, finding the notion of manipulation distasteful, but could not to see it otherwise.

"But all's well that ends well," Nahia sighed, turning toward the terminal.

"And following an end, there is always a new beginning—"

Nahia froze. She closed her eyes in rigid concentration. *It can't be!* She waited for any repetition or sign she might have imagined it—her nerve endings crackled, wholly unprepared for such a twist.

From behind came a pair of strong arms to encircle her waist. "You disappeared without a word," Sendoa whispered very near her ear. Nahia shuddered from head to foot.

A myriad of replies, excuses, and apologies vied to come out of her mouth, but Nahia's exhaustion, her fears, and the uncertainty she'd experienced in the last weeks all had come to a head upon hearing Sendoa's voice. She suddenly felt like a child, grateful the ordeal was over and glad to have an adult on whose shoulder she could unburden herself.

Nahia cried with abandon, seeming to revisit the most frightening moments of her odyssey, as if determined to get rid of the whole. She sobbed uncontrollably for the better part of fifteen minutes, and Sendoa held her until the worst of the storm had passed. When she'd been reduced to sniffling and her breathing had stabilized, he led her over the airport terminal and onto the beach.

The three-quarter moon lent a fluorescent glow to the foamy crests of the waves. Nahia and Sendoa sat on the sand, listening to the hypnotic tune of the surf. They told each other how things had played out in their respective parts of the world, and Sendoa filled in the details of what Nahia hadn't been able to glean from Maité's dreams.

"That is a courageous, determined girl, Maité, to have crossed Wizard's Pass on foot. But she made it and she arrived to meet with the council— how like Celeste she looks," Sendoa said as if he still couldn't believe the resemblance (Nahia grinned). "And Aintza meant to disclose everything about your history with Calisto, and tell Maité she is a descendant of yours. But your cousin, reckless as ever, dropped in from the sky and murdered half of the council members, including Aintza, before anything was really revealed," Sendoa said grimly.

"I saw it happen in Maité's mind," Nahia sniffled, thinking what a stroke of luck it was that Ederne hadn't learned the truth about Maité's heritage.

"Amets whisked Maité away and Ederne followed—I know that did not end well for our friend, but you must know he was very brave, and a lot like his old self, convinced as he was Celeste had returned. Those of us who survived the attack regrouped in Handi Park, and I told the troop I meant to go in search of you."

"But what happened with the council?"

Sendoa nodded, "Before I left, we called for new appointments to replace the three lost in battle—we are back to six council members who will oversee things in your absence, and Nahia, they are aware of what must happen in seven years' time."

The eastern sky blushed pink announcing the arrival of a new day. A cold shiver crept up Nahia's spine—the promise she'd made to her dying mother quivered foremost in her mind. *Bide my time. Keep Basajaun safe until the seventh seven-year cycle is complete. Give Basajaun a new magical body.*

All too soon, she'd have to make good on that promise.

CHAPTER 26
THE LONG WAY HOME

Seven years to go, Nahia thought, rocked by a tremor of anticipation and dread. If forty-two years had passed so quickly, seven more would be gone in the blink of an eye. In the meantime, Basajaun rested safely over Maité's breast; it had been so since she'd discovered the pendant in Santa Clara. As for the magical vessel, Maité and David's budding romance, and the timing of it, pointed to them as the likely gateway.

Although Nahia longed to visit directly with Maité, she had continued to pass up opportunities for Lucid Dreaming, to avoid a confrontation over leaving her alone to face Ederne. But she could not be in the dark about Maité either, so in cowardly fashion, Nahia began sneaking into Alba's dreams to clear all her concerns there. That was how she learned that Maité would pursue higher education, and only afterward would she marry her David.

Fascinated by how events seemed to be lining up, Nahia derived a degree of satisfaction in telling Sendoa the Realm could not possibly be accused of interfering now. Whatever happened in the next seven years would be all Maité's doing.

"There isn't much of this island we haven't already seen," Sendoa remarked offhandedly one morning; it had been a month since Alba and Sósimo had left. "Don't you think it's time we head back?"

From her spot on the sand, beneath the shade of the sea grape trees, Nahia cricked her neck turning to Sendoa—she hadn't realized how wildly different their thoughts on the subject were. "Do you really mean that?"

Sendoa scowled, "What else can we do? I was actually thinking it might be good to start preparing the Realm for reawakening."

"Seriously? You want us to do housekeeping for seven years?" Nahia said, outraged. The thought of seeding, sweeping, pruning, and sprucing up in general was something she assumed would be completed in mere days. Anything longer than that horrified her. "Really, the concerted efforts of our troop of fifty should be more than enough to complete the task in less than a week!"

Sendoa cracked a smile. "So what should we do then?"

Nahia shimmied her shoulders and raised her eyebrows suggestively. "Did you know the Caribbean is littered with islands? And then there is the mainland—I think we can see all of the Americas in seven years."

Sendoa made a whistling sound, but then he winked at her and leaned in. "I suppose *we* can do whatever we want."

Nahia looked away, flustered, thankful her tanned skin hid the blush creeping up from her neck to her face. Her mind bounded back to the fateful morning, decades ago, when she was sneaking out of the Realm to be with Calisto and Sendoa had let her go, but not before he kissed her. From then on, the feel of his mouth on hers had cropped up over the years at the oddest moments.

Like at present; on hearing the wistful intonation he'd given the word "we," it occurred to Nahia Sendoa had been waiting for her to take the initiative. He had not made any advances, ever. He must've not considered it his place to do so; after all, she was the heiress apparent, soon to be queen. And it was up to her to choose a consort.

Nahia couldn't bring herself to look at him. Turbulent sensations and his pleasing qualities tripped over one another, all clamoring to be acknowledged by her. Nahia's heart raced when she felt Sendoa's hand on the back of her neck. She responded to the slight pressure of his fingers and turned to face him.

His eyes glinted silver in the shade, and Nahia experienced a sudden rush of irritation over his adherence to protocol. Nevertheless, with measured voice and steady aquamarine gaze, the Faery Princess nodded and said, "Yes, you and I can do whatever we want."

She took the initiative and kissed him, catapulting their relationship to another level. In one moment, the right moment, their friendship transitioned smoothly to an engagement of their hearts. Nahia suspected the seed of change had been planted years before, when he had kissed her to save her from a fate worse than death.

Sendoa readily agreed to Nahia's plan. As they both shared a deep love of the coast, they didn't bother going inland anywhere and instead they swooped down to Punta Arenas, at the southernmost tip of Chile. After that, they climbed up the Pacific Coast of South America to Colombia. They loved the Pacific so much, they pressed on along Central America to México. They crossed into the United States and continued up to Canada's west coast until they reached Alaska.

A chilly October in 2015 found them on the island of Sitka, where the scenery and the proximity to the mountains put Nahia in mind of Santa Clara and the Pyrenees. The length of her absence suddenly weighed heavy on her. As subtly as possible, Nahia had continued to monitor Maité's dreams over the years. She knew Maité had become an architect, she'd married David in 2014, and she was now six months pregnant, which meant the baby, the magical vessel, would be born in January 2016. Ederne, for all accounts and purposes, had dropped from the face of the planet.

"I'm not looking forward to winter here," Sendoa said, looking across the bay at the mountains already dusted with snow. "Should we start making our way back—maybe on a southern route?"

Nahia nodded, head full of passing thoughts without any semblance of order. "The years have breezed by, haven't they?" she said, staring into the distance.

"Mm-hmm"

"And the moment is almost upon us. I wonder if Maité will have a boy or a girl—"

"Does it make a difference?"

"I don't know," Nahia said, a crease forming above her nose, "only that we'll have a male or a female unicorn, I suppose." If she were honest with herself, the sex of the baby did not matter—what mattered was the *revulsion* she felt, yes, that was the word, when she thought about Maité's child becoming a vessel. To deprive the child of a normal life would create such bitterness among family. They would never recover; the relationship couldn't possibly be salvaged afterward. *Could turning Maité's baby into a unicorn be construed as harm?*

"What are you thinking?" Sendoa whispered, drawing closer to her on the boulder of a private jetty where they'd gone to watch the sunrise.

"You don't really want to know—"

"Is that so?"

"Do you honestly see me sacrificing an innocent baby?" Nahia demanded, feeling at her wits' end. "I can't take it upon myself to change someone's destiny like that, from one species to another!"

"And I thought you were mulling over our return flight path," Sendoa said with a nervous grin. "That is some heavy thinking you're doing, but you're not considering going against your mother's wishes, are you?"

Nahia's brow went up, she wrinkled her nose. "I don't know," she groaned, feeling out of her depth and wondering why she'd left these considerations to the last minute. "I should've been thinking this through for the last seven years."

Sendoa gathered her to him in a tight embrace. "Your mother was very traditional and practical. My feeling is she told it to you exactly how it needed to be, and you shouldn't try to interpret otherwise."

Nahia stared at him wondering why she had said anything about it in the first place—this was her burden to bear alone.

Sendoa seemed to catch on to her thoughts and quickly added, "You can look at it this way too: you still have three months before the forty-ninth year begins, and six months from there until the summer solstice, when all this will be sorted out."

Nahia wiggled and wedged herself against his chest. "You're right," she sighed, "and as for our return trip, how about we jump on one of those international flights, see what that's like."

"Which is the nearest, most international airport around here?"

"I'm betting the one in California—Los Angeles," Nahia said, feeling a ripple of excitement over flying on an airplane. How it eased her mind to know the trip back would be accomplished in under twenty-four hours.

PART IV

2016 TO 2017

What lies behind us and what lies ahead of us are tiny matters compared to what lives within us.

Henry Stanley Haskins

CHAPTER 27

THE WILLING ABDUCTEE

Mansión María Celeste in San Sebastián positively glittered. Light poured out of every window as Nahia watched it from across the street, crouched like a gargoyle on one of the ornate lampposts lining the bridge over the Urumea River. The thick veil of memories clouding her vision made her wonder if she should've asked Sendoa to come along. Nahia had misjudged the impact it would have on her to be in the city again, to see the house with all its changes.

Nahia's eyes narrowed; the wondrous sight seeped into her as if for the first time. Maité's architectural magic had brought forth all the changes Nahia had hoped for when she was lady of the house. The city around the mansion had changed too; in her time, mostly horse-drawn carriages had rumbled across the bridge and streets, causing a wholly different bustle from present-day motor vehicles.

She shook off the wave of gloom sinking her into the past and focused on the moment.

It appeared the María Celeste's inaugural feast, along with the christening of Maité's daughter, had been a success. The breeze carried snatches of laughter and conversation to Nahia as guests left, while through the windows she caught glimpses of Maité with the baby in her arms. She had named her Aintza, meaning *glory*, and Nahia heartily approved—the baby's namesake had been a magnificent head of the Faerie Council.

Nahia reminded herself to relax a little, for the prospect of seeing her girls had her in a state of painful agitation. She took a deep breath and shifted her attention to the cluster of people lingering in the foyer; after all, this was the first time she had seen them, outside of Maité's dreams.

Maité handed the baby to David and put her arm around a lanky girl Nahia recognized as Emily, Maité's best friend. Of course, she recognized Alba and Sósimo right away too. The rest she identified from dream snippets; Emily's husband, Finn. Maité's grandfather, David's father and Emily's parents, all were there for the occasion. It appeared the two younger couples would stay at Mansión María Celeste, while the older ones would stay elsewhere. Santillán Manor, Nahia guessed.

David took the baby around to all the grandparents so they could kiss her goodnight, and then Nahia lost sight of Aintza as he walked away, presumably to put her in bed. The older couples climbed into the two vehicles waiting for them at the curb, and having waved them off, the younger ones went back in the house.

Nahia rose from her crouching position on the lamppost and soared over traffic on the avenue toward the nursery window on the third floor. The faery blew in with the song of the late summer breeze, rustling the chiffon hangings as she passed—heart hammering in her chest.

Aintza slept in her crib and Nahia stared at her, dazed by how much of Maité she could see in the baby's three-month-old face, and by the little bits of Celeste she could see in her too. The faces of so many dear women drifted in and out of focus in her mind; the existence of each one had shaped the moment at hand, and all had Oihana's dormant spark.

"*Kaixo*, little one, I am Nahia," she whispered the greeting in a trembling voice to the newest addition to the family tree.

The door opposite opened and Maité came in. Nahia retreated to a corner and watched her lean over the crib. She kissed her baby's forehead and tucked the blanket snug around the small form. When she turned to leave, seemingly satisfied all was fine, Nahia decided the time had come to make her presence known. Her sea-green aura sparkled in anticipation, and Maité seemed to catch a flash of it out of the corner of her eye. She froze with her hand on the door handle and turned slowly.

Nahia hovered above the crib for a moment before she deliberately turned her gaze on the sleeping child. Unable to break from tradition, she quickly rattled off the binding words for Lucid Dreaming, except for this child there would be more. Nahia placed her hands over the cradle and the song she'd been rehearsing for weeks spilled out of her:

> *The world welcomed you in the dead of winter,*
> *When nature slumbers full of dreams and promise*
> *Yours is the force of creation that sleeps with purpose*

To nurture and replenish, that when the earth again looks for the sun
It may sing and flourish in the boon of spring
Constant and vital you are, to you we shall turn
That we may carry on.

The faery sealed the gift with a fragrant shower of jasmine petals, aware of Maité's rapt expression; she seemed to be listening with her entire body while Aintza slept, undisturbed.

I knew you'd come back, Maité's sparkling eyes told Nahia. She pulled back the hood of her cloak and saw relief spread over Maité's face as the faery's golden curls streaked with turquoise tumbled over her shoulders. Their eyes locked and in the brief, silent exchange, Nahia knew Maité had been waiting for this visit as anxiously as she had. Nahia might even be forgiven for her absence.

"Maité?" David's voice took them both by surprise. His arms encircled Maité's waist, and he kissed her neck. In her ear he whispered, "Is she asleep?"

"She is," Maité replied, though she didn't break eye contact with Nahia.

"Then are we ready?" He nuzzled her below the ear, oblivious to the faery's presence.

Nahia could see that even after seven years, Maité experienced the same palpitations as when she had first met him. Again she was reminded of Celeste and Etienne's romance, down to begrudging David how much of Maité's heart he had. *It is considerably diminished from what it was with Etienne,* Nahia argued inwardly.

"I'll be down in just a minute," Maité said, kissing him before he tiptoed out of the room, and in an instant she rounded on Nahia. "Where have you been all this time?" Maité scolded. "It's been years, and I haven't heard from you, or seen so much as a—"

Nahia felt the justice of the reproach and was ready to make amends. She immediately offered, "Let's you and I talk."

"Now?" Maité stammered.

"Yes—let's you and I go back to the woods where it all began," Nahia said, amused by a newfound level of interaction; it seemed Maité's dominant streak of Glamour recognized Nahia's, strengthening their connection and allowing them to experience Lucid Dreaming while awake and in each other's presence. Nahia heard the sudden explosion of frantic reasoning in Maité's head and grinned.

"Surely you can't schedule a later appointment or a conference call with a faery! And what about David and Emily? Em's my baby's godmother, for crying out loud!"

"But I am her faery godmother," Nahia countered and Maité blanched.

The faery's eyes flicked to the heavy pendant resting in plain view over Maité's breast. The three stones, two onyxes and one ruby, sparkled in the amber glow of the nursery. *Basajaun.* Nahia placed her hand on Maité's solar plexus to trigger the shape-shift, and the girl's indecision between staying and leaving dissolved into silent laughter. Nahia felt Maité shudder as the cells in her body unfurled to redirect energy. Large wings began flapping in their bellies, followed by the thrilling sensation of the body turning into liquid and being poured into a reduced version of itself.

Like Nahia, Maité seemed to welcome it. She let out a long whoop but immediately cringed; the thought of the baby monitor streaked across Maité's mind and they both knew her shriek would wake up Aintza and alert the others downstairs—all the more reason to dash away. Nahia clasped Maité's hand and together they shot out of the open window into the starlit sky.

Aintza cried, and David raced back up the stairs with Emily and Finn close behind.

Maité laughed out loud and Nahia joined her, incapable of containing her excitement. As they looked back toward the window, Maité called out to David, "I won't be long." Nahia knew the message would dissipate in the breeze before a note of it reached him.

David stood at the open window with Emily and Finn on either side of him. Three pairs of eyes followed them in the dusky sky, Nahia could feel them and returned Maité's anxious squeeze of the hand.

Although she uttered it in the quiet voice of her mind, Nahia heard her plea to David, "Take care of our baby girl."

"Come home soon," he replied and Nahia caught it. He said it with such understanding, it tore at the faery's heartstrings. It dawned on her how much they must have discussed Nahia's return and what it would mean to Maité. David had known he'd have to let her go one day, and all he hoped for was her swift return.

Nahia swallowed the knot in her throat and tightened her grasp on Maité's hand, ignoring the twinge of guilt squeezing her insides. She made a revolution around Santa Clara Island and then headed east, toward the mountains. The crisp alpine scent soon replaced the humid, salty air.

Basajaun sparkled in the moonlight against Maité's skin. Energy pulsed between them, palm to palm.

CHAPTER 28

HOLDING BACK

"It's cold," Maité cried out. Nahia laughed, relishing the cool mist as they blasted through it. An upward air current caught them and slingshot them over the waterfall. The faery stalled in the open sky above the plunging water and let out a gleeful shout—this was her favorite part of the journey.

"On to Moon Dancer Lake," Nahia sang, glancing sideways at Maité, who appeared more stunned than impressed.

Maité let out a long "Okaaaay!" as Nahia wrenched her over the jagged rocks and into the undergrowth. Afterward, all Nahia could hear were Maité's gasps and groans as they crisscrossed in the shadows, seeming to ricochet from tree trunks to branches without touching any of them.

Nahia did not let up until the canopy overhead began to thin, and even then, the faery sped up for landing. She blew out of the shrubbery in a flurry of leaves and hit the ground like a pebble skipping on water. Maité got three huge lunges in, trying to keep up, and would have slid on her belly on the sand had Nahia not held her up.

"Ugh!" Maité let go of Nahia's hand after steadying herself. "You could've warned me!"

Nahia's brow creased. "Sorry. Did you not like it?" asked the faery, not feeling sorry at all but becoming suddenly aware she'd been showing off, as she had often done with Celeste—really, they could be twins. Perplexed by how the likeness seemed to be enough to make her revert to old patterns, Nahia clucked her tongue impatiently and with a sheepish grin began picking leaves off Maité's windblown hair. "I like to fly fast."

"I can tell," Maité said, twisting her long hair, tangles and all, and tying it high with a band she pulled out of her pocket. She stood on the sand, looking expectantly at Nahia though her eyes darted distractedly toward the starlit surface of the lake.

Nahia fought the urge to further amaze Maité with her skills. Refusing to spiral down into the sisterly dynamic she'd had with Celeste two hundred years before, she admonished, "I'm going to shift to human height now, so don't be alarmed or feel dwarfed when I do it."

The warning still hung in the air when the shift happened.

"Whoa! You're too fast for your own good," Maité exclaimed, jumping back a few steps the better to see the giant faery.

Nahia smirked, liking the compliment she'd fished for, though realizing Celeste, who knew her best, wouldn't have surrendered it as easily as Maité had. Her expression sobered—if she didn't separate the two women now, the seven weeks they had until the summer solstice would be whittled away in pointless daydreams.

"Do I get a turn? Or will you carry me the rest of the way?"

Forced to get over her ruminations, Nahia looked down and grinned at Maité. She stood on the sand, hands on her hips, looking defiantly up at her. Just like Celeste would've done. "Yes, yes, but I expect you to do this on your own pretty soon," she said, bending down and placing one hand on the small of Maité's back and two fingers over her solar plexus to trigger the shape-shift. Nahia gave Maité a warning look just before she released a surge of energy through her fingers. Then she stood back to watch her handiwork.

Maité let out another long whoop. She distended to a larger version of herself in four seconds flat. "Geez! Will I get to catch my breath tonight?" Maité complained, although the twinkle in her stormy gray eyes betrayed her excitement.

"You will for sure, because we're walking from here to a private entrance to Handi Park."

"A private entrance?"

"Yes. Into the Queen's chamber because I don't think tonight's the night for you to meet the council or the rest of the troop," Nahia said, thinking there was so much she needed to get Maité acquainted with.

"Oh, Nahia, it would be such an honor to meet your mother."

The faery paused disconcerted—but of course, Maité couldn't know. "The Faery Queen passed into the light nearly fifty years ago," Nahia said solemnly.

Maité grimaced, "I'm so sorry—I had no idea."

Nahia shrugged and wagged her head dismissively. "It happened long ago, before you were even born."

"So does this mean you are the Faery Queen now?" Maité said nervously, as if unsure of the protocol to be applied.

"I'm the heiress apparent," Nahia said, dipping her chin and peering up at Maité, who at human height was taller than Nahia, just like Celeste had been. "I won't be queen until the Realm is reawakened."

Maité frowned and glanced at her surroundings as if expecting to hear the hills and trees snoring placidly. "What do you mean by *reawakened*?"

Nahia motioned for Maité to follow her into forest. They walked single-file on the meandering trail while Nahia explained, "Ederne has been up to no good for more years than I care to count. She was responsible for my mother's death, and for the death of the unicorn."

"You mean the Keeper of the Forest, right?"

Nahia nodded. "The death of that magical creature caused the Realm to go dormant for forty-nine years, during which there really is no point in there being a queen."

"But why forty-nine years?"

"It takes seven seven-year cycles for the Realm to mend—"

"Lucky number seven," Maité murmured.

"More than lucky, it's magical and powerful," Nahia replied without slowing her pace. "Anyway, at the end of that cycle, we will be ready for a new Keeper of the Forest, who will magically bind us in the collective consciousness that has sustained us in the past."

"Where in the forty-nine years are we? When did the unicorn die?"

Nahia smiled inwardly at Maité's use of the word *we* in her question; she was already counting herself as one of the Realm. "We are there. And we must be ready for the new Keeper of the Forest by this coming summer solstice," Nahia said importantly.

"So now what needs to happen? What can I do to help?"

Nahia did stop this time and she turned to look at Maité, moved by her eagerness yet cringing with the knowledge of what she was *supposed* to do to help. Nahia put her hand on Maité's shoulder. "We're here to talk about all that—I promise to fill you in because there is a lot you don't know. But let's get to my mother's chamber first—there is something there I need to show you."

Nahia resumed walking and could feel Maité keeping time a couple of steps behind her. For a few yards nothing was said, and then Maité broke the silence, an unmistakable note of accusation in what was nearly a whisper.

"It's been seven years since Ederne almost killed me."

"I know," Nahia replied feeling the full weight of what Maité hadn't said. *I did leave her alone—maybe she's not forgiven me, or forgotten*, she thought. Trying not to sound defiant, the faery countered, "But they have been seven wonderful years during which you have enjoyed your parents. Haven't you? And you married David, and you even brought a lovely daughter into the world."

"You're right. Of course you're right," Maité sputtered. "Thank you for what you did—for giving my parents back to me."

"You're welcome," Nahia said, hearing Maité's steps close behind as they bypassed Paloma's pond on their way to Handi Park. Nahia sidled away from brittle branches and prickly pine needles hemming them in, comforted by Maité being so close, copying her moves.

The keen sense she should've been there seven years ago, in person rather than just in dreams, wouldn't let up. However, determined to lessen her guilt with her own view of the circumstances, Nahia continued, "I *am* sorry I left you on your own to face Ederne, and I don't expect you to understand, but the truth is I might not have done as well—you seared away all the Glamour in that petulant faery. You spared her life, but reduced her to living out her remaining days as a human. Quite clever."

The words came out grudgingly and Nahia hated herself for it. *Why is it so difficult to give credit where it's due?* She wondered irritably if she would ever mature and become truly kind and selfless. If it hadn't happened in forty-nine years, she doubted it could happen in the next seven weeks. *And if it doesn't, how can I be sure I will be effective when the solstice arrives?*

"So you stayed away because there was no point in coming to me until the forty-nine years were up?"

Thrown off by the question, Nahia scrambled for a reply. It hadn't occurred to her she'd have to explain her seven-year absence. Suddenly it seemed childish to say she stayed away because Maité had once considered the Faerie Realm's interference *petty*. She stammered, "I think so. Yes, what was the point of bringing you to our sleeping kingdom? And I'm sorry I broke into your home tonight, unannounced and unexpected."

"I'm not fishing for apologies," Maité said, and her tone ignited a defensive spark inside the faery, who realized she'd already said "sorry" twice. "I just want to know and understand everything."

Nahia stopped and turned again. In the starlight, Maité's gray eyes glinted fiercely. "I know you're not looking for apologies, and I certainly didn't bring you here to proffer them," Nahia declared with a surge of aggression that fizzled out as soon as the reason for being there resurfaced in her head. Suddenly seven weeks seemed an awfully short time.

Nahia clucked her tongue. "I *will* tell you everything I can, just as soon as we get where we're going."

A crease formed between Maité's brows as she lilted, "Everything you can—do you mean there is stuff you can't tell me?"

Nahia turned away, pursing her lips and resuming the walk. "Everything I can is everything I know," Nahia said mulishly, "and it will be told over time—tonight won't be long enough."

Nahia, who knew the terrain like the back of her hand, glided easily over it. Maité, despite her long legs, trotted to keep up while posing a steady flow of questions, to which Nahia responded patiently.

"Are you really two hundred years old?"

"Technically speaking, I'll be one hundred and ninety-seven this year," she replied, remembering Maité had read *Faery Sight*, where Xiomara had revealed many details. "You know Celeste and I were born on the same night, in 1819. What you may *not* know is faeries age like humans only until we are fifteen. After that, our bodies change at the rate of one year for every fifteen of theirs. So really, by that reckoning, I'm only twenty-seven."

"What about the streaks in your hair? Do they always match your eyes, or is it a choice?"

"They always match. Every faery's hair is streaked to match the color of her eyes. My mother's were the color of amethyst—quite celebrated at court."

"Do you think it will all be again like Xiomara described?"

"You wouldn't think so, to look at these gnarled trees, and all the brittle, prickly shrubbery," Nahia remarked on her surroundings, fully aware of the desolate state they were in. "The smell of decaying vegetation makes it hard to even breathe—but the repair work won't be as bad as you might think, especially if you have a clear image in your mind of what Xiomara described."

"Yes, but *how* will we do the repair?"

Again, the use of the word *we*. Brimming with satisfaction, Nahia took a look around and quickly spotted a small clearing between the pines. "For centuries, faeries have known this place as the *bulb patch* of the Arboretum. My mother consigned it to a very old faery whose time to return to the light was nearing. She wanted nothing more than to spend her last days (which turned out to be innumerable still) nurturing bulbs.

"Under her care, the clearing became an open gash of color among the somber conifers—she cultivated every variety of tulip, hyacinth, daffodil, iris, narcissus, and even her own peculiar grafts," Nahia said, kicking the dirt around the clearing and even getting on all fours in some sections, searching for a surviving bulb.

When she finally spotted one, aided by the light of her aura, she motioned for Maité to come closer.

"What is it?" Maité asked, kneeling beside her.

Nahia picked up a dry bulb and peeled off its brittle covering to reveal the smooth, pebble-like surface. "Now watch," Nahia said as she buried the seed and placed her hand, palm down, over it. "The old faery once grew a beautiful variety of tulips here; they had velvety apricot-colored petals. Try to see them in your mind."

Maité nodded and Nahia continued to embellish the imagery in a singsong voice. "Silky-petaled flowers on long stalks, waxy, green blade-like leaves . . ." said Nahia until the vision in her head became the pervasive intention directing her creative energy.

Nahia pictured shimmering, cool blue tendrils unfurling from her solar plexus, traveling through her body with increasing strength until they reached the palm of her hand. From there, the tendrils visibly penetrated the ground in sparkling trickles, waking the bulb and bidding it to seek out the moisture and nutrients around it.

Moments ticked by without anything happening aboveground, but when at last Nahia heard the indefinable breath of life stirring, she seized upon it and commanded it to hasten—she envisioned every molecule of the buried bulb eagerly replicating, and within seconds, a bright green shoot poked out through the loose soil.

She heard Maité catch her breath, and the faery smiled satisfied.

"Is that what we have to do to restore the Realm?" Maité said, giving her surroundings a distressed look, "one flower at a time?"

Nahia's furtive glance fell on the pendant. "Yes, but all will be done on a much larger scale—the cleaning, designing, and seeding. The whole troop must share the workload to ready the foundation for a new Keeper of the Forest, without whose magic our dimension cannot be sustained."

Maité blanched. "But how do we do it—where do we get a new unicorn?"

Nahia let out an involuntary laugh at Maité's startled expression.

"It's not funny! Are you saying we're going to hunt down a unicorn—do you know where one is?" she demanded, her eyes bulging slightly.

"Do calm down," Nahia said patiently, convinced that in a few seconds she'd become some sort of quack in Maité's opinion. "We won't be needing virgins or golden bridles to catch our unicorn—we're going to *make* one."

Chapter 29

Enlightened

Nahia shook her head the moment Maité opened her mouth to speak. "Don't ask me how, yet." She was glad that although a fleeting scowl darkened Maité's expression, she did not persist on the daunting question of how a unicorn would be made. "We're almost there," Nahia soothed, picking up the pace considerably as they began climbing a steep slope.

The faery stopped at the summit, where stood the base of a well amid dusty conifers. "Through here is the only other entrance to Handi Park," Nahia said, jutting her chin toward the ring of stacked stones. "The main entrance is a ways from here, near an Aspen Grove."

"So, we are above Handi Park right now?" Maité said eagerly, patting her feet on the needle-strewn ground.

"We are. Are you ready?"

Maité visibly tensed, and Nahia did not disappoint. She reduced Maité's height and darted upward in one swooping motion. She hovered long enough to let her see the opening below, and then plunged through the center of the well. Maité let out a loud *aaaaargh*.

Nahia stopped the free fall before they hit the ground; the thin layer of air between their feet and the floor acted as a squashy sponge that kept them from shattering their knees.

"Uggh!" Maité said, touching solid ground and trying to stay upright after the abrupt stop.

"Here we are," Nahia said, awfully pleased with the precision of her landing. She released Maité's hand, inviting her to examine the Faery Queen's octagon-shaped room suffused in fragrant candlelight.

Nahia followed Maité's glance as it roved over the tiled floor, and the deep-lilac ceiling with its upward vortex ending in a skylight. She ambled about the room, caressing the textured walls and ornate furnishings and stopped in front of the large hearth, directly across from Oihana's tapestry of her girls.

"Beautiful!" Maité sighed, whirling toward the faery.

Nahia agreed. She conjured a fire in the grate and guided Maité toward the table and chairs before it, inviting her to sit. A pitcher and two glasses were already there.

"Chamomile infusion," Nahia said when Maité frowned and raised an eyebrow at her. "Nothing more sinister than that," the faery assured her as she poured the drink.

Maité raised her glass. Nahia mirrored her and they both drank.

"My mother died in this room," Nahia began, glancing toward the bed as if the Faery Queen might materialize in the sputtering firelight. Maité's eyes flickered to the bed but quickly returned to Nahia. "Right before she passed into the light, she told me the story I'm about to tell you."

Maité drew up her long legs and wrapped her arms around them, in a very Celeste-ish way. Nahia's voice vibrated with emotion as she began the tragic tale of the Faery Queen's first family. She got as far as Oihana traveling from Italy into Spanish territory without interruption, but at the first mention of Monte Perdido, Maité tensed and interjected.

"When I met David, my husband, he was researching a genetic anomaly he and his team had discovered in Monte Perdido—"

"I beg your pardon?" Nahia said, perplexed.

"A genetic anomaly is like a different code in the internal structure of people."

Nahia sat up straighter, agitated on discovering humans studied such things, but also aware that at the mere mention of Monte Perdido, the color had risen to Maité's cheeks—the beginning of a smile had quivered on her mouth like a subtle illusion.

"You mean you can see people's cells and find differences in them?"

"Uh-huh," Maité replied hurriedly. "Do you think it's the same place? I mean, Oihana and David's Monte Perdido?"

Nahia nodded curtly, thinking of the young boy, Nino, who'd been left behind. "I believe it might be."

The narrative continued, while in the back of her mind Nahia pondered what might happen to the Realm's privacy if humans identified and labeled their differences. Would her troop be hunted down and trapped, to be studied, or destroyed? But obviously, David had been discreet with his findings; maybe Maité had begged it of him. Certainly in the seven years since he'd made the discovery, no human had stomped above Handi Park looking for them.

Nahia relaxed, pleased to see that as the story progressed, Maité's eyes darted toward the tapestry on the wall—comprehension quickly dawning on her. "My mother kept track of all her girls, and I kept up her practice after she passed," Nahia said, excited for Maité to take a look.

She let go of her knees and relaxed her limbs; her stormy eyes flashed, motioning toward the tapestry. "May I?"

Nahia assented, and they rose together. She leaned against the wall to one side of the tapestry, the better to watch Maité's reaction.

She scanned the map in front of her, rocking back and forth as if to release her nervous energy. The contents were embedded in Nahia's heart, and so just by looking at where Maité had trained her glance, she knew the name being read.

Just as Nahia had done all those years ago, Maité reached out and ran her fingers tentatively over Nere's embroidered name. "This is near Marseille," she whispered.

Nahia nodded. "That is where Eleanor took her after their flight from Monte Perdido."

Maité rubbed the tips of her fingers distractedly and then placed them again over the name. "It's like hot water bubbling on my fingers, and then—then . . . ."

"You see her," Nahia said, knowing full well Nere's existence had passed in golden flashes before Maité's eyes.

"Yes, it's like highlights of her life . . . ."

"*Highlights*," Nahia repeated thoughtfully. "That is a good word for the most precious moments of our lives, and my mother fixed them there with just a lock of hair and her Glamour . . . ."

Tears gleamed in Maité's eyes as she traced over each name. Nahia could tell when a surge of heat happened, triggering the magical reaction that allowed her to see Oihana's girls. Together they followed the lineage: Nere, Juliette, Émilie, Adèle, Camille, Rose, Angèle, Naomi, until they arrived at Paloma's name. Nahia looked up expectantly to see Maité had paled.

"Celeste's mother—has to be. So close to San Sebastián!"

Nahia stood statue-like against the wall. "Touch it," said the faery, and Maité obeyed.

She pinched her eyes closed, possibly to better see Paloma's highlights, which of course included Celeste, Nahia, and Oihana herself. In a few moments, she opened them again and stared narrowly at Nahia. "I suspected, I mean, I knew you and *Anahí* were the same person, or faery. Seven years ago David and Emily helped me confirm that. But I had no idea—" she paused. It seemed her mouth had gone dry and could not articulate her astonishment.

"There are two drafts of faery blood in you," Nahia confirmed. "From my mother to Paloma, and then from Celeste and I, all the way to you and Aintza. I knew nothing of my mother's history when I fell in love with Calisto. I pursued him, conquered him, and tried to make a life with him in *his* world, only to be discovered, and punished for it with our eventual separation."

Maité listened attentively until Nahia concluded her own tale of desertion, her history with Alaia and Calisto, and her eventual return to the Realm. Any doubts Maité may have had about her ancestry had been whisked away, and she was suddenly choking down tears. In an understandable daze, Maité stumbled back to the table; she grabbed the chamomile infusion and gulped down what was left in her glass. She slung Basajaun aside on its chain and massaged her breastbone, as if to slow the rapid beating of her heart.

Their eyes met. Nahia said, "Yes. We go further back than you realized."

Maité took two strides and threw herself in the faery's arms.

"Oh, Nahia, I don't know what to say—we really *are* one," she gushed even as she pulled away and held the faery at arm's length. "What I just saw is like a door swinging open for me. I always sensed a connection to something larger, I always felt there were things I hadn't really learned on my own and now I see I'm genetically threaded to these women's lives! That's where the knowledge comes from, even if it's only subconscious wisdom. It's almost like I lived their lives myself, and all of it is recorded in the cells in my body. I carry Oihana's genetic imprint in me, and yours too," she said in awe. "And so does Aintza . . . ."

Maité released Nahia's shoulders; her arms dropped to her sides and her eyes glazed as if focusing inwardly. Nahia recognized the symptoms of someone who'd grasped a critical revelation in a short period of time; she was about to remark on it when Maité spoke again.

"How pointless is the amount of energy we waste complaining about what we have, envying someone else's life, or wishing for something else— how blind we are! How blind *I* have been, when the truth is we already have everything we could want, each one of us is everything and everyone, all the time, the good and the bad."

"I never understood it that way," Nahia said, a little unnerved. She had always taken her unique status for granted. Yes, she was part of a community and a family, but she never felt she was *one with everyone*. She saw herself as a separate individual who made choices and had experiences without affecting those around her.

Nahia opened her mouth to express her own views but stopped herself just in time. Did she really believe her choices and experiences hadn't impacted others? The faery rolled her eyes and clucked her tongue, annoyed. Here stood Maité—very real evidence of the consequences of her actions.

Nahia sighed. "I see what you mean," she said, secretly acknowledging she might have been jealous of Celeste; her romance with Etienne, the family they'd built together, had driven Nahia, at least in part, to emulate it with Calisto. "But I can't say I have experienced someone else's life as if it were my own."

Maité tilted her head doubtfully. "Haven't you ever benefited from the experience of people, or faeries, around you? You know, taken advice, applied it? That's mostly what I meant."

Nahia rolled her eyes again, not wanting to confess how generally unreceptive she was to the ideas of others while favoring her own trial and error method. "I tend to consult my own wisdom," she replied tersely, suspecting but not caring that Maité might be judging her.

"At your age, it's probably a great deal of wisdom."

Nahia's eyes narrowed. Was Maité being like Sendoa, reminding her how old she was and how much more was expected of her because of it? She stopped herself from uttering a defensive reply and instead went to Maité, remembering she had to correct a previous omission.

"When I gave you your Cradle Gift, I did not bring back a lock of hair for your place in the tapestry," Nahia said, tugging lightly on the loose strand brushing Maité's cheek. She showed her the couple of inches she'd detached.

"I didn't feel a thing." Maité grinned.

Turning back to the tapestry, Nahia placed Maité's lock of hair beneath Alba's. She held it down and focused her thoughts on drawing a swirl of energy from her solar plexus and releasing it through her fingertips. She intoned the charm Oihana had taught her, causing the fibers on the tapestry and the strands of hair to weave into a satin-stitched leaf.

They stood back to admire Nahia's handiwork, and together they placed a fingertip over Maité's leaf. The happiest moments of her life succeeded one another in a glittering mist, from her birthday celebrations at home to meeting David and reuniting with her parents, and to her daughter being born.

Maité wiped her tears with the back of her hand. "Thank you, Nahia. This—all of it—means so much to me."

Nahia embraced her, unable to say a word because of the knot in her throat. She couldn't stop seeing the last image of Maité and David on the tapestry—smiling peacefully, talking in whispers, watching their baby asleep between them on their bed. *And I will destroy that?*

"Now will you tell me about making the unicorn?"

Jolted out of her dark thoughts, Nahia released her, eyes darting again to Basajaun on Maité's chest. Consciously or instinctively (Nahia couldn't tell), Maité made a fist around the pendant.

"Do you remember when you found it?"

"Of course I do. It was seven years ago in the underground cave in Santa Clara."

Nahia nodded. "I left it there for you to find, inside the chest with other family heirlooms."

"This pendant was in its own compartment with a piece of paper," Maité recalled and immediately recited like a child at lessons, "It said, 'His return will signify the Realm may flourish. Look upon us with your favor once again, O Basajaun. May the beating of your heart infuse renewed life to that which has been dormant for years past. O Basajaun.'"

Nahia nodded again, perturbed by the moment of revelation being so suddenly upon her, after forty-nine years. She declared, "The name of the slain Keeper of the Forest was Basajaun."

Maité frowned but then her eyes grew wide and she held out the pendant on its chain: two onyxes, one large ruby. "This makes me think of eyes, and a heart."

Nahia hastened to confirm, "Indeed. The powerful magic residing in those precious organs needed forty-nine years to compound, while the Realm slept. On the eve of the upcoming summer solstice, in seven weeks' time, Basajaun's eyes and heart will inhabit a magical vessel and the new Keeper of the Forest will look upon us again and bind us with renewed life."

"All these years—" Maité said, fervently pressing the pendant to her breast with the palm of her hand, "I've worn it—every day, and I told myself I was imagining it, but I *did* feel something. I felt protected, sometimes *invincible*, and now I know why."

Something cold and unpleasant shocked Nahia's insides upon hearing the hint of regret in Maité's voice. The imminent separation from Basajaun must have caused it, and if that was so, Nahia could not fathom how Maité would react when she discovered the other sacrifice expected of her.

Best not to dwell on it now, she thought, and returned to Maité's remarks. "I felt it too when I wore the pendant," Nahia admitted. "When I passed it on to you for safekeeping, I had no idea that Basajaun would keep you safe when you confronted Ederne, but I thank the stars he did."

"That fiery lance she aimed at me bounced right off his heart," Maité said, bringing it reverently to her lips and kissing the ruby.

"You needn't part with it just yet," Nahia said kindly, deciding on the spot to let her keep it a while longer. She was relieved to see Maité's expression clear, but then felt the need to admonish, "We have seven weeks before the solstice and then, no matter what, and we will wake the Realm."

"OK, yes. But between now and then, will I meet the council?" Maité spluttered as if fearing Nahia would change her mind about letting her keep the pendant. "And tell me, the two drafts of royal blood, does that mean I can, you know, *do* what you do?"

"Yes, you will meet the council and, as to what you can do, keeping company with Basajaun these seven years can only have strengthened your innate abilities," Nahia told her, glad to delay the troubling moment of full disclosure.

Maité beamed. "So do you think I can change my size at will? Can I fly?"

"Shape-shift, fly, make things grow, Lucid Dreaming," Nahia ticked the abilities off on her fingers, grinning as Maité's delighted smile widened. "All you need is a little direction. You must discard insecurities, master concentration, so it becomes your nature to focus without effort. You must never doubt."

"You say that like it's the easiest thing in the world—"

"When you do it enough, it *is*. Let's go outside now and practice your basic shape-shifting."

"What—now? How? I never . . . ."

"Yes you have," Nahia countered. "Lots of times—in your dreams, with Amets when he saved you from Ederne, and tonight with me."

"But everyone can do stuff in their dreams, and you and Amets changed me and carried me."

"You just needed a little nudge."

Maité gulped and took Nahia's proffered hand.

Unlike previous displays of skill, this time Nahia started her gracefully off the ground and into the vortex in Oihana's room, traveling slowly toward the skylight. "You focus your energy in your solar plexus," Nahia explained as they ascended. "I always envision whirling stardust in my core, spinning with such force as to propel me in whatever direction I need to go."

Maité's free hand rested gently over her diaphragm as they continued to float upward. "I think I feel something—are you doing that, or am I?"

"I've triggered a surge of energy, but you must help it expand and tell it what to do."

"How?"

"You need to picture in your mind the shape you want to become or the place you want to arrive at—I used to imagine the complete journey, landmark by recognizable landmark on the way, but then I realized that only served to slow me down." Maité's puzzled expression prompted Nahia to expand. "On my way to San Sebastián, for instance, my thoughts paused at the pond, then at the edge of the forest, at the waterfall, and so on. But those were all unnecessary stops and eventually I figured out I could save time by trusting the collective consciousness of the planet. If I *saw* my destination, *focused* intently on it, and *told* the swirling stardust in my belly to get me there, it would tap into the map-keeping energies of the world and take me there."

"So where are we going?" Maité said eagerly.

"Let's go back to Moon Dancer Lake."

"Oh my!" Maité gasped.

"See what I mean?" Nahia laughed, for as soon as Maité pictured the sandy shore, her focus had sharpened and by extension, the speed with which they advanced toward their destination. Already Oihana's skylight was a tiny lilac point of light below.

They alighted on the starlit sand and as soon as Nahia let go of Maité's hand, the girl whooped, exhilarated. "This is mind-blowing," she sang, twirling on the spot. "Can we practice shape-shifting?"

The sky had begun to lighten in the east and Maité looked worn out, exhausted from lack of sleep as much as from attempting to master concentration and focus.

"I can't do this unless your hand is on me," Maité complained.

"That's your insecurity speaking," Nahia replied for the twentieth time. "If you practice like this for a few more days, you'll have a set energy path, and you won't have to work so hard at it anymore."

Maité hadn't even finished *humph*-ing when all at once (and by the looks of it, involuntarily) she distended to her full height. "Aaaargh!"

191

Nahia shook with laughter as she rose from the sand to be at eye level with her.

"I don't know what I did," Maité said frantically. "Was that you?"

"No—but you *are* making progress. You need to relax—instead of squandering your focus in multiple directions, come up with a single, consistent method."

Maité's knees seemed to crumple and she slumped on the sand. "I'm so tired!"

"Let's get you back home then," Nahia soothed. "We have plenty of time to work on this."

"Emily and Finn are here for another two weeks and I would really like to spend time with them."

"Of course you would," Nahia replied, careful to keep ominous undertones out of her words. "I know she is family to you and you should treasure your time with her."

Nahia shifted to human height and offered her hand to Maité. They flashed across the sky in the predawn gloom, ahead of the storm clouds blowing into San Sebastián.

CHAPTER 30

MAITÉ

DOWNPLAYING REALITY

Maité looked but couldn't find the crying baby in the shadows. *Calisto*. Where had Nahia put him? Then she remembered the faery had left him alone on a huge bed, in Paloma and Celeste's grotto, while she went to find milk. She should try to calm him down until Nahia got back.

Yes—a hungry cry, Maité thought, fumbling toward the sound and wishing she could move faster. She tried to pick up the pace and had a shock realizing she wasn't even on her feet. She was lying down, her head on a pillow. Hadn't she been sitting on a chair, across from Nahia, in the royal chamber?

Maité sat up, bewildered. She was on the fourth floor of the María Celeste, by the pool. Aintza's lusty cries came out of the baby monitor beside the lounge chair where she had been sleeping. The dismal light filtering through the glass dome told her the sun had come up, but the heavy storm clouds were bound to prevent it from shining on San Sebastián.

Disoriented, though beginning to dispel the dream about Calisto and Nahia, Maité stumbled off the chair and headed to Aintza's room. She was still wearing the clothes from the christening ceremony the day before, which reminded her of the previous night's departure with Nahia. "She really stole a baby," she muttered, perplexed and uneasy. In the dream, Alaia had seemed as unpleasant as Nahia described her, but even so, Maité felt sure she would react the same way if something like that happened to Aintza.

She hurried down the hall to the nursery, noticing her own baby wasn't crying anymore. She went in and found David there, finishing up the first diaper change of the day. Maité leaned on the doorframe and smiled as David scooped up their daughter.

"All done, *amor*," he said to Aintza kissing her neck and making her giggle.

The sight of her little family warmed her all over. Maité crossed the room in three strides.

"Good morning to you both," she whispered, putting her arms around David's waist and looking over his shoulder at the baby.

"You're here! I was afraid I wouldn't see you again for—I don't know how long." He made a half turn and put his arm around Maité, holding tight to his girls. "When did you get back?" he asked, punctuating each word with a kiss.

Maité rolled her eyes and snuggled close to him. "I think it was close to five in the morning. Nahia dropped me off by the pool upstairs, and I have no clue why I didn't come straight to bed; instead I fell asleep on one of the chairs up there."

"So what happened?"

"I'll tell you while we take a shower—I really want to change out of these clothes."

"Deal."

Maité told him about Oihana being dead, about Nahia being the crown princess and immediately after, burst out with the story of Monte Perdido (*his* Monte Perdido, the place where he had found the genetic anomaly for which Maité was a match).

"So it's confirmed," David said, wearing a towel around his waist while combing his hair. "You're royalty."

Maité grinned, pulling on a sweatshirt and her favorite jeans. "You won't guess what I was able to do before my visit with Nahia ended," Maité said, as modestly as she could, though her glittering eyes betrayed her excitement. "I shape-shifted! But I *do* think the magic of the place, or even Nahia, had more to do with it than my own ability."

"Mm-hmm, but it could also be that all you need is some practice to be able to do it whenever and wherever you like?"

"That's what Nahia said."

"What else did Nahia say?" David asked, kissing her forehead—dressed and ready for the day.

Maité breathed in his clean scent, got on her tiptoes, and kissed him on the lips. "Lots of things," she said with a flustered grin, overcome with a sudden urge to keep quiet about the dormant Realm and the problematic notion of having to make a unicorn.

She busied herself making their bed, telling him the story of the old faery with the tulips. Inwardly, she questioned if her new sense of discretion had to do with Nahia's desire for secrecy, or if she, Maité, preferred to cover it up because it sounded ludicrous.

But who was she kidding? She already believed in faeries, why not unicorns? Maybe *finding* one would be more palatable to her brain than *making* one? *Yes*, Nahia had chosen the wrong verb, that was all.

"I shared a dream with Nahia in the couple hours I slept by the pool," she improvised when nothing else of what Nahia had said or done came to mind. "She must've been asleep too so I was able to sneak in. Anyway, I think she was dreaming about the day she stole Calisto, when he was a baby. I had no idea that happened . . . ."

Noting David's creased brow Maité immediately wished her words unsaid, and a mental struggle ensued. *Should I have kept quiet about that, too?*

"A baby abducted into faeryland?" David remarked with a grim hint of humor. "I guess the earth is flat and we've fallen off the edge of it."

Maité scowled in mock contempt while fluffing the pillows; she punched them a couple of times each before tossing them on top of the freshly made bed. *Nahia acted like any faery of legend would*, Maité thought reasonably. She picked up the baby from the playpen and they headed downstairs.

In the kitchen, Maité fed Aintza while David brewed coffee and chopped fruit for breakfast. Emily and Finn would be coming down shortly.

"When are you going back?" David asked cautiously, placing four mugs on the counter.

Maité pulled the empty bottle from Aintza's mouth and held the baby against her chest. She began rubbing her back in a circular motion. "I guess a summer solstice celebration requires lots of preparation, and I offered to help. But I told Nahia Emily and Finn would be here for a couple of weeks still, and I wanted to hang out with them." Aintza let out a healthy burp. "I do want to surprise her, though, by getting myself up there at least once in the next two weeks."

"You mean, because you shape-shifted the one time?" David frowned and before Maité could even answer, he expounded on his feelings about it. "It sounds to me like your one shape-shifting experience *was* unintentional, and I can see how encouraging that might seem, but I do worry you haven't considered the risks of doing it on your own. What if you shrink yourself partially, I mean, just an arm or a leg. Would you know how to get back to normal? And what if you *do* get airborne but your concentration hiccups and you drop to the ground, from say, six, ten stories?"

Maité pulled a face. The possibility hadn't occurred to her. She cradled Aintza, who had begun to fuss, and stuck the bottle back in her mouth. Her inability to offer a sensible rebuttal right away encouraged David to press on.

"I really believe you should delay, at least until you can have some serious, *supervised* practice with Nahia. In the meantime, can't you two stay in touch, safely, through some kind of mental-gram or your shared dreams?"

Maité looked at him, torn between arguing and wanting to laugh. "Really? A mental-gram?" She grinned. "And here I was, foolishly hoping you and Emily and Finn could help me practice."

"*Bom día*," Emily yawned coming in through the swinging door. "Holy smokes—you're here! And I thought you'd been abducted for years to come."

Maité laughed and David said, "We don't speak Portuguese."

"I know that," Emily said breezily, "and you should know (your wife does) how important it is to know at least basic greetings in as many languages as possible. Tomorrow I'll surprise you with Basque or maybe even Spanish." She held her arms out and Maité gave her the baby. Emily began swaying on the spot. "Did I hear we are supposed to practice something?"

"Good morning," said Finn, unlike Emily, he was already showered and dressed.

They finished preparing breakfast and sat at the table while Maité recounted her experiences of the night before, editing them just as she had for David and finishing up with the exciting prospect of a summer solstice celebration—a page right out of *Faery Sight*, she rhapsodized to Emily, imagining she'd move to the Realm with Aintza as soon as Emily left. She'd be there for five magical weeks, until the middle of June. David, of course, would come to her on the weekends.

Then Emily, the voice of reality, drew her from her happy plans. "So it's confirmed, Anahí and Nahia are the same person," she said, adopting the forensic tone Maité had learned to associate with a distressing logic. "And in a zany plot twist, Nahia's mother is the reason for the Monte Perdido anomaly, which means Calisto was what—Nahia's *nephew*?"

Maité stared, momentarily stung. David and Finn exchanged a humorous glance. "Only very, *very* distant," David said.

"Yeah," Maité jumped in, recovering a bit of confidence. "Genetically speaking, they were twelve generations and over three hundred years apart, and besides, Calisto had already died when Nahia found out about Monte Perdido," she said, looking to David for support.

He nodded, addressing Emily with an amused expression. "You can discard inbreeding, if that's where you were headed, and focus instead on the fact that we're having breakfast with royalty."

Emily pursed her lips and squinted at Maité. "I guess," she conceded. Picking up her fork, she resumed devouring her meal.

When they had finished and were sitting around the table enjoying a second cup of coffee, Maité again expressed her wish to pay Nahia a surprise visit. "So Em, what do you think about helping me practice shape-shifting?" Maité asked, her eyes flashing guiltily toward David.

Emily ran her tongue over her teeth, apparently checking for bits of food she hadn't swallowed. "Yeah," she said, "because we've done it loads of times ourselves and, you know, we'll be able to correct your mistakes." She rolled her eyes.

David smacked his fist on the tabletop. "Yes! Glad you see things the way I do."

Maité's head whipped toward him, and by chance, Aintza mimicked her mother's movement, which caused Emily and Finn to grin and David to wince, a little alarmed.

"What—am I not allowed to worry about you? All I want is for you to have professional supervision before you start changing your proportions, which I think are perfect, by the way."

"Really—professional supervision? Way to make her sound unfit," Emily said under her breath.

"Did Nahia ever say you needed it? Supervision, I mean," Finn wondered.

Maité pondered it for a moment. Nahia hadn't even hinted at such a thing, but it was probably because she was so self-sufficient she couldn't conceive of a beginner, much less of her stumbling blocks. Maité shook her head. "She *did* say that I needed to practice, that I should come up with a single consistent method to focus and direct my energy until the process becomes second nature to me."

David exchanged another look with Finn, who shrugged as if saying, *It's out of our hands.*

"I guess," Emily said, unconvinced, "maybe, just in case, you should walk us through the process, verbally first, so we can write up a procedure."

"Seriously?" Maité retorted, aghast. "You don't mean you want to flow-chart this thing—do you?"

"Well, she's got a point, *amor*," David interjected and Maité leaned back in her chair, subconsciously distancing herself from complications. "With a step-by-step process you can eliminate the worry of missing a key element—at least in theory."

Maité stared off, arguing with herself about how open her mind might be and how closed David's was. In the end, she acknowledged the wisdom of her husband's suggestion.

The clock of Emily and Finn's visit began to tick quickly and the inmates of the María Celeste spent their time doing everyday things. They talked, played with the baby, did laundry, and ventured out occasionally to do some sightseeing (when San Sebastián's squally spring weather allowed).

Maité repeated Nahia's instructions countless times, and Emily got it in her head from the beginning that the fundamentals of yoga were involved. When it became clear the ladies would apply that discipline to their practices, David and Finn excluded themselves. They would not partake of the morning and afternoon routine of breathing, screaming, stretching, and meditating, to which Maité and Emily had subscribed with fervor.

Every night before she dropped off to sleep, Maité meditated on Nahia and usually succeeded in bringing the faery into her dreams. During those nights, she picked Nahia's brain about setting up a consistent method to channel energy. It gradually sank in, until one morning, Maité woke up dazzled having had an epiphany: *Channeling energy is as easy* and as hard *as visualizing a series of steps and executing them in the same order, every time.*

"First, I see a silver spark, which for some reason starts in my chest," Maité said to Emily one afternoon.

"Like in your heart?" Emily said tilting her head.

The color rose to Maité's cheeks, a sure indicator of how awkward she felt, yet she nodded briskly and plowed through the steps she had come up with. "Then I see another spark, and another, until every cell in my body glitters. This is how I picture the energy inside me. Then I see each point of light spiral in every direction until they concentrate right here," Maité said, placing the palm of her hand over her solar plexus.

"When all the energy from my head, limbs, and every part in between is tangled up and buzzing right there, I tell it to relax and sync into an even pulse, like large wings flapping, the way Nahia taught me. Then I see me at my destination. Or if I want to shrink or return to my normal height, I tell myself how tall I am," she said, searching Emily's eyes as if for approval, knowing she had to overcome her insecurity if she would ever gain the confidence to succeed.

Emily reached across the table and squeezed Maité's hand. "You have to believe it, M," she said with her usual ability to hone in on the core problem.

Maité's shoulders sagged. "I know—believing is seeing."

"What's the problem?" Emily said, sounding rather stern, "Sorry, M, but you can't have flown out of the upstairs window with a faery, been to a Faery Queen's room, and seen a family tree you never knew you had, where you find not one, but *two* faeries in your lineage, and *not* believe! That was just a few days ago, but if that's not enough, let's take a minute to remember what you saw and did seven years ago."

"I *know!*" Maité repeated, blinking away the tears pooling in her eyes but unable to confess the root cause of her doubts—the dead unicorn, and Nahia proposing to *make* a new one. How could it be done? She was sure Emily's head would explode at the mere mention of it, but then she would regroup and things could go one of two ways: Emily might binge-read *Frankenstein* and be ready to follow Nahia into the unknown. Or she could laugh herself silly over such fiction. Wouldn't complete disbelief resonate more with Maité's own feeling on the subject?

Were the three stones really the eyes and heart of a once living unicorn? And how were they to be turned back into a whole, magical creature again? She must ask Nahia to explain herself. Or she should at least try to recover the conviction she'd experienced at the Realm—she hadn't doubted then; she had felt the magical influence inside of her. *Why can't I just believe?*

Aintza let out a raspy cough, interrupting Maité's tortured inner dialogue. Maité and Emily turned toward the baby monitor on the counter and waited to hear if the baby would settle back down.

"That sounds awful, but it does seem like it's clearing," Emily said to Maité, who kept staring at the monitor.

A whimper, a bout of wheezy coughing, and Maité stood up. Emily followed her out of the kitchen and up the stairs to the nursery. "It's been three days already, if she's not better by tomorrow, I'm taking her to the doctor," Maité declared.

"I guess the good news is she doesn't have a fever," Emily said reasonably.

They tiptoed into the nursery and watched Aintza from afar. The cough was an obvious discomfort but apparently not enough to fully wake her. The bout calmed and she settled down, breathing through a stuffy nose.

"It has to be some kind of virus," Maité whispered as they retreated out of the baby's room. "Who knows what's blowing out there in that crazy wind. And stuffed up as she is, she can't be getting a decent rest."

Emily grimaced. "I know, I hate it when I can't breathe through my nose, especially at night."

Maité installed a humidifier in the nursery, coated Aintza's back and chest with mentholated cream, and gave her teaspoons of cough syrup, to no avail. The stuffiness and coughing didn't worsen or improve over the next three days. Dismayed, she and Emily took the baby to the pediatrician, who after a thorough examination left them more frustrated than when they got there.

"She said it's a flu-like virus that's been going around, and we should keep up what we're doing to relieve the symptoms. Basically, let the thing run its course," Maité whispered to David that evening while Aintza dozed on his chest, looking pathetic.

"I guess that's all we can do—although maybe we should try your mom's red onion cough syrup. She said nothing worked better for you when you were little," David suggested in the spirit of leaving no stone unturned.

"Maybe," Maité said, feeling the baby's forehead with the back of her hand.

Aintza shuddered drowsily, her breathing a disturbing, phlegm-plagued rattle.

CHAPTER 31

MAITÉ

LEARNING TO FAERY

By the next morning, the winds had died down and, as if to confirm the doctor's theory, Aintza awoke noticeably decongested. Flooded with relief, Maité put away the onion syrup she'd made, just in case, and her thoughts returned to shape-shifting practice, determined to put her discussions with Emily to the test.

After Aintza went down for her nap, the four of them gathered in the spacious family room looking self-conscious. Maité removed a vase and a couple of knickknacks from the marble table before she sat on it, legs crossed like a pretzel. With an awkward grin, because she knew she made an unusual centerpiece, Maité eyed the others who occupied the chair and loveseat facing her.

"Yup—totally weird, people, but this is happening . . ." Emily said and everyone seemed to loosen up. David eased back in his chair while Finn squeezed Emily's hand and held it.

Maité grinned nervously, seeming to get a renewed understanding of how alien this must be to them—and for that matter, to her as well. Were they going to add this level of magic to their lives? Could house cleaning, doctor's appointments, careers, *really* be interspersed with weekend flights to a hidden Faerie Realm? Could shape-shifting be incorporated to mundane routines like changing outfits and grocery shopping?

For the first time, Maité saw her husband's apprehension, and Emily and Finn's uneasiness like a blatant, brownish haze hanging about them, and wondered if she was emitting her own fog too. Maité detected a fleeting glance exchanged between Emily and Finn; it seemed to say, *Our friend has gone over the edge.* It didn't lift her spirits much. When Maité met David's eyes for a few seconds, an understanding seemed to pass between them about an irrevocable separation. The implications momentarily neutralized her—*what is he saying?* Did he believe their genetic differences would divide them forever?

Maité thought, *Yes. That must be how he feels.* Otherwise, why had he been so surprised when her first visit to the Realm turned out to be only overnight? It was as if he had expected her to be gone for good. She sat up straighter, placed her hands, palms up, over her knees and took a deep breath, determined to prove to her husband her ancestry would not split them up.

"So . . . What I want is to change my size—I want to be a foot tall," Maité said.

"Proportionate," David interjected, "you want to change your size proportionately."

"OK—and the rest of us need to visualize her already short, she will have to do all the work of ordering her energies around, but it will help if we picture her reduced," Emily said bossily.

Before she closed her eyes, Maité saw the three of them lean toward her in concentration. The corners of her mouth quivered upward and she began the process she'd described to Emily. A single spark pulsated to the beat of her heart. Now, to multiply it . . . .

The minutes piled on slowly, making her aware of the heat coursing through her. She considered it an encouraging sign, although the wry thought of it being just a natural, nervous reaction *did* cross her mind.

Maité tightened her core and doubled over again, straining to bring on the height reduction, convinced she'd done it because her folded legs were tingling. Like before, she opened one eye, saw she was still at eye level with the others, and stubbornly straightened her back to try again.

"I'm not sure, but it looks to me as if you're not focusing," Emily whispered, not twenty minutes into the fruitless attempts.

"I swear I am," Maité cried, brushing her hair away from her sweaty face and feeling hot all over. "But my legs are falling asleep and it's distracting," she said, scooting to the edge of the table and sitting properly, with her feet on the floor.

"You said Nahia helped you by putting her palm over your belly," David said. Maité nodded, slightly arching her back and putting her hand over her stomach.

"Yeah, your solar plexus," Emily added while Finn grabbed the notebook she'd dropped on the rug.

"Let's take a look in here," Finn said, leafing through Emily's notes until he found what he was looking for. "Here we go—the third chakra at the solar plexus is all about who you are: your personal power, your confidence, your will power—the power to transform and harness energy," he said, looking expectantly at Maité.

"That's exactly what I'm focusing on!" Maité glared at him, wondering what she'd missed and thinking, suddenly troubled, she might be doing it all wrong. *Emily's yoga lectures the past few days can't have been for nothing,* she thought, frustrated.

"Let's just keep trying until Aintza wakes up—it hasn't even been a half hour yet, and I'm sure you'll start making progress very soon," David coaxed.

"OK," Maité said, giving her husband a grateful look and squaring her shoulders, ready to try again.

The strenuous efforts that followed went from frantic visualizations to a silent struggle to overcome mounting insecurities. If she could only replace them with confidence. But Maité kept floundering in a swell of doubts, and by the time Aintza's cooing noises reached her through the baby monitor, she was good and dejected.

Maité glanced at the still form of David, asleep beside her. She sighed and stared at the ceiling again. *Am I just not ready for this, is it too soon?* No—she had managed shape-shifting already; Nahia said she hadn't helped, and the magical powers of the Realm hadn't contributed either. She, Maité, had the power inside her. It had come to her from two royal ancestors who'd shared their magical DNA.

Restless to the point of irritation, and having decided to meditate (and practice on her own) by the pool on the fourth floor, she kissed David's shoulder and climbed soundlessly out of bed. Maité felt as if she were back at school, with a surprise test sprung on her. She groped in the dark for fragments of wisdom she hadn't realized would be so critical at this point in her life—she wished she'd taken up yoga seriously and been as devoted about it as Emily had been for years.

Maité paced along the edge of the pool assailed by self-deprecating thoughts mingled with Emily's earlier counsel. She shook her head irritably. *If I judge and criticize myself I'll be depleting my third chakra, and there goes my will power,* she berated herself. *I need a balanced solar plexus chakra—how else will I be able to really value myself? I have to be confident in what I do, I have to love and accept myself. It is OK to express power, and I can direct my own life!*

Maité wrung her hands anxiously, getting a first glimpse of her deficient self-esteem. It angered her to think she'd been so unconscious of it up until then. She thought her doubts and insecurities had always been within the scope of normal, but tonight she saw that by believing in that normalcy, she had in fact become more insecure.

I have to unlearn it all, she thought, daunted by the enormous task before her. What did it matter if, as Nahia said, she had the tools she needed to succeed, but she couldn't unlock the toolbox? Even though she wholeheartedly wished she could.

"I believe in myself, damn it," she muttered, and her own voice, though quiet, startled her in the silence. Maité stopped pacing.

Through the glass dome, the light of the moon sparkled on the still water of the pool. She took a deep breath and quieted herself—her hand rested over her belly. Something Maité hadn't felt before had started. *Could it be?* She closed her eyes to isolate the deep fluttering inside, at a loss for what exactly had triggered it, but she dared not get sidetracked to figure it out.

Don't stop, she thought over and over, refusing to open her eyes in case it broke her focus.

The fluttering strengthened and soon became a deafening heartbeat, at her throat and in her ears. *That's more like it*, she thought, ecstatic—how had she ever confused her legs falling asleep with this? But she must not dwell on it too much or it might stop. And in any case, another happy thought occurred to her: the new sensation was different than when Nahia had triggered it.

Nahia's intervention felt like large flapping wings—an eagle taking off. This felt like a hummingbird had been set off in her belly. As soon as she pictured it clearly, her insides trilled with the frantic beat of wings. Could this be *her*, developing her own style, her own path?

Something solid pressed on top of Maité's head; shocked, she opened her eyes. She had floated upward over the pool until she was bumping against the dome. She didn't know how she kept her wits about her, but in the fraction of a second it took to see herself crashing into the pool, she also glimpsed an open window and saw herself flying out of the building instead.

The thought and the deed were instantaneous.

The cool night air struck her and in the next moment, she'd turned her body due east, not sparing a thought to whether or not she was full-sized or reduced. All her energies were focused on envisioning Paloma's pond and getting herself there.

The flight seemed to take mere seconds. Maité zipped across Moon Dancer Lake and over the forest, anticipating a rough landing.

Quicker than expected, brittle branches slashed her arms and face as she plummeted from the sky. *Shit!* Maité had aimed for the small clearing by the mighty oak, but clipped the edge of the forest instead. She hit the ground hard, dropping and rolling haphazardly, like some parody of a fire drill. Maité got on all fours and stood up cautiously, as if checking nothing was broken. Satisfied she was still in one piece, she tramped onto the thin blanket of morning glory beneath the oak, breathless and with her insides still vibrating.

There was no doubt in Maité's mind—she'd gotten herself there faster than Nahia had. She dissolved into laughter thinking back to her frenzied departure; she had flashed out of the María Celeste in such a state of panic over breaking her concentration that she had paid no attention to form or speed. Maité's laugh attack redoubled as she pictured herself hurtling through the air in complete disarray, screaming the whole way.

She was startled into silence, however, by two floating turquoise orbs, eerily iridescent and staring at her from between the knobby branches of the oak.

CHAPTER 32

INCOMPLETE TRUTHS

Unable to sleep, Nahia wandered out of her chamber and drifted over the dimly lit gardens in Handi Park, wondering if she'd eaten something that made her restless. She hadn't seen Maité in dreams in over three days and was worried Aintza's cold might have developed into something serious. Nahia hovered over the jasmine shrub, momentarily struck by a horribly cold thought: was she losing sleep over the baby not being healthy enough for the solstice ritual?

"I couldn't sleep either."

"My stars!" Nahia yelped, startled out of her ruminations by a husky whisper. "What are you doing here?" she demanded.

Sendoa's silver aura glittered mischievously. "I told you—I fancied a stroll because I couldn't sleep either."

"Fine, but did you have to hide and jump out at me like that?" Nahia complained, irritated by the prickly adrenaline still spraying her insides.

"I wasn't hiding. I've been sitting here for a few minutes, and I actually thought you had seen me," he replied.

"Well, I didn't."

"Then tell me what's on your mind? You're definitely distracted."

Nahia quirked her brows, thought better of keeping quiet, and launched into what was troubling her. "Am I unfeeling and heartless if there is only one way to do what I must? I *have* to do what my mother said, and there is no choice in the matter, for me or for Maité!"

Sendoa's humorous expression drooped. He began drifting along the pebbled lane, and Nahia fell in beside him. "I don't think you're heartless. I think you care very much—I know you love Maité and her baby as if they were Zorione and Mireya all over again."

Two fat tears trickled down Nahia's cheeks, which she quickly wiped off. "Sometimes I think it was just yesterday that I had Zori with me, and Mireya and the others," Nahia sniffled, not caring if her crying gave away the uproar her feelings were in. "I feel so close to them, as if my mind and heart are chained to all those girls, and maybe closer to Maité, because we've shared so much, even if it was mostly in dreams.

"And my interest in Aintza *isn't* just because of what must happen in five weeks; it is also because she is my granddaughter and Maité loves her, and because she—actually *we*—have to accept making a sacrifice no mother should ever have to make."

Sendoa, who had been listening quietly, reached out and tucked a loose curl behind her ear and grazed her cheek. "Are you wishing there was a way you could leave your latest children untouched in this affair?"

"How am I to tell Maité what must happen with Aintza?" Nahia paused, momentarily dazed to find herself outside of Handi Park. She'd been so caught up in telling her troubles, she hadn't noticed they'd exited. Making a quick decision to visit Paloma's pond and the two graves at the foot of the oak, she continued in that direction. "Maité won't accept it without a fight, no matter how excited she is about her ancestry."

Sendoa nodded gloomily, making Nahia feel grateful for a friend she could siphon her worries to, and guilty at the same time—how selfish of her to involve him when there was nothing he could do to help.

They wended silently under dappled moonlight and between dusty boughs. As they entered the clearing by the pond, Nahia caressed the trunk of the mighty oak, where now rested not only Paloma's but Calisto's remains too. Dragging her fingers over the rough surface, she rose to one of the lower limbs and settled on her favorite crooked branch. Leaning against the trunk, she watched Sendoa pace away and back toward her.

"We all have a job to do here," Sendoa said. Nahia strained to make out his expression but had no luck through his silver aura and the leaves obscuring his face at the farthest end of the branch. "And while some of us might have flexibility with ours, you do not."

Nahia bristled, "I don't see that—why should that be?"

"Your job is to be queen, simple as that. The blood tie between you and Oihana is closer than—"

Nahia had risen from the crook of the branch ready to oppose, when something flashed out of the sky like a shooting star, emitting a short oath. The sound of branches cracking immediately followed. "Maité?"

Nahia descended from the branch to see better. Indeed, Maité was crawling around, laughing riotously. The faery allowed a brief glimmer of her aura to make her presence known and to gloss over the clutter of mixed sensations—delight, foreboding, pride. Sendoa's aura dimmed guardedly but he did not leave.

"I made it," Maité cried out excitedly looking up at Nahia. The faery grinned, won over by the girl's radiant satisfaction. "I didn't think I would be able to, but I did," Maité said breathlessly as she slapped dust off her flannel pajama pants and picked pine needles out of her hair.

"Just as soon as you decided you could, I'm sure," Nahia observed, floating level with Maité's face. "Looks like you had some trouble with the shape-shifting."

"What?" Maité said as if shocked by the news she'd managed even a degree of it.

"It looked like you had shrunk to about half your size, but when you landed and fell to your knees, you distended to your normal height—it looked *involuntary.*"

"Totally involuntary! It must've been a wild reflex because I didn't even know I'd made myself smaller," Maité admitted with a nervous giggle.

"A degree of style will come in time," Nahia assured her, choosing to stay at faery height. "It is both remarkable and encouraging you are unlocking your potential so quickly."

"I was so excited to surprise you, and I thought I might not be able to even though I'd been practicing with Emily. Also, with Aintza being so sick, I wasn't sure I could get away."

Nahia swallowed hard but didn't comment.

"Emily and Finn are going back home in two days, but I wanted to tell you I won't be here on the twenty-first like I promised. I want to wait for Aintza to be fully recovered—I'm sure she will be in the next week. The thing is, I want to bring her with me, and we'll stay and help until it's time for the solstice. David can come and stay on the weekends. What do you think?"

A whole apple seemed to have wedged itself in Nahia's throat. She thought she saw a faint glimmer of silver light up the leaves above their heads and fancied Sendoa sensing her distress. Things were lining up as if commanded by an unseen force. In a few days' time, Basajaun and the magical vessel would be in the Realm, awaiting the solstice and its full moon.

How do I tell Maité what fate awaits Aintza? How will I bear the hate and betrayal I'm bound to see in her eyes when I force her to become the fearsome defender of her daughter?

Refusing to look Maité in the eye, Nahia smiled grimly. "It would be delightful. I'd like nothing better than for you and your family to claim your place in Handi Park."

Scarcely had the words left Nahia's mouth when Maité hugged her affectionately. She stiffened at first but quickly gave in and returned the embrace. "I want you to know that I love you like a daughter."

Maité drew back and peered at the faery. "I love you too—" she said, but then her face split into a huge grin. "I love you more, because in a roundabout way, you are my mother, but also a grandmother, and sister, and cousin—you could be my aunt, too!"

Nahia laughed, "And don't forget, I'm your faery godmother as well."

As Nahia and Celeste had done centuries before, Maité walked a wide circuit around the pond, with Nahia perched on her shoulder, while the faery recounted her first trip to the United States, to bestow upon her a Cradle Gift.

Midnight had come and gone. The moon no longer brightened their path and a cold mist hovered over the ground. Although Nahia had tried to diminish the dread and dismay she'd experienced at the hands of Ederne on that adventure, Maité, who'd been listening intently, picked up on it.

"As much as it cost you," Maité said, tilting her head toward Nahia, "I'm really thankful for my Cradle Gift. I wouldn't have been able to do what I did without it."

Nahia kissed her. "It's getting late."

"I know, and I need to get back. I'm so sorry I won't be here for another week, but even then, we'll still have three weeks before the solstice—did you know the last time the summer solstice and a full moon coincided was in 1967?"

"I know—that was the year my mother died and when Catalina married your grandfather."

"Really?" Maité's stormy eyes sparkled, reflecting Nahia's aura. "I'll have to look more closely at my mom's family tree."

"Would you like me to take you back to town?"

"No—no, I really need to practice, thank you so much, though," Maité replied but then added, "Maybe a little help to fully reduce my height?"

"Of course," Nahia said. She soared off Maité's shoulder and descended to the height of her midriff, where she reached out and pressed her palm above

Maité's solar plexus. The moment the energy was discharged, Maité yelped and crunched involuntarily. When she straightened up she was already a reduced version of herself, bobbing in front of the faery.

"Will you be able to get yourself back to normal?" Nahia asked, her aquamarine eyes twinkling full of humor.

Maité nodded.

"Trying not to talk?"

Maité nodded again.

"Because you don't want to break your concentration?"

Emphatic head bobbing.

"Be on your way then," Nahia said as Maité closed her eyes.

The execution was swift—Nahia heard a clipped gasp and then Maité was gone.

"You didn't tell her," Sendoa whispered, so close to Nahia's ear she recoiled as if scalded. Her aura emitted a powerful deflecting gust, which sent Sendoa sprawling sideways.

"Stars in the sky," Nahia cried, with no traces left of a smile.

His aura pulsated with contained laughter over having startled her, even as he righted himself from a near hit with a withered elderberry bush.

"Yes. It was cowardly to keep quiet," Nahia admitted, glaring at him as he advanced toward her. "But you heard Maité; she's coming in a few days—*with* the baby, to help with preparations."

After a few seconds, Nahia had to look away from Sendoa and his eyes full of silent reproach.

Chapter 33

Maité

Unexpected in the

Aspen Grove

A swooping, hollow sensation filled Maité's belly the moment Nahia took her hand away. She bobbed for a couple of seconds, stressing over weight scattering and height reduction —*I must learn to do it on my own*. The familiar hummingbird wings began to vibrate inside her, calling her to attention. "Be on your way then," was the last thing Nahia said, and Maité closed her eyes.

A crisp image of the fourth floor at the María Celeste overtook her. She shot up above the canopy of trees and then, as if pulled by a great magnet, she flashed helplessly west.

Maité blew in through the same window she'd exited a few hours before. The temperature of the pool had noticeably warmed the air, making her realize how chilled she was. Two questions popped into her mind: where to put down, and how to return to her normal height. She stalled above the pool, her brain hiccupping between a lounge chair and the pebbled walkway surrounding the pool. Should she sit on one, or stand on the other? At either one, she meant to be five feet seven inches tall.

The instant's hesitation thinned out her focus. She plunked into the water, but by the time she kicked back and her head broke through the surface, she had stretched to her full height. Maité pulled herself out of the water and dripped over to the changing room. She peeled off her wet clothes, wrapped herself in a warm towel, and headed downstairs.

It was near four o'clock in the morning when she climbed into bed next to David without waking him. She sighed and closed her eyes, exhausted. She drifted off, still feeling the slight pressure of Nahia sitting on her shoulder, the elusive scent of gardenia clinging to her hair.

The faery's eyes looked like two pools of Caribbean blue water in the blinding midday sun. Groggily, Maité wondered where the moonlight had gone and how did it get to be noon when she couldn't remember dawn. But Nahia laughed from her spot on Maité's shoulder, her eyes growing wider. *Impossible*, thought Maité, *how like water they look.*

"Dive in," Nahia said and Maité squinted into her eyes, failing to even detect a pupil. Before she knew it, she'd been sucked into Nahia's aquamarine irises.

Maité's heart kicked wildly in her chest. She didn't hit a white sandy bottom as she had expected; instead she was shooting through a winding water tube, outside of which raged a formidable lightning storm. The thought of optic nerves and synapses flitted vaguely across her consciousness. In a remote corner of her mind she understood she was going deep into Nahia's memories.

At last, through the crystalline water and the terrific fireworks, Maité stopped at a garish moment in time—the whole forest had stopped to mourn the immobile figure. The noble heart of the unicorn had stopped beating. Riveted, Maité watched Nahia deftly separate the tissue around the eyes and the heart, until the glittering organs floated outside their rightful body. No birds chirping, no breeze rustling leaves, only Nahia's singsong voice trapped among the trees. Maité shuddered, realizing she understood the words.

O Basajaun
A comet your passage has been
Fleeting yet magnificent in this life's din,
You leave us with the memory of your light.
And I beg of thee, a gift before you take that final flight.
Your eyes, that your vision may again be carried out
Your heart, that your love may flourish eternal, beyond any doubt,
O Basajaun.

Maité tossed in her bed. The moment of waking loomed—she recoiled from the hairy limb she brushed with her foot. *David's leg*, she thought sleepily and rolled away on her side to continue dreaming. The forest, the dead unicorn, and Nahia's song were gone, and now she saw and heard Oihana, the Faery Queen.

"To recover from what has been done, the Realm must go dormant for seven cycles of seven years—the Keeper of the Forest must be brought back only then—Basajaun will be ready for a *new magical body*—one will enter our dimension forty-nine years hence."

The weight of David's arm, draped over her waist, woke her. Maité rolled and snuggled closer to him. Oihana's words receded to a remote corner of her brain suffused in fragrant candlelight.

"Good morning," he said.

The baby monitor crackled and Aintza coughed. "Morning." Maité gave him a peck on the cheek and they both got out of bed.

Over breakfast, predawn dream completely forgotten, Maité gushed about her accomplishment to David, Emily, and Finn, and she delighted in their surprise and congratulations—David hadn't even noticed she'd been gone.

"Good for you!" Emily clapped her on the back, "because, really, how embarrassing to be part faery, a royal one even, and not be able to fly."

Aintza seemed to have borrowed her mother's radiance and looked healthier than she had as of late, which amplified the sense of well being throughout the household, at least for a few days.

"We're lucky sevens this trip," Emily said, shaking the wrinkles from a T-shirt before folding it. She and Finn were flying back home that night so they were doing laundry.

"Seriously, did all this stuff fit in one suitcase when you came out?" Maité teased.

"Mm-hmm. Well, Finn has his own," Emily said dismissively and added, "When I checked us in this morning, they gave me the seat assignment for the last leg of the trip. Now all three flights match. We're on row seven all the way. How weird is that?"

Maité laughed, "The universe says you'll have no turbulence for sure, and you'll get there on time."

Mention of sevens caused an instant recall of the dream she'd had a few days ago, and in the middle of folding clothes, Oihana's words slid into Maité's mind. *Seven cycles of seven years—a new magical body—one will enter this dimension forty-nine years hence.*

"Are you OK?"

"Yeah, sure." Maité averted her eyes, sifting through the basket, intent on finding a lone sock's match. She thought back to Nahia's reply when asked where they were in relation to the forty-nine years. "We're already there," she had said. But what was the magical body Oihana mentioned? Nahia hadn't said anything about that.

Troubled, but unable to think it through amid the chaos of friends departing, baby under the weather, and a working husband, Maité put the question out of her mind, meaning to revisit it soon.

Emily and Finn flew back home, leaving the María Celeste emptier and devoid of Emily's lively chatter. Maité might have thought it peaceful had it not been for Aintza's renewed and worsening symptoms.

Once again, Maité had neglected her Lucid Dreaming with Nahia; she told herself it was because of the stress of Emily leaving and Aintza relapsing, but the more she thought about it, the more she caught herself dwelling on Oihana's words—had there been an ominous negativity? *Yes*, something to do with the magical body.

Her thoughts flitted from one possibility to another without settling on any one. *It has to be a faery's been born in Handi Park, or is about to. It could be a horse, or a deer or some other creature already living in the Realm, couldn't it?*

Cold and barbed, a suspicion slipped into her belly—hadn't Aintza been born in 2016, exactly forty-nine years after the unicorn had been slain? Wasn't Aintza a partly magical body?

"No," Maité hissed. "Nahia wouldn't dream of it, and I'm a vile betrayer for even thinking it."

"Did you say something?" David walked into the room holding the baby.

"No—no," she said, rising from the couch to greet them. "My goodness, she still reeks of onions," Maité exclaimed after kissing Aintza—they had resorted to Alba's remedy after all.

David grimaced. "Red onions are potent, but I can't believe they've not gotten out of her system yet. We discontinued the stuff twenty-four hours ago."

"And we only gave her two teaspoons—this is so frustrating," Maité grumbled, feeling Aintza's neck and forehead for a fever. She had rushed her to the pediatrician the day before to show the doctor the welts outlined with pustules on Aintza's belly, worried about how quickly they seemed to be spreading to the chest and neck. The pediatrician told them to stop the homemade syrup at once, insisting the baby had chicken pox. She claimed the virus could mutate and not always appear as little blisters.

"Pox *could* look like this," the doctor had assured Maité with a twitching nostril, while touching Aintza's welts with gloved fingers. "Bathe her with oatmeal soap—should clear up in about a week," had been her dismissive recommendation.

But Aintza showed no signs of improving. In fact, she was deteriorating right before her parents' eyes. Her cheeks weren't nearly as plump as they used to be, there were dark circles under her eyes, the sweet timbre of her voice seemed to have deepened for good, and most disturbing of all, wherever a welt dried up, it left behind a patch of leathery skin that looked depressingly permanent.

Desperate for fresh air and sunshine, after an entire week of blustery spring showers, Maité bundled herself up and packed Aintza into her stroller, where she had made a nest of blankets to keep her warm. She raised the hood to protect her from the sun, lest it further damage her skin, and mother and daughter set off.

Maité crossed the street at the intersection to walk along the Urumea River, looking forward to a long stroll, possibly all the way to Paseo de la Concha. But she hadn't gone a block when two men assaulted her.

They charged. She instinctively bent over the stroller to shield Aintza, but one of the men grabbed her by the hair and yanked her head back. She saw the flash of a blade and a scream gurgled in her throat. The weight of the backpack lifted—he'd sliced off the straps and relieved her of it. One last tug of her hair and then a rough release nearly sent her sprawling. She righted herself and heard their footfalls on the sidewalk racing away. Through eyes full of tears she checked Aintza—besides her skin condition, she was unharmed.

The attack had lasted thirty seconds, and as she caught her breath the uncontrollable shaking began. Aintza started to fuss and Maité wanted to cry out, but to what end? The men were gone. She pulled her cell phone from her back pocket and called David. He told her to go to the police immediately and he would meet them there.

"I got here as quickly as I could—how are you?" David hugged and kissed her and hugged her again.

She had already given her statement by the time David arrived at the station. "I'm fine—really, and so is Aintza," Maité assured him when he hugged her a third time.

"Were you able to describe them?"

"I did the best I could—the whole thing was so quick. All I had in the backpack were diapers and a bottle—my ID and a credit card were in my pocket, so they didn't even get anything of value."

"Bastards!" David said through gritted teeth, his gaze drifting anxiously over his wife's face.

"What is it?" Maité asked, puzzled. David's anger had turned to sudden dismay.

He reached over and tucked a loose strand of hair behind her ear. "You cut your hair," he said mournfully.

"What?" Maité exclaimed, turning her head and frantically reaching back. The thick ponytail hanging down her back had been severed. Comprehension dawned like the replay of a desecration; with the last tug, the attacker had sliced her hair below the band and left Maité with a shoulder-length mane, at best. "He cut my hair. One of those guys cut my hair! Why?"

David shook his head in mute outrage.

They amended Maité's statement to include the last, unsettling aspect of the attack, and were assured the case would be investigated. Maité and David exchanged a resigned look. No valuables had been stolen, a haircut (regardless of how defiled she felt) wasn't considered *bodily harm*, and they had no hope of cracking the attackers' mysterious motivation.

They returned home dejected and perturbed; Aintza, unnaturally tranquil in spite of the leathery, painful-looking stripes crisscrossing her body. Maité carried her to the nursery, aware she didn't want to look at her own daughter or hold her closer than absolutely necessary. She told herself it was a natural feeling, especially after such a violent experience—she was bound to return to normal in a couple of days. If only Aintza would too!

Maité lay awake in bed that night, and she could tell David was too. Like her, he seemed intent on not speaking. The bitter, syrupy silence coated her mouth and stomach; how was she to rinse it off? It discouraged her and filled her with distress bordering on physical pain.

The rims of her eyes burned with tears. She wiped them off and sniffled, thinking she might get herself a glass of water, when like a star twinkling through the mist, a happy thought occurred to her. What if Aintza didn't have chicken pox at all? What if she'd been suffering from some bizarre hybrid-faery condition all along? And Nahia could probably fix her hair too!

I shouldn't have delayed my return to the Realm. I should get myself and the baby there right away. "Ugh! I'm such an idiot," Maité grunted, slapping her forehead and startling David, who rolled toward her.

"What's happened?"

Maité propped herself on her elbow, facing him in the shadowy room. "I think I should . . . ."

The baby monitor on the bedside table crackled to life and a croaky sound, unlike any they'd heard to date, broke through, flashing a bolt of alarm up Maité's spine. She and David sprung out of bed and darted across the hall to the nursery. In the gloom of a single night-light, terror-stricken, Maité saw a small shape sitting inside the crib—Aintza hadn't learned to do that yet.

Maité started toward it, determined to pull her baby out of the crib, but David gripped her elbow. "Something's in there with her," he hissed.

Maité shook her head and whispered urgently, "I can't make out if Aintza's in there. Can you see her?"

The figure in the crib turned its head, bit by bit, and stared right at them through ghoulish, gleaming eyes.

"Shit!" Maité and David swore in unison. He let go of her arm and flipped on the light switch.

A couple of frantic blinks were enough to adjust to the light. A quick glance told Maité Aintza wasn't there, not even shoved into a corner of the crib. She squeezed David's arm and together they inched closer. Craning, Maité looked inside—only Aintza's pajamas lay crumpled there.

"*Eraman nazazu etxera, s'il vous plaît,*" the creature wheezed in both Basque and French, making Maité and David jump back, aghast. *Take me home, please.*

They exchanged a startled look and for a moment could do nothing more than stare wearily at the thing in the crib. It sat with short, bony legs stretched out in a V—a wooden creature with knobby joints and cracked skin. Its eyes bulged (Maité tilted her head doubtfully and yes, one was bigger than the other, and neither had lashes), and each rattling breath blew out of the creature's chest as if through a flute stuffed with mucus. The head shaped like a coconut had a few twine-looking strands of hair sticking out like wire, and Maité could see no protruding features such as a nose or lips.

"Oh my God. It's wearing Aintza's diaper!" Maité exclaimed rounding on David. "Chicken pox, my ass," she swore, a second time in less than five minutes.

"What—what do you mean?"

"This *is* Aintza—look, she's wearing her diaper. I think she has some weird faery illness, and I know Nahia can fix it."

David stared at her, thunderstruck. His eyes swiveled toward the crib just as Maité reached in and snatched the baby, but held her at arm's length.

"You are home already," she assured the unrecognizable baby, trying to disguise the revulsion she felt.

The gash that was supposed to be a mouth opened, letting loose the hideous rattle again. "*S'il vous plait.*"

"I don't believe this is Aintza," David shook his head vehemently. "She's not even four months old—as of today she hadn't learned to talk yet, and tonight all of a sudden she can speak Basque and French? I'm not buying it!"

Maité paused, casting a suspicious glance at the sturdy body she held by the armpits. "That *is* weird," she admitted, lowering it back into the crib. The thing blinked with a faint clack of its eyelids and then peered at them resignedly. "But the welts Aintza had, they looked so leathery, and they were getting rougher to the touch. They could've turned into this, no?" she speculated, motioning to the reddish-brown, bare chest.

"I guess they could, but I don't know—if that really is our baby, I'd be more likely to believe she's been shape-shifted."

Maité frowned, "The more reason I should have Nahia take a look at her."

"So what do we do? A mental-gram?"

Maité bit her lip. She had been deliberately avoiding dreams with Nahia for days, and now she would have to attempt it while only one of them was sleeping. "I'm going to try it. . . I guess it will be just like I did with you, years ago when I was trapped in the cave in Santa Clara and you came to rescue me."

After several attempts, however, Maité was forced to conclude she was too agitated to meditate properly. It was nearing two o'clock in the morning and desperation set in. "I'm going there, and I'm taking the baby with me."

"I'm not letting you out of my sight, and you're not doing this by yourself."

Maité thought it over quickly. She had no hope of shrinking David and the baby, much less fly them to the Realm, so Maité opted for the next best thing. She would call from the Aspen Grove near the old Citadel of Santillán, same as Alaia had done centuries before.

They dressed quickly, taking turns to watch Aintza. Maité picked her up again, but only to gingerly strap her into the car seat. "Are you sure about this?" David said, as he put the car in reverse, ready to pull out of their garage.

"You bet."

David backed the car out to the street and shut the automatic gate. "Who are you texting?"

Maité hit *send* on her mobile. "Em," she said. "I'm letting her know where we're going and why. She'll fill in the rest of the family if for some reason we're delayed."

They drove on near-empty streets and highways in silence broken only by the wheezy, labored breathing coming from the backseat. *Nahia will fix her,* Maité assured herself. The road became even more desolate as they left the suburban sprawl behind. They snaked through dark canyons, crossed misty valleys, and finally began their ascent to the mountains.

"So . . . Will any tree in the Aspen Grove do?" David said, interrupting the monotonous rumble of the car climbing in low gear.

"That's what Nahia said. I just have to make a gash on the trunk and tell it my message," Maité replied, eyes flicking nervously to David—she may as well be suggesting they mail a letter to Santa Claus.

"I guess that's the faery Interweb then."

Maité chuckled. "We should plant an Aspen Grove in our backyard and have Nahia link us to their network."

They both laughed, releasing some of their pent-up stress. Maité opened a bag of almonds to snack on, and their banter continued in that vein until they reached the summit. Soon they'd gone through the last pass, and the mountains opened up to Santillán valley. The stone walls of the Citadel gleamed in the waning moon. Maité leaned forward in her seat.

"I think the dark mass to the right of the wall might be the grove," she said eagerly.

"You might be right."

Streetlights and porch lights gleamed here and there as they passed the sleepy town in the direction Maité had pointed out. "I guess not even cows get milked at this hour," she said wryly. The digital clock on the dashboard read 4:22 and there were no signs of life out there.

Not one quarter of a mile from the Citadel, David maneuvered the car so the headlights hit the cluster of trees. Maité recognized the bleached, spotted trunks with the heart-shaped leaves right away. Aintza snored loudly in the car as Maité and David got out and stepped a few feet into the grove. He pulled out his Swiss Army knife and made a three-inch horizontal gash on the chosen tree.

Maité stepped forward and put her hands on the trunk as if she meant to slow dance with it. For a few seconds, she stood there quietly, trying to feel, she didn't know what, from the tree—a current of energy or something. But she only felt the rough, cool surface. Uncertain about the proper procedure, wondering how it would even work (she didn't know if there was a designated someone at the other end, listening at all hours of the day and night), she pressed her lips to the cut and began speaking.

"Nahia, something's wrong with my child. *Please* help us!"

CHAPTER 34

NOT AGAIN!

"I haven't heard from Maité in over a week," Nahia complained to Sendoa one deceptively sunny afternoon. The squally weather had finally let up, and after being cooped up for days in Handi Park, Nahia gladly shivered in the crisp chill, determined to take the fresher air aboveground. "Do you think the baby is getting worse?"

"I hope not," Sendoa said distractedly. He was focused on shaping the elderberry hedge with a series of complicated moves of his hands.

For several weeks, the troop had been scouting the Arboretum to refresh the landscape in preparation for the solstice. Nahia had to admit, the sustained rains had been great to wash off all the dust, even if she'd been forced to stay underground to keep dry. At the moment, everything looked green and vibrant, and for the first time in decades, Nahia glimpsed how magical it would all look again in only twenty more days.

Out of the corner of her eye, Nahia saw something move. In the fraction of a second it took for her to look properly, Sendoa let out a clipped growl. She whirled back in time to see him launched by an unseen force and crumple at the base of a tree. Nahia braced herself for the attack, but it didn't come. Instead, something caught her over the head and forced her to the ground—someone had cast a weighted net.

Perplexed, Nahia tried to stand but the weights lining the edges kept her in a stooped position. The sight of Sendoa's inert body sent shockwaves through her—she hoped more than knew he was breathing. Nahia struggled against the golden net, testing it, considering the best way to rip it apart and free herself.

"Don't be doing anything stupid now—you don't want to be breaking any promises."

Nahia froze. She recognized the coarse voice, and the odd warning clanged in her head for a few seconds, until she understood it. She pinched a section of the net between her fingers and found it wasn't rope or thread. Thin braids had been cleverly knotted to make the flexible latticework.

This cannot be. This can't happen to me twice! Nahia thought, staggered, yet she was certain the brute speaking to her and his partner (who had shown himself and was now kicking Sendoa's foot as if checking him for signs of life) had been present on the day Oihana had been mortally wounded, and also on the day the unicorn had been slain.

"That's right, little princess," the rough voice went on, "we know you won't harm that human, not even a hair on her head."

"Ha!" said the other one, and once started they couldn't stop their bark-like laughter.

Nahia stared horrified at the braids—*whose hair? Has to be Maité's. But how did they know?* "What have you done to her?" she demanded, letting go of the net and glaring at her captors, fully intending to extract a truthful answer with the force of her stare.

"Figured it out, have you? Well, you'll see."

Unexpectedly, he swooped down on Nahia. In one fluid motion he gathered the ends of the net and hoisted it over his shoulder like a sack. Nahia righted herself and poked her fingers through the latticework, holding on as his feet parted with the ground and he set off at a bumbling pace through the woods. The second thug brought up the rear; he leered unpleasantly at Nahia, and she glared right back. When she refused to look away, he poked her with a crooked stick, which Nahia dodged. They repeated the annoying exchange half a dozen times until, tired of getting poked in the back, Nahia's transport rounded on his partner and told him off.

They descended into a ravine, and although Nahia couldn't see where they were going, she recognized the landscape they passed. She knew the Realm like the back of her hand—they were headed for the swamplands, probably to the labyrinth of caves she and Celeste had often explored in their childhood.

The darkness suddenly enfolding them made the cold sunshine they left behind seem warmer by comparison. Nahia's eyes grew wide, adjusting to the gloom. She dispelled the illusion of her captor managing to move faster inside the labyrinth, reasoning their closeness to the dirt walls was a likely cause of the effect.

He moved as clumsily as ever; it had taken him an hour to get there. Nahia rolled her eyes, certain she would've made it in fifteen minutes.

Grasping the braids tightly, Nahia swayed against her captor's back, studying her surroundings. She detected a reddish glow illuminating the protruding roots above her—she guessed they were approaching a widened section of the tunnel in which a fire burned.

Soon the grumbling speech of a third thug reached her and Nahia pricked her ears, hoping for news of Maité. She gasped when she heard cooing noises instead. *What is happening?* Nahia wondered, caught unawares. *Do they have Maité and Aintza?*

As she had foreseen, they at last arrived at a wide space where a fire crackled. She took in the rustic furnishings as they passed, a cauldron dangling above the hearth, a table and chair, a makeshift curtain, either shielding something from view or dividing it from the rest of the area.

Her world spun and crashed all of a sudden. "Ugh!" Nahia righted herself again after her transport had whipped her off his shoulder and lobbed her on the dirt by the fire. The other brute watched her, sniggering. She glared at him.

"Where'd she go?" grumbled the one who had unloaded her unceremoniously, and one of the others answered with an unintelligible grunt.

Nahia coughed and wiped the dust off her eyes, wondering how dense they were—she was right there where that imbecile had slung her. She looked up to remark on it and through watering eyes she saw the curtain move aside. A fourth someone emerged, and Nahia's jaw dropped.

Chapter 35

Maité
A Mother's Nightmare

Maité stepped away from the tree, unsure what to expect. She looked at David and shrugged.

"What now?"

"I have no idea," Maité said. "Maybe we give it fifteen minutes?"

David paused mid-nod. "Or less," he said, pulling her toward him and pointing into the grove.

Maité peered through the tree trunks illuminated by the car's headlights. She saw a man approaching. He was broad-shouldered and gave the impression of having a muscular build beneath the loose pants and shirt Maité would have called loungewear. He gazed steadily at them as he wended through the grove, and she realized he was conveying at once a greeting and a reassurance of no harm meant.

"I heard your message," he said gruffly, stopping not three feet from her and David. "My name is Sendoa."

"I am Maité, and this is my husband, David." She curtseyed awkwardly in response to his bow. Beside her, David inclined his head. "Did Nahia send you? Why couldn't she come?"

A furrowed brow darkened Sendoa's expression. "Nahia has disappeared."

"What?" Maité gasped, fumbling for and grasping David's arm. He had flinched on hearing the news.

"Please permit me to take you into Handi Park where we will be safe, and I shall tell you what I know."

Maité and David exchanged a worried look. "Of course we'll go," Maité said, "We'll just get Aintza and—"

"We'll get the car into the woods, out of sight," David said, and Sendoa nodded.

"Well, this was unexpected—about Nahia, I mean," David said under his breath, pulling her by the hand toward the vehicle, away from Sendoa's ear.

"You're not kidding," Maité murmured, wondering if David blamed her—did he expect her to know what was going on?

They climbed in and drove a few yards to a copse they figured would provide sufficient cover. Maité unstrapped the sleeping baby, picked her up, and pressed her awkwardly to her chest. She couldn't get used to the creepy, solid feel of her. They locked the car and walked back to Sendoa, guided only by the silver glow he emitted and which they could see now the headlights had been shut off.

The faint clack of eyelids told Maité Aintza had awakened, and the slight turns of the coconut-shaped head meant she must be staring groggily about. Maité felt her tense up, as if on alert, realizing they were out of doors. She tightened her grip, fearful Aintza might wriggle out of her arms.

"Non gauden? Gara etxera?" croaked the creature when they'd reached Sendoa. He looked sharply at it, then threw a questioning glance from Maité to David.

"We don't know what's happened to her. . . she didn't even know how to speak yesterday, and all of a sudden, a few hours ago, she started talking in Basque," Maité rattled off anxiously.

"And in French," David added, "We thought maybe Nahia could set her right."

Full of mistrust, Sendoa eyed the thing in Maité's arms, who continued to ask "where are we?" and "am I home?"

"This is not your child," he declared in a perturbed voice, setting off alarms inside Maité. "It is a changeling."

Maité cricked her neck, whipping her head toward David—he was staring at Sendoa, jaw clenched. Unable to drop the creature but equally incapable of having contact with it, Maité scooted closer to her husband, holding the changeling at arm's length, offering it up to Sendoa.

Dozens of questions cluttered Maité's mind, some of the more prominent ones were: How long had she been caring for this thing believing it was her baby? Where was Aintza? Who was responsible?

The creature wriggled trying to free itself. The tips of its fingers felt like pencil erasers pinching Maité's forearms. Her nose wrinkled involuntarily. "What do I do?" she pleaded.

"Let it go," Sendoa said. "It will find its way back to wherever home is."

"But, are we sure?" David interjected before Maité could release the creature. "What if this *is* Aintza, only she's been shape-shifted or something."

"A changeling can be a number of things: a gnome, a troll, a wizened faery or even a piece of wood shape-shifted to look like the stolen child," Sendoa explained. "The charm lasts a few weeks at best, and from the looks of this one, it must've been swapped three weeks ago, not more than four," he said, shaking his head to discourage further argument from the duped parents.

David scowled at Sendoa but he didn't say any more.

"So what's this one?" Maité asked, dropping her glance to the creature she was still holding by the armpits. "Is it a piece of wood?"

"If it was, it wouldn't talk—my guess is it's a troll, and a very old one. Probably its family got tired of caring for it," Sendoa glowered.

The changeling wriggled more forcefully and Maité let it go, disgusted. As soon as it hit the ground, it scuttled away with an ungainly limp. "Sorry," Maité called after it, feeling guilty she may have hurt it. The creature disappeared into the grove and soon its grumbling complaints faded away too.

"Don't fret about it," Sendoa said of the changeling. "It's us I am worried about now, and we are not safe out in the open. Let me take you to Handi Park."

Maité grabbed David's hand while Sendoa performed a swift scattering of their weight, followed by a simultaneous height reduction. Besides a hoarse gasp he apparently couldn't repress, no other outward reaction came from David, not even when their feet left the ground and they bobbed, momentarily unaffected by gravity. Sendoa held out a tethering hand to Maité, which she took while tightening her grasp on David's with the other. Sendoa immediately pulled them above the grove and up the side of the steep mountain.

They traveled efficiently and in silence. Maité welcomed the chilly headwind, reflecting on how different Sendoa's confident style was compared to Nahia's breakneck approach and her own haphazard beginner's performance.

Recognizable landmarks flashed below—a waterfall, a lake—but Maité felt no inclination to remark, and she assumed the other two were as immersed as her in their own concerns. She wondered what Sendoa was to Nahia. Had she misinterpreted his grim expression when he told them Nahia had disappeared? Had it been the look of a tormented lover, or the look of an aggrieved subject?

Sendoa dipped into the vegetation, dragging Maité and David with him. She made out a clearing up ahead where sat a shadowy dome-like mass. She thought it might be the formal entrance to Handi Park, which Nahia had avoided on the eve of Aintza's christening. Could it really be like Sendoa said, her baby had been taken over three weeks ago?

Maité glanced at David—had he felt the gravitational shift too? An irresistible force, maybe Handi Park's tractor beam, sucked them into the tangled ivy mound with mind-blowing precision. Roots, vines, stems, all of it seemed to clear out of the way on their approach. In mere moments and without a scratch on them, they emerged at the top of a huge shaft carved with spiraling walkways. They descended right through the center of it to a grand entrance hall ten stories below.

A minor pause allowed Maité to register a circular hall with pebble-encrusted floor and a spring bubbling in a rectangular pool. They were surrounded by a series of doorways, each marked with a glowing lantern. The progression of color from one lantern to the next both pleased and suited Maité's structured mind. White blushed into pink, deepened to red, then warmed up to orange and yellow, only to cool off to green, blue, and lilac, and back to white.

The doorway marked with the sea-green lantern opened without anyone touching it, and Sendoa dragged them through it. The passage led to an archway beyond which sprawled a white sandy shore, and of all things to find underground, a replica of Bahía de la Concha.

Sendoa halted and gave back to Maité and David the weight he'd dispersed for the journey. They touched down on the sand and could do nothing but look around, openmouthed. "This is our Tablinum," Sendoa said, and recognition dawned on Maité—she'd read about it in *Faery Sight*. "Please make yourselves comfortable while I go summon the others." Sendoa motioned toward a cluster of chairs around the rectangular table on the boardwalk.

"Sorry—the others?" David asked.

"The six council members," Sendoa replied gloomily, "who in Nahia's absence must decide what's to be done."

Maité and David exchanged a wary glance. "Are you thinking what I'm thinking?" he whispered as soon as Sendoa was out of sight.

"If you're thinking it's crazy we've not had our baby for nearly a month, and we didn't know it, then yes," Maité said, but that was all they had time for.

Sendoa returned, accompanied by six other faeries—three females and three males. Maité didn't recognize any of them from the group she'd met seven years before. With a heavy heart she recalled so many had been destroyed by Ederne—only Amets had survived long enough to get her to safety. But Ederne had caught up with them in the end and destroyed him too.

"This is our troop's council," Sendoa said, causing the six members to bow or incline their heads. Maité and David mirrored them. "This is Celeste's descendant, Maité, and her husband David."

"We are glad you are here," said one of the males, whose eyes were a deep shade of green and who had shoulder-length hair streaked to match. Maité and David once again inclined their heads but they didn't comment. She wasn't sure yet how she felt about being there. The seven colorful faeries, who made Maité feel sadly monochromatic, approached the table and took their seats, motioning for her and David to take the remaining two.

Without preamble, Sendoa began speaking in a sober tone. "I have already informed the council, but to bring you two up to speed, I will say again, Nahia and I were attacked yesterday afternoon, while in the Arboretum."

Maité inched forward on her chair. David put his hand on her shoulder blade and rubbed it distractedly as he listened.

"I was knocked unconscious by an unseen force. When I came to, Nahia was gone. I inspected the area and surmised there'd been two attackers. I saw evidence of a scuffle, and it appeared a bundle, I assume Nahia, was dragged and hoisted, at which point they must've gone airborne, as there were no prints leaving the area in any direction."

"Do you think they've taken her somewhere within the Realm?" said one of the council members, a female.

"I have no idea in which direction they flew, but my guess is they *are* hiding in the Realm," Sendoa replied, rubbing his lower lip with his index finger as if something troubled him. His gaze shifted toward Maité, drawing the attention of the council to her. She glanced awkwardly around the table. "I will let her tell you what has happened to them."

Maité cleared her throat and in a voice shaking with emotion as much as nervousness she said, "Aintza, my daughter, is gone too." She proceeded to relate the whole tale, from when they thought she had a cold to a few minutes ago when Sendoa had identified the changeling.

As soon as she finished her story, Maité could tell everyone in the room knew something she and David didn't. Sendoa and a female member of the council, with fluorescent, carrot-colored eyes and hair streaked to match, exchanged a meaningful glance.

"My name is Esti," said the orange-tinged faery, addressing Maité and David. "I'm sorry to hear you've lost your child—"

"We *haven't* lost her," David interrupted. "Has my daughter been abducted by one of you? Are the legends true?"

A frisson seemed to go around the table. Sendoa looked positively tormented.

Esti replied in a steady voice, "We have reason to believe Nahia did it."

"That can't be," Maité burst out heatedly, but then she frowned and held her tongue. Hadn't she suspected it too?

Sendoa rose from his seat, hands balled into fists. "Nahia would not have faked her own kidnapping," he growled at Esti. His glance shifted pointedly toward Maité and his voice softened before he continued. "I know she meant to tell you everything, she wanted it all to be done with everyone's understanding and agreement."

"What needs to be done? I don't understand," David said, betraying a degree of frustration for the first time.

Maité cringed. Now he would hear from others all the fears and suspicions that had been troubling her. *I should've told him myself!*

"The Realm has been dormant these forty-nine years," Esti said to David in a calming voice, "and now the time is at hand to reawaken it. For that, a magical vessel, and the pendant Basajaun, must be united at the full moon, during the summer solstice."

Maité's worst fears were about to be confirmed. She made a fist around the pendant and sought out David's eyes but when she found them, all she could do was shake her head in mute denial.

"Forgive me," David said, wrenching his glance from his wife. "What does my daughter have to do with it all? And is the pendant you mentioned the one Maité is wearing? If Nahia needs it, all she has to do is ask."

"Is that what happened? Nahia took our baby to ransom her for this?" Maité pleaded, holding the pendant for Esti to see. Inwardly, her mind erupted with questions: Was she to blame? Had she been wrong to suspect Nahia, or had it been wrong to feel protective of her? Maité had done both, and more—she had chosen *not* to confide in David. *Oh, Basajaun, help me, please!*

All eyes fastened on Basajaun, but Sendoa was first to speak. "Nahia didn't take the baby—she believed you when you said you'd come to the Realm, *with* the baby, to help us all."

David rounded on Maité, eyes narrowed. "You said that to Nahia?"

"I did—I said I'd come with Aintza as soon as she recovered from her illness, because I wanted to be a part of the project. And I wanted you to come too, but the baby wasn't getting better and then, well . . ." Maité hesitated, feeling suddenly foolish for implicitly trusting the family bond with Nahia. Had she been manipulated? Should she refuse to trust—did she want to? Why did her loyalties have to be at odds between husband and family? And what if David rejected her because of family relations?

"So Nahia took the baby because you took too long to deliver her?" David asked, determined to find a culprit.

"I don't know," Maité said, struggling to settle her position.

Sendoa shook his head and insisted, "Nahia didn't take the child. But she *is* needed, together with the pendant, to bring back the Keeper of the Forest."

Esti said, "The child, Aintza, is the magical vessel of royal descent who arrived at the end of the seventh seven-year cycle."

"But what does it mean she is a magical vessel? And where is the Keeper of the Forest? Where is he coming back from?" David insisted

Tears welled in Maité's eyes, combing over Oihana's words in her dream—had she said anything about royal descent, or just a magical body? She couldn't recall. Meanwhile, Esti and Sendoa confirmed to David that the Keeper of the Forest was a unicorn that had been slain. They told him Nahia had removed the eyes and heart, transmuted them into a pendant so as to keep the organs safe for forty-nine years. And now they must be deposited into a new magical body to bring him back.

"So Nahia is going to turn my daughter into a unicorn?" David asked, aghast.

Maité put her hand over his, approving the question. She gazed steadily at Sendoa and at the council members, waiting for their reply. Whether of royal descent or merely a magical body, it seemed Oihana had predicted Aintza's birth, right on target, to become the necessary sacrifice. As if driven by a curse or a spell, an inner confrontation ensued between her maternal instinct and a genetic urge to comply with what her faery blood asked of her.

David squeezed her fingers—no doubts plagued his mind; he was simply a father fighting for his daughter's life. Maité needed to do the same; there was no curse or spell, there should be no conflicted thoughts. She could *not* allow Aintza to be sacrificed!

"It falls to Nahia to reawaken the Realm at the appointed time, according to what Oihana foresaw, that is all," Esti said, unmoved, although she did glance at Sendoa as if looking for his support.

Again Maité wondered what Sendoa was to Nahia—he wasn't a council member, yet they seemed to defer to him, perhaps because of sentimental ties?

"What can we do to find Nahia?" Maité asked the room at large, feeling her decision to come to the Realm had been like walking into a trap. How could she use Basajaun as leverage if she was a prisoner in Handi Park? How were she and David to escape? She must identify her advantages, if any. "Do we assume she'll be back with the baby to collect the pendant and unite them both?"

Sendoa shook his head and clucked his tongue. "Or, we realize Nahia has been abducted. If we don't find her, we will miss our opportunity to awaken the Realm. Please think about what you're saying—the charm on the changeling fully wore off yesterday, which means your child was swapped weeks ago. Nahia has been in Handi Park, worried about the illness you reported. Everyone here is witness to her efforts to prepare the landscape while she waited for you, and she has been present to us, not gone for hours at a time to presumably care for an infant—"

David threw a doubtful look at him but Sendoa persisted. "Nahia is bound by her word to the descendants of Celeste Santillán; she shall never harm any one of them, not even a hair on their head."

Maité's hand went to her shorn locks automatically, drawing attention to herself. As David had at the police station, Sendoa remarked on it, sounding regretful. "You cut your hair."

"I didn't," Maité declared and told them of the incident that had prompted their distress call from the Aspen Grove.

Once again, the council members exchanged troubled glances amid tense murmuring. Sendoa's eyes wouldn't leave Maité, seeming to mentally piece together the events, but it was Esti who voiced her conjectures. "If the baby's abduction, your hair, and Nahia's disappearance are all related events, which Nahia did *not* orchestrate, the picture changes dramatically," she said, looking at everyone around the table as if trying to tap into their suspicions. "But if Nahia isn't behind it all, who is?"

"And why?" Sendoa was quick to add. "The timing, so close to the summer solstice, is quite distressing. I feel certain whoever it is knows what we are up to."

Clearly, Sendoa wanted to release Nahia from suspicion, while Esti painted Nahia as being determined to do what must be done. Maité caught David's eye, wishing they could speak freely—he looked as tense as Sendoa and Esti, though neither faery could see into her husband's heart. Maité alone understood David's overwhelming need to recover his family and return home, possibly to pretend none of it had ever happened. Discomfited, Maité acknowledged she was in the thick of it, still trying to recover her faith in Nahia, scrambling to find a way to save her daughter and the Realm.

My daughter, the Realm, and *my marriage,* she hastened to add, distraught by her delayed inclusion of that third, equally vital, priority.

Chapter 36

The Magical Vessel

Nahia bit back the rant rioting in her brain, her fists tightened around the thin though tough braids as her cousin, Ederne, sauntered toward her. *How had she managed it? Here she stood in the Realm, albeit the swamplands, but in the Realm nonetheless, shrunk to her old faery height. Was this the work of her three underlings? How did she manage to find and recruit them again?*

The baby's gurgling noises made Nahia pause her inner rant. What condition was she in? Was it indeed Aintza? A wild hope Ederne had taken the wrong child flitted across her mind, yet for fear of betraying too much concern, Nahia didn't dare look. As for Maité, unless she was gagged behind the curtain, Nahia assumed she wasn't there.

Despite the initial shock, her cousin's decrepit state and shabby human garb, afforded Nahia a glint of wicked pleasure; dirty T-shirt, frayed denim, the skin on her bare arms covered in gooseflesh—Ederne felt cold! Without her temperature-regulating aura Ederne was subject to whatever conditions Mother Nature was in the mood for.

Ederne's last two strides put her nose to nose with Nahia, who stood her ground—never mind the fact that she felt like a fish caught in a net. She got an eyeful of the wilting skin and dull head of hair—all the litheness and allure of old, gone. Nahia found it hard to believe this feeble, unkempt woman had once been known as the Beautiful One. And Maité was responsible for Ederne's current condition. Not that Nahia suddenly felt sorry for her cousin, but she could see why Ederne had chosen to take her baby—she'd always been a vengeful faery.

Nahia choked down the desire to gloat, considering her current vulnerable position, but she couldn't keep the condescending smirk off her face when she finally spoke. "I suppose squalor within the Realm is better than trying to make the best of your *human* life in the fresh air," she needled Ederne, hoping to draw out the details of how she'd come to be there. "Did it take three whole goons to shrink you and bring you here? I noticed they couldn't manage it with the child," Nahia said, casting an offhand glance toward the basket turned cradle, and downplayed the flood of relief on confirming she *was* Aintza and she was unharmed—filthy, but unharmed.

"I see you haven't lost your penchant for blathering," Ederne said, grazing the braids with her fingers. "Pity."

"Pity you? Very well, I shall," Nahia said smartly, ignoring Ederne's irritated eye rolling. "You do look pathetic. But it hasn't stopped you from coming up with some new plan to take over the Realm, am I right? You've troubled yourself with this baby, just to bait me."

"Third time's the charm," Ederne sneered. "Except this time there are three things I want instead of one."

"Do tell," Nahia said, fairly confident she knew what two of the demands would be.

A few feet from Nahia, from the frayed basket they kept her in, Aintza seemed to watch the proceedings attentively. She was close enough to the fire as to benefit from its warmth, which eased Nahia's mind.

"That child is dead," Ederne threatened, jerking her chin toward Aintza as she began enumerating her demands, "unless you restore my powers, you renounce the crown and cede it to me before the Faerie Court, and you bring back the Keeper of the Forest."

Nahia stiffened. *How much does Ederne know?* Her eyes flickered toward Aintza and back to her cousin.

"What makes you think I—"

"One. Two. Three," Ederne cut her off frostily. "Fail any one of my demands, and this human dies."

Nahia's nostrils flared and her lip twitched. "You have no idea what it takes. If you did, you'd know there is nothing I can do from here."

"Always puffing yourself up," Ederne jeered. "No one ever believed your skills were as unique and as complex as you made them seem. I grant you will need ingredients for potions so I'll make sure you have them, but you best produce the stones—yes! I saw you draw them out of the unicorn before it died, and I'm sure they are needed now."

"He didn't die, you killed him!" A frustrated snarl disfigured Nahia's face, unnerved by her cousin's audacity and her heretofore-unknown powers of deduction. Ederne's laughter, full of spite, further enraged Nahia, but she held her tongue. *Is there no end to her comebacks?* Nahia's mind spun with self-reproach over how ineffective she'd been at getting rid of Ederne over the years.

For the second time in her life, Nahia wished she could act against her own nature and send the Beautiful One into the light, or the dark—preferably the latter, for good.

With mild interest, Ederne watched the silent changes darkening Nahia's expression. At length she spoke. "I think we understand each other. Do you know, I think I can even see us working together," she added flatly, not a hint of intent to collaborate. "You will make a list of ingredients for the potions. You will tell me where you've hidden the stones, as I don't see them on you. And you will get to work right away because we must take advantage of the new lunar cycle when it begins.

"And, oh—I am through taking care of that brat. It is your turn now. You will be allowed to clean and feed the child three times a day, but only if you can show me you've made decent progress on my demands."

Nahia trembled with rage. It would seem her cousin's deviousness had been fortified with some serious wisdom; the new moon was indeed only days away. Her eyes flicked to Aintza again, wondering how long since they'd taken her from town. Judging by how dirty and calm she looked, it might already be a few weeks. Had they limited contact and nourishment? Is that why she seemed so defeated and resigned in spite of her youth? Did they have her sedated?

Nahia rounded on her cousin and fixed her with a steely glance. "Either I have the baby with me every minute of the day and night, or I do *nothing* for you."

Ederne looked for a moment as if she were chewing the inside of her lip. Nahia stared unyieldingly until Ederne gestured to something Nahia couldn't see. "Suit yourself," she said.

Nahia heard the labored grunts before the thug emitting them came into view, dragging a cage. He'd taken the precaution of gripping it with leather pads, which told Nahia it was made of iron, and the path of flattened dirt it left behind further evidenced its considerable weight.

Once again she marveled at her cousin's uncanny foresight. Nahia's energies would dwindle gradually inside the cage, but they would also revive proportionately under the influence of the waxing moon, enough for Nahia to function but not enough to perform unforeseen feats, like breaking out of prison, or at least getting the baby to safety to deprive Ederne of her leverage.

The brute released a latch and the gate dropped like a drawbridge. They poked and prodded Nahia, net and all, to climb into her new quarters.

Once inside, Nahia demanded, "Bring me the baby."

"You may have noticed my assistants aren't as talented as I would like them to be."

Nahia frowned but then understood what her cousin meant. With a swift motion of her hands, Nahia directed a blast of turquoise-glittering energy toward Aintza. The baby bawled, obviously startled by the swooping sensation of being reduced to faery height. Nahia floated the crying baby toward the cage. No sooner had the basket settled on the wooden floor than the gate clanged shut, making Aintza wince with yet another shock.

Once the prisoners were secured, the brute that had previously been her transport did a clumsy charm to release the weights lining the net. Nahia scuttled out from under it, rolling Maité's braids carefully into a thick coil and setting it down inside the basket. She picked up the baby, cradled her, and began swaying on the spot to calm her. She addressed the same thug who had locked them in. "Get me a basin with water and a wash cloth, and a ration of whatever you've been feeding her."

Out of the corner of her eye, she saw Ederne give him a curt nod authorizing him to act.

Nahia lost herself in caring for the baby, feeling she must make up for whatever neglect she had suffered at Ederne's hands. She bathed Aintza, refreshed the soiled clothes, and the smelly basket too. Satisfied with cleanliness, Nahia warmed the milk with little effort and fed her. The baby drank in a dazzled state, more over the attention than out of hunger. Nahia spoke softly and Aintza listened as if she understood every word.

"This will be over quite soon," Nahia told her, taking the empty bottle out of her mouth. Eyes wide, the baby continued to suckle distractedly a few moments more. "You'll be in your mother's arms again in no time."

As she spoke, Nahia's thoughts flitted between past and present. This could be Zorione, Mireya, or any one of her other daughters. For a moment, she supposed it was the fault of the iron, already draining her and making her see things that weren't there, but she really could see the others in Aintza's eyes.

A knife seemed to twist in her heart as doubt seeped into the cage, and

Nahia began to question herself. Did she really mean to deliver Aintza safely and unchanged back to her parents?

And if I do, Nahia thought, looking at the baby, *how will I bring back the Keeper of the Forest?*

The magical vessel cooed sweetly in her faery godmother's arms.

CHAPTER 37

MAITÉ
PIECING IT TOGETHER

"Lucid Dreaming," Maité said thoughtfully. "That was the Cradle Gift Nahia gave me when I was born. I can use it to find Aintza! I guess I didn't think of it before because I didn't realize I had a changeling."

David squeezed her hand. "Can you try to reach Nahia as well?"

"Her receptive ability will depend on where she's imprisoned," Sendoa persisted.

"Our Celestial Observatory was designed to favor astral projections. You are welcome to use it, as it will enhance your ability and give your gift every advantage," Esti offered, and Maité couldn't tell what had motivated her. Was it a desire to soothe the worried parents, or was she representing the Realm's interests?

Whatever the case, Lucid Dreaming was the only thing Maité could think of doing. "Thank you for your support," she said. "Would it be all right if David and I sleep there?"

"I will take care of it," said one of the council members, standing up and bowing curtly within his amber-colored aura.

Maité and David murmured their gratitude in unison and the meeting came to a close. Everyone stood up, and Sendoa waited while the council members wished them good day. The Tablinum, whose bright blue sky spoke of the early morning hours outside, emptied gradually until only Sendoa was left.

The night's exertions seemed to catch up with Maité all at once. "I need to lie down," she sighed to David.

He put his arm around her and kissed her forehead. "No doubt, you'll want to dream as soon as possible."

Maité smiled sleepily.

"I will take you to the Celestial Observatory. Light refreshment awaits you, and something to help you sleep for a couple of hours," Sendoa told them kindly. "You must be exhausted from the sleepless night, but it won't do for you to sleep away the entire day."

Sendoa drew closer to Maité, giving her an appraising look. She squirmed uncomfortably under his scrutiny and winced, fleetingly distrustful, when he reached around her head with both hands. He grabbed handfuls of her short hair and said, "I can fix this, if you let me."

Maité relaxed a little and said, "OK." Sendoa didn't quite close his eyes; he blinked slowly instead, as he tugged four times. "Goodness," she gasped, feeling her scalp tingle—her hair had grown a few inches with each tug.

"It's all back," David exclaimed when Sendoa had released Maité. Her thick, wavy hair hung down her back, as it always had. "Thank you, thank you so very much!" he said, vigorously pumping Sendoa's hand.

"Don't mention it," Sendoa chuckled, and Maité beamed, momentarily forgetting the seriousness of their circumstances in the bright interval brought on by his gift.

Hand in hand, they followed him out of the Tablinum with more compelling words of gratitude. Tickled, Maité continued to run her fingers through the recovered locks. From the circular hall, Sendoa guided them through the doorway marked with a sapphire lantern, onto a pebbled meandering footpath. As they advanced, Maité saw the expanses along the narrow passageways like bulky knots in a rope, in which clusters of faery dwellings had been terraced into the earth. She remembered well Xiomara's description of this cheery part of Handi Park. There should have been colorful balustrades, overhung with bougainvillea, overlooking the walkways carpeted with mounds of phlox in every dazzling color imaginable, and luxuriant gardens with flowering shrubs.

But no such sight greeted her. Instead the dwellings were deserted, evidence of how the troop had been decimated by Ederne. Weeds grew unchecked, choking the untended landscape and spilling onto their footpath. Maité glanced mournfully at it as they passed, wishing it could all be returned to its former splendor—

Only not at the expense of her daughter's transformation.

She followed Sendoa, pulling David with her, into a chamber bathed in

239

a soothing bluish light. The sapphire glass tiles on the floor and on the walls gleamed like moonlit water. Once again thanks to Xiomara, Maité knew they were in the place where Celeste and Nahia had been taught to observe the night sky. In the center of the room stood the reflection well whose base and rim had been crafted out of clear glass blocks, and directly above it was the shaft of a petrified tree.

A bedstead sat to one side, overflowing with a feather mattress, pillows, and blankets. A spindly table and chairs were arranged with the promised refreshment and a pitcher filled with a golden liquid, still swirling, as if someone had just pulled out the stir stick.

"If there is anything you need, just say my name into this mirror and I will hear you," Sendoa told them, pointing to the frosted glass frame fixed to one side of the entryway.

He bid them good day, promising to be back as soon as they asked, and he left them alone at last.

David rounded on Maité. "What do you make of all this?"

"I believe Sendoa. I think Nahia has been kidnapped." David shook his head but Maité pressed her view. "I don't think Nahia knew anything about Aintza being kidnapped. Like Sendoa said, she believed me when I told her I would come here, with the baby, to help—"

"Did you really offer Aintza to her?" David said appalled.

"No! It was not like that. I didn't know our baby was supposed to be a magical vessel—I mean, Nahia *did* say we were going to make a unicorn, but I never imagined—I mean, I knew this necklace," she said as she grabbed Basajaun and held it up, "was what they said, you know, the eyes and heart of the dead unicorn. But I had no idea a royal vessel was needed too; I thought there was some magical way to do the thing. I really thought my part would be to help landscape and organize the base structure of the new and improved Handi Park . . . ."

The more she spoke, the more foolish it sounded to her own ears and the more withdrawn David became. But their reality could no longer be denied or dismissed; the gory faerytale was unfolding for them. Their child had been abducted and replaced with a changeling. Only hours before, they had used a tree network to contact the child's faery godmother. They themselves had been abducted into the Faerie Realm and now they were underground, having just finished a meeting with the full Faerie Council about their situation.

David had listened intently, seeming to process every bit of his wife's words. When she finished, the dark expression in his eyes confirmed to Maité he felt betrayed. And how could he not? She couldn't even make out if her magical blood was stronger than her love for him. How she wanted the two loyalties to simply coexist.

David's eyes hardened as if he'd made up his mind. Maité tensed, bracing for his answer.

"I won't lose you, or our baby, over this."

She stared, momentarily stunned by the unexpected declaration. Every cell in her body exhaled and she voiced her heart's simple truth. "I love you!"

Maité stepped into his embrace and started kissing him. In time they would discuss what he meant and what she had understood by it—she fervently hoped they wouldn't be too off the mark. He grabbed a fistful of her newly regrown hair and crushed her to him.

Feeling lighter than they had in several days, they broke apart at the same time and their glances fell on the spindly tabletop. The refreshment turned out to be a small pyramid of lemon cookies sprinkled with lavender. They ate all of them, to the last crumb. They drank a cupful of the golden liquid, smacking their lips and remarking on it tasting grassy, though obviously sweetened with honey. They peeled the outer layer of their clothes and climbed into bed. The mattress molded deliciously to their bodies, giving them a weightless feel.

David dropped off to sleep right away. Maité smiled dreamily beside him, certain the drink had been concocted to guarantee two to three hours of blissful sleep, from which they would wake rested and refreshed. With a pleasurable groan, she sank deeper into the mattress and closed her eyes, summoning an image of Aintza, in her christening gown.

Not until she buried her face in Aintza's neck and kissed her to make her giggle did Maité realize how much she'd missed her baby. She scooped her up and spoke softly while Aintza patted her face with a chubby hand. "You have grown so much, and I've missed it! Where have you been?" she said, grinning broadly. It appeared she was inside a basket lined with soft blankets; a cord sat coiled to one side of Aintza's head.

Maité became aware of the scent of gardenia—the baby smelled of it, as did the blankets and the space inside the basket. Subconsciously and in her dream, she connected the aroma to Nahia, and she knew they were together. Either Nahia was responsible for the kidnapping or a third person had abducted both of them for their own reasons.

"Where exactly are we?" Maité asked Aintza, rocking her gently. A fire burned nearby, making shadows move, and coloring everything in an orange glow. It took a moment for her to realize the lumpy walls were dirt. With some trepidation she understood they must be in some sort of burrow. She further realized she was looking at everything through bars. Maité gasped.

Holding tight to Aintza she whirled, confirming in a sweeping glance they were inside a cage. A strangled scream wedged itself at the top of her throat; a pair of turquoise orbs stared at her from only inches away. The baby had not been caged, alone! "Tsssnnt mmmee."

As other sounds poured out, the rest of Nahia materialized around her eyes. "Eddneh ssbk."

"What's wrong?" Maité hissed, bouncing the baby and then it hit her: she was inside Aintza's dream and she was hearing from Nahia only what a four-month-old baby could understand.

Nahia continued to make unintelligible noises, which Maité tried to decipher, but the baby wriggled in her arms. The harder she focused on Nahia's eyes and hand gestures, the more sluggish her understanding became. She stopped cradling Aintza and held her against her chest but the baby tensed as if trying to look at Nahia too. Maité flipped her to a forward-facing position and the baby's chubby hands immediately reached for the faery. Nahia allowed her to grab on to her little finger while with the other hand she pointed to the cord coiled inside the basket.

Maité realized it was a braid made of hair—her hair!

"Eddneh ssbk," Nahia mumbled.

Chapter 38

Preparations

It took a few minutes for Nahia to calm Aintza after the excitement of seeing her mother. Even after she began to doze, Nahia continued to pace inside the cage with the baby in her arms, brooding over how she and Maité might communicate if they couldn't understand each other inside Aintza's dreams. Nahia's abilities had been acutely diminished by being underground and exposed to iron, but the braid had at least served to strengthen the connection between mother and daughter. Nahia clucked her tongue impatiently. "We just have to come up with a way to let your mother know what's happening."

Aintza opened her eyes drowsily and made gurgling noises in so earnest an attempt to reply, Nahia had to smile. She kissed the baby's forehead and put her gently inside the basket, saying, "Very well, I will let you get back to sleep."

Ederne's three underlings had left early that morning to collect the ingredients Nahia requested. Shortly after sending them off, with dire warnings not to bother returning with an incomplete supply, Ederne had disappeared behind the curtain, leaving Nahia and the baby to themselves. After the excitement of Maité's visit, the rest of the day spent itself in the silence and gloom of the cave, where the only cheery anything came from the crackling fire that never stopped burning.

Changings and feedings succeeded one another uneventfully, and although she couldn't see the sky, Nahia tracked the hours, sensing the temperature and the angle of sunrays seeping through the layers of earth above her. When night fell, out of sheer boredom, Nahia yielded to sleep and wallowed in fretful dreams. Sometime during the night, she became aware of the thugs having returned, but she would not acknowledge them. When she opened her eyes in the morning, the cave was quiet again. The thugs had already left and another tedious day began. The only excitement she anticipated involved a possible spat with Ederne, or maybe a one-sided conversation with Aintza.

While the baby dozed in the afternoon, Nahia started pacing again, tabulating her advantages in hopes a plan might reveal itself.

Though limited, she *did* have contact with Maité through the baby's dreams. Ederne would *have* to let her out to work on the potions, which would give her a few hours' window to reach Maité or Sendoa and communicate a plan (assuming she came up with one). Although Nahia had been forced to tell Ederne that Maité had Basajaun (she resented even the appearance of conceding an advantage to her), it appeased Nahia her foolish cousin had welcomed the news as a positive development. *Nothing could be easier*, she had said, *we'll simply exchange the child for the pendant on the night of the solstice.*

Above all, Nahia considered her top advantage to be Ederne's ignorance. She didn't know Maité and Aintza were of royal blood and therefore more qualified than her to become Queen of the Realm. She didn't know Aintza was the designated magical vessel either.

Nahia paused her cataloguing, suddenly assaulted by a crisp recollection of Oihana on her deathbed. Overcome with the intensity, for she fancied she detected her mother's lilac scent in the air, Nahia chased down the elusive notion of an alternate meaning—a different interpretation of the instruction Oihana had given her.

Who would've thought it—nearly fifty years after she'd uttered them, Oihana's beseeching final words opened up a new possibility. Nahia tilted her head and squinted at the fire, transported. Her mother's body flickered between mass and light, her cool fingers grazed Nahia's cheek, and in an agitated voice Oihana said, "*You are the rightful queen; that is your destiny no matter what the cost.*"

Nahia held her breath. The new theory unfurled; what if Oihana couldn't bear to sacrifice her daughter—the one daughter she knew and loved best. The one who'd been with her from the day she was born. Better the sacrifice be an unknown descendant who'd appear forty-nine years hence.

Could it be Nahia had a choice? She refocused on Aintza, who continued to sleep in her basket. The vessel must be of royal descent, and obviously it could be watered down. But could watered down be an acceptable condition for the rightful queen? No doubt the degree of separation between Nahia and Oihana outstripped Maité and Aintza's but . . . .

"Tomorrow is the new moon," Ederne said, jerking Nahia out of her conjectures.

"I know, and I can't do anything until you get *everything* I need," Nahia snapped back, directing a look of deepest loathing to where Ederne lounged with one leg over the armrest of a chair near the fire, sipping the liquor she claimed warmed her.

"They'll have gathered all the herbs by tonight," Ederne said, jutting her chin toward a makeshift table where copious leaves, roots, and flowers had been laid out the night before. "And they'll be mining quartz tomorrow."

"If I don't have it before dusk on the first night of the waxing moon, they may as well not bother," Nahia said grumpily, knowing she had to turn the blue quartz into a mortar and pestle before she could even start on the potions. "Timing is everything, and I can't believe you're willing to risk the entire Realm missing its opportunity."

"They'll bring it," Ederne replied lazily, seeming to derive amusement from Nahia's frustration. "The Realm is only at risk if, as usual, you try to inflate your performance with unnecessary steps and rituals."

"Don't pretend you know what it takes—"

Ederne rose from the chair and strode toward the cage. "Just do your job!" She grabbed the bars and glared at Nahia. "Do it right or the child will die. I have half a mind to finish off the lot of them if you don't give me what is rightfully mine," she snarled.

Nahia stood her ground though inside she cringed. Her mind winged to Maité and her mother, Alba. Unthinkable Ederne should lay a hand on them! "I better have the blue quartz before dusk—in two days' time," she said through gritted teeth.

Ederne shoved off, giving Nahia a filthy look.

With glittering eyes and indulging in murderous thoughts, Nahia watched her cousin until she disappeared behind the curtain. *What if Ederne, like her father—a known member of the Unseelie Court—can't pass into the light when her life ends?* Nahia wondered huffily, *and what if the darkness she created when she killed Basajaun swallows her? She would have to do her life over again as a unicorn, so as to learn her lesson.*

But Nahia's triumphant grin slipped off her face—even if Ederne died of natural causes, her death would have to coincide with the birth of a unicorn and Nahia knew only a *thundersnow* could bring that about. The odds of that natural phenomenon occurring at the same time Ederne died were not even remotely favorable. One hadn't happened in Nahia's living memory, nor in Oihana's, who would've been close to eight hundred years old, if she still lived. The unreliability of such an event was precisely what had put them in their current predicament.

Nahia's hopeful anticipation further deflated with another dead end thought. Ederne was too cunning to be tricked, and to forcibly entrust Basajaun to her would be an outrage—a creature so magical and pure of heart, as had been the Keeper of the Forest, could not exist in an unclean vessel permeated with greed, selfishness, and malice like Ederne's.

A rustling sound drew Nahia's attention toward the basket, where Aintza had begun to fidget.

"So," Nahia whispered crossly, picking up the baby and holding her against her shoulder, "we won't be saving our home by turning my crazy cousin into a unicorn."

Aintza cooed and patted Nahia's chin and lips with her hand.

"Just like your great-grandmother couldn't see me as a unicorn, I can't see you being one either. Although, you *would* make the most beautiful, gifted, utterly sweet-natured baby unicorn that ever lived." Nahia smiled, punctuating her words with kisses on the chubby fingers that continued to playfully pinch and prod her mouth. "Of course, my mother is no longer here to see me do or become anything anymore."

Aintza burbled sweetly and Nahia kissed her forehead.

Early in the afternoon, before the waxing moon had risen, the carrying echo of clumsy footfalls preceded the thugs by several minutes (heeding Ederne's warning, they hadn't bothered returning the night before). Eventually they entered the expanse in the tunnel where Nahia and the baby were caged.

One of them tossed the lumpy leather sack on the floor as Ederne came out, surely to see about their success. Four decent-sized lumps of quartz tumbled out of the bag when Ederne emptied it. "Well before dusk," she said, rounding on Nahia.

"Luckily," Nahia muttered, but her heart rate increased, caught in the sweeping current of upcoming change and opportunity for action. Soon she'd be outside, free of the cage! The prospect thrilled her, even with the time constraints. Since Ederne refused to make concessions for what she called "unnecessary rituals," Nahia knew she wouldn't be allowed out before the sun set.

She quickly shoved Maité's rolled-up braid inside a fold of her cloak and with renewed optimism, she dimmed her aura to conserve even more energy—once free of the debilitating effect of the iron cage, she mustn't take too long to replenish her strength. Time was of the essence and she had a great deal to accomplish on her first night. She must transmute any negative energy within the stones into positive, shape them into the tools she needed, and then call on the universe to raise her creative vibration to the powerful currents of the waxing moon, to endow her potions with the strength and purpose she intended.

But before any transmuting happened, before any potion making began, Nahia meant to sneak a message to Maité.

CHAPTER 39

Maité
The Seven-Day Search Begins

The small flame struggled to shine through the dirty glass windows of a lantern dangling from a branch. Through gaps in the undergrowth, Maité glimpsed a sliver of the crescent moon pasted to the starlit sky. In the inky gloom, beneath the canopy, she opened her eyes as wide as she could to make out her surroundings.

Starved trees emerged from puddles of filmy water, like the rigging of phantom ships, draped with hanging moss. Dizzy with the buzzing song of the cicadas, she rubbed her eyes sleepily. A dark shape, stooped near the base of a tree trunk, came into focus. She advanced toward it, bypassing a swarm of whirling dragonflies and waving off the tall reeds tickling her elbows as she cut a path through them.

The stench of rotting leaves rose from the ground and went thickly into her lungs. Her heart hammered a quick beat in her ears; she put her arm around the tree trunk for support and peered over the hooded figure's shoulder. It held a rock aloft with both hands (Maité thought it an oversized mango) and brought it down hard against a flat stone on the ground.

With a muffled crack the rock split into halves. A singsong chant issued from beneath the hood while the figure cupped one half of the rock and rubbed a circular pattern over it with the other hand. Soon the rubbing became a dipping movement and Maité understood the rock was being hollowed out. An intensifying blue glow pulsated around it, transforming it, until the rock became a bowl.

The figure repeated the process with the second half, and soon two brand-new bowls sat on the leaf-strewn ground. The figure removed its hood and turned toward Maité. Her breath caught in her throat—two disembodied points of turquoise light gleamed, but then the rest of Nahia's features became more distinguishable in the glow of her characteristic sea-green aura.

"Aintza is safe," Nahia said, though Maité hadn't seen the faery's lips move.

"I can understand you," she exclaimed, dropping to her knees in front of Nahia. "Where are you—what is this place? Where is Aintza?"

Nahia smiled patiently at the flurry of questions and showed Maité the coiled braid. She understood it was her cut hair and frowned, momentarily confused. "How did you get this? Was it you who sent those men to cut my hair?"

Nahia shook her head. "Tell the council Ederne is behind this—"

Maité gasped. "How can that be? I stripped her of her powers. She's supposed to be living like a simple human. How could she surface now and find a way to kidnap Aintza, and you too?" Dragonflies swarmed around Maité, unsteadying her with the beat of their wings close to her ears.

Alba, gathering a shape from the hovering mist, kissed her daughter's forehead and breezily said, "Nothing to worry about, sweet girl. A dragonfly warns you of upcoming transformation, nothing more."

Unconvinced, Maité shrank from the insects and turned away from her mother to question Nahia. "Where is Aintza?" she moaned, swatting and catching the vibrating body of a dragonfly with her fingertips. She cringed and withdrew her hand. "She's with you, isn't she?"

"I will return her to you untouched," Nahia said, her eyes trained on the rows of twigs, leaves, and roots she had arranged in a half-moon shape on a slab. A smooth pestle lay between them, made of the same blue stone as the bowls.

"Promise me—"

"We must be ready for the solstice celebration; bring me Basajaun at the appointed time, and I will bring Aintza."

A dragonfly burrowed into Maité's hair and a gurgling scream came out of her throat. She swatted at it frantically—it reached her neck. She made a fist around its body, not caring she had a clump of her hair too, and started pulling.

"Wake up . . . You're dreaming." David's voice reached her through the buzzing cicadas and croaking toads.

Maité's eyes snapped open and she jerked to a sitting position. "I'll have to cut it . . . the hair, the dragonfly," she rattled off, still breathing fast though the dream had begun to dispel.

David's face, half worried, half amused, came into focus. Bewildered, Maité released his finger—she'd been gripping it with disgust, mistaking it with the nightmarish large body of the insect she was about to snap in half. David had been trying to wake her by smoothing away the tousled locks from her face and neck when she grabbed him.

"Are you back now?" he asked, studying her face as if looking for signs that she had regained her senses.

Maité nodded as things gradually came back to her. She was in the Celestial Observatory. She had retired to it shortly after dusk, really hoping Aintza might be napping so they could see each other.

"I didn't get to see her," she told David, giving up on the clump of hair she'd been running her fingers through, convinced there might be dragonfly parts still tangled in it. "But I saw Nahia, and I saw my mom—oh, David, how long have we been gone?"

"Five days," he said, startled as if just realizing time had flown. "But I'm sure Emily has given everyone an update. Did Alba look worried in your dream?"

"She didn't," Maité said, mollified. "All the same, I'm going to try to tell her myself what's going on, especially because it looks like we'll be here a few more days."

"I figured as much," David sighed. "So, if not Aintza, did you see Nahia then? Are we nearer to recovering our baby?"

"Oh my! We need to talk with the council before I forget everything I saw." Maité jumped out of bed and went to the mirror to summon Sendoa. "This dream was so much more helpful than the last!" Inwardly, she repeated key words to help her anchor the details: crescent moon, swamp, bowls, herbs, Nahia.

By the time Sendoa fetched them and they arrived at the Tablinum, the council was already there. Maité repeated her short dream to them.

"It would seem Nahia might be in the swamplands, and tonight *is* the first night of the waxing moon," Esti observed skeptically, as if she believed Maité's dream only in part. "Most auspicious for potion making."

"But why is she making two potions? Only one is needed to bring back the Keeper of the Forest," Sendoa interjected, looking at Maité, who suddenly realized she'd forgotten a key piece of information.

She announced it to the room at large, "Nahia said to tell you Ederne is behind all this." The few seconds of stunned silence were followed by an eruption of dissent, cries of surprise, and accusing looks directed at Maité. "I'm not making it up—it's what Nahia said!"

Sendoa hushed the loud objections with a halting motion of his hands. "But that's impossible. How could Ederne be back in the Realm after what you did to her?"

"I don't understand it either—and another thing, Nahia showed me a braid made with my hair. I think that is how we connected in the dream. I asked her if she had sent the two men to cut my hair and she told me Ederne was behind that too."

"Maybe it wasn't two men who cut your hair," Sendoa said, again with the narrow glance he used to fit imaginary puzzle pieces together. "Over the years, Ederne has been known to work with three trollish brutes. She recruited them centuries ago, during one of her self-imposed exiles. On her orders, they could've assumed human form to attack you, and she must've known about Nahia's vow—"

"Not to ever harm a descendant of her birth sister, Celeste Santillán, not even a hair on their head." Esti recited, giving Maité the impression that as head of the council she'd been required to memorize a biography of her royal leader.

"Do you think the second potion is meant for Ederne?" Maité addressed Esti, trusting her to know more than the others about faery lore. "Can it give her back the power I wiped out—can that be done?"

Esti pursed her lips, seeming to ponder her reply before conceding, "Nahia is a gifted potion maker and she outclasses anyone in the troop when targeting energy. I believe she *is* capable of reversing what you did."

"But she will *not* do it," Sendoa grumbled, causing heads to tilt quizzically around the table, assimilating the implications.

David broke the silence. "I don't know what Nahia will or will not do—at this point, we're not even sure what she has already done." Maité squeezed his hand, wishing he would tone down his aggravation in the interest of keeping faith *and* allies. Particularly Sendoa, whose scowl gave away his dislike of hearing anything against Nahia. "Let's consider for a moment she does intend to give Ederne her powers back—"

"Not even under torture," Sendoa interjected fiercely.

David gave him a placating nod but continued in that vein. "If she is indeed in the swamplands, I don't see why we can't discover the hideout before Ederne's powers are restored. We rescue Nahia, recover our baby, and we take Ederne back into town. Kidnapping is a punishable offense in the human world."

The corners of Maité's mouth quivered upward, but she swallowed the chuckle. With a witty raised brow she said under her breath to David, "Hmm . . . Ederne in a human jail, serving a life sentence?" He gave her hand a squeeze before turning his attention back to the council.

"We have fourteen days until the summer solstice, which in this year coincides with the full moon," Esti explained in full consideration of David's suggestion. "If Nahia, as Maité assures us, was making mortars tonight and exposing ingredients to the energy of the waxing moon, we can safely assume potions will not be completed sooner than seven days hence. You see, for full potency, a potion must be left to mature at least until the half moon appears in the sky."

"Seven days is hardly enough time to poke around every crack and crevice of our swamplands," Sendoa pointed out reasonably. "If Nahia were here, she could sniff out traces of Glamour along the way to help her discover the hiding place. No, I'm more inclined to believe she would as soon trick her cousin, than cave to whatever demands have been imposed."

Maité digested Sendoa's fervent remarks and surmised, "Ederne took my child to bait Nahia, I'm sure of it. She must be forcing Nahia to give her back her powers, and bring back the Keeper of the Forest, or else she'll kill Aintza."

Heads bobbed in agreement around the table.

"But you said Nahia promised to give Aintza back, untouched," David reminded his wife. "How can she manage to bring back the Keeper of the Forest if she won't use Aintza as the vessel?"

"She said I was to bring Basajaun to her at the appointed time, and she would give me Aintza," Maité repeated thoughtfully. "I assume the appointed time is during the full moon, on the shore of Moon Dancer Lake?"

Esti nodded. "Do we trust Nahia might have an alternate plan then?"

For all his earlier championing of Nahia, Sendoa had grown silent and suddenly looked pale. Troubled, Maité wondered what could be going through his mind—had he thought of a way Nahia might bring back the unicorn without using Aintza? Did he not approve? Maité longed to ask him.

"We will make every effort to discover them in the next seven days," Sendoa said resolutely, confirming Maité's suspicion that he must have guessed Nahia's intention and was determined to stop her.

David offered to join the search party. "I can't just sit and wait—I have to do something."

Meanwhile, Maité rested easy knowing Aintza was under Nahia's care. Her energies would be spent on the Realm's finishing touches prior to reawakening, trusting that when the night of the full moon arrived, she would have Aintza back in her arms.

But what was Nahia's intention—what did Sendoa fear?

CHAPTER 40

NAVIGATING HIDDEN TRUTHS

A perfect half moon rose on the eastern horizon and, as expected, Ederne demanded the potion that would restore her power.

"I'm surprised at you," Nahia scoffed, belittling her cousin's urgency to purposely delay. "You would risk consuming an underdeveloped potion when your magical nature is at stake?"

Ederne's pupils contracted but the red smolder did not flood her irises as it had often done (when she was a faery) in moments of extreme rage. Nahia observed this failing and grinned loftily, causing Ederne to lash out.

"I warned you, I would not tolerate procrastination! Everyone knows the half moon is sufficient time for—"

"But for such a potion as this, to restore damaged magical cells," Nahia cut her off with superior disdain, "only exposure to the *complete* lunar cycle will guarantee potency. Because when the time comes, you know you and your flawed cells will be of *no* help in directing energy, much less saturating it with intent, so all the work will be on me. That being the case, I *want* the strongest potion I can work with, and I don't care what you think or tolerate."

"I don't trust you," Ederne snarled. Nahia started to rejoin but her cousin growled unexpectedly. "Get the child out of there!"

The moment's confusion shook Nahia; the thug was already at the gate, grunting and fumbling with the latch when she understood what Ederne meant to do. He dropped the gate with a clang and Aintza started bawling. Resenting more than ever the weakening effect of the iron, Nahia braced herself to engage in a physical struggle, if necessary, to defend the baby.

She blocked the entrance to the cage with her body and addressed Ederne over Aintza's cries. "Touch the baby, remove her from my side, and I will not give you my best effort," Nahia said calmly, knowing it was a gamble and hoping her cousin would concede the bit of leverage.

Livid, Ederne's eyes flashed from Nahia to the thug poised to enter the cage.

The seconds stretched, with neither cousin backing down. Nahia would not lose ground. She caught Ederne's eye and leveled at her the powerful thought pounding in her head—*You are in my power, you miserable wretch!* She imbued it with as much conviction and menace as she could to tip the scale in her favor. At length, Ederne's shoulders sagged and she looked away. But Nahia relaxed only when she jerked her chin toward the thug, signaling him to stop.

With a grunt, he slammed the gate shut and Nahia picked up the baby, who had worked herself into hysterics from being ignored. Nahia stared after Ederne, not caring if she had heard the words, or if she had only felt the strength of the thought Nahia had leveled—it was a win and nothing else mattered.

Near midnight, Aintza had calmed down sufficiently to eat. After a quick sponge bath and a change of clothes, Nahia cradled and rocked her, humming softly, until she dozed. The minutes turned to hours as Nahia gazed broodingly on the sleeping child, again seeing traces of Zorione, of Mireya, Catalina, Alba, and Maité—they were her legacy to the Realm, her royal descendants, the ones Ederne knew nothing about. Nahia was convinced her cousin's ignorance of that fact would be her undoing. Even restored powers would serve no purpose. Nahia couldn't cede the crown to Ederne when there were three viable royal successors, no matter how watered down their bloodline; their two drafts outstripped Ederne's any day. But it was imperative Ederne remain ignorant. If she knew about Alba, Maité and Aintza, she wouldn't scruple killing them all.

The critical moment would come on the night of the full moon. Nahia had concocted her cousin's potion with the intent to *invigorate* only, making it crucial to convince her to wait until the very last minute. Otherwise, the fact her faery cells weren't repaired would become obvious too soon, exposing Nahia's trickery. She was counting on Sendoa and the council to make short work of Ederne and her thugs as soon as they showed their faces.

The potion for the Keeper of the Forest, however, had been formulated to bring about transformation and to bind species. It would age to perfection until the day of the solstice, so when Nahia met Maité and united Basajaun and the potion under the full moon, on the shore of Moon Dancer Lake in front of the entire troop and council—

"Do tell," Ederne slurred as she swirled the drink in her cup, looking askance at Nahia. "Who's the vessel the council is preparing? Anyone I know?"

Nahia stopped pacing and took a deep breath, resenting the interruption. "What do you care," she fumed, trying not to completely lose the thread of her thoughts. "When the full moon comes, you, the pendant, and the vessel will come together for your long-awaited big night."

Oblivious, Ederne continued to goad, her voice full of spite. "Sendoa would make a formidable Keeper of the Forest."

The sudden mention of his name knocked the wind out of Nahia—her mind conjured so vivid a vision of Sendoa she couldn't think straight. She wished to be in his presence, in his arms, and his voice soothing away all her worries.

She rounded on Ederne with half a mind to tell her the truth. She would not get her powers, she would not get a crown, she would not get the Realm! But how foolish would that be? Oihana would never give in to rage like that.

Nahia decided to hold her tongue about what Ederne wouldn't get. Instead, with a surge of fierce loyalty for Sendoa, and wishing never again to hear his name come out of her cousin's mouth, she said, "Sendoa is overqualified. You, on the other hand, tell me why it hasn't even occurred to you to repay your debt to the Realm? *You* should be begging to become the unicorn. A life for a life!"

Ederne let out a bland laugh. "I'd forgotten what a sense of humor you have—really, a faery from a royal line such as me, and a beast, on equal footing? I don't think so."

Provoked past endurance Nahia strode to the iron bars and stood as close as she could (without touching them) longing to throttle the woman on the other side to within an inch of her life. "You are right, you're not fit to be such noble beast as a unicorn," Nahia said, biting back the urge to add that Maité and Aintza came from a bold, compounded royal line, next to which Ederne was a step above peasant, if that.

The heat emanating from the iron added to the hot irritation coursing through Nahia's body. She took a step back, telling herself to breathe. She'd be an idiot to fall for her cousin's badgering. When she felt ready to speak, without the angry quiver in her voice, she resumed her jabs.

"You'll do well to cut down on your drinking," Nahia said, relishing her cousin's immediate reaction—the narrowed eyes, the pursed lips, confirmed how poorly received the advice was. Nahia pressed on. "If you don't stop now, in seven days, no matter how strong the potion, it won't heal your pickled insides. And don't you want to be in full possession of your faculties? Look at you. I bet you can't even walk a straight line."

Ederne glowered but did not reply.

"If you stay inebriated, you might take the wrong potion. I wonder how you'd look with hooves and a horn sticking out of your forehead," Nahia insinuated wickedly.

"I don't trust you," Ederne repeated, "but you will do your job—and you will do it right, or I will track down every last one of them."

Nahia wagged her head and sat by the baby's basket, a satisfied smirk on her face. Ederne didn't suspect the potion was the lie. *I guess I really can't be trusted*, she thought, more amused than disturbed. *Who needs Ederne's trust anyway?*

Do I have Maité's trust? Nahia wondered. *Is it wise to continue the connection?* After she let her know Aintza was safe, she'd connected with Maité two other times while working on the potions. How much information was Maité privy to when in a Lucid Dreaming state? Nahia suddenly worried about Maité's dominant streak of Glamour, would it allow her to hear her most private thoughts?

Aintza continued to sleep. Ederne had retired behind the curtain (to sulk, Nahia hoped) and the faery could sense the sun had come up—she hadn't slept a wink the entire night, but didn't feel tired or grainy eyed. *I'll leave the braid with Aintza from now on*, Nahia resolved, fearful Maité might catch a whiff of her latest reasoning and sound the alarm with Esti or Sendoa. *I won't be argued with*, Nahia thought huffily. *When she made her prediction, my mother wasn't thinking about the vow I made to protect Celeste's descendants. To transform Aintza would be to harm her, and that cannot happen by my hand.*

When night fell, Nahia tucked the braid under the basket's pad, feeling a twinge of anxiety over leaving Aintza at the mercy of Ederne, even for half an hour, which was how long it would take for her to do the nightly ritual over the potions.

As on previous nights, Nahia refused to fly, to annoy her cousin as much as to lengthen her exposure to fresh air. How she wished Aintza would be allowed to go with her. But Ederne would never relinquish her leverage.

"The exertion of flying defeats the purpose," Nahia derided her cousin, rolling her eyes as if tired of repeating herself. "Walking under the stars helps me build up the strength I need to do my job."

Also as on previous nights, Ederne gave in reluctantly, and Nahia was once again escorted outside by one of the thugs. They set off and had barely made it out of the tunnel when the wheezes and grunts coming from behind had annoyed Nahia enough to make her forgo a leisurely pace. She regretted she couldn't stuff each of his nostrils with thick dragonflies to shut him up.

They arrived at the clearing within a cluster of aspens, the dappled rays of the moon shone obliquely on the glass coffer atop a pedestal. Inside, the potions gleamed crimson and gold in their blue quartz mortars.

"Stay back," Nahia told the thug. He obeyed and she approached the pedestal. Without the braid on her person, she felt safe from possible intrusion by Maité.

She opened the lid and pulled out the small vial with the power oil. She'd emulsified enough of it for the fourteen nights of the lunar cycle. Nahia anointed her forehead and wrists; immediately the scent of cypress, juniper, and frankincense overwhelmed her. She replaced the vial in a corner of the glass box and she laid her hands, palms down, over the potions. With complete abandon, Nahia called down the white light from the heavens to bring up her vibration and to amplify her strength before the empowering mantra began. Nahia didn't need to see it to know her aura had started glowing, not in her traditional sea green but under the powerful influence of the moon, it shone silver. She pushed away all thoughts of Sendoa, which her temporary aura had put her in mind of.

The song began. First, to reinforce the enchantments she'd laced into the mixtures. Then she moved on to the tedious though critical portion of the ritual, to fortify the spiritual qualities of each raw ingredient.

Chapter 41

Maité

Acting Alone

When the half moon appeared in the sky, the troop exhaled a collective, dejected sigh. The search party had failed and the council was divided. Had Nahia given Ederne her powers back? Or had her plan, all along, been to delay until the full moon?

Sendoa expressed his contempt for anyone who believed the former and adamantly voiced his intention to find the hiding place. He crossed his arms over his chest, daring anyone to question or try to stop him.

No one did. In fact, David stood up to show his support, which pressured two others into resuming the search with them. For their part, the rest of the council and the adult members of the troop returned to their preparations for the solstice. Their approach forcibly reminded Maité of her mother's fastidiousness when she expected guests, and couldn't make out if she was exasperated or charmed. Either way, Maité was suddenly pining for her parents and for a normal home.

Although the myriad of chores, underground and out of doors, should've been enough to distract her, each day further embittered Maité's heart with corrosive uncertainty. Five days after the half moon, she gave up and had to accept she'd lost contact with Nahia. She didn't want to believe it, but it seemed Nahia had deliberately stopped using the braid. Or perhaps it had been taken from her?

Meanwhile, Sendoa continued his obsessive search for Nahia, while a fevered David followed in his wake, determined to find Aintza. Maité listened to their reports and began thinking of them as the faery and the human, both

259

committed to win the race that would save their heart's desire. She cried for her husband's tenacity, and blamed Nahia's silence—it had bred enough bitter distrust for Maité to believe that even if David found Aintza, they had no hope of rescuing her from the fate planned for her.

Maité began avoiding the others, not just because she didn't want to see the disappointment in their eyes when she had no new dreams to share, but because neither the council nor Sendoa would understand the suspicions Nahia's silence had set off.

As outdoor tasks dwindled (flower beds were budding, streams had been cleaned, the wood had been swept, the lake shore had been raked, hedges had been trimmed) Maité's help wasn't required as much, so she spent longer periods of time alone in the Celestial Observatory.

"The solstice is two days away," Maité murmured to herself. She sat on a chair, two feet from the bedstead, staring at the clothing old Usoa had delivered from her workshop just that afternoon. She'd left them on top of the bed; a dress for Maité, a tiny frock for Aintza, and a pair of pants and shirt for David. Did they really expect her to recover her daughter, and immediately dress her for sacrifice? Yes, she had volunteered to help prepare for the event, but that had been when she still believed in Nahia and thought she and her family would be closer to the out-of-town-guest category at the festivities.

Maité leaned forward and fingered the purple dress meant for her. Had she not been in such a brooding mood, she might have appreciated it was made of silk, spun right there in Handi Park, and she would've been bowled over by the artistry of the diaphanous bodice threaded with tiny glittering beads.

Instead, all she could think of was Usoa and her explanation of how in this special year, for the rebirth of the Realm, and as requested by the council, they would dispense with tradition. There would be no individual designs and no flimsy materials in every color of the rainbow—symbolism would be favored.

"Purple is the color of royalty and nobility," Usoa had said. "Nahia's, of course, will be the same color as yours, dear. The council will wear blue, for loyalty and wisdom. David, along with the rest of the troop, will wear shades of green—the color of harmony and freshness, darker for males and lighter for females. And Aintza will wear white—" Usoa paused uncomfortably, but Maité had had no trouble plucking the end of the sentence from the air. *White symbolizes innocence, light, and goodness—everything a worthy vessel should be.*

She leaned back on the chair, drew her legs up and wrapped her arms around her knees. "What do you mean to do?" she whispered to the empty room, half expecting Nahia to respond.

For an answer, Maité got a vivid recollection of the last dream where she had seen Nahia, and during which she'd felt like a mere spectator, unacknowledged by the faery. The smell of cypress, juniper and frankincense filled her nostrils and Nahia's lilting voice seeped into her brain—*four-leafed clover, connect me to nature's spirits—thornapple, break open my mind that I may see beyond light and dark—edelweiss, raise me to the heights that I can embrace my destiny—ivy, ground me to the earth mother—yellow iris, strengthen my resolve to keep my vision—*

Unaware of it, Maité rocked slowly on the chair, listening to Nahia's song, knowing the faery had been methodically strengthening the individual properties of each ingredient, meaning to take advantage of the entire lunar cycle so when the time came, the potions would be at full potency.

If only she'd been able to see how many potions were still in there, she could've told the council what Ederne's condition was.

Maité studied their surroundings inside the recollection. She panned past Nahia, noting the unusual silver glow of her aura above the pedestal and the glass box. The milky moon peeked through the branches. They were in the center of a clearing. And all the trees around them—all the trees had bleached, spotted trunks with heart-shaped leaves.

Maité's eyes snapped open and she dropped her feet to the floor. "There is an Aspen Grove in the swamplands!" She put her hand to her chest to calm her beating heart. As clearly as if the canopy had suddenly parted to reveal a vast starlit sky, so was Maité able to see inside Nahia's mind. The faery's intention during the dream had been to continue the empowering ritual of *two* potions until the night before the solstice. *Ha!* Maité thought, *at least Sendoa was right on that count.*

"Does it matter, though? If Nahia cut off communication, it's because she doesn't mean to keep her promise," Maité said under her breath, going right back to her briefly interrupted gloom. "She won't return Aintza untouched—David was right to mistrust her."

"No luck," David said, startling Maité out of her hostile conjectures.

She got off the chair and went to him, glad that the bluish lighting in the room hid her flushed cheeks. "But Sendoa won't stop looking?" she inquired mildly.

"We will go out tomorrow, and the day after too, until right before dusk if necessary. If we haven't found them, then we'll be prepared to meet them lakeside."

Maité nodded but didn't say anything more. The lakeside plan had been discussed repeatedly and she was displeased with how her family would fare there.

Maité could hardly sleep that night; the fate of the Realm and Aintza's fate weighed equally heavily on her. When dawn arrived, Maité had made up her mind. She sent David off with a kiss and wished him luck. This time, she didn't feel even remotely guilty to have kept information from him. *I haven't identified Aintza or Nahia's location—I only know where the potions are*, she reasoned inwardly, *and that's not what they are looking for.*

Maité ambled on Handi Park's pebbled walkways, avoiding the area cluttered with dwellings where the reduced troop had chosen to make a neighborhood. She only joined them for meals, as that was family time, and she would not break the faery tradition. But even then, Maité kept to herself. Only seldom would murmurs of "the poor dear" reach her, and Maité easily ignored those.

During dinner, Maité chewed her food distractedly, looking at the gleaming pitchers filled with colorful beverages. Her eyes lingered on the dark red, giving her a sudden craving for a glass of wine and making her lament the pitcher was likely filled with eggplant or grenadine juice. She took a gulp of her water instead, and her glance drifted toward the golden liquid in a small decanter. *Just like what Sendoa gave us the night we got here*, she thought, swallowing her food.

Before she retired to the Celestial Observatory, she filled two vials with the red and gold drinks and stuffed them into a fold of the cloak she'd taken to wearing. Maité couldn't see the nearly full moon on the reflection well—it hadn't reached its zenith yet, but in her mind's eye, she could see Nahia, hovering over the glass box, palms down over the bowls, empowering the potions one last time.

She fell asleep and didn't hear David return, nor did she feel him climb into bed next to her. She dreamt on, curled into a ball. The slight crease on her brow denoted the tension contracting her muscles, including her heart.

"Ma-ma," Aintza said, patting Maité's cheek with her chubby hand.

She opened her eyes, which immediately filled with tears—how she missed her baby! And she was beginning to talk now, barely five months old. Maité sniffled, rolling over on her back and staring at a sliver of sky visible through the skylight. The day of the summer solstice had dawned.

It was now or never—a shudder of doubt rattled her—what if Nahia had taken the potions already? *She hasn't*, Maité decided. She kissed David's shoulder and got out of bed without rustling the covers. She threw the cloak over her cotton nightdress and tiptoed onto the glass blocks framing the well.

In over a fortnight of assisting the troop and the council with preparations, Maité had perfected her ability to direct energy and to fly. Her visualization skills too, had become second nature, as Nahia had predicted. She exhaled and, with upturned face, Maité focused on the twinkling stars above, imagining them overlaid on the glittering surface of the potions. As Nahia had taught her, she trusted the map-keeping energy of the planet and she told the frantic beat of hummingbird wings in her solar plexus, "Get me there."

She was airborne. The vials clinked in the fold of her cloak as she sped toward the marshes opposite Moon Dancer Lake, on the east end of the Realm's basin. The moon ducked in the west, eluding the rising sun, as Maité descended on the misty clearing among the cluster of trees. There stood the pedestal and the glass box.

CHAPTER 42
SOLSTICE AND FULL MOON

The blinding curve of the rising sun broke the horizon. In the underground prison, Nahia opened her eyes, dazed. She propped herself on her elbow and peeked inside the basket; Aintza slept placidly. She was about to lie back down when she felt a prickly heat spread from her neck to the rest of her. Nahia instinctively turned to see where the energy current came from and choked down a startled gasp. Ederne sat like a statue at the table, glowering at her.

"Happy summer solstice," Nahia said scornfully, aiming to rile her cousin, who on the eighth day of not drinking looked as bad-tempered as ever. "You are up early . . . or did you not sleep last night?"

"The stage is set at Moon Dancer Lake," Ederne said, ignoring Nahia's inquiry, "but I have decided you will return my powers before we go. I will not risk any ill-conceived plans from the council or from your consort, or even from that human—I still cannot believe you entrusted Basajaun to her!"

"I've told you already. She found it and thought it a family heirloom come to her directly from Celeste." Nahia's glance narrowed. "But you will do well to keep your word, or I *will* defy my very nature and put an end to you."

"Empty threats," Ederne laughed blandly and Nahia struggled to keep calm. "I will take you to the clearing before dusk and you will do your job," Ederne said. "Then you and the child will be brought separately to the lake, just to make sure you don't have a change of heart."

Nahia appraised her cousin in silence, feverishly reckoning Ederne's new demand with the timing she'd been counting on. She concluded that the invigorating potion would likely fool her long enough for them to get to the lake. Furthermore, she trusted the council would quickly overpower Ederne. So Nahia said, "If you like."

Two hours before sunset, Ederne had done waiting for lunar cycles and reassurances of potency. She walked Nahia out of their hideout, on a leash made with Maité's braid, and set off to the clearing. As she walked, Nahia put a hand over her belly to settle the nervous flutter and catch her breath. She blamed her cousin's infectious distress for her discomfort.

When they arrived, Nahia noticed with fiendish satisfaction that her cousin recoiled from the pedestal. *Figures,* Nahia thought acidly, *now the moment is at hand she hesitates—coward!* But then it occurred to her, maybe Ederne's senses *did* serve her well. What if they were screaming a subconscious warning? Telling her this was the beginning of the end? *Good for her if they are,* she thought huffily. *They won't save her, though.*

Nahia willed herself to the top of the pedestal looking like a balloon at the end of a string. She lifted the glass lid and froze—*something is not right.* A scowl darkened her expression for a brief moment. *Who? Ederne's underlings wouldn't dream of it. Who then?* Careful not to spill, Nahia pulled out the blue quartz mortars, cradling them one in each hand. She descended to where Ederne stood holding out the two empty vials they had brought for the transfer. Nahia focused on directing the mortars to tip their content into the respective vials. *Sendoa? Esti? Maité?* Nahia wondered, listening to the bogus liquids trickle in until the last drop had been transferred.

"Which is mine?" Ederne said, eyes flicking anxiously toward the red one, surely reminded of the Bordeaux she was so fond of.

Nahia humored her, she jutted her chin toward the vial filled with red liquid. Thinking quickly, she sent a well-aimed flash of energy and transmuted what looked like beet juice into a more palatable wine-flavored drink. Ederne stared at it greedily, licking her lips as if she could almost taste it and feel the power it would unleash within her. Meanwhile, Nahia grabbed the other vial and conjured a wax seal for it. She did it strictly for Ederne's benefit because looking at it up close, Nahia had no doubt it was a plain old drowsy draft.

Do I let her drink it? Nothing will happen—she won't even feel invigorated, Nahia thought frantically. Maité's braid around her neck seemed to tighten. *She'll know I duped her; she'll kill Aintza with her own hands!*

Ederne smacked her lips, the empty vial in her fist. "Now what?"

Nahia's eyes refocused on her cousin, realizing the choice had been taken from her. She stood there, momentarily stricken, with her dashed plans and unfinished conjectures crashing like waves against the inside of her skull.

Nahia growled inwardly but she shook off her misgivings. She told herself it was liberating to lose control, exciting to suddenly have to scramble to anticipate and follow someone else's lead (if only she knew whose). Nahia squared her shoulders, pocketed the drowsy draft and replied, "Now I bolster restoration of your cells."

Nahia put forth her best effort, surprising even herself, for she never imagined she would one day want to gratify her horrible cousin, on purpose! If not her faery powers, Nahia would give Ederne her looks back.

Nahia called on her finest thoughts and feelings and sharpened them into a creative current to drench Ederne's every cell. She amplified the intoxicating effect of the wine, causing Ederne to experience exhilaration. She commanded every molecule to regain elasticity and to rejuvenate. Delighted, she observed the immediate tightening of the skin, the hair rippling, as if each follicle had suddenly become a spring from which vibrant nourishment and color poured out to saturate and renew.

Their eyes met, the breeze parted the leaves of a tree, and a fiery ray of the setting sun struck the side of Ederne's face. For a second, Nahia thought her cousin's eyes had smoldered red—*a passing illusion*, she told herself.

"It didn't work," Ederne frowned.

Nahia glowered back, nonplussed. "Look at yourself—"

"Yes, yes, I see I've recovered my looks," Ederne said irritably, "but you should be unconscious at the foot of that tree where I tried to heave you."

"You miserable wretch. I shouldn't bother telling you this. I should just let you squirm in anger and suspicion," Nahia spat, gaining confidence with the prospect of telling an even taller tale. "But for the sake of the Realm I will repeat myself. A complete cycle is needed, you idiot. The full moon must seal the effect of the potion by imprinting its power on each restored cell."

Ederne looked like she'd swallowed regurgitated wine. "I don't trust you!" she fumed. Her face, contorted with rage as it was, made it easy for Nahia to read the inner struggle. She had no choice but to believe Nahia's story—she would have to see it through at the lake.

Nahia couldn't savor the small victory for very long. Unexpectedly, the leash tightened around her neck, almost snapping it, and she hit the leafy ground. Ederne had coiled the slack braid around her wrist and dropped to one knee, yanking Nahia along. Her chin was already on the ground, yet Ederne tightened the braid with one more twist. Nahia's eyes rolled upward to glower at her cousin.

Ederne's sour breath puffed over her face when she snarled, "Do not lie to me, or I will make you regret it."

"Let—go—of—me," Nahia hissed, doing what she could to free herself, but Ederne held her down. Once again, the cousins stared at one another, refusing to back down.

At last, Ederne stood up, pulling Nahia up with her—she dragged her by the neck back to the tunnels.

They made a grim convoy, bumbling over treetops on their way to Moon Dancer Lake. Nahia, on a short braided leash, led the way. Ederne, whose weight had been dispersed for the trip, followed inches behind Nahia on borrowed power. Two of the thugs held the iron cage between them, with Aintza inside, while the third brought up the rear.

The western sky still blazed, for the sun had barely sunk. Nahia got her first distant glimpse of the lake, already littered with lanterns. Though she craned, she couldn't make out the crescent-shaped beach, much less the troop—perhaps they'd set up the terrace closer to the edge of the forest and they were all gathered there. She sped up but Ederne immediately tugged at the braid.

It dawned on Nahia the council would have placed sentinels to secure the site and to sound the alarm on their approach. With renewed excitement she scanned the canopy and the horizon, to no avail. She flew on with a pang of disappointment.

They left behind the Arboretum and the forest. All was silent. They reached the edge of the trees, and almost immediately below, on the shell-shaped beach, was the terrace with its ornate balustrade—no sign of the troop though.

Lanterns bobbed on the lake. The white sand looked rosy under the orange sky.

"Land us in the center of the terrace," Ederne ordered. Nahia obeyed, a little unnerved by the absence of the council, and of the whole troop.

Nahia and Ederne touched down lightly. The underlings carrying the cage landed noisily, with groans and a muted clang. Aintza didn't make a sound, as she was likely in bewildered awe over being aboveground.

"What have you done? Why is no one here?" Ederne hissed, yanking Nahia's leash.

"I've done nothing but make potions for you!"

"So you say," Ederne muttered, eyes flashing toward Aintza. "We'll know soon enough how much you value that human's life. If I don't have my powers back as soon as the full moon comes out, she'll be dead."

Nahia paused—had she been wrong to trust the council? What about

Sendoa? A quick eastward glance told her the moon was minutes away. She'd been counting on their assistance. *Where are they?* A strange sound reached Nahia's ears, like logs pummeling the sand with an impossibly rapid beat. Ederne whirled toward it, wrenching Nahia along.

The giant came out of the forest. He streaked across the strip of sand and bounded onto the terrace. David, at human height, made short work of the startled thugs. He flung them headlong over the balustrade and snatched the cage in one sweeping motion, pausing only to peer inside and make sure the baby was fine.

Nahia wedged her thumbs between her neck and the leash to release some of the pressure. Ederne hadn't reacted yet to David's sudden appearance, but whether on purpose or not, she was nearly strangling Nahia. A frustrated growl issued from Ederne.

Nahia would have laughed out loud had her throat not been so constricted or had she not been worried about the conspicuous absences. "You have no power over David," she wanted to sing out, even as the pressure around her neck increased. Aintza was safe, and Ederne had no troop to threaten or thugs to order around, for the moment.

Ederne turned, using Nahia as a shield and allowing her to see the council had just landed on the terrace. *Finally!*

"Let her go," Sendoa said. Nahia grinned in spite of her current discomforts.

"Not on your life," Ederne replied confidently. "You will not risk the rebirth of the Realm, so you will bring us the pendant and the vessel. Tell them, cousin—"

Nahia pulled on the leash with her thumbs to get some relief. "The moon will soon rise. We must do as she says," Nahia choked out the words, looking wildly about for Maité. She was nowhere to be seen.

The mere thought of her name seemed to summon her—the girl's voice seeped into Nahia's brain, "I'm at Wizard's Pass—come find me." Driven by a jarring hunch of what Maité meant to do, Nahia sprung into action.

Her eyes flashed a signal to Sendoa before she kicked her elbow into Ederne's rib cage. While her cousin doubled over in pain, Nahia unraveled the leash from her wrist and freed herself. Sendoa pounced on Ederne before she could recover.

"Thank you—she has nothing!" Nahia called out, hoping he would understand she had not restored Ederne's faery powers.

CHAPTER 43

TRYST GONE AWRY

The eastern horizon lightened with each passing minute. Nahia took to the air, and with dread in her heart, she dashed to the waterfall. Behind it lay hidden Wizard's Pass, through which, Basajaun, had allowed a pregnant Paloma to enter the Realm of Faerie 197 years ago. *Why does Maité want to meet where it all began?*

Nahia landed a few feet behind her. Maité stood on the edge of the precipice, staring at the swirling mist veiling the waterfall. The thunderous roar seemed to drown out even the thoughts in Nahia's head. Maité looked so fragile.

"I am here," Nahia said, her voice steady in spite of the heap of emotions cluttering her heart.

Maité remained motionless with her back toward Nahia, but her right hand, which had been balled into a fist, relaxed. From it dropped a glass vial. Nahia knew immediately what it was, and her insides quaked. She marched toward Maité, furious, livid. With a last wild hope she picked up the vial, wishing it to be the crimson potion, that she'd chosen the wrong one. But she held it up and saw a single milky drop left—she had consumed it all!

Her faculties deserted her.

Nahia grabbed Maité by the shoulder and forcefully turned her around. "How could you? You stupid, *stupid* girl! The stars forgive me," Nahia thundered, enraged. Of its own accord, it seemed, Nahia's hand struck Maité across the face before she could stop it. The mark of her fingers throbbed angrily on the girl's smooth cheek. Her gray eyes filled with tears but Nahia's wrath would not abate.

"What are we going to do now? Do you realize you have destroyed our chances to renew the Realm. All that waiting, our work—wasted!" she couldn't keep down the hysterical note in her voice, "SAY SOMETHING," she cried out, shaking her.

"Nothing is ruined, Nahia," Maité replied coolly, tucking a lock of unruly hair behind her ear.

"For the stars in the sky," Nahia exclaimed, taking a step back, looking her up and down. "I simply cannot believe it."

The tears dried and Maité's gaze hardened—her eyes became two steadfast pewter orbs as she spoke. "I know the Realm needs a new Keeper of the Forest, and I know what Oihana told you to do, but I won't let you take my daughter."

Nahia's hands went up to the sides of her own head, appalled. She grabbed fistfuls of hair in a fit of ultimate frustration. *I shouldn't have stopped communications!*

"My mother had her motives to say what she said, but they don't matter anymore because I promised *you* I would bring Aintza back, untouched. Do you not trust me?" Nahia cried out, injured. "I meant to become the vessel myself, and I meant for *you* to take my place as queen!"

Maité's eyes grew wide with surprise. She squeezed the base of her throat as if the potion might still be there in a pending bubble, waiting to be expelled. But it was not.

At length, Maité shook her head and exhaled, resigned. "I am not the rightful queen, Nahia, you know that." Nahia shook her head stubbornly but Maité pressed on. "I *will* be responsible for keeping the Realm alive. I want to do it—I feel the task was meant for *me* all along."

A groan of despair came from the depths of Nahia's heart and she began to cry. But the upper arch of the rising moon, about to break over the horizon, jolted her out of her sorrow. Through her tears, she saw Maité had started blinking between visible and invisible.

Maité frowned and turned a pleading eye on Nahia. "It's happening!"

The faery couldn't respond. She stood there paralyzed by conflicting sensations.

"We're wasting time," Maité cried, snapping Basajaun off the pewter cord around her neck and relinquishing it.

Nahia stared at it as if it was a horrible insect, but then she took it. Heartbroken, angry, and nowhere near resigned, she kissed Maité's lips. "I love you, blood of my blood," she said in a tremulous voice.

Maité nodded and collapsed to her knees; all the while her body flickered between solid and mist. "Love you, too," she stammered and lay down on the grass, beneath the dusky sky.

With the loose stones already released from their setting, Nahia waited for Maité to solidify again. When she did, she placed the two onyxes over her closed eyelids and the ruby on her chest. The stones stayed in place, even as Maité began to vanish from sight again.

CHAPTER 44

UNPRECEDENTED CRADLE GIFT

The frequency and intensity of the episodes increased rapidly—just like contractions increase and become more intense as the moment of birth approaches. Nahia began chanting:

> *O Basajaun*
> *Your return signifies the Realm will flourish.*
> *Look upon us with your favor once again,*
> *O Basajaun*
> *May the beating of your heart infuse renewed life*
> *to that which has been dormant for years past.*
> *O Basajaun.*

For a moment, Maité's entire body disappeared and only the stones remained, hovering in the place where her frame had sustained them before. Slowly, her hair, lips and skin began to materialize again and Nahia's attentiveness intensified—no detail could be missed. She noticed her clothing was gone and she understood Maité must have been helping—targeting energy only to the necessary organs.

"Tell them I love them—David and Aintza," Maité said with great effort. Stricken, the faery nodded but had to continue the ritual.

"Look upon us with your favor once again . . ." Nahia said and Maité opened her eyelids without disturbing the onyxes—rather she took them into her, and looked at the faery through new eyes. They were black. A stab of pain pierced Nahia's heart—she would never more see the beautiful storm-cloud eyes.

"O Basajaun . . . May the beating of your heart infuse renewed life to that which has been dormant for years past . . . ."

After two more episodes the ruby at last sank into her, and Nahia saw it begin to glow within. During a third episode, the steady beating started and Maité's own heart was no more.

"Oh, Basajaun." Nahia sobbed bitterly for the loss of a child of hers.

Even as Maité's lovely sepia coloring became silvery and pelt-like, Nahia wished she could undo it—if only she could take it back. But Maité began to display a bizarre new symptom, tearing Nahia from her futile wishing. Her body appeared to bubble all over—Nahia pictured thousands of marbles flowing in her bloodstream, wondering with intense discomfort if it hurt. "Oh, let it not be so!"

When Maité again solidified, her hands and feet looked like they were balled into fists, but the illusion soon dispelled as Nahia realized what she saw at the ends of her limbs were hooves. The long mane was sucked into her skull, and the head and neck seemed to elongate in one fluid sequence. "Stars in the heavens," Nahia whispered, astonished by the rapid transformation.

For over a fortnight, Nahia had believed this would happen *to her*, and seeing it happen to Maité, now, was torture of the acutest kind. Every change tore at the faery's heart because it meant another beloved attribute of Maité's went into nonexistence. The flickering spasms ceased at last. The fiery sky had waned into cool blue. Over the horizon, the upper quarter of the full moon saw the deed done.

Nahia knelt beside the baby unicorn—a steady stream of tears spilled onto her dress. She placed her hands on the shivering creature before her and it occurred to Nahia, regardless of this being a beast, the fact remained *it was newly born*. Not only that, this was blood of her blood, flesh of her flesh. And furthermore, she had made a promise to Celeste, over two hundred years ago, to look after her offspring so long as she lived.

And for crying out loud, isn't Maité my offspring too?

Nahia pressed her lips together to keep from smiling—somehow it didn't seem right she should laugh at such a moment, but the thought of granting a Cradle Gift to *this* particular newborn, struck her as inspired, revolutionary.

What would mother say? Nahia wondered, feeling somehow she should ask for permission—after all, it had never been attempted—to give a Cradle Gift to a beast?

"I don't care!"

The baby unicorn lay still beneath her hand. She seemed to sense the turn

273

of Nahia's thoughts and blinked sleepily. Nahia welcomed the surge of giddy excitement pulsating inside of her. "I don't even know if this will work," she said recklessly, "but as your faery-great-grandmother used to say, the bleakest regret comes from unattempted tasks."

A new song for the infant unicorn poured out of Nahia. Although unrehearsed, not a piece of her soul was missing from it:

Infant dear, with the steadfast heart and the selfless foresight,
I give you tonight a gift unique;
by the silvery light of the moon, every midsummer night
you shall break this bond and stand on two feet.
Shape fully recovered—you shall be as you were before your
noble sacrifice,
and through human eyes once again see the world you sustain,
that your loved ones may look upon you, and share with you a
moment frozen in time.

The unicorn wriggled beneath her touch and Nahia released her. She stood on wobbly legs, leaving the aura of jasmine petals on the ground where she had lain. The new Keeper of the Forest nuzzled Nahia and she cradled the innocent face. "I love you, baby girl." The unicorn leaned into the faery—the gesture was as close to a hug as could be had between them. Nahia wrapped her arms around the small neck and they stood like that for a few sweet moments before Nahia scooped her up and took to the sky again.

As they approached Moon Dancer Lake, Nahia's heart filled with trepidation. How was she to announce what happened? How would David take the news? Would they believe her? Would they think she had tricked Maité? She landed on the terrace where the council and the rest of the troop had gathered around David. He was holding Aintza in his arms as if he might never let go of her again and his glance immediately fell on the baby unicorn in Nahia's arms. David's tears gleamed in the combined light of the lanterns, auras, and the full moon, which by then had fully cleared the horizon.

Nahia couldn't take it anymore. "Forgive me. Forgive me!" she cried, holding the unicorn as tight as David held Aintza. She let the details, as she knew them, rush out in disconnected declarations. "She didn't believe me. She drank the potion before I even reached her—she didn't trust me. I should've told her what I meant to do!"

David turned to Sendoa, who immediately understood and took Aintza from him. "She never told me about the potions," David said gruffly, as if explaining a complicated problem to himself. "She acted alone—probably because she knew I would not have agreed. But you, she tried to believe in you until the very end. Only when you stopped communicating did she feel distrust."

"Please forgive me," Nahia murmured, grieving anew for the loss of Maité, and for the irony of how alike their behavior had been in the end.

David held out his arms, and Nahia gave him the unicorn. He buried his face in her neck and sobbed quietly. The faery put her arms around both of them, whispering Maité's last words to him.

The troop and the council formed concentric circles around David, Maité, Aintza, Nahia, and Sendoa; their glittering auras blended into a pure light as the moon continued its trajectory. Esti started the binding song, and the outer circles picked it up, swelling its intensity like a wave toward the center. Nahia's voice joined theirs, causing the song to rhythmically wash from inner to outer circles, back and forth.

The song spoke of rebirth, of the arrival of a new Keeper of the Forest, and of a new age. The age of Nahia—queen of the Faerie Realm of the Western Pyrenees. While it lasted, all those present (even Ederne in the cage where Sendoa had locked her) felt linked by the powerful energy swirling around them.

By the time the song stopped, David's tears had dried. He seemed to have been comforted, perhaps by the power of the unicorn he still held in his arms, and by Nahia's, who held tight to both of them. He set the new Keeper of the Forest on the ground and stood back. The troop's and the moon's energy currents continued to revolve around the newborn unicorn. She watched them swirl attentively, and seeming to understand what must be done, she shook her mane. It unsteadied her for a moment, but she recovered and immediately began drawing the tendrils of energy into her small body.

They held their breath as one; the unicorn pawed the terrace with tiny hooves and then shook her head again. A thin aura began to gleam on the silvery pelt, but it expanded quickly, with magic so strong the orb soon covered the terrace and the lake. As Nahia and the others whirled in awe, they witnessed the inclusion of the whole cradle of the Western Pyrenees: forest, mountains, cliffs, all were encompassed beneath the restored dimension.

The baby unicorn clopped off the terrace with hesitant steps. She pranced joyfully on the sand until the scent of the forest seemed to call her. After a couple of tentative sniffs she frolicked toward the trees, reminding Nahia more of a playful pup than a foal, and soon she was gone from their sight.

CHAPTER 45

REAWAKENED REALM

The new Realm is a year old today. Tonight is the first midsummer's night since the birth of the unicorn, and I haven't slept for three days, thinking about it. I have endured hot and cold flashes every time I recall the Cradle Gift I bestowed, and merciless doubts assail me as to whether or not it will work.

David and the baby, Aintza, who is now seventeen months old, will be arriving shortly to join in the festivities. They are my special guests. The stars help me, I haven't said a word to him about the Cradle Gift, because what if it fails? I couldn't bear to cause him such a disappointment. Preparations are under way and were it not for the pronounced absence of such beloved people as Celeste and Paloma, my mother, Oihana, and Amets, this could very well be any midsummer's day, two centuries ago.

I have seen Maité once or twice over the year, though she shirks my company, I have seen enough to note she has grown taller and sinewy. I don't know if she resents me or has simply misplaced her human memories. Maybe she has fully meshed into the nature of a unicorn and no longer holds any of her human qualities. Her magic is as strong as Basajaun's ever was. Moon Dancer Lake is a delicious, warm pool one can bathe in even in the dead of winter, and our Arboretum thrives as it always did during my mother's reign.

Our population increased when word got out the Realm within the Cradle of the Pyrenees had been restored and members of the old troop, who had escaped Ederne's last stand, came back from their exile. I'm proud to say my troop now exceeds three hundred, and our heritage is quite diverse.

At noon, the appointed time, I descend to the waterfall on the Santillán side of the old territory. David and I agreed to meet here because I would not

276

have him chartering a helicopter and drawing attention to this place. Although skeptical, he agreed to let *me* fly him and the baby over to the Realm.

I hardly have to wait. Soon I hear a rumbling engine climbing over the rough terrain. So many feelings clutter my heart and mind at the sight of him. How Maité loved him. Does he blame me? Does he hate me? Could I have stopped her? I still feel guilty about it.

He steps out of the car and grins. This is a good sign. He walks around the car and releases the baby from her safety seat in the back. She is beautiful! More so than the last time I saw her six months ago, when I went to San Sebastián to extend my invitation.

I stand stock still a few feet from them. Aintza is sleepy and her head rests on his shoulder as he carries her toward me. "So good of you to come," I say and impulsively hug him and the baby. "So good to see you both!"

He pats me awkwardly on the back and stammers, "Yes, you too. Thank you for asking us."

I can't begin to think what he's feeling and I am about to ask, when Aintza looks straight at me. Her eyes are so like Celeste's—translucent dark honey with sunshine. "Nahia," she says, and I'm speechless.

David looks from his daughter to me and explains. "She dreams about you nightly. She says she rides her 'horsey' chasing after you while you fly through the trees."

I can't hold back the tears—so Maité has managed to keep her original Cradle Gift.

"Do you think we will be able to—um, see the unicorn?" David asks.

"I can't make any promises." I confess to him I haven't seen much of Maité but I keep my speculations to myself as to why.

"Well, let's get this show on the road then," he shrugs disinterestedly, but it seems like he's keeping something from me. When I squint suspiciously at him, he adds, "I dream as well."

Aintza giggles through the entire process of shape-shifting, quick though it is, and then laughs out right as we fly over the waterfall and toward Moon Dancer Lake. Even David has a thrilled grin on his handsome face. I am pleased.

I land us on the shore nearest the forest where I return them to human height. We stroll through the woods for Aintza's benefit—I'd like her to explore to her heart's content. I guide them through meandering trails to the pond, and then into Celeste and Paloma's old dwelling. As the afternoon draws to a close, I take them to Handi Park, where they will be able to rest, take refreshment and get ready for the evening's celebration.

As dusk approaches, Sendoa and I meet our guests in the grand courtyard. Aintza toddles around looking fairer than any faery child within Handi Park, who at present anyway, are looking quite sullen over the exception made for Maité's baby—a solstice celebration is strictly for those fifteen and older. And David, well, he is the kind of handsome that makes humans believe in angels. I do believe if Maité sees him, he will have to contend with a lovesick unicorn following him around for the rest of his life.

As soon as we exit Handi Park, I shift us all to human height. With well-practiced skill I disperse their weight and, grabbing each of their hands, I fly us to Moon Dancer Lake, where our traditional ivory terrace has been constructed, complete with balustrade. I choke down a sob as memories overwhelm me. This seems a repetition of the first solstice celebration Celeste and I attended.

On our approach, I see on the terrace dozens of males and females of the troop, resplendent in their finery, laughing and talking with one another. Some walk, some float arm in arm, while others sway to the melodies drifting in the breeze. I squeeze David's hand but he won't look at me. His eyes are riveted on the activity of the multitude of luminous eyes and bodies we are descending upon. We touchdown and the colorful auras instantly converge on us: blue, yellow, orange, green, silver, purple, all mesh into a compounded glow of gratitude that suffuses our senses. This is the troop's welcome, a gift of color and warmth so intense it becomes palpable—they know who David is, they know who Maité is and what she did for us.

"It tickles," Aintza squeals and the troop's laughter further intensifies the healing glow.

I see David blink away tears and I know he must be feeling as I do; so much gratitude fills one's heart to bursting.

Bom-Bom Bomm! The booming call of the timpani startles Aintza so badly she yelps and clings to my skirt. I let go of Sendoa's hand to scoop her up into my arms and think of Celeste, who had had a similar reaction, all those years ago—she hadn't seen the drummers directly behind the terrace.

Bom-Bom Bomm! Instantly all eyes turn to the east with raucous acclamations, as do I, pointing to the horizon for Aintza's benefit. *Bom-Bom Bomm!* The excitement crests as a sliver of the full moon becomes visible, inching up behind the distant, jagged cliffs. *Bom-Bom Bomm!* The moon rises, bright yellow at first, although it will soon become milky white, and before long, it will bathe everything in its silvery light.

How close I feel to Celeste on this night, while holding our latest descendant in my arms—I let the tears flow and hold tighter to Aintza.

The air is electrified with anticipation. *Bom-Bom Bomm!* The lunar disk completely clears the ridges to whooping cheers from faeries floating about the terrace or standing on the sand. The last beat of the drums still resonates through the balmy air when a powerful neigh rings out, and we turn as one toward the sound. The unicorn paws the air, its mane flailing in the breeze. She makes a striking figure beneath the moonlight.

"Horsey," Aintza cries and wriggles from my arms. I let her go.

Beside me, David whispers, "Maité."

The unicorn shakes its beautiful head and paws the air again, but instead of dropping down to stand on four legs, it remains upright, caught in the moonlight, between sand and sky. A collective gasp issues from the troop and I hold my breath—*could it be?*

My eyes don't deceive me. With prodigious swiftness, she seems to draw a shape for herself from everyone's mind, and why not; I wager at least David, Sendoa, the council and myself are picturing Maité precisely as she was in human form. The equine limbs are in fact turning into human arms and legs! And the straight mane becomes Maité's unruly long hair. I don't want to miss a thing so I try not to blink, but I have to because I'm blinded by tears.

I can't believe it! There she is, whole and radiant in a starlit gown. I'm about to soar over the balustrade—I want to hug and kiss her, tell her how much I've missed her. And I have so many questions, and I want to tell her how much I love her. But catching David's movement beside me, I stop. Surely the priority is his.

David vaults over the balustrade, and on his way he scoops up Aintza, who had managed to climb down the steps and is already on the sand, toddling toward her mother.

I did it, I congratulate myself, even as I laugh at the sight of Maité, patting her arms, legs and face in disbelief. Our eyes lock for the briefest of moments and our identical thoughts cross in the charged atmosphere: *it worked!* I feel Sendoa's arms around my waist and I stay there, safe and warm, my eyes on Maité.

She stops checking herself because she has spotted David and Aintza; she breaks into a sprint toward them and my throat tightens with emotion at the site of their reunion. My heart bursts with happiness—the turquoise radiance exploding from me competes with the silver light of the moon, encircling and binding us all as the family we are.

THE END

EPIL⊕GUE

Nature does not hurry, yet everything is accomplished.

Lao Tzu

Thundersnow is a rare natural phenomenon where lightning and thunder occur during a heavy snowstorm or a blizzard. There are only a handful of recorded instances, which have served to amuse atmospheric scientists across the globe, but for those who know of thundersnow's magical qualities, such a phenomenon is the stuff of legend.

One afternoon in early February, 2023, word reached Nahia a thundersnow event had occurred at Wizard's Pass; a magical gateway under the binding power of the Faerie Realm's Keeper.

Lightning struck the frozen waterfall, breaking off a pristine chunk of white ice, causing it to melt with the heat of the bolt. In spite of it being the dead of winter, the pure water did not freeze again, rather it alchemized into the most magical creature ever to grace the face of the earth—a natural born unicorn.

On that same afternoon, David was notified that the woman, Ederne, had died in the human prison cell where she had been serving a long sentence for kidnapping and attempted murder.

Nahia's and David's thoughts converged on Maité.

Deep within the dusky forest, the white unicorn rose on its hind legs and pawed the air; a victorious neigh issued from her.

www.ingramcontent.com/pod-product-compliance
Lightning Source LLC
Chambersburg PA
CBHW020957120726

47905CB00009B/2736